JONATHAN JANZ

THE DARKEST LULLABY

This is a **FLAME TREE PRESS** book

FLAME TREE PRESS
6 Melbray Mews, London, SW6 3NS, UK
flametreepress.com

Distribution and warehouse:
Marston Book Services Ltd
160 Eastern Avenue, Milton Park, Abingdon, Oxon, OX14 4SB
www.marston.co.uk

Thanks to the Flame Tree Press team, including:
Taylor Bentley, Frances Bodiam, Federica Ciaravella, Don D'Auria,
Chris Herbert, Matteo Middlemiss, Josie Mitchell, Mike Spender,
Cat Taylor, Maria Tissot, Nick Wells, Gillian Whitaker.

The cover is created by Flame Tree Studio with
thanks to Nik Keevil and Shutterstock.com.
The font families in this book are Avenir and Bembo.

Flame Tree Press is an imprint of Flame Tree Publishing Ltd
flametreepublishing.com

A copy of the CIP data for this book is available from the British Library.

HB ISBN: 978-1-78758-271-2
PB ISBN: 978-1-78758-270-5
ebook ISBN: 978-1-78758-272-9
Also available in FLAME TREE AUDIO

Printed in the UK at Clays, Suffolk

JONATHAN JANZ

THE DARKEST LULLABY

FLAME TREE PRESS
London & New York

No one who, like me, conjures up the most evil of those half-tamed demons that inhabit the human beast, and seeks to wrestle with them, can expect to come through the struggle unscathed.
Sigmund Freud

"I want to run with the children outside," said the little boy. "But I don't like the Night."
"I'll introduce you to the Night," said Dark.
"And you'll be friends."
Ray Bradbury

This one is for my amazing wife. Honey, you've been with me from the beginning, and you've helped me weather years of rejection and frustration. More importantly, you've been my true love, my best friend, and an incredible mother to our three children. Thank you for everything. I love you with all my heart.

BEFORE

October 14th, 1982

Susan saw Brad signal a left turn and figured he was just making a joke in bad taste. But when the car actually started to slow, she said, "Not funny," though a contraction reduced her words to a whisper. It was irritating enough that he'd chosen this circuitous route to Ravana, but the fact Brad was more interested in playing unfunny tricks than he was in getting his pregnant wife – hell, his *delivering* wife – to the hospital spoke volumes about his lack of maturity.

Mom called it, she thought for the thousandth time. *Knocking a girl up doesn't make a boy fit for marriage.*

Susan compressed her lips. If only she hadn't been so stubborn.

The Mustang continued to decelerate.

By the time she realised where they were, Brad was steering them toward the forest, the wheel ruts embracing their tyres like a pair of obsessive lovers. She'd been reclining in her seat and concentrating on her breathing the way her YWCA classes had taught her, but now she sat up and glared at her husband in disbelief.

"Where're you taking me?"

"Relax," he said and gave her the lopsided smile, the one that used to make her stomach flutter but now only made her doubt his intelligence. "The big guy'll take care of you."

At his words her windpipe constricted and the seat beneath her seemed to drop away. "What are you talking about?"

He rolled his eyes and blew out a disgusted puff of air, like she was his probation officer and not his wife. "See, I knew you'd be that way, all woe-is-me and how-dare-you-do-this-Brad." He shook his head and made a little whistling sound. "Jesus Christ, honey, it's like you believe a third-rate hospital's the only place people can have babies."

He continued on that way, and as he talked, a detached part of her was able to pull back and watch him – really watch him – for perhaps the first time. The brown mustache and sandy blond hair, a combination she once found irresistible, now made him look to her like one of those sleazy actors in the video he'd brought home the other day, an adult movie he'd shown her in the hope it would kickstart their sex life, and though she'd played along with his fantasy for a while, her back had started in hurting again, which of course was the reason she hadn't been in the mood lately to start with. Being pregnant, she tried to tell him, was hard on a woman's body. Brad couldn't seem to grasp this.

Her thoughts broke off as a nasty contraction dug in and knocked the wind out of her. She imagined a pair of sadistic hands in there seizing her uterus and kneading it with calloused fingers. The bitter taste of hot bile scalded her throat.

Brad took in her tortured expression, said, "Now, aren't you glad I brought you here? If we'd kept going we'd still be ten minutes from town."

Through clenched teeth, she said, "Turn around."

He laughed softly. "Honey, you aren't thinking—"

"*Now,* dammit."

For a moment, he stared back at her, his face stricken. Then the arrogant porn star grin bled into his features again, the expression that said she was just a hysterical woman, what the hell did she know anyway? He threw the Mustang into park and killed the engine.

"Come on," he said, opening his door. She turned and stared at the horrid black house, its windows lit up like some scorched and sinister jack-o'-lantern. She shot a desperate glance at the ignition, but he'd snatched the keys on the way out of the car. Another contraction ripped through her, and she moaned at the pain. Her door swung open and Brad's handsome, vacant face swam toward her. Though he was still grinning, there was a tightness in it, a *Don't you screw this up for me* quality that made her yearn to slap him, to ask *Who the heck matters right now? Aren't your wife and baby as important as your cult friends?*

He clenched her arm and muscled her out of the car. The cloying odour of pine needles enshrouded her. The ancient trees reefing the yard beckoned her forward, forward, like ushers at some blasphemous wedding. Making her halting way toward the house, she recalled the time she'd accompanied him here, the ghastly things she'd witnessed. Most of all she remembered the man and woman who lived in this place.

The big guy'll take care of you, Brad had said.

A shudder plaited down Susan's back at the thought of the man. His large, powerful frame. The broad, tan forehead and the mad eyes that made her think of drowning. She glimpsed someone stepping onto the front porch to welcome them, and she thought, *No, please let it be someone else.*

But it wasn't.

Gerald Destragis smiled and spread his arms. "I'm so glad you've decided to experience this moment with us."

Susan jerked her arm free of Brad's grip. "I didn't decide to," she said, glaring at her husband. "Brad brought me here."

The man's huge hands folded before him. "How far apart are your contractions, dear?"

Susan searched the man's blue eyes, the face that by all accounts was sixty-some years old but remained attractive and virile nonetheless. She wanted to trust him, wanted to believe he could bring her child into this world without harm. Yet...she'd heard so many terrible things. And the night she spent in the clearing with Destragis's people... Had she really seen what she thought she had, or had that been the mescaline at work?

She doubled over as the worst contraction yet crawled through her, sent blazing spears of pain shooting through her body. Her knees buckled, but strong, gentle hands took hold of her. Panting, the cold sweat dripping from her nose, she leaned against Destragis, who'd somehow caught her before she fell.

"We don't have much time, dear," Destragis said in his deep, resonant voice. "I could drive you to town, but I suspect we'd be too late."

As if confirming this, her stomach clenched again, and before she knew what was happening, Destragis had swept her into his arms and was striding across the porch with her. A man Susan recognised as a custodian from Ravana High School opened the door for them as they passed. She sensed Brad behind them, trailing along like a scrap of toilet paper. Then Destragis was easing her onto a mattress someone had arranged in the middle of the living room. The sheet on which she lay was white and rubbery, and next to her sat a bucket of water, several folded towels. Half a dozen tall lamps tossed hot yellow gazes down at the mattress.

She glanced at Brad, who'd knelt beside her. "You planned this?"

"That's crazy," he answered, throwing uneasy glances at the people who had appeared out of nowhere. Susan spotted Mike McClure and Juliet Joel, two kids from their graduating class. Beside them, the Anthony twins, cheerleaders who still attended Ravana High. There were older people, as well, but none of these were familiar.

Then the crowd opened up and she saw the tall woman.

"I want to leave," Susan said, but her voice came out a dry croak. "*Please*," she whispered to Brad as the woman's face loomed closer. The scent of the tall woman's perfume drowsed over her, the placid expression on the still-beautiful face somehow tranquilising Susan, assuring her that she and her baby would be just fine.

"Please get her clothes for me," a voice said, and Susan turned to see Destragis standing shirtless beside her. He was sliding on a pair of rubber gloves, the sinews of his arms jumping like eager serpents. Susan felt her maternity shorts unbuttoned, the uncomfortable denim slithering down her legs. The woman's hair, Susan noticed, was mostly auburn with wisps of grey at the temples. It was drawn back with tortoise shell barrettes. Susan focused on the amber and black whorls as the woman's slender fingers hooked beneath the waistband of her underwear, then removed them. A distant part of her felt embarrassed to be half naked before all these strangers, but the pain had diminished, and she was too grateful for that to worry about modesty.

"Fully dilated," Destragis said, and Susan lifted her head to discover him between her legs, his muscular shoulders flexing in the lamplight.

"Is it a boy?" Brad asked. No one bothered answering.

Destragis said to the woman. "Is she comfortable?"

Susan saw the woman nod and smile down at her. The smile warmed her, so unlike the feral intensity Susan had witnessed that awful night in the clearing. She remembered these two – the strong man and the tall woman — stripping naked, caressing each another. The woman's eyes rolling white, some fell spirit seeming to seize hold of her, the still-firm body trembling in ecstasy, the pale skin appearing to grow younger as she drank from the silver chalice. The crimson fluid dripping from the corners of her mouth, her shark-white teeth gleaming...

"It's coming," Destragis said.

The woman's smile broadened, and she bent over Susan, took both her hands and whispered words of comfort. Dimly, Susan felt an urge to push, which she did, and eventually there was screaming and a lovely, newborn wail. Susan raised her head to see Destragis cradling her baby, the pinkish-yellow umbilical cord glistening with blood.

The woman moved toward Destragis, who was beaming down at the baby in his arms. It was a boy, Susan now saw, the penis sheathed in some whitish substance. A sudden urge to hold her son gusted through her, and without speaking she reached for him, the dull ache between her legs as nothing next to her desire to hold her child.

"Hold still, dear," the woman said. Brad held Susan's shoulders as the woman's slender fingers opened a pair of what looked like sewing shears and severed the cord. Rather than staunching the flow of liquid spilling from the raw umbilicus, Destragis only rocked the screaming child and whispered soothing words. Susan reached for her baby, but the woman stilled her with a glance. "Soon, dear," she said, but something in the woman's face disquieted her. Destragis's muscled chest was stippled with drops of blood and afterbirth, but it was the man's eyes that transformed her uneasiness to dread. He stared down at the baby with an unnatural fervour, his avid blue gaze predatory.

"Give him to me," Susan said, but Destragis was rising, her baby nestled firmly in the crook of one great arm. The woman rose too, and to Susan's infinite alarm they passed her by and moved toward the door.

"*No!*" Susan screamed and wrenched her shoulders free of Brad's grasp. He grunted in surprise and attempted to pin her to the mattress. She lashed out, raked his face, her nails leaving bloody contrails in their wake. Though her legs were weak, she pushed to her feet and staggered after the man and woman, who were now gliding through the front door and descending the porch steps. A voice shouted at her to stop, but she paid it no notice. She was possessed, hellbent on taking back her boy, on stopping those fiends from stealing him. If what she'd heard was true, if the rumours really were fact... *Oh, Jesus*—

She uttered a choked sob as she slammed open the screen door and shambled down the steps. She spotted them immediately as they passed the Mustang, moving toward an opening in the woods.

"*Give him back!*" she screamed, but neither of them turned. She set off across the yard to catch them but something struck her in the middle of the back, and she was driven face first to the grass. She shot an elbow at whomever had tackled her, but they were on her now, too many of them, their hands pawing at her, dragging her back to the house.

The last thing she saw before the couple disappeared into the woods was one of her baby's feet. Then the tiny pink toes were devoured by the forest.

PART ONE
PURIFICATION
CHAPTER ONE

Ellie's attitude had been reasonably positive, it really had, before they made the turn onto the eerie forest lane. But from that moment forward her thoughts were an ungenerous maelstrom of resentment and anger, her body worsening matters by staging an open revolt. She'd heard about motion sickness before – her older sister Katherine used to suffer from it on long family trips – but Ellie had never actually experienced it until now. It was almost as if a primitive part of her sensed a wrongness with this place and was reacting to it.

Give it a chance, Ellie heard a voice say as they bounced down the lane. *It might not be so bad.*

Behind her shut lids she imagined the nausea roiling like a hazy green fog in the back of her throat. A cold patina of sweat had formed on her forehead, her upper lip.

"You okay over there?" Chris asked.

Ellie opened her eyes and some of the carsickness dissipated. "Surviving."

"Something you ate?"

"I had the same thing you did."

"But you've never been carsick—"

"I know."

She could feel Chris's eyes linger on her. "You need me to stop?" he asked.

The Camry rocked as they trundled over a bridge.

Ellie palmed sweat from her face. "You might slow down a little."

As Chris reduced their speed, the clanging in her skull grew louder, a maniacal backbeat to the clenching of her gorge.

"Is it much longer?" she asked.

"Almost there."

I hope so, she thought. Deep down she'd been dreading this moment all day, so perhaps it was a mercy she had the motion sickness to take her mind off it. This way Chris might not see the disappointment in her face when they arrived at the house.

She clenched her teeth and thought, *He deserves to see your disappointment. It's his fault you're here in the first place.*

Stop being a jerk! the voice in her head chided.

Ellie nodded faintly, but the movement brought her closer to puking.

Chris gestured toward the windshield. "What do you think of the woods?"

Diplomacy, the voice reminded her, and this time she recognised it as Katherine's. Though Ellie hadn't seen her sister in years, she heard Katherine's voice more and more often lately.

Ellie took a steadying breath and said, "I think we'll have plenty of privacy."

Chris smiled, and despite the nausea, despite all her misgivings about moving here, his good-natured grin cheered her.

But when they rounded a curve and she saw the house, she said, "Is this it?"

Chris's grin faded. "I did say the siding had darkened some."

"It looks black."

"With age, Ellie. What'd you expect?"

Three storeys high, like something out of a children's cautionary tale, their new home rose like a gaunt spectre among the forest trees.

She grunted as the Camry dropped into twin wheel ruts and bottomed out. If she didn't get out of the car now, take in some fresh air, she'd paint the dashboard with what little she'd eaten for supper.

Chris angled toward an outbuilding to the left of the house. The car was stopped before she realised it was a garage.

"It's not attached?"

He opened his door. "Most houses built in the 1800s didn't have need for attached garages, honey."

He got out and came around to her side. Ellie blew out air and rummaged through her purse until she found her phone. She turned it on and stared with disgust at its glowing face. No bars, no coverage.

"You ready?" he asked, bending toward her window. She caught the trepidation in his voice and felt herself thaw. A little.

She shouldered her purse, opened her door, and gazed up at the woods. The enormous spruce boughs bordering the yard drooped like pilloried thieves. She climbed out and shivered. It was April, yet it was only, what? Thirty-five degrees outside? Forty? And the sun hadn't even set.

Ellie followed Chris toward the covered porch, which was a ruin of sinking cinderblocks and rotting two-by-fours. Chris mounted the steps and opened the door, but Ellie stood a moment and gazed up at the house.

There were windows enough, she supposed, but despite the dull glimmers of glass, it was as though she faced an unbroken wall of darkness. She shivered again, and this time it had nothing to do with the chill of impending night.

"You gonna stay out here?" he asked.

"Is the inside as bad?"

"The rooms are painted black."

"Not funny."

He stepped down from the porch and took her hands. "I know you loved Malibu, but give it a chance." He searched her face. "Just think – a couple days ago we were sharing walls with four different neighbours. Now you've got twenty-three hundred acres all to yourself. That's damn near five miles square."

He put his arms around her. His tall, muscled body was warm, his size comforting in this wilderness.

She pressed against him. "Is it always this cold?"

"Give it a few weeks."

"Guess I don't have a choice, huh?"

He gave her a squeeze, drew away and before she knew what was happening, he hoisted her in his arms and carried her toward the open front door.

Laughing, she said, "What, are we newlyweds again?"

"The apartment didn't count. This is our first real home."

If it doesn't cave in on us, she thought.

★   ★   ★

The interior was better, but not by much.

The walls of the foyer were festooned with hideous skeins of torn wallpaper. Beneath the pink roses and faded damasked patterns were more flowers, more designs. To worsen matters, the ceiling had split open at some point and had been poorly repaired. The warped wooden planks underfoot confirmed the water damage.

"It gets better," Chris said, but he was staring up at the patched ceiling, his face plagued with apprehension.

They entered the dining room. No water damage that she could see, no warped floorboards. No table either, but that would be remedied by tomorrow when the movers arrived. The day after that at the latest. She refused to entertain the possibility of it taking longer than that. Surely God wouldn't be that cruel to her.

A spider scuttled across the floor, its bulbous brown body the size of a Calamata olive.

Eyeing it, Chris said, "The kitchen's an eat-in, so I figured we'd use our table in there and buy a new one for here."

"With what money?"

He didn't have an answer for that.

She reached out and peeled off a faded strip of wallpaper, burgundy and gold with a fleur-de-lis pattern that once might have looked regal.

"Comes off easily enough," he said.

"You ever removed wallpaper?"

"Uh-uh," he said. "You?"

She shook her head and moved through the room. "I've heard it's an awful job."

"Can't be that bad."

Ellie kept quiet. She opened the door and was assailed by a draught of sour air, a withering brew of spoiled milk and old must. She felt along the inner wall and thought, *Please don't let this be the—*

"Here's the kitchen," Chris said as a spill of jaundiced light flooded the room.

It was old and it was ugly and it smelled as though the last occupants hadn't bothered to clean out the fridge, which was the same drab green as the ancient stove. The cabinets were a murky brown that flirted with black, and the countertops were splotched with innumerable burns and scars.

What a disaster.

"The table could go over here," he said, standing by a window. When she didn't respond, he added, "Or somewhere else if you want."

"How about Malibu."

"Ellie—"

"Is this place safe?"

He groaned.

"Holes in the ceilings, water damage everywhere—"

"Just in the foyer, Ellie."

"—animals living in the walls—"

"I had an inspector here."

"He must've been brave."

He opened his mouth to respond, but rather than speaking he dropped his head and went out the back door.

Ellie watched him go, and though she knew she should say something to stop him, make some sort of apology, she didn't. She blew hair out of her eyes and sighed. He'd be back in a couple minutes. She could say she was sorry then.

Unless he gets in the car and leaves your sorry ass out here, her sister told her.

"Shut up, Katherine," Ellie said and went upstairs.

*   *   *

Ten minutes later Chris opened the bedroom door, the sleeping bag slung over his shoulder. "Ready to camp?"

"Thanks for putting up with me," she said.

He shrugged. "We were on the road so long, I don't blame you for being grouchy."

"Still..."

"Carsickness gone?"

"Mostly," she said and eyed the bedroll. "You bring pillows?"

"In the trunk," he said. "I'll get 'em while you make yourself comfortable."

A corner of her mouth rose. "Who says I'm not comfortable?"

Grinning, he went out.

The heating was slow, but the temperature had grown bearable. She was anxious to explore the third floor, but her skin ached for a hot shower. Ellie left the bedroom, flipped on the bathroom light and saw the clawfoot tub.

She reached into the curtainless shower, twisted on the water and began undressing. The water smelled of eggs, but the thought of rinsing her greasy hair made her dizzy with anticipation. She clenched her jaw, hooked her thumbs under the edges of her underwear and slid them off.

She stuck an open palm under the shower spray and felt the warm water. She twisted the cold water lower until the shower began to steam. Taking care not to slip, she climbed over the edge of the tub, gasped as the hot spray assaulted her skin. She ducked under the showerhead, relishing the burning on her scalp, the exhilarating heat racing down her temples.

There was a knock on the door.

"Open," she said.

Chris entered. He looked at her, startled, and said, "Oh, I bought a shower curtain before we left. It's in the car."

"You're not really wearing that." She nodded at his belt buckle, a gift from his students. The word LENNY was stamped on it to commemorate their reading of Steinbeck's *Of Mice and Men*.

He glanced down at it. "Sexy, huh?"

She cocked an eyebrow. "Not the word I'd choose."

"I'll get the curtain."

As he turned to leave, she said, "Chris."

He stared at her dumbly a moment. Then his expression began to change.

"Join me?" Ellie asked.

Chris unclasped the belt buckle.

CHAPTER TWO

Sighing, Chris opened his eyes and checked the phone. Four-thirty in the morning. He wasn't sleeping anymore and that was that.

As cautiously as he could, he squirmed out of the sleeping bag, knelt and kissed his wife on the cheek. He hung there, breathing in the warm smell of her flesh.

She stirred in her sleep, mumbled something unintelligible.

When he pulled away, the clouds broke for a moment, and a ghostly pool of moonlight illuminated her profile.

Beautiful, he thought. *Just beautiful.*

He often watched her sleep. Sometimes he worried she'd catch him and think him a pervert, claim he'd somehow violated her. He doubted he could explain just how lovely she was when she lay on her side, her brown eyes shut and her hair flowing behind her like ripples of dark water. Below, the exhilarating curve of her lower back and her perfect rear end.

God, the sight of her made him ache. Sitting next to her in the gloom, he wondered again if he'd made a mistake.

When he'd come to this place shortly after Aunt Lillith's death, the idea of living here, of uprooting Ellie and the life they knew was the last thing on his mind. After he and the inspector made sure the house was still livable, he'd hired Doris Keller, a local real estate agent, to help him sell it. Land in this area, Doris explained, went for five thousand an acre. But estates of this size were rare nowadays, and as a result, they'd have to temper their expectations.

Two million, then, was their asking price.

No one bit.

They reduced the land to a million-five.

Meanwhile, the high school at which Chris taught cut wages. Their credit card bills swelled alarmingly. They downsized to one car, and soon they had to give up eating out, going to concerts. It was only in the budget if it was free.

Then Ellie quit her job at the insurance agency.

Chris couldn't blame her, had actually expected it for a while. Her boss spoke to her, Ellie explained, like she was a prostitute. Had Chris not worried about getting arrested and losing their only source of income, he would have kicked the man's teeth in.

After eight months without an offer on the land, they dropped their price to a million.

It was around that time he first mentioned the idea of moving to Indiana. He'd enjoyed growing up there, he told her. It was a good, wholesome place.

"You're joking," was Ellie's response.

"Think about it," he said.

"I don't want to," she answered.

Another month passed. Their rent unpaid. The calls from their creditors grew hostile.

Chris asked Ellie about moving again, and though she didn't dismiss him out of hand this time, the look on her face made him sick inside.

You're failing her, a voice in his head insisted. *You're a shitty provider. You two want kids? How the hell will you support them?*

"Think of all the money we'd save on rent," he said one day as they sat brooding on the beach.

She wouldn't make eye contact, only stared at the sand as though a bleak, joyless future were projected on its beige contours.

He sighed. "It's really not that bad a place, Ellie."

"Then why hasn't it sold?"

He shrugged. "It's a big piece of land."

"What if we lower the price?"

"We've lowered it."

"Better than living on it."

That night on the phone, sitting in the bathroom with the fan on so Ellie wouldn't hear him, he told the Realtor to sell it for half a million.

"It won't matter," she said. Doris had been amiable the first few months of their correspondence. Now she sounded like a principal preparing to expel an unruly pupil.

"What do you mean it won't—"

"No one's going to buy it."

"When we put it on the market you said—"

"I was wrong."

Running a hand through his hair, which had begun to thin over the past few months, he said, "Maybe if you add more pictures to the website, change the description a little."

"There's nothing wrong with the listing, Chris."

"Maybe we should get another Realtor."

She hung up.

The next day he came home from work to find Ellie crying.

Sitting beside her on the couch, he asked, "What happened?"

"I took a pregnancy test."

He put hand on her back. "And?"

"Another negative."

A sick coiling in his belly, the hand on her back going numb. Her face was wet with tears and snot, and he couldn't think of anything to say. They'd been trying for more than a year now; what if it was him?

She laughed without humour. "It's not like we can afford a baby anyway, right?"

A thickness in his throat. "It'll happen, Ellie."

He held her while she wept. After a time she asked, "If we moved, what would we live on?"

"I'll get a job."

"Teaching?"

"Or writing. Money goes a long way in Indiana," he answered. "We'd only have utilities and food."

"And car insurance, and house insurance, and—"

"Diapers."

She stared at him. The pridefulness had gone out of her face, replaced by a naked longing. For the first time he could see her considering it.

"You should see the land, Ellie."

She averted her eyes. "The pictures make it look like the setting of a horror movie."

"Only because it's isolated." He stroked her hair. "It's really quite lovely."

She nodded, the reservations plain in her face, but the possibilities there too.

"You could be a stay-at-home mom," he added and felt a twinge of guilt.

A slow smile dawning.

He kissed her and it lingered.

That was late January.

In February, he arrived home to find her humming and making dinner, the smell of basil thick in the air. On the table were freshly cut flowers and the glow of several candles.

"What's the occasion?"

He noticed her outfit. Tight khaki slacks and a red shirt that clung to her breasts, a sharp contrast to the baggy clothes she'd worn since she quit her job. She approached and handed him a glass of wine.

"What's this for?" he asked.

"Let's give Indiana a try," she said.

*   *   *

Now, remembering her smile that day, a palpable sense of guilt grabbed hold of him. Chris forced himself to stand, his knees popping in the dark, and ambled over to his clothes. He put them on as quietly as he could, though the car keys jangled in his hip pocket. He grimaced and cast a quick glance at Ellie.

Still asleep.

Moving quickly, he went downstairs and out the back door.

The wintry night air acted like a tonic on his frazzled nerves. Stiff blades of grass crunched under his shoes, a sound he found oddly soothing.

He turned and regarded their new home. The clouds had dissipated, and in the gleaming ivory moonlight its façade didn't seem so black. Dark, yes, but nothing like the forbidding death's head that had greeted them at dusk. No wonder Ellie had been so hesitant.

A rustling to his left cut off his thoughts. He turned and glimpsed a large shape moving into the forest.

Unthinkingly, Chris took a step in that direction. Something in the creature's gait had reminded him of Petey, the black Labrador retriever who'd been his companion for eight years until one terrible summer afternoon as Chris sat watching television there came the bone chilling sound of squealing breaks and the muted thump of metal on fur. When Chris went outside, Petey lay unmoving, his pink tongue lolling in a spreading lake of red.

He brushed off the memory and waded into the tall weeds.

"Hey," he whispered. "You don't need to run from me."

He stopped and heard breathing, harsh and rapid. Chris crept nearer. Soon a gigantic blue spruce filled his vision. Beneath it, something stirred.

He paused, straining to distinguish the dark shape amidst the darker shadows, and as he did he heard a pitiful whimper. He was ten feet away when the dog raised its head and stared at him.

"Hey, guy," Chris said. He knelt and smiled, but the dog – a black lab, he noted with surprise – rose up as if to bolt if Chris came any closer.

"Listen," Chris said, "I know you're scared."

Chris continued, emboldened by the animal's stillness. "My parents used to make fun of me for talking to Petey – he was my dog once, and he looked a lot like you – but I knew he understood me."

He reached the prickly edges of the spruce branches, the dog a few feet away. He lowered to his hands and knees, crawled forward. "I promise I won't hurt you."

As Chris extended his hand, the dog eyed him with barely restrained terror. The lab sniffed his palm, whined. Very slowly, Chris reached out, caressed the smooth black fur.

It lunged at him, but before he could raise an arm to ward it off, he felt the warm tongue lap at his cheek. Laughing, Chris went over on his side and the dog came with him, licking his face as though it were the world's most delicious treat.

Moments later, Chris angled back toward the house, hoping the dog would follow him. It did, the lab's large paws padding softly over the frosty earth.

When they reached the driveway, Chris fished out the keys, opened the Camry door, and half-turned the ignition in order to check the time. The digital green numerals told him it wasn't yet five in the morning. He sighed, his white breath pluming out the open door, and regarded the dog, who sat obediently on the gravel.

"Wanna check out Ravana?" Chris asked.

Before the words had finished, the lab bounded through the gap between Chris and the wheel, the muscular black haunches bumping Chris against the seat.

Laughing, he said, "I'll take that as a yes."

CHAPTER THREE

When she awoke she didn't know at first where she was. Instinctively, she reached behind her but Chris wasn't there. She sat up but something restricted her movement. Bewildered, she batted and kicked at the warm, membranous barrier and didn't remember the sleeping bag until her left hamstring tightened in a frightful cramp. Despite the pain, she pushed down the sleeping bag and scooted her way out.

Ellie rolled over, reached back and massaged the back of her leg, but the knot of muscle only squeezed tighter. It felt like a judgement. Moaning now, she lay prostrate and babbled incoherent prayers for mercy.

Slowly, the muscle relaxed, though Ellie remained very still so the cramp wouldn't return.

She opened her eyes and peered about the dark room.

Her head ached. The cold, probably, plus the fact she was dehydrated. Travel often did that to her. She reached over, checked the time on her phone. 5:35, she saw.

Ellie shivered. She couldn't quite see her breath, but she suspected the temperature had dipped below sixty. Surely the furnace hadn't failed. Had Chris even checked it?

She paused, a bigger question stopping her.

Where was Chris?

She went into the hall and saw the bathroom was unoccupied too. Then where was he? The lights were off in the other bedrooms, which meant Chris was almost certainly downstairs.

If he's here at all.

No way, she thought as she descended the steps. No way he'd leave her all alone on their first night here.

Would he?

A shudder coursed down her back. The silence folded around her like the arms of some cruel and implacable ghost. Barely suppressed terror whispering at the nape of her neck, she checked the living room, the kitchen, but the first floor appeared deserted as well.

The basement?

To hell with that, she thought.

As she stood in the foyer, debating, an unfortunate cinematic memory arose: *The Texas Chainsaw Massacre*. Leatherface and his cannibalistic family, the maniacal laughing and the roaring chainsaw, the—

Would you stop it for chrissakes?

Struggling to corral her galloping heart, she listened for her husband.

Nothing.

Her skull throbbed, the headache worsening.

Ellie went upstairs to the bathroom and found what she was searching for right away — the extra-strength pain relievers. She shook two out and popped them into her mouth. She leaned down to sip enough tap water to wash the pills down.

She made a face at the metallic tang of the water. Chris had prepared her for it, but even so, the well water was a shock to her system. She bent and drank again, remembering something Chris had said: *Sometimes you'll smell manure from the pig farms, and the humidity can be brutal, but the water will be cleaner in Indiana, and...*

"...it'll be better for our babies too," Ellie said and wiped her mouth.

When she opened the cabinet to put the bottle away, something between the first and second shelves caught her attention.

She couldn't believe she hadn't noticed it before, but built into the dingy cabinet interior was a small metal door, about two inches wide and one inch tall. She pushed the cool metal surface and glimpsed the darkness within.

What on earth?

Propping up the tiny door with her fingers, she braced herself on the edge of the vanity and brought her face as close as she could to the opening. She couldn't imagine what its use could be. A peephole? A laundry chute for mice?

An idea occurred to her. She left the bathroom and entered the bedroom that shared the wall. She crossed the room, opened the closet door, and gasped as something lunged at her legs.

The yardstick clattered on the wood floor.

Ellie put a hand to her mouth and suppressed laughter at her skittishness.

She yanked the pullstring, and light flooded the closet. It was a small space, scarcely wide enough for her to enter without having to turn sideways. Straight ahead, level with her ribcage, Ellie spotted a tiny wooden knob affixed to what appeared to be a small wooden door. The medicine cabinet, she calculated, would be exactly that height. She grabbed the knob and pushed. For a moment the door slid easily to the left. Then it caught and wouldn't budge no matter how she tried to joggle it. Still, the aperture was wide enough she could slip her hand inside, which she did, feeling around the narrow compartment for some clue to the thing's purpose.

The tip of a finger brushed something.

Vague thoughts of secret treasure cavorted through her mind. Childhood memories of playing pirates with Katherine recurred as she reached deeper, determined now to retrieve something of worth from the compartment.

She brought her body flush against the wall, her bare arm skimming the smooth wood within. Ellie paused. Her fingers had touched something cold and hard lying at the bottom of the compartment. A coin? Straining, she pushed farther inside and got hold of something very thin. Sharp even.

A bead of sweat oozed down Ellie's temple, her shoulder beginning to ache from the contortion. God, she wished she had Chris's long arms now. She straightened her elbow as much as possible, slid her arm inside another couple inches. She turned her hand, got hold of the object with her index finger and thumb, tugged. It slipped a little, so she pulled harder, and within the compartment something shifted, and her thumb erupted in a starburst of pain. Crying out, Ellie jerked her hand away, a hideous fire searing through her flesh.

Her knees became jelly when she beheld the bright red lines on her forearm and the razor blade sticking out of her thumb.

She hissed as she extracted the razor blade from the soft pad of skin.

The wound was deep. It ran the length of her thumbprint and ended just shy of the nail. Within the dark compartment she could see a gruesome mass of razor blades, many of them rusted with age, some speckled with what might have been dry blood. One blade tumbled out and clittered on the floor an inch from her bare feet, as though it too wanted a sample of her blood. She grimaced and dropped the blade that had cleaved her flesh.

She sucked on her thumb, the coppery taste making her queasy. Then she stopped, eyes widening.

What the hell was she thinking? She hadn't sliced her thumb open on an envelope or a piece of clear plastic, she'd cut it on a goddamned razor blade, a razor blade with rust or blood or God knew what caked all over its filthy mean edge.

A litany of horrific possibilities crashed down upon her like hailstones:

Tetanus.

Lockjaw.

Hepatitis.

AIDS.

Was AIDS even around when the razor blades had been discarded here? She scrambled through the dates, calculating with panicked rapidity. The last tenant, of course, was Aunt Lillith, and though Ellie had despised the old goblin, she doubted Lillith had been afflicted with any diseases.

But what did that prove? Just because Lillith had been healthy didn't mean the owners before her had been. Anyone in the last hundred years could have used this disgusting razor blade disposal system and consigned Ellie to a life of disease and a slow-suffering death.

Unconsciously, she'd begun to suck her bleeding thumb again.

Revolted, she jerked it out and spat, brought up the belly of her tank top to clean her tongue with.

She was shivering all over, her thoughts dissolving in a sick, fatalistic haze.

Think, Ellie. Think.

Katherine's voice, for once a welcome sound. *Get your tush in the bathroom and wash your wound. Apply pressure to stop the bleeding.*

Automatically, Ellie obeyed. She strode into the bathroom. Using her uninjured left hand to twist on the water, she thrust her thumb under the cold flow and winced as the dull throb increased.

"*Ooo,*" she said, walking in place. "*Damn damn damn damn damn.*"

Eventually the water warmed, but she held the thumb under the misty spray as long as she could stand it, the vague notion that hot water would kill the razor's germs raising her pain tolerance to a level far above normal.

When she could endure it no longer, she shut off the water and held her dripping hand above the sink. A bright red drop pattered in the white basin and coalesced, swirling, into the rivulets of water spiralling toward the drain.

She swaddled her thumb in a moist washcloth and stood, exhausted, before the open cabinet. She eyed the metal door and fought an insane urge to strike it with a hammer.

Ridiculous, she knew, to take out her frustration on an inanimate object. Besides, she had no idea if they even had a hammer.

Her thumb pounding, Ellie glared at the rectangle of metal.

She'd find a hammer in the morning.

CHAPTER FOUR

After exploring Ravana for a while, Chris went to a store called Ike's and splurged on groceries. When his cart began to overflow, he checked his watch and realised that seven a.m. was fast approaching. He didn't want Ellie to awaken in the new house alone.

The clerk watched him impassively as he began unloading his cart on the conveyor.

"You Ike?" Chris asked.

"Do I look like an Ike?"

Chris smiled. "Sorry. I just assumed you were the owner."

The man started scanning Chris's items. "Please, I'd rather eat dirt than own a business in this town."

A bunch of bananas refused to read. The clerk passed it over the dark glass again and again. As he did, Chris noticed the thinning black hair, shiny with too much gel. The hairy forearms. He detected a faint trace of old sweat and resolved to breathe through his mouth.

"Well, damn," the little man muttered and began typing in numbers.

In his peripheral vision Chris saw someone approach. He turned and saw a tall, broad-shouldered woman who quickly averted her eyes. He blinked a moment, the lack of sleep finally getting to him, when comprehension dawned.

"Doris?" he asked.

She froze as though debating whether or not she could keep walking and pretend she hadn't heard. Apparently deciding there was no escape, she faced him, her cold expression altering to something that wasn't quite friendliness.

She said, "I take it you decided to go through with it."

"We got in last night, and hopefully—" He knocked on the steel rim of the counter. "—the movers will arrive today."

"I wouldn't count on it," she said, smiling. "Those companies can be awfully unreliable."

"So I've heard," he answered and was irritated to note the clerk had stopped scanning to better hear their conversation.

Doris examined a bottle of shampoo from a centre display. "Shame we weren't able to sell your property."

Chris folded his arms. "I'm sort of glad it didn't sell."

"You're not the one who's moving into the Martin house," the clerk said.

Chris returned his gaze. "That's right. Lillith was my aunt."

The little man glanced at the real estate agent and something passed between them.

Doris said, "I feel we should have a talk, Mr. Crane. For closure."

She was only a few inches shy of his six-foot-three frame. He remembered seeing her photo on the real estate website, but nothing could've prepared him for the real thing. The woman was intimidating as hell, her large breasts crowding him, her small grey eyes rife with accusation.

Grateful for an excuse to avoid her gaze, Chris ran his debit card through the keypad and typed in his PIN number. "I don't see the need for that, Mrs. Keller. You did your best to sell the house."

"That's not what I'm talking about."

Her words were clipped and too loud by half in the otherwise deserted store. He noted with wonderment how fierce her expression had become, how aggressive her posture.

He faced her. "When would you like to meet?"

"I have showings until Friday. Come to my office then."

"Seems to me," Chris said, "since you're the one who wants to talk, you should come to our house."

She pursed her lips. "Friday around noon then," she said and walked away.

Chris looked at the clerk. "You wanna let me in on the secret?"

"What do you want to know?"

"For starters, why no one wanted to buy the land."

A cunning smile played over the man's lips and was replaced by a seriousness Chris knew was feigned. The clerk asked, "Have you heard of Gerald Destragis?"

The name meant nothing to him. He said so.

The little man nodded. "Might be a good place to start."

Chris opened his mouth to ask another question but a bloodcurdling wail from outside stopped him. For a long moment he and the little man stared at one another uncertainly. Then Chris remembered the dog in his car and started for the door.

*   *   *

When he first spotted the man bent toward the Camry's window, his face mere inches from the gap in the window, Chris thought he was taunting the animal. His blue work shirt, denim overalls and stovepipe hat gave the man a mischievous appearance, like a ceramic garden gnome come to life. Furthering the impression was the man's posture: hands on knees, red-bearded face jutting forward, the flesh of his cheeks ruddy and gleeful.

The man was saying something to the dog, which was baying wildly and scratching at the window. As he approached, Chris realised the man was attempting to mollify rather than provoke the animal.

"…a good dog…he'll be back for you soon…shhh…"

"What's going on?" Chris asked. Dog and man looked up at his voice, and though the man was smiling broadly, the dog's efforts to claw his way out of the car redoubled.

"Doesn't much care for being alone," the man said.

"Guess not," Chris answered and opened the door. A black blur leaped out and nearly sent him sprawling. The dog skidded awkwardly, scrabbled for footholds, and jumped at Chris again. The man laughed as the animal hurled himself against Chris's body as though they'd been apart for years rather than minutes.

"Easy," Chris said. "Easy, boy."

"Take care," the man said and went toward the store.

Kneeling before the dog, Chris called, "He just start howling like that? For no reason?"

"None that I could see," the man said and came back over. "I didn't even notice him when I got out of my truck. When he started in I must've jumped a mile in the air."

Now that the triphammer of his heart had subsided, Chris was able to survey the length of the man's beard, the plainness of his clothing. A German Baptist, or what his parents called Amish.

The man asked, "New in town?"

"My wife and I arrived last night. We moved into my aunt's old home."

"Yeah?"

"It's east of town. A black house in the woods."

For the merest fraction of a second the man didn't respond. Then his grin returned and he said, "Sure, I know the place." He offered his hand. "Name's Daniel Wolf."

Chris told the man his name and shook, the large hand gripping his firmly.

"We're neighbours, Mr. Crane," Daniel said.

"Chris."

Daniel nodded at Chris's belt buckle. "Figured your name was Lenny."

Chris smiled and explained the buckle's origins.

Daniel nodded. "Your land ends at Deer Creek Road – mine begins across the way."

Chris opened the Camry door and ushered the dog in. Closing it, he asked, "Are you a farmer?"

Daniel grinned, regarded his scuffed work boots. "I cash-rent a little. Mainly I work on houses."

"Like a handyman?"

"If people need that, sure. Mostly we do renovations, but occasionally we'll do a new construction."

"We?"

"Me and my brother. I do custom cabinetry, Aaron's a wiz with plumbing and electric."

The dog pawed the inside of the window, whined at them.

"Just a second, pal," Chris said and smiled an apology at Daniel. "You in the yellow pages, Mr. Wolf? We might be needing you guys soon."

"If I'm not mistaken, Aaron did some work there."

Chris nodded and hooked a thumb at the dog. "I better get going before he eats the seat."

"Hope you like it here," Daniel said and walked away.

Chris got in but before he could fit the key in the ignition, the dog assaulted him with a flurry of slobbery licks. Chris shielded his face, nudged the dog back toward the passenger seat. "All right, all right, I was only gone a few minutes."

The dog whined and shook his posterior excitedly.

Chris made to start the car, but paused. "I gotta get my groceries," he said. "Be back in a couple minutes."

After returning with his paper sacks and arranging them in the trunk, Chris got in. The dog set to licking his face again, and once Chris had him calmed down, he slid the key in the ignition.

"I've been thinking about names," Chris said. He started the engine and glanced at the dog. "How about Petey?"

*　　*　　*

Nestled in the sleeping bag, Ellie heard the Camry approaching and thought: *He better have food.* Then she recalled the incident in the closet and the sleep fog burned away.

Ellie got up and went downstairs, and through the kitchen window saw Chris pop the trunk. He hefted several plastic bags and jogged to the back door. Reluctantly, she went over and opened it for him.

"Don't hit me," he said as he passed.

She peeked inside a couple of bags and felt much of her anger melt away at the sight of eggs, apples and bagged lettuce.

Setting everything on the counter, he said, "I was hoping you'd sleep until I got back."

She was about to relay her bad experience when a large yellow sack caught her eye.

"Dog food?" she asked.

"Oh yeah, I forgot to tell you."

"That sounds ominous."

But he was already by her, down the steps, and flinging open the Camry's back door.

The black dog was enormous.

Worse, it was bounding toward her like some kind of heartland panther, its eyes gleaming with idiot ferocity.

"Chris?" she said.

But he was laughing as the dog torpedoed her mid-section and almost knocked her down. She pivoted and made to escape but the dog shoved its nose up the crack of her ass. She straightened and let out a cry. And Chris, goddamn him, was laughing as though it was the funniest thing he'd ever seen. She hated when dogs did this, when they jumped on you and treated your crotch like their own personal wonderland.

"Down, boy," Chris said, finally coming over. "Down, Petey."

"Petey?" she asked as she tried to ward it off. The dog continued bouncing, his nose boring between her legs.

Chris laughed. "Friendly, isn't he?"

She covered her privates but the dog battered himself against her hands and nearly bent her double.

She backpedalled. "Chris…can you…"

"All right, Petey, stay down."

"You sure he's safe? He's been living in the wild."

"The wild? Come on, honey, this is Indiana."

She watched her husband soothe the eager animal and fought the ridiculous feeling that she'd been replaced. The dog surged forward but Chris wrapped it up before it could assault her again.

Ellie backpedalled to the screen door and grasped the handle in case Petey broke free.

"Can't you give him a sedative or something?"

"I think he likes you."

Petey finally gave up trying to reach her and contented himself with licking Chris's face.

Ellie made a mental note to withhold her good morning kiss. As if to affirm her thinking, Petey left off slobbering on her husband and immersed himself in licking his own testicles.

"Charming," Ellie said. "He doing that when you found him?"

"Kind of impressive, really."

"So we're keeping him," she said. "That's what you've decided."

Chris made a pained face. "Come on, don't be like that."

She chewed her lip. "You could've consulted me."

"You were dead to the world."

"I wasn't," she said, holding up her bandaged arm. "But I might be."

"Oh hell," he said, moving over to her. "What happened?"

"I'll share the gory details over breakfast," she said. "You get pancake mix?"

He wrapped his arms about her waist. "I got everything."

He leaned in to kiss her, but she stayed him with a hand on his chest.

"What?"

"I'll kiss you later. Right now you smell like Petey's balls."

⋆ ⋆ ⋆

A couple hours later, she changed her mind about the dog.

After scrubbing rust stains out of the bathtub and sweeping the floors with a broom and a dustpan that looked so old they might have been part of some archaeological dig, she began the job of putting her clothes away. She'd been unpacking a suitcase when she found a purse she'd stuffed inside before they left. Though she hadn't used the purse in years, there were a few items within, one of which was a crumpled photograph of Kat and her children. Ellie had seen the picture before, of course, but the last time had been before she and Chris had gotten serious about having their own family.

And here they were, still childless.

The sight of Kat – hugging her two girls and her son – blindsided Ellie, caused her to slump on the bedroom floor and cry slow tears of self-pity. She hated herself for reacting this way, and she hated Kat for winning yet again. Most of all she hated the fact that another year of prime childbearing was flying by, and she and Chris still hadn't gotten pregnant.

Then Petey came in. The animal still shook with anxious energy, and sitting as she was on the floor, she hadn't the strength to resist his friendly overtures. He nosed her hand until she petted him. He whined happily.

Petey flopped down beside her and thrust his heavy head into her lap. She scratched him under the chin. And as stupid as it was, within a couple minutes, she'd forgotten all about Kat and her family. Gazing into Petey's trusting, guileless face, she realised she wasn't alone. At least she had a husband and a dog.

She stroked Petey's fur and was almost able to smile.

CHAPTER FIVE

By the time the sun had burned away the last of the morning dew, Chris and Petey were a mile from the house. The trail they followed was a tortuous earthen corridor overhung with branches that frequently smacked Chris in the face and nettles that bit through his jeans like eager teeth. Suspicious-looking weeds slithered up his pant legs, tickling his ankle hair with spiderlike delicacy.

Petey bolted away through the forest.

"Hey," Chris called after him. He did his best to follow Petey downward into the darkest stretch yet, a shadowy, marshy swale that would no doubt soon become host to a million mosquito eggs. His tennis shoes, already damp, soaked all the way through as he squelched through the standing water. He thought briefly of quicksand, of childhood cartoons that used to scare the hell out of him. In those shows quicksand was never far away, and once one fell prey to it, the speed at which a person sank was equal to the vigour of his struggles. In spite of his relative surety that there was no quicksand here, he nevertheless found himself eyeing the standing water with growing suspicion.

A shrill bark made him jump.

"Relax, boy," he muttered at Petey, who watched him impatiently. "What's the emergency?"

The black lab danced about, his strong body tensed in a half crouch. He retreated a few feet and stopped, his back paws jittering.

Chris frowned. "What's eating you, pal?"

The dog uttered a sharp bark, retreated again.

"You want me to follow you?"

Another bark.

Chris glanced back up the hill. "Gimme a break this time. I don't want the wife waiting for me all—"

Sharp teeth clamped over his hand, and Chris jerked away from the dog in surprise. "*Hey*," he said. "That hurt, dammit."

Petey continued to shake his hindquarters, his head low and expectant. A barely perceptible growl had begun to emanate from the dog's corded throat.

"All right, all right," he said. He grunted, moved farther into the marshy thicket. "But wherever it is you're leading me, it better be worth it."

*   *   *

For a moment all Chris could do was stand at the edge of the forest and gape. Prior to this moment he'd suspected that on a property this expansive, there must be clearings in the forest. He'd even wondered whether or not there existed a more suitable place to build a new house, a site with a better view and higher ground.

But this was breathtaking. Acres upon acres of treeless land, slightly longer than it was wide, the gorgeous meadow rose gradually toward the middle, then sloped into a wide dale that meandered toward the woods bordering the eastern edge. Chris set off at a run up the hill with Petey in tow, and once there he realised that, yes, his suspicion had been correct. Before the woods once again reclaimed the land there lay a circular pond at the edge of the clearing, the water itself at least two acres in diameter. A family of mallards patrolled the brown water, the baby ducks floating like grey cottonballs.

Amazed, Chris paused at the top of the hill and wheeled about, taking in the jawdropping view around him. He'd dreamed of a place where he and his children could run and tumble in the grass, and though this meadow was overgrown, it looked infinitely more inviting than the weed-strewn horror of their current yard. Petey galloped around him in delighted circles, his mouth open in silent laughter.

"You like it, boy?" Chris asked and stared down at the glimmering surface of the pond.

Something to the left arrested his attention. He squinted and shielded his eyes to better make it out.

Another clearing, but much smaller. A half-acre at most. A short trail serpentined into the forest for a short time before opening upon this second cleared space. A nagging worm of unease wending its way through his excitement, Chris began to walk slowly down the hill in that direction. Unaccountably, a bitter brew of gastric juices began to percolate at the back of his throat.

He reached the path and stared into its shadows.

He turned, expecting Petey to be watching him, but the black dog was resting now, chin on paws, dozing languidly by the pond's edge.

Strangely disappointed, maybe even hoping Petey would give him a reason to head back, Chris squared up to the path and noticed for the first time how clean its lines were. No thorny undergrowth here, no brambles or deadfalls of branches. Just a neat, open swath about four feet wide that looped gradually to the left before disappearing into the enshrouding darkness. Behind him, an odd stillness had fallen over the meadow. As if bidding it farewell for the last time, Chris scanned the rise, allowed his gaze to linger on every detail of the rolling ground.

Then, with no reason to wait longer, he entered the lightless path.

CHAPTER SIX

Something's gone wrong, he thought. *You took the wrong trail.*

Had to have, for the one he glimpsed from the hill ran for no more than fifty yards before terminating into the smaller clearing. But he'd been walking for several minutes now, and there was no sign of a break. If anything, the foliage here was denser than any he'd yet encountered. And though he knew he was being paranoid, he found it odd that he hadn't yet spotted another living creature in this eerie corridor. Perhaps the animals were afraid of this place, too.

He wished Petey had come. The dog's presence would have been a salve for his escalating apprehension. Chris was more frightened than he had been since he was very young, and the fear made him angry at himself. Lips thinning, he resolved to follow the trail to its conclusion, to by God see what he'd come here to see and not let his quailing nerves get the better of him.

He peered up at the overhanging boughs and saw why it was so dark on the trail. The trees here grew in two tiers, the old growth giants – oaks, elms, sycamores – on the upper level; younger trees and shrubs forming the lower. Yet despite the surfeit of plant life, there was nothing impeding his progress, no branches here to strike him like switches brandished by stern headmasters, no nettles to set his skin aflame with their pinprick assaults.

Almost like the path was cleared for you.

Chris swallowed. Despite the growing darkness, his eyes were adjusting, and he wasn't at all sure this was a good thing. A sentience seemed to lurk here in the wooded corridor, one that regarded him with barely restrained hostility. Strange designs began to clarify on the ancient brown trunks, and though most were oblong whorls, a few resembled faces. One in particular...

He moved closer to get a better look.

At first the swirling lines on the immense oak tree reminded him of knights jousting, their lances raised as they thundered together. Then their armour faded and took on the shape of modern garb – tuxedos replete with bow ties and cummerbunds.

His breath caught in his throat. He no longer discerned just a pair of figures – he could make out eight of them. They were dressed for a wedding. And what they raised in the air were not jousts, but golf clubs. The eight clubs formed an inverted V, a tunnel through which the groom could pass.

And yes...there *was* a figure emerging through the tunnel of clubs, grinning, the handsome features smug and chiselled. The face he'd seen a thousand times in his nightmares, the ones in which Ellie left him to return to...

...to return to Jason Halladay. Her ex-husband.

It was the same picture, right down to the grinning faces of the groomsmen, that he saw on the dining room wall at his in-laws' house every time he and Ellie came to visit. Even after it became plain that Ellie and Chris were an item, even after they got *married*, for chrissakes, the goddamn picture stayed on her parents' wall, for what purpose he could only guess. To warn him Ellie might someday divorce him too? To remind Ellie she'd already screwed up once, that this was her second marriage and her parents would brook no more failures? To confirm they preferred Jason to Chris? That they wished Ellie and Jason had stayed married because he'd been a better provider?

He became aware of sharp pain in his hands. He glanced down and discovered he'd been digging his fingernails into his palms.

Lighten up, he told himself. *Good lord, it's just a tree.*

Yet it wasn't. The clarity of the design was uncannily true to the wedding photo. He'd hated the picture the first time he'd seen it, and not just because it reminded him Ellie had once been married, had been through the process of courtship, engagement, of planning a wedding, of exchanging vows, and then the wedding night, the honeymoon—

Stop it.

He hated the picture because it perfectly summarised Ellie's ex-husband: Jason Halladay with his charmed life, his full ride to UC-Irvine on a golf scholarship, his cushy job working for his father.

His half-a-million-dollar starter home in a gated community. Jason Halladay, grinning at Chris in triumph.

His breathing was growing ragged, but that had nothing to do with the heat. His rage had grown murderous, a shrieking red cloud that ate through him like acid, that made him long for something, anything into which he could pour his frustration. No, goddammit, it wasn't just the *fact* of the picture that bothered him, it was the *symbolism* of it as well. He'd once tried to explain it to Ellie, but she'd rolled her eyes at him as though he were an overimaginative child.

But staring at Jason's form passing under those raised golf clubs, all the groomsmen grinning at him with pride and deference, the old insecurity welled up in Chris like a poisonous geyser. Yes, Jason looked like a king in the picture, a lord and master, and wasn't that exactly what he'd been? *It doesn't matter what you do*, his grin seemed to say, *it doesn't matter that you're legally married to Ellie now. Because I was there first, pal. I met her first. I made love to her first. She gave herself fully to me, willingly, passionately—*

And hadn't she once confided in Chris – back before he had any idea he and Ellie would become a couple, back when they were just two people who'd met by chance at the beach – that her relationship with Jason had been largely physical, that the sexual chemistry between them was what led to their marriage, as well as the element that sustained it for five years?

That's right, Jason's voice echoed in the shadowy glade. *She and I made love too many times to count, and it was better than it'll ever be between you and her. I was better than you'll ever be. Just ask Ellie.*

He almost had, God help him, one night as they planned their wedding reception. Yet he'd been too terrified of her answer to pose the question, terrified her brutal bluntness would forever feed the tumour of jealousy gnawing away at him.

Jason's wheedling voice: *You're thirty-seven years old, Chris. Four years older than Ellie. You told yourself the age difference didn't matter, but what if it does? What if that's the reason why she's still not pregnant?*

Oh God, he thought, a hand going to his throat. His airway had dwindled to capillary thinness. He tried to look away from the tree but could not, for now he heard a sound that bewildered him, a baby crying, and though he knew the sound was coming from his imagination, he was unable to escape it.

It's you, Chris, Jason Halladay whispered. *You're the reason you can't conceive. You're shooting blanks, buddy, and if Ellie'd stuck with me we'd have a handsome brood by now.*

No.

You're quite a catch, you know it, Crane? Poor, sterile, unemployed. It's no wonder Ellie's unhappy.

Chris shook his head. *Not unhappy.*

Discontent is her middle name, pal. And dragging her out here to the middle of nowhere just might prove to be the clincher, the move that sends Ellie to the courthouse to rectify the mistake she made when she married your sorry ass.

Shut up.

Can't give her a child, can't make her moan in bed the way I did, can't even pay the bills to maintain that shitty apartment you two had.

Chris dug his fists into his eyes.

Did you really think it would work? Isolating her? You know in your heart she'll wander, don't you? No matter how far away you try to keep her from other men, there'll always be someone better than you, someone who'll sense in her that frustration, that wildness, and when it happens, there'll be nothing you can do about it. Who knows, buddy? Maybe it's happening right now.

"*Shut up!*" he shouted. He sank to his knees, whimpering, a forearm over his eyes, over the stinging tears. He stayed like that a long while, kneeling abjectly on the soft humus of the trail.

*   *   *

After a time he got slowly to his feet, sniffed, rubbed the mucus from his nostrils. Licking his lips in disgust, he glanced at the tree and was amazed to see the design gone, ordinary bark having taken its place.

Now he was glad Petey hadn't come. He wouldn't want anyone, not even a dog, to see how he'd behaved. The sweat on his forehead had cooled, and the hair at his temples and the base of his neck was wet and sticky. His flannel shirt clung to his chest. He unbuttoned it, peeled it off his shoulders and tied it around his waist. The air here felt good, the forest stifling any breeze that might chill his bare skin.

He moved on, certain now he'd chosen the wrong path – he should have long ago come upon the clearing. But this didn't worry him. It wasn't as though his steps would be difficult to retrace. This trail reminded him of a topiary maze he'd visited as a child, its green walls stately and impeccably manicured. The only difference was that inside the topiary he could follow a strip of blue sky as he walked. Here there were only intermittent reminders that there was a sky overhead at all. His nostrils tingled with the crisp fragrance of new vegetation, the moist scent of groping roots.

Ahead, the trail widened.

His pulse speeding, Chris jogged down the path. He spotted occasional breaks in the forest now, malformed splotches of sunlight piercing the forest wall. Beneath the padding thumps of his footfalls he discerned another noise, but it was so faint he was forced to slow down so he could hear it better.

A woman's voice. Humming.

The song was sweet, beguiling. There were no words, but the melody intoxicated him, made his flesh tingle and his nipples harden. A heat developed between his legs, his blue jeans suddenly too restrictive. He had a delirious urge to shed them, to strip naked and dash forward into the clearing.

The song grew louder, beckoning him forward.

What are you doing? a voice asked dimly, but the words scarcely registered beneath the tumult of his senses. And besides, wasn't it obvious? This was a mystery, a golden, glistening mystery not unlike the myths that used to spellbind him as a child. Some ethereal creature had happened into his world, and he'd be foolish to let it escape without making some sort of contact.

Ahead, the trees began to thin, the sunlight slanting through in a dozen places. Chris beheld the mottled mouth of the clearing, but an ugly buzzing now mingled with the lovely melody, sullying it, transforming it into a dirge. His vision greyed, and his legs tingled as if they'd been asleep. He staggered against a bush and hissed as its sharp appendages gored his shoulder. He reeled down the trail toward the clearing, but he could hardly see now, the dimming veil strangling his consciousness.

A figure flitted across the trail. It was slim, naked, but Chris couldn't continue any longer. He sank forward on buckling knees. As his face dipped toward the earth he heard the voice again, but this time it was laughing. He rolled over, struggled to open his eyes, but the torpor deepened, a cruel lassitude anesthetising his lids.

Then, as he descended into the velvety folds of dream, he felt fingernails caress his stomach.

CHAPTER SEVEN

It had been a taxing day, with the movers unloading for the better part of the afternoon and then Chris behaving distantly. But now, as Ellie lay in bed, all the exhaustion and worry melted away. She rolled onto her belly and moaned contentedly at the warmth of the sheet on her face. She dozed, sweet images of their honeymoon in Cancun replaying in her memory. The need to urinate dragged her unwillingly back to the present, but the cosiness of the comforter on her back, the peaceful susurrus of her sound machine forbade her from rising and emptying her bladder. Smiling, she let her hand dangle over the bed's edge.

She became aware of pressure on her fingertips. Wet, yielding.

Ellie frowned, full consciousness tugging at her like an insistent child.

Something was licking her fingers.

Ellie groaned. It was a cruel irony that Petey had chosen her injured thumb for his sloppy ministrations.

"Stop it," she whispered. "Go away."

But the licking became more determined, her nostrils filling with the stink of Petey's hot, foetid breath. Her fingers felt dipped in cooking oil.

"Chris," she said, her voice louder. "Get your dog out of here."

The Band-Aid slid off her thumb, the stupid animal actually pushing his tongue into the aching slit of her wound. Hissing with pain and revulsion, Ellie shoved away and pushed to her knees. She patted the bed for Chris, but, dammit, he was gone again.

Leaving her with Petey.

"*Out*," she yelled at the dog and pointed at the door. "*Now!*"

She listened for the clatter of toenails on wood, the steam engine chug of Petey's breathing.

But the room was silent.

Was the dog watching her in the dark?

"Petey," she said, a whisper of fear tingling the nape of her neck, "I want you to leave this room at once."

Great, she thought. *You sound like a nineteenth-century schoolmarm.*

She breathed deeply, hoping it would give her courage.

Be firm. Let him know who's boss.

"I'm going to turn on the lamp now, and when I do—"

"What's going on?"

She cried out at the voice and perceived a large figure standing in the doorway; then light flooded the room and Chris was crossing to the bed.

"Ellie, what—"

"Where were you?"

He spread his palms. "I was downstairs having a snack."

"You told me you put the dog out."

He stared at her. "I did."

"The hell you did," she said and drew up her legs. "I woke up and found Petey dining on my thumb."

He shook his head and grinned incredulously. "Honey, that's impossible. I put him out right after dinner. You saw me do it."

An icy mist of dread engulfed her. "Stop scaring me. It isn't the least bit cute—"

"Ellie—"

"—and it isn't funny either. Do you have any idea how repulsive it felt to have his tongue burrowing into my thumb? Like he was getting a taste for it?"

Chris scratched the back of his neck, let his arm drop. "Come with me."

"Where're you going?" she asked and hated the break in her voice.

"To call Petey in," he said, walking to the door. "You don't believe he's outside, I'll prove it."

Ellie's heart pounded. "You swear you didn't let him in?"

"Of course I didn't. Jeez, you think I'm that stupid, playing a practical joke when you already hate the place?"

She gathered the sheets to her chest. "Then what was it?"

"You must've been dreaming."

"I wasn't—"

"They can be really vivid."

"Dammit, I wasn't dreaming. Don't you think I know the difference?"

"What else could it be?"

"*I don't know*," she shouted.

"Okay," he said, coming to her. "Okay, let's both calm down. I'm sure there's an explanation…" He searched the bedroom a moment before seizing on something. "The vent." He pointed to the wall opposite the bed. "The furnace kicked on and started blowing hot air and you thought—"

"It wasn't the furnace."

"How do you know?"

"A furnace doesn't have a tongue."

He threw up his hands, the rational man beleaguered by the hysterical woman.

"Or saliva," she went on, "or stinking dog breath, or—"

"It's an old house, it's bound to smell."

"Where's my Band-Aid then?" She held up her thumb. "Did the vent take that too?"

He shrugged. "It fell off in your sleep. It's probably in the bed somewhere."

She flung the sheet away and swung her feet to the floor. Kneeling, she jerked up the blankets and stared under the bed.

Nothing.

She crossed to the hallway.

"I'm telling you," Chris said, following, "he's not in here."

She jogged down the stairs and began switching on lights. The living room bloomed in a dim amber glow. Empty. The family room. The screened-in porch. No sign of the dog.

Chris passed her on the way to the door.

"Where're you going?" she asked.

"To get Petey."

"Wait," she said, but he'd already opened the door, was bellowing the dog's name into the still April night.

Within seconds she heard a sound that made her stomach clench, Petey's eager breathing, the muted thump of his paws on the frosted earth. The dog appeared, moving slower than usual, as though the exertion of his approach had expended all his energy. Petey moved sluggishly up the steps and rather than jumping on Chris, slumped down next to his feet.

"Hey, fella," her husband said a bit too triumphantly. Chris knelt, scratching the dog's ears, and glanced up at her. "Well?"

"Well what?" she said. "I was wrong." She turned and went to the kitchen.

She filled a glass of water, her hands trembling, and downed half of it in a swallow. Rather than calming her, the frigid liquid drove a hatchet into the centre of her forehead. She leaned against the counter, blanching at the pain.

"Relax, honey," he said. "I'm sure there's an explanation."

"Explain it then."

But he didn't say anything, only eyed her wound. Ellie glanced at it too, and as she did she had a vision of a fanged creature spreading wide the flaps of skin and swallowing her blood in a gush.

Later, she'd remember that vision and marvel at how apt it had been.

CHAPTER EIGHT

Doris's car reminded Chris of the woman herself: big, white, imposing. Through the living room window he watched the big sedan crunch to a stop as though to draw any closer might taint Doris or her gleaming white car.

"She's here," he called over his shoulder.

"Goody," Ellie called back.

He put on a smile he didn't feel and opened the front door. Doris climbed out of her car, shouldering a large beige purse. She wore a red business suit, the skirt stopping just north of her thick calves.

"Hope you brought your appetite," he said from the porch.

"I've eaten," she answered as she climbed the steps.

"I thought you said—"

"I said lunch time, Mr. Crane. Not that I'd eat lunch here."

Ellie held open the door, an expression of welcome on her pretty face that Chris would have believed had he not known her so well.

"You must be Doris," she said.

The Realtor nodded. "Ellie."

He stepped inside after them, Ellie going left into the dining room, Doris making no move to follow.

Ellie said, "There's iced tea, Diet Coke—"

"I'm not staying."

Ellie looked at him and he explained, "She's already eaten."

The skin around Ellie's mouth drew tight.

Chris asked, "Would you be comfortable in the living room?"

The realtor sighed. "It's as good a place as any, I suppose."

When the woman moved past him he saw Ellie's mask of cordiality slip, and it took all he had not to burst into laughter. She raised her middle fingers at the woman's back. Doris sat primly in the green velvet chair and smoothed her skirt.

"What can we do for you?" he asked, sitting across from her on the futon. Ellie sat beside him.

The Realtor folded her hands on her knees, which were pressed tightly together as though she feared Chris might try to peek up her skirt. Now that he observed her in the softer light of the living room, he could catch the merest glimmer of her girlhood self. Not a beautiful face — not at any age — but one that had perhaps long ago contained a species of crude eroticism.

Doris glanced out the window. "Too bad we couldn't find a buyer."

"I don't get it," Chris said. "It's gorgeous out—"

"The property's desirability has nothing to do with aesthetics."

He grunted. "Then what is it? There a landfill nearby?"

She regarded him levelly. "You don't know anything about this place, do you?"

From the corner of his eye he could see Ellie staring at him, sensed the worry in her face, and thought, *Don't screw this up for me, Doris. I already have enough to contend with. Don't tell us this house is full of ghosts or something.*

"I came to tell you about the previous owner of this land," Doris said. "A man named Gerald Destragis."

For reasons he couldn't explain, a trickle of acid began to scale his oesophagus.

Doris said, "He came to America in 1932 and bought this land from a local farmer. Soon after, he met your aunt. She was the closest thing he had to a long-term relationship."

Chris felt faintly nauseated. He'd never seen Aunt Lillith with a man, had never considered the possibility she had any interest in them. On more than one occasion, Ellie had raised the possibility that Aunt Lillith preferred women.

Doris crossed her legs, her voice taking on a pedantic air. "The two of them formed a cult."

Chris smiled. "What?"

"You heard me, Mr. Crane."

"Aunt Lillith was the leader of a cult."

"Destragis's scripture revolved around pagan legend, the gods of the Celts and the Romans. He contended Satan was a minor figure in the religious landscape, that the real power lay with spirits far, far older.

He also wanted to dispel commonly held beliefs regarding demons."

Ellie frowned. "Commonly held beliefs?"

"Most believe that demons are separate entities from ghosts... that demons are, well, demonic, and that ghosts were once human in nature. Most who study that sort of thing associate demons with the devil, and ghosts with human beings who haven't yet...crossed over, I suppose."

Doris pursed her lips, studied the hands folded on her knees. "Destragis believed man could willingly enter the demonic realm, that nature itself could serve as a passageway between life as we know it and a different kind of existence."

Chris chuckled. "What a crock of shit."

Ellie fluttered a hand, as if shooing a persistent insect. "You said 'nature itself could serve as a passageway'."

"Gerald believed demons were people who had, over time, become one with nature, one with the ancient world and its energy."

Ellie's voice was wondering. "That's why he came here."

Doris stared at her a moment before tilting her head and asking, "Do either of you believe in reincarnation?"

"No," Ellie answered.

Doris hardly reacted, merely raised her chin a fraction of an inch and favoured Ellie with an appraising look. "Then I don't suppose you believe in vampires either."

Chris uttered a laugh that came out half an octave too high.

"Gerald Destragis believed in them," Doris said with the merest hint of a sneer. "He believed he'd died and returned as a vampire." The sneer grew. "Twice, actually."

Doris let it sink in a moment before continuing. "In the first reincarnation, he was reborn as a feral, bloodthirsty creature. The sort of beast one sees in horror films."

Ellie started to say something, but Doris was already going on. "The second rebirth – the life with which we here in Ravana were familiar – that was a more refined existence. He appeared to be a regular man. Eating, breathing, interacting the way men do. Preying upon human beings, but only infrequently. As a ritual, a preparation. Not for sustenance."

The feeling was growing upon Chris that the women had forgotten his presence. He heard himself saying, "The romantic vampire."

Doris turned to him.

Chris said, "I feel like I'm on one of those hidden camera shows."

"You sound frightened, Mr. Crane."

He flailed a hand in the air. "Lillith didn't believe in vampires, demons, whatever you want to call it."

"Demonic evolution."

There was a silence.

"Demonic evolution," Ellie repeated.

"It's all in his book," Doris explained. "I'm sure Lillith had a copy."

"My aunt wouldn't have gone in for this stuff. She'd have known Destragis was a fake." He shook his head. "Some freak masquerading as a twice-resurrected monster."

"You misunderstand, Mr. Crane. Lillith Martin believed she'd also lived two previous lives."

Chris could only stare.

"You don't believe me," Doris said, "because you didn't know your aunt. That was clear to me the first time we spoke."

"I knew her a hell of a lot better than you did."

"Lillith Martin was a bloodthirsty harlot."

Chris felt his body go rigid, the muscles of his forearms bunching like steel cables. "We're done here, Doris."

"What's the book called?" Ellie asked.

"*The Lust*," Doris answered and turned to Chris. "Lillith drank the blood of infants."

He stood. "Listen, I don't know why you're making this crap up, but—"

"I want to buy the land from you."

For a long moment no one said anything, but Chris could sense a change in Ellie. When she spoke, her tone was full of a restrained eagerness.

Goddammit, Doris, he thought. *Get the hell out of here before you spoil everything.*

"How much would you offer?" Ellie asked.

Chris put a hand on Ellie's arm. "Hold on a second."

"Enough to help you buy a new house."

"Ellie, she's—"

"One that doesn't need tens of thousands in repairs," Doris went on. "One that isn't stuck out here in the middle of nowhere."

"How much?" Ellie repeated.

"Ellie—"

"Two hundred thousand," Doris answered.

Ellie's eyebrows rose.

"*Ellie*," he said, "she's trying to rip us off."

"Imagine it," Doris said. "Two hundred thousand to spend on whatever house you want, wherever you want."

"That's less than a hundred an acre," Chris almost shouted. "What the hell?"

Doris finally glanced at him, and as she did he understood how deftly she'd managed it, how she'd driven a wedge between him and Ellie. Her look of cold triumph did it, put him over the edge.

"I'm not going to tell you again," Chris said. "Get out of my house."

The cold smile never leaving her lips, Doris gathered her purse. "You two can discuss it in private."

"There's nothing to discuss," Chris said, but when he glanced again at Ellie he could see the offer had grabbed hold of her. She sat as if in a trance, her gaze turned inward.

Something about the woman's expensive-looking purse sent a galvanic jolt of energy through him. It started as a vague thought but within moments crystallised into an unshakeable certainty.

"Who owned this land?" he asked.

Doris paused a fraction of a second before answering, "Why your aunt, of course."

"Before that."

"Gerald Destragis owned it for many years," Doris said, but her smile had thinned.

"That's not what I asked."

A subtle but unmistakable patchwork of blotches had appeared on the woman's neck. "It's all public record, Mr. Crane. You're free to investigate it on your own."

"Why don't you save me the trouble, Doris?"

Her smile vanished. "I'll be going."

But Chris followed her to the foyer. "How do you know so much about Destragis?" he asked.

Doris reached for the door. "Though he cheated on her for decades, he was legally married to my mom."

Chris's mouth fell open.

Doris smiled without humour. "Which made him my biological father."

Chris could only stare.

Doris's eyes were cold. "Any more questions, Mr. Crane?"

"Your mom…"

"Yes?" she asked, the bitterness twisting her face into an ugly mask.

"She was the one who got the land, wasn't she. When Destragis died?"

Doris opened the door and went out.

Chris followed her. "How much did she charge Lillith for the land?"

"Look it up."

Doris was down the steps in an instant. He said to her back, "How much?"

"Four million," she said.

He felt as though he'd taken a sledgehammer to the gut. "Four million…Jesus Christ, that could have been mine."

Nearing her car, Doris said, "But it wasn't."

"You stole from me—"

"It's a fair offer," Doris said.

"—now you're trying to steal again. You're playing Ellie against me."

"I've done my duty," she said. "Now you know what horrible things your aunt and her lover believed in. Their intention was to return again, only in perfect form this time." Doris's eyes shifted toward the woods, and with incipient misgiving Chris saw Petey padding toward the big white car. "Human, vampire… Destragis believed both were stages in demonic evolution. He and Lillith believed the demonic realm was the ideal fusion of both."

Chris hooked a thumb at Ellie, who'd appeared on the front porch. "You're poisoning her against this place."

Doris was halfway in the car when she held up an index finger. "I forgot to tell you one thing—" she began, but her eyes suddenly shifted to Chris's right. He turned that way, and as he did a large, black object shot past him toward the Realtor. Chris stumbled back in shock as Petey seized the woman by the arm and dragged her out of the car.

For a moment he was frozen, the sight of the flailing woman and the growling dog like a surrealist painting of damnation. Then he lunged forward and got Petey around the neck. But the Labrador was immoveable, its sleek head shaking Doris's arm like a long, red chew toy. The woman was slapping at Petey's snarling face and moaning in terror.

"Stop it, goddammit," he said, battering at the dog's shoulders now. "Stop it *right now*, Petey."

Wild-eyed, Doris twitched her head at him. "*What did you call him?*"

Chris got an arm under the dog's jaw, seized a handful of the lab's neck fur and reared back. The dog yelped and opened its mouth enough for the Realtor to break free and scuttle, crablike, toward the car.

Ellie was beside him now, helping with Petey. The engine revved and as the white car's rear end backed into the yard, Petey lurched forward, dragging Chris and Ellie several feet before they corralled him and held him in place as the car fishtailed in the grass and leaped back onto the lane. Petey uttered several strident barks at the receding car and strained to break free of their grasp, but after the car disappeared he finally seemed to calm a little. Chris petted the Labrador's smooth, black neck, whispered soothing words. He sensed Ellie watching him, knew what she was thinking.

"She's a thief," Chris said without looking at his wife.

Ellie didn't answer.

He continued stroking Petey's fur, the dog like a bulwark between Chris and his wife's desire to be rid of this place. *No*, he thought. *We're going to stick this thing out. We're not going to let some farcical tale about demons and vampires deprive us of what we might have here.*

Ellie stood up and moved toward the house. Still on the ground beside Petey, Chris watched her go.

PART TWO
THIRST
CHAPTER ONE

Sheriff Troy Bruder struck Chris as the type of guy who had probably been immensely popular in high school. A football player, maybe a wrestler too. Bruder had a dark complexion, thick brown hair trimmed to a nearly militaristic shortness, blue eyes and a muscular physique. A muggy cloud of Brut aftershave attended him.

After introducing himself, Bruder folded his hands respectfully and said, "I guess you know why I'm here."

Chris said, "Doris," and Bruder nodded.

"I don't know what got into Petey," Ellie said.

"That the dog's name?" Bruder asked.

"He kind of came with the place," Chris said and ventured a smile. Bruder didn't return it.

"What are you going to do?" Ellie asked.

Bruder eyed her grimly. "If we go by the letter of the law, I'll have to destroy the animal and fine you a thousand bucks."

Chris's heart sank. The panic on Ellie's face made it worse.

Bruder scuffed a shoe in the gravel. "I suppose, though, that in this case we can skip the fine."

Chris said, "What happens to Petey?"

Bruder was silent a long moment. Chris's breathing thinned. *Oh no*, he thought. *Not that.*

But the sheriff's eyes confirmed it. "I'm sorry, Mr. Crane. You two seem like nice people, and I'm a big dog lover. Got three of 'em myself, two collies and a black lab."

"Petey's a black lab," Ellie said.

"I know, ma'am. Doris said so."

Chris compressed his lips. Doris. The vengeful bitch. If she hadn't stuck her greedy nose in their business, none of this—

Movement beyond the sheriff caught Chris's eye. At the woods just beyond the police car, he spotted Petey peering at them through the weeds. Chris quickly returned his gaze to the sheriff, terrified he'd given Petey away, but Bruder apparently hadn't noticed.

"You ready, Mr. Crane?"

"For what?"

"I'll need you to accompany me."

For the first time he felt a spark of anger. "I have to watch you do it?"

Bruder seemed embarrassed. "I need a witness. Either you or your wife." He regarded Ellie. "You're welcome to come, too, ma'am. I only thought…"

"No thanks," Ellie said and Chris was surprised at the thickness in her voice. He took her hand.

She asked, "Isn't there some other way? Can't you say you got rid of Petey and let us keep him on a chain or something? He really is a sweet dog."

Bruder looked doubtful.

"We could have a fence built," Chris said, "and make sure he doesn't get out."

Bruder scratched the back of his neck. "I feel for you, I really do. And if I thought I could get away with what you're suggesting, believe me—"

"No one has to know," Ellie urged.

Bruder heaved a sigh. "Experience is a tough teacher, Mrs. Crane. I've learned the hard way. Believe me, someone always finds out."

Chris's gaze shifted to the edge of the forest, where Petey had emerged from the weeds, was sitting in plain sight. *Oh man*, he thought. *If Bruder turns around…*

"Something wrong?"

Chris swallowed and struggled to meet Bruder's eyes. He could see, just beyond the sheriff, the dog's friendly form watching them, oblivious to the danger he was in. *Get your ass out of here*, Chris wanted to shout. If only there were some way to communicate telepathically, to mentally nudge the dog back inside the enclosing safety of the forest...

Ellie's hand squeezed his. Chris glanced down at her. She'd noticed too.

"I just remembered," she said in a tight voice. "I left a pot of noodles boiling."

Bruder frowned. "Oh. If you need—"

Chris put a hand on the sheriff's arm, and though the man tensed, it took his attention further away from Petey.

Eyes on Chris's hand, Bruder said, "Mr. Crane."

"I'm sorry," Chris said, pulling his hand away. "It's just...that dog means a lot to us. Isn't there anything we can do?"

"There isn't," Bruder said in a considerably frostier tone. He didn't tell Chris not to touch him again, but the threat was plain in his eyes.

Go, Petey, Chris thought. *Hide or you're gonna get shot.*

And to his amazement, Petey turned and disappeared into the forest.

Chris blew out a tremulous breath.

"If you're ready, Mr. Crane," Bruder said.

"Do I need to bring anything?"

"Just your voice," the sheriff said. "I'll need you to call him."

Chris nodded and gestured behind him. "Petey usually plays in the western part of the property."

Bruder followed Chris through the yard, and as they neared the edge of the forest, Chris looked back and saw Ellie watching him with grateful eyes.

*   *   *

Ellie picked up her paperback but couldn't concentrate on it. The spectre of an impending gunshot loomed over her, scattered the words she read, reduced the plot of the book to a series of desultory words and phrases. Sighing, she set the book aside and ambled through the living room searching for a job to distract her. A dozen projects presented themselves, none of them pleasant. The ratty carpet needed to be washed, or better yet, torn up and replaced. Of course, that would cost money. The cabinets needed stripped and refinished, though they too should be removed and replaced. Fat chance of that.

Think smaller, she told herself. *Find something that'll divert you for the next hour or two — surely Chris and the sheriff won't be gone longer than that.*

She caught sight of her reflection in the windowpane above the sink, studied the crease between her eyebrows. It made her look ten years older.

With an effort, she relaxed her face and the crease disappeared.

Ellie crossed to the sink, leaned forward, and peered out the window. No sign of Troy Bruder, no sign of Chris.

No sign of Petey either.

She considered heading outside and finding him on her own. She could locate the dog, take him to a safe place — the basement maybe — and make certain Bruder wouldn't shoot him.

No, Katherine reminded her, *he didn't say shoot. He said* destroy.

Ellie rushed from the kitchen and out the back door. She stood on the lawn, debating.

She had to find Petey, had to do something, goddammit, rather than quail on the sidelines. Chris was doing his part, leading the sheriff in the wrong direction. A fleeting wave of pride for her husband surged through her. With any luck, Chris would take the sheriff far from wherever Petey was now.

But what if the dog wanted to find its master?

Possible, she thought, but not likely. The property was over two thousand acres. The chance of Petey finding them was...

...was very good if Petey *wanted* to find them. *He's a dog, for Christ's sake; that's what dogs do, they find things. They follow their sensitive noses until they catch what they're after.*

But Petey went in the other direction, she reminded herself. *He's a smart dog.*

Kat's response, dryly pragmatic: *He's smart for a dog, yes, but his escape earlier might've been luck. Do you really think he'll hide out like some fugitive until Bruder leaves?*

The thought got her moving. She had no idea where Petey might be, so she headed toward the rear of the shed, the place from where she'd often seen the dog emerge. The trees here were dense, the weeds taller than she was. She cast about for a place to access the forest but couldn't find one. Suddenly irritated with herself for not yet exploring the woods, she set her jaw, lowered her head and pushed into the wall of undergrowth.

Her clothes absorbed the moisture from the weeds, her sweatshirt and jeans immediately leaden and cold against her skin. There came a painful tug on her wrist. She stopped and saw a thorn embedded deep in her skin, right where all her veins shone blue. Baring her teeth, Ellie slowly extracted the thorn from her flesh, then rubbed her bleeding wrist with a hand that trembled.

Movement in front of her.

She stopped rubbing and bent over to peer through the thick brush. Nothing was immediately visible, but several yards away...

Yes. There was a subtle tremor there, a stirring in the snarled tangle of weeds and dead branches. Despite their desiccated brown hue, they reminded her of mouldering bones.

"Petey?" she whispered.

Ellie gasped as a chipmunk darted out of the deadfall and passed within inches of her feet. Laughing softly at her skittishness, she exhaled and felt her composure return. The deadfall rustled again, whatever lay within a good deal larger than a chipmunk.

She took a cautious step forward, winced at the cracking of a brittle branch, and knelt to see if she could spot the animal.

Her eyes widened.

A faint scent tickled her nostrils, and at first she couldn't think why it should fill her with such suffocating dread.

Comprehension dawned.

Diorissimo. Aunt Lillith's perfume.

Kneeling there in the forest, the smell of the scariest woman she'd ever met wafted over her, cloying, chillingly sweet.

A memory of Lillith the night Chris had introduced Ellie:

Smiling with her mouth only, scrutinising Ellie, listening politely and asking all the right questions until Chris left the room to make drinks.

Turning to Ellie with a look of unfathomable coldness.

"You're not good enough for my Chris."

Ellie gaping at her.

"Don't try to hide the fact you've had multiple lovers, dear. I can smell it on you."

Ellie shaking her head, unable to respond.

"Men will marry whom they want, and Chris is no different. But I'll be watching how you treat him."

Ellie finally saying, "Listen, I don't know why—"

"Hush, dear."

Lillith leaning forward, pencilled eyebrows raised, speaking the words that would repeat in Ellie's memory innumerable times in the years to follow:

"Christopher has always been my boy, and no vulgar little slut is going to wrest him from me."

Ellie's mouth hanging open in shock.

Lillith's cruel mouth twisted in a wrinkled grin: "Christopher will always belong to me."

The sound of a snapping branch jolted Ellie out of Lillith's living room and back to the forest where, unaccountably, Diorissimo was filling her throat, gagging her.

A soft crunch in the weeds directly in front of her, very much like a footstep.

Oh Jesus, she thought. *It can't be.*

Ellie pushed to her feet and bolted away. She'd gotten disoriented, confused, and that was why such a bizarre memory had been triggered.

But the perfume lingered in her nose, and she could taste it, and ahead, thank God, she saw the forest thinning, the peeling paint speckling the garage like leprous skin.

Ellie hurdled a fallen log and landed in the yard. Though it was wild and overgrown, it was safe and as she raced forward, she spotted the two men, Troy Bruder and Chris back from their search. As Ellie drew nearer, all thoughts of Lillith, of her sickly sweet perfume, evaporated and were replaced by her fear of Petey being killed, Petey whose only crime was tackling a woman who was in desperate need of it.

The men turned and watched her approach.

Chris said, "What happened to you?"

"I'm fine," Ellie said and struggled to catch her breath. "Any sign of Petey?"

Chris averted his eyes, but Bruder watched her for a long moment.

"We didn't find him," Bruder said.

Ellie felt her muscles go slack but she kept a neutral expression. "So what's next?"

Rather than answering, Bruder continued to watch her, his nice blue eyes clouded by some emotion she couldn't immediately identify.

She looked at Chris. "What is it?"

Chris made a face. "The sheriff here thinks we're hiding Petey inside."

Ellie faced Bruder and folded her arms. "You want to check?"

Bruder looked abashed. "I didn't say you were—"

"You implied it," Chris said.

Ellie gestured toward the house. "Come on in, Sheriff."

"Mrs. Crane," Bruder began.

"Search your heart out," Ellie said and began walking toward the back door.

"That won't be necessary," Bruder said, and when she glanced back at him, he looked as though he'd caught a whiff of something rotten. His cheeks were flushed, and he was slouching like a shy boy at the junior high dance.

Chris said, "So...what do we do now?"

Bruder heaved a weary sigh, kicked the driveway gravel. "You swear you won't let it happen again?"

"You have my word," Chris said. "Any time someone visits, we'll lock him in the basement."

She turned to the sheriff to see what he thought, but he was already nodding and regarding his shoes. "I better get going."

"What'll you tell Doris?" Chris asked.

Bruder shrugged, favoured him with a rueful grin. "I'll tell her we couldn't find him. If she wants something done about the dog, she can do it herself."

CHAPTER TWO

Petey watched her from his spot on the kitchen floor.

"We've gotta hurry, boy," she said. "Daddy will be down any minute."

She took the simmering pan off the burner and killed the gas. Clutching the glasses in one hand and the bottle of Merlot in the other, she returned to the dining room and set everything in the middle of the table beside the vase of magnolia blossoms she'd picked off the tree outside their bedroom. She'd brought the salad in earlier, and now she filled two small bowls with it. A fine sheen of sweat coated her forehead. She rubbed it away, then stood back and examined the table.

Perfect.

The Thai meatballs were Chris's favourite. He much preferred beer to wine, but she didn't think he'd mind this once.

Staring at the bottle of Merlot, Ellie chewed on a thumbnail.

Though wine sounded delicious, it was just possible she was pregnant. Not likely, of course, but possible.

Better play it safe.

Creaking noises from above.

Chris.

She moved back a little. She wanted to see his face when he came in and discovered the candlelit layout.

Ellie gave a start as she remembered the apron. She hurriedly untied it and lifted it off so he could see the black sundress she'd picked for the occasion. She liked the way its silky fabric lay on her chest, her thighs. God, it felt good to wear something other than jeans.

His footsteps descended slowly, the way he often moved after working out. She hoped he'd be wearing a short-sleeved shirt so she could see his arms. After he lifted, they always seemed so full, so chiselled.

Chris rounded the corner and gaped.

"How's my baby?" she asked.

He gawked at the glowing candles, the wine-red tablecloth she hardly ever pulled out. A bemused smile curled the corners of his mouth.

"What's all this for?"

"For us," she said. "For you, mostly."

His eyebrows arched. She resisted an urge to go to him, to kiss him lingeringly. He'd worn a T-shirt – just a plain white one – but it showed his body to perfect effect. She could make out the broad curves of his pecs, the round tautness of his shoulders. The seams of the short sleeves grabbed the skin just above his biceps, so that his brawny arms hung at his sides like some professional athlete's, a power-hitting right fielder or a linebacker.

Easy, girl, she told herself. *Don't want to leap into the main event before you've even tasted supper.*

Chris looked better than supper.

She reached up and laced her hands behind his neck.

"I didn't do anything special," he said as his arms encircled her. "Unless you consider showering an amazing feat."

"I wish you hadn't," she said, standing on tiptoes to kiss the side of his neck. "I like the smell of your sweat."

Below, she felt him hardening against her.

"I'll keep that in mind."

"Please do," she said, kissing him again, just under the jaw.

His hands caressed the smooth fabric of the sundress, slid from her lower back over her rear end.

"Keep this up," he said, "and there's no way I'll be able to concentrate on eating."

She reached back, grasped one of his hands, and drew it around her hip until his palm rested against her sex. She rubbed his hand against her, moaned softly into his ear. His hand moved on its own now, and Ellie spread her legs to give him room to explore. His other hand dipped to the base of her buttocks, worked its way under the sundress, rubbed against her naked rear end.

He drew away, face stamped with surprise. "No underwear?"

"That a problem?" she asked and kissed the side of his mouth. His face moved with hers and then their tongues were together, tasting, mouths open and hungry. She reached down, unbuttoned his jeans, drew down the zipper. Her fingers dipped inside his boxer briefs and closed over his penis.

They made love.

After a time, she slowly slumped forward and lay against him, her chest against the side of his panting face. Runnels of sweat slid down his temples, mingled with hers.

"Thank you," he said as his breathing slowed.

"I'm the lucky one."

"That was…"

"Magnificent?"

"Uh-huh."

Against her skin, she felt his face spread into a smile.

* * *

They ate dinner and Chris drank wine. They made love again before showering together and returning to bed, where Chris surprised her by going down on her and making love to her a third time.

When they'd finished, Ellie slipped into her favourite nightshirt, a navy blue one that had once been his. Lying beside him in the dark, breathing in the soapy scent of his skin, she said, "When do you think we'll renovate this place?"

"Big job."

"We could do it in stages."

"How about a brand new house?"

She regarded the silhouette of his face. "You mean tear down this one?"

He shrugged. "Maybe."

"But to build a new house…"

"There's a site deeper in the forest."

She propped herself on an elbow. "You serious?"

"You should see it."

"Go on."

"Think of a giant oval meadow," he said.

"Okay," she said and lay back.

"On the western end of the oval about fifty yards from the woods there's a ridge."

Ellie pictured it, her mind painting the scene at sunset.

"The house will face west. We'll still have a covered porch, only it won't be warped and rickety."

"Shucks."

"Behind the house, where the ground slopes, there'll be a walkout basement, a big deck for entertaining."

Ellie waited, a warm mist of goose bumps electrifying her skin.

"There's an in-ground pool, bigger than the one at your parents' place."

"I like *that*," she said. In fact, the pool was the only thing she missed about her childhood home.

"It can be whatever kind you want—"

"Kidney-shaped."

"That'll work."

"And heated."

"Of course."

"More," she said.

"The hill continues to sweep eastward about a hundred yards or so, till you come to a pond."

"Pond?"

"Where I'll take our kids fishing."

She shivered happily. "Boys love to fish."

"Girls, too, if they're given the chance."

Ellie abhorred the thought of impaling an earthworm with a steel hook, but she kept quiet.

"I don't know if the pond is stocked, but if it isn't, we'll stock it with bluegill, trout, some catfish. At the moment it's ringed with cattails and weeds, but we'll mow it all down so you can see the water from anywhere. And there'll be a bench where we can sit and watch the waterbugs dart around."

She could see it all, even the bugs. The main detail, though, was their children, their tiny bodies in constant motion. They'd have bonfires down there, roast marshmallows and hot dogs, do all the things of which Chris had spoken fondly when reminiscing about his childhood in Indiana. It had been impossible for her to visualise back in California, the ocean and constant sun too dominant to allow her to construct a world so alien. But now, God help her, she really was growing excited about the possibilities.

"I'm thinking," Chris said, "that you should have a gourmet kitchen…"

They went on that way a good deal longer, dreaming about a future that seemed very possible, very real.

Days later, after it all went bad, and later still, after it got much, much worse — unimaginably worse — she would look back on that night and think of it as the happiest she'd ever been. Happier than when they'd met. Happier than their wedding day. Happier even than the time she'd gotten a false positive from a pregnancy test and had believed for three wonderful, deluded hours.

She'd look back on that night and remember the feel of her husband's arms around her, the sound of his voice in the gloom. Their lovemaking.

She would remember these things and hold them close to her like talismans against the onslaught of darkness.

But they would prove useless.

In the end, everything did.

CHAPTER THREE

Chris had only been at the library ten minutes before a stirring on the hackles of his neck told him he was being watched. He paused in his skimming of *A History of Iroquois County* and looked up. The man who'd been staring at him slipped behind a tall bookcase, but not before Chris glimpsed a gnomish belly, the thick disdainful eyebrows: the grocery clerk from Ike's.

Without thinking Chris put the book down and pushed away from the table. He heard diminishing footfalls, the muffled thuds rapid enough to suggest the man wished to escape. Chris rounded the bookcase and caught a hint of black hair bobbing down the steps to the library's basement.

As he reached the bottom of the steps, he saw that the basement was devoted to children's books. The low ceiling was mitigated by the expansiveness of the room, the load-bearing ivory pillars the only encumbrances to his vision. It was behind one of these pillars that Chris glimpsed a leather-coated shoulder, a sliver of nose poking out.

Chris approached the clerk and stopped directly opposite him, a chest-high bookcase the only thing dividing them. Eyes downcast, Chris said, "Read a lot of young adult books?"

The clerk's voice was defiant. "Some."

Chris bunched his lips, nodded. "I like it. Some of it, at least. When you teach freshmen, you better have an idea of what they read."

The clerk said nothing.

"What do you like? Sci-fi? Fantasy?"

The clerk's doughy face was flushed and miserable. Dewdrops of sweat glistened on his high, pale forehead. "Is there a reason you're badgering me?"

Chris shrugged, ran a finger over the book spines before him. "I saw you spying and figured I'd find out why."

The clerk's eyes narrowed, his recessed chin tilting up. "Is it happening?"

"Is what happening?"

The little man pretended to study his fingernails. "Have you seen her yet?"

Chris glanced around, but the only other people down here were a pair of mothers chattering away while their toddlers drooled on the stuffed animals lying about.

"I don't know what—"

"You've slept with her, haven't you?"

The air in the low-ceilinged room was molten, oppressive.

"You're drunk," Chris said and began to turn.

"Hope your wife doesn't find out."

Chris stood rigid. He felt suddenly feverish, a moist furnace superheating his flesh.

"How many times have you been with her?" the man asked. "Half a dozen?"

Chris glanced over at the mothers, who were still oblivious of everything save their chatter. The toddlers played on happily.

"It's your secret from the little lady, isn't it?" the clerk asked. "Your own sweet place."

Shut your goddamned mouth, Chris thought. He could feel the muscles of his forearms knot and jump like ravening wolves pinned under tarps of flesh.

But the little man seemed not to notice, only spoke louder. "Of course, you're planning on bringing the wife one of these nights, right? Such a lovely spot, I'm sure she'd like it."

Chris swallowed. Didn't the man realise how loud he was being, how easily one of these chattering women might hear? Or were their too-polite faces concealing the truth, that they heard every word and would soon divulge all this to Ellie?

"Bet she was amazin'," the man said, his voice adopting a mordant country drawl. "Best lovin' you ever had."

Lost in the memory of the clearing, the pale flesh of the woman's thighs, Chris grew faint.

"She speak to you, Chris? Did she whisper about immortality?"

Chris staggered against a shelf, and though the man made no

move to help him, he felt the clerk's presence reaching out, enshrouding him. The books breathed a heavy haze of must and browning paper. The overhead fluorescents blared down at him in feverish condemnation. He pushed away from the bookcase, his body listing, and then he was hurrying toward the stairway, his hands clutching the rail as though he were infirm. When he reached the top of the stairs and burst through the first set of double doors, he was sure he'd escaped the man's unctuous voice, but as he shoved through the second set of doors and started down the steps he heard footsteps behind him. Raindrops began to darken the sidewalk, but they restored little of his clarity. From the west came an ominous rumble, a bad storm approaching.

"Fess up, Chris," the voice behind him insisted.

"Leave me alone," Chris muttered. Ahead he could see the Camry, parked on a side street. Just a few seconds away.

"Your aunt understood. She knew Destragis's secrets. That's why she bequeathed his gifts to you, don't you see?"

"*Campbell!*" a voice shouted from behind them.

The little man froze. Wobbling a little, Chris turned to see who it was.

Daniel Wolf, the German Baptist carpenter he'd met at the grocery store. Only now the smile and friendly demeanour were gone. The man stood in the middle of the sidewalk, arms rigid at his sides.

"Get away from him," Wolf said.

The little man, Campbell apparently, took a step backward, but his upper lip curled in a petulant sneer. "This has nothing to do with you."

Chris viewed the scene through a gauzy grey curtain. In desperation he stumbled the last few steps to the Camry. As he struggled to extract the keys from his jeans, he heard Daniel Wolf's voice: "...won't happen. You better stay away..." But the majority of it was lost in the sound of rushing water that assailed his ears. The rain was falling steadily now, an icy needling that helped him focus on getting the damn keys out and pushing the unlock button. He heard Campbell yelling something at Wolf, but it was cut off as he slumped in the driver's seat. He pulled away from the curb, but as he did he glimpsed Daniel Wolf swinging at Campbell, the Amish man's face a hateful rictus.

Chris stopped the car and stared in the overhead mirror as Wolf lifted the little man, reared back, and slugged him in the face. Through the shut windows he could hear Campbell's head snap back.

He cut the engine and climbed out. As he approached he saw Wolf's fist rise and fall, rise and fall, and beneath him the clerk flailed his hands to ward the larger man off. Wolf aimed a haymaker that barely missed Campbell's face.

"Take it easy," Chris said, venturing closer.

Wolf reared back, swung again, and this time his fist sliced between Campbell's upraised hands. The blow caught the little man above the left eye, and blood immediately began to pour from the gash.

"That's enough," Chris said. He interposed his body between the struggling men. Campbell was weeping. Wolf shoved Chris aside as if he were a child and set to work again pummelling the helpless clerk.

From behind, Chris got Wolf in a bear hug and struggled to drag him away, and though it took several moments, in the end he was able to separate them.

Wolf spun, and when Chris beheld the flaring nostrils, the hairline soaked with sweat, he was sure Wolf would start in on him too. Then the man's eyes seemed to clear.

Wolf dragged a forearm across his mouth, looked around and found his hat, which he picked up and put back on. Wolf glanced at Campbell's curled-up form. "I'm sorry he had to dredge all this up again."

"You'll regret this," Campbell said between sobs. "Bruder will pay you a visit tonight."

"Not likely," Wolf answered. "He'd rather you were somewhere else, too."

He turned to Chris. "Go home now, Mr. Crane. Forget you ever met this person."

Campbell had gotten to his feet, was staring at Wolf with fear and rage. "She came because she wanted to."

The black look returned to Wolf's eyes. "Not another word."

Campbell lowered his gaze, turned and moved away, occasionally glancing back to make sure he wasn't going to get knocked down again.

Wolf eyed Chris a long moment. Then he said, "Keep an eye your wife," and walked away.

CHAPTER FOUR

She'd driven halfway to town before she got a single flickering bar on her phone, and when Ellie heard the voice in the message, she didn't immediately place it.

Then she realised it was Katherine.

"Hey, El, just calling to make sure you're still alive." A cynical laugh. "I guess if something really had happened to you I'd feel guilty for joking about it, huh?" A pause, Katherine preparing to get down to business. Ellie steeled herself.

"I know you're not my biggest fan, but I've been worried about you lately. Now that you're within driving distance of Ann Arbor, it's ridiculous for us to keep acting like we don't know each other. Anyway, what I was thinking—"

Ellie pressed seven, erasing the message. Her chest hurt, and her stomach had soured the way it always did when she thought of Katherine. It occurred to her that there had been two messages, but she wouldn't risk listening to the second one; if it was Katherine again, she might just toss the phone out the window, stop, and back over the damn thing.

Her eyes began to water. She became aware of a persistent throb in the base of her skull, the pressure reminding her of an elementary school classmate, his name long forgotten, who used to torture her during recess by chasing her down and pinning her face on the sparse playground grass, the dust that puffed into her mouth a welcome reprieve from the boy's terrible ketchup breath. His thumbs would delve into the vulnerable flesh just below her skull, digging and prodding like some crazed masseuse, until her eyes were muddy with tears.

Might as well go home, she thought. She veered onto a side road and made a U-turn. She signalled, cranked the wheel to the right and had just nosed onto the county road again when a deafening blare sent both feet stomping on the break, the open-bed semi roaring by her in a clattering blast of outrage.

Ellie sat immobile, her breathing an arrhythmic flurry. The truck had missed the front end of the Camry by less than a foot. Though the semi had travelled more than half a football field already, she could still see its back end swishing like the tail of a receding shark.

Focus, Ellie, a voice reminded her.

Placing her hands at the ten and two o'clock positions for the first time since driver's ed, she drove on. A film tasting of warm milk coated the inside of her mouth. She stared fixedly at the unspooling road and waited for the painful squeeze of her heartbeat to subside. After what seemed an interminable period of driving, her turnoff appeared. She switched on her blinker and guided the Camry onto the puddled gravel of County Road 1200. She winced as the wheels dipped and jounced in the multitudinous chuckholes pockmarking the road. Closer to the forest now, Ellie felt a tightening in her chest, a feeling very much like being submerged from the neck down.

The woods loomed before her, and soon the dense trees encroached on both sides. The heavy sensation in her chest grew, made breathing difficult. She reached over, thumbed down her window a crack, and immediately regretted it. Not only was the air in the Camry still gravid with the portentous aura that had plagued her all day, but now her skin was lacerated with a blade of freezing April wind. She rolled the window up and, with a combination of claustrophobia and sorrow, spotted the turnoff to their house ahead.

Ellie had completed the turn and driven fifty yards when she saw the black dog in the middle of the lane.

She depressed the brakes, the Camry skidding a little before halting twenty yards in front of the Rottweiler. Behind the dog she distinguished the frail bridge, and she was reminded of all the fairy tales wherein trolls or evil knights guarded bridges forbiddingly against safe passage. The huge animal's eyes reflected her headlamps, lent the creature a spectral intensity. Her foot on the brake grew numb, her hands on the wheel tingly. Though she told herself it was imagination, she was certain the low growl she heard was real and not just the Camry's idling engine.

Stop being a wimp, El. Drive forward and the damn thing will scamper back to wherever the hell it came from.

She compressed her lips, wished death upon her sister for taunting her at such a moment. Yet she did ease her foot off the brake pedal, rolled slowly forward thinking the dog might bolt in self-preservation. Fifteen yards away now. Ten. Five.

The black dog stood in the lane, absolutely unmoving.

Ellie heaved a sigh, brought the Camry to a stop. Shoving the gearshift into park, she thought, *What now, Katherine? Any more bright ideas?*

If the goddamn lane weren't so narrow she could simply sneak around the animal. She eyed the muddy shoulder, the dead leaves and the standing water, and dismissed the notion. The last thing she needed was to get stuck here, a mile away from home with a useless phone and a vicious dog the size of a Bengal tiger.

It couldn't hurt to try the phone again, could it?

She raised her hips, reached into her jeans pocket for the cell. Her fingers had just touched its smooth surface when the animal leaped onto the hood.

Ellie screamed, flailed her hands at the snarling beast. She watched in disbelief as its thick yellow claws clattered and scratched over the windshield, smearing dirt and what might be blood all over the glass. Its immense muzzle rammed the windshield, a gout of viscous slaver splattering in a messy streak. The curved fangs snapped in idiot need.

"*Goddamn you!*" she screamed at the dog and drew back, gasping, as it lunged at her, its flared nostrils the size of bathtub drains.

Drive, you moron, drive!

Momentarily grateful for Katherine's scolding, she popped the Camry into gear and stomped the accelerator. The back wheels skidded a moment, the animal's ferocity momentarily giving way to confusion. Then the tyres grabbed the muddy lane and the Camry lurched forward. The animal yelped in surprise. One black shoulder smashed the windshield as the dog was hurled off balance. As the Camry picked up speed, the dog pawed the air in an effort to regain its feet. The car cleared the bridge.

Now.

She slammed on the brakes and watched in triumph as the dog

tumbled off the hood and somersaulted for twenty feet. In an instant it was up again, snarling, tensed for another assault on the Camry.

"Fuck it," Ellie muttered and floored the gas.

The car bore down on the animal, but rather than moving, the Rottweiler actually galloped forward, apparently meaning to ram the grill head on.

"*Jesus*," she gasped and jerked the wheel at the last moment. The Camry swerved toward the shoulder, the animal actually snapping at the car's front corner as it whipped by. There was a dull, sickening crunch and a wet wail of agony. She spun the wheel back to the left, but only succeeded in swinging the car sideways, a tree rushing at the passenger's window. The Camry struck it, the door imploding like an accordion, Ellie thrown sideways as glass pelted her face, the airbag punching her body and whipping back her head.

The car settled and Ellie lay unconscious in her seat.

*   *   *

When she became aware of the ticking sound, her first thought was of the grandfather clock in her parents' house. Beneath that she heard the pattering of rain on the roof. Something pressed down on her, and from her neck came a needling pain.

She remembered the crash.

Ellie moaned. She felt like hell. The airbag had mashed her boobs flat and pinioned her to the seat. A wave of claustrophobia swept over her. She had to get out of the car soon or she'd be screaming like a lunatic and thrashing to get free.

She opened her eyes, reached out, and after several frustrating moments, was able to nudge open her door. By wiggling her hips and pushing against the console to her right she was able to scoot sideways toward the open door. With an effort she swung a leg outside and winced when her foot squished in mud. Heavy drops of rain smacked her left leg, her shoulder, but despite the frigid shower, her focus remained on getting out of the car. With one final wrench, she yanked free of the airbag and sat panting on the edge of the seat.

When she'd caught her breath, she glanced back at the imploded passenger door, though moving her neck cost an effort. Her preliminary and completely unmedical diagnosis was that she'd sustained no serious injuries but would be sore for days. The Camry was in better shape than she'd thought. Had she been travelling faster when she slid off the lane, things might have been much worse – for her and the car. Fortunately, the sparse gravel had given the tyres something to grip, and the damage had been limited.

Get back to the house, Ellie. Get your husband.

Take it easy, she thought. *Just take it easy a second. It's not like—*

A low growl ripped through her thoughts. She looked up and saw, ten yards away, the Rottweiler dragging itself toward her.

Can't be, she thought, but it obviously was. The huge black dog was in bad shape – dying even – yet it continued to limp forward on three legs.

At once she realised what the crunching sound had been. The back left leg, she saw, had been snapped in half by her rear tire. It flopped uselessly behind the Rottweiler as it made its slow, inexorable way toward her. It was a good thing she'd awakened when she had...had she been out any longer, the vicious bastard would have been right beneath her door when she opened it, and then—

Stop it. You did *wake up in time. Now get your ass out of the car and get home!*

Ellie pushed to her feet and nearly crumpled when she put weight on her right leg. She moaned, hung on the open door for a moment and rode out the spires of pain rocketing up her leg.

Not broken, she thought, but definitely bruised. Bruised badly. Man, what luck she had.

A guttural bark made her jump. The Rottweiler had halved the distance between them, would be upon her in seconds if she didn't get moving now.

Grimacing, Ellie sidestepped the door, hopped on her good leg to the end of the hood. The dog continued to lurch closer, its growling a throaty, raspy sound. The animal's head was lowered, its eyes never leaving hers, its expression a mixture of wrath and loathing.

It got her moving. The first few yards she nearly collapsed because of the pain. Somehow, she kept her balance. The pitted lane slowed her, the lurking craters forbidding progress. She shot a look back at the Rottweiler and was stunned to see it rising, leaping forward. Then its bad back leg gave way and it nosedived into the lane.

Ellie smiled grimly and pushed ahead.

She had limped for nearly a minute before looking back again, and this time when she did she glimpsed the animal dragging its broken body toward the woods.

I hope you die in there, she thought and felt no guilt at all. She loved animals and attempted to be kind to them as a general rule, but when one tried to tear her to shreds, all bets were off. The son of a bitch.

I hope you die, she thought again as the animal disappeared into the forest.

I hope you die.

*   *   *

Chris's first thought upon hearing the front door bang open – a thought for which he would later feel guilty – was: *Not now. Please, of all times, not now.*

For once the writing was going well. He had no idea what the story was about, nor did he even have a skeleton plot. But he did have a scene – an eerie one at that – and that was *something*. That, at least, was a start.

He typed on as long as he could before Ellie's heavy tramping on the stairs vanquished his hold on the scene. The muscles in his arms bunched. He swivelled in the chair, laced his fingers in his lap, and watched the door with unmasked asperity. She needed to see how furious he was, dammit, needed to understand how fragile his concentration was. The last thing he needed was her stomping through the house like a Nazi stormtrooper.

She opened the door and his anger drained away.

Rising from his chair, he noted the blood streaking her face and neck. She took a step in his direction, winced, and leaned against the doorjamb for support. He got an arm around her.

"Jesus, Ellie, what the hell happened?"

He started her toward his vacated chair, but she shook her head. "Bed."

He nodded, leaned lower to support her weight as they approached the stairs, but their height disparity made it terribly awkward. Ellie gasped as she put too much weight on her injured right leg.

"Ah, to hell with this," he said, and scooped her into his arms.

"Ohhh," she groaned. "Please don't drop me."

"Don't worry," he said. "You don't weigh as much as my writing desk did."

"Good to know I weigh less than a gigantic piece of mahogany furniture."

She whimpered as he barked her ankle against the banister.

He grimaced. "Sorry about that."

After a few more ginger steps, they were in the bedroom. Rather than laying her on the bed right away, he contrived to push the covers down with one of his knees. When that only jounced her body and made her hiss with pain, he abandoned his efforts and laid her as gently as he could on the made bed.

"What happened, El?" he asked and pushed a lock of brown hair out of her eyes. He could smell the sheen of fear on her. Her skin was moist and unnaturally cool.

"Had an accident," she muttered.

"You crashed the car?" he said and gritted his teeth in self-reproach at his choice of words. *Nice one, Chris. Why don't you just yell at her and threaten to dock her allowance?*

But if she was irritated by the question, she didn't show it. She nodded, a sweaty arm coming up and covering her eyes.

"Oh, baby," he said and touched the side of her face that wasn't crusted with blood. "What can I do? Call an ambulance? I can drive you to the hospital."

She shook her head slowly, as if in a fog. "Just banged up."

"Think your leg's broken?"

Another head shake. "I don't think so." She took a shallow breath and swallowed, her throat clicking dryly.

"Water?"

She nodded.

Glad to finally have something to do, he pushed away from the bed, jogged to the bathroom, and found a coffee mug she'd left beside the sink. Ordinarily her habit of leaving drinking glasses all over the house drove him nuts, but now he was grateful for it. He washed out the old coffee and filled it with tap water. Returning to Ellie, he noticed she'd risen to her elbows, was staring down at her legs.

"You're still in one piece," he said and offered her the mug.

"Barely."

After she'd sipped a couple times, he asked her what happened.

She told him, his worry changing into astonishment, then incredulity. "And this dog's still out there in the woods?"

"Yeah," she said. "But he's in bad shape. Even worse than me, if you can believe that."

He wetted a washcloth and dabbed at the cuts on her face. All of them appeared shallow, but in two or three places there seemed to be glass embedded under her skin.

"We need to get you looked at," he told her.

"Ah, crap," she said. "Do we have to?"

He frowned at a pea-sized lump on her right cheekbone that had already begun to purple. "Unless you want scars on that pretty face of yours."

That was all the convincing Ellie required. She talked him out of calling for an ambulance, and though she still limped, they made it outside. It wasn't until they got to the driveway that they remembered she had crashed the Camry.

"Oh man," he said, and despite himself, he joined Ellie in weary laughter. She sat heavily on the back porch and laughed, one hand clutched to her side.

When he'd gotten control of it, he said, "Wait here."

He was about to hustle out to the Camry when he paused and regarded his wife. "You okay for a minute or two?"

She cocked an eyebrow at him. "You mean, am I worried about that Rottweiler coming back to finish the job?"

He waited.

"He's in no shape to hurt me again. Besides, I'm right here by the door. If he does show up, I'll slip inside and let you do battle with him."

A black shape appeared to his left and he whirled, expecting to see the offending animal dragging its injured leg across the driveway. But it was Petey, returned from the forest, his muzzle gleaming in the overcast light.

Chris walked over to him. "What gives, boy?"

He reached down to scratch Petey on the back of the neck, but stopped when he saw a drop of blood patter on the grass between the dog's paws. The dog's toenails, too, he now saw, were splashed with blood.

From the porch, Ellie called, "You get him, boy?"

Petey bounced in place a moment, uttered a piercing bark.

Chris eyed Ellie, saw the wry smile on her face, and began to grin.

Scratching Petey on the back, he said, "Guess no one messes with Mama, huh?"

CHAPTER FIVE

Though the Camry looked terrible, it still drove. Because the passenger's door was utterly destroyed, he had to put Ellie in the back seat. On the way to the hospital, he tilted the overhead mirror so he could keep an eye on her.

The emergency room doctor at the Ravana Health Centre – a gaunt man in his early forties – seemed competent. Chris held Ellie's hand as the doctor carefully tweezed minute bits of glass from her skin. She hissed a couple times and nearly broke his hand when the doctor extracted a crescent-shaped sliver from her cheek.

Ellie's leg, the doctor told them, was bruised, just as Ellie had insisted. He prescribed a painkiller, which they picked up at the drug store on the way out of town. By eight-thirty they were home.

Chris put Ellie to bed, and when he was sure she was sleeping deeply, he bent, kissed her on the forehead, and went downstairs. He stepped outside and surveyed the sky. The storm clouds had receded and left a clear blanket of stars in their wake.

He drifted through the yard until he found himself on its eastern edge. Though he hadn't cleared the path here, it seemed a good deal less overgrown than it had last week when he'd ended up in the clearing

(and the smaller one)

where the idea of building a dream home had occurred to him, where he and Ellie and their children could go

(to the other clearing)

and play tag in the meadow, lug rods and nightcrawlers down to the pond and catch that evening's supper, explore the forest and

(find her, find the one you heard)

flit between the trees, chase lightning bugs, gather fallen branches and mossy logs to burn

(the one who touched you)

His skin suddenly tingling with nervous energy, he took another step forward and screwed up his eyes to see into the woods. He could have sworn...

Yes. The path had been cleared. Whether he had done it by passing through here the other day or Ellie had done some trimming without mentioning it, the path was wider now than it was before.

But still dark. He peered up at the night sky. The moon was nearly full, and there were a good many stars out, but all the same, it would be difficult to see in the forest. He'd need a flashlight.

Excited now, he hurried back to the house and into the kitchen. Under the sink he found the flashlight he'd purchased at Ike's. On a whim, he reached into the fridge and gathered a few cans of beer. One in his hand, one for each jean pocket.

Petey meandered in from the dining room.

"Hey, boy. I'm going for a walk, wanna come?"

Petey watched him noncommittally.

"C'mon," Chris said. He held the screen door open, but rather than going out, Petey sat on his haunches.

"No?"

Petey's head twitched up, and for a fleeting instant, Chris was convinced the animal had gestured toward Ellie, sleeping upstairs.

"I see," Chris said. "You want to stay back and watch over Mommy. That it?"

Petey regarded him evenly.

"Gotcha," Chris said and went out.

On the way through the yard, a pair of small birds fluttered by him before disappearing into the forest. At the edge of the path, he sucked in his stomach and stashed the flashlight between his boxer briefs and the waist of his jeans. He cracked open a can of beer, inhaled its pungent aroma and took a sloppy gulp. He wouldn't need the flashlight yet, especially with the path so open. Later, though, when he ventured deeper into the forest, he'd be glad he brought it along. Hell, without it he might get lost and not make it back until morning.

You might get lost anyway, he reminded himself.

True, but if he did, what was the big deal? Petey was guarding Ellie like Cerberus guarded the gates of hell. She was safe.

He took another swig of beer and moved into the engulfing woods.

*   *   *

She'd taken Vicodin one other time, and despite the doctor's assurances that the pills were perfectly safe, she met the onset of sleep with an atavistic dread and a fervent desire for Chris to come back and lie down beside her.

Ellie knew there was a problem when the bed began to cant beneath her. Her saliva grew viscid and tasted vaguely of the shitty grape cough medicine her parents used to force-feed her. She began to perspire. Oh hell, she thought, her fingers digging into the sheets, it was all happening again, just as it had the time she'd wrecked her dad's car and been given Vicodin in the hospital. That night had been a fever dream of edgy paranoia, and this night would be just as bad.

Though she was aware of the bedroom around her, the air ovenlike and damp, she also recognised the beginning of the dreams that weren't quite dreams, because in them she still sensed her prone body here in the bed, still laboured under the glaze of discomfort that made her wish she could leap out of her own skin.

At first there was very little, just the tidily landscaped backyard of her childhood home. Then there was Katherine at maybe seven years old, far too tall for her age and making Ellie feel more than ever like a runt, an afterthought.

Katherine frolicked through the sprinkler the babysitter had set up – Dad was at work, Mom was probably shopping – and though Ellie tried to keep pace with her, Kat bounded away like an antelope evading capture. As ever, Ellie felt weak and hopeless, but soon the scene melted into Kat's high school graduation. She'd gotten valedictorian, of course, and received her adoring crowd in a manner befitting royalty while Ellie brooded at a card table tucked in the back corner of the yard, an uneaten plate of metallic-tasting pineapple chunks and dry carrot sticks her only companion. She remembered thinking how nice it would be for her sister to die of intestinal cancer when a hand on her shoulder made her jump. Kat embraced her, her sister's smooth cheek pressing hers, saying, "I'll miss you next year,

El. I know I don't show it, but I'm sick about being apart." Ellie surprised herself by tearing up and hugging her sister back.

And that was Katherine. Regal and infuriating, but occasionally the brown eyes would fill with love, and all the hurt would be washed away by the warmth and the lovely smile.

Another memory, this one from Katherine's first year of grad school, out with Katherine's friends, Ellie just a few weeks removed from her twenty-first birthday and not very good at holding her liquor.

Barhopping with Katherine's set, thinking one of Katherine's male friends – Derek, his name had been – was incredibly handsome. Flirting with Derek and getting mixed signals, the guy nice enough but once or twice exchanging glances with Katherine that pissed Ellie off. They rode from bar to bar, the six of them, two guys and four women, and at those odds Ellie worked extra hard to stand out, drank more beer to show she could handle it. One guy clearly falling for one of Kat's girlfriends, Derek pingponging between Kat and Ellie. A competition, familiar and savage. She read on her big sister's face the quiet confidence that Derek would choose her over Ellie, the unwavering belief in herself that made success an inevitability. Ellie linking her arm with Derek's on the way inside a bar called Harry's, a name that struck her as hilarious. She laughed with Derek about it and drank shots with him, and at some point they were kissing and she was straddling him on a barstool, Derek getting into it as much as she was. Until the stool tipped and she and Derek were lying on their sides, laughing, the pitcher of beer overturned and splashing over half a dozen bystanders.

Katherine curt and embarrassed, saying to someone, "Get Derek up, I'll get my sister."

Ellie on her back staring up at her stormy expression: "Don't be jealous, Kat. Other boys might prefer you."

Kat telling her to shut up and hauling her to her feet a trifle too roughly for Ellie's liking. Ellie shoving her sister into Derek, who was staring at Ellie with a kind of fascinated disgust. Ellie saying to Kat, "You should have told him your GPA, he might have been interested in you."

Kat's face going hard, the entire bar ogling the scene: "For someone who gives up on things so easily, you sure don't know when to quit."

At the words Ellie came half-awake in bed, groaning, the sweat trickling over her jaw. Where the hell was Chris? She needed him to be here, to hold her hand, to slap her cheeks and rescue her from this maelstrom of hurtful memories before it could pull her down again, the sheets drenched and clinging to her calves, dragging her down...

...to Ellie's first wedding reception. After returning to college and finishing up in a total of five years – something she considered an accomplishment given the fact she'd dropped out once and changed majors three times – she'd married Jason Halliday. Dreamy, affluent Jason Halliday, whose short game had garnered him an All-American honourable mention in golf, the boy whose dad owned several of the most successful Mercedes dealerships on the West Coast.

The boy who got drunk before his own wedding.

That part of him had excited her when they were dating, the rebel who didn't give a damn what people thought of him and did whatever the hell he pleased. She'd gone to bed with him on their second date, though it hadn't really been a date at all, just a party at his fraternity. From the beginning Jason Halliday had been different, his supreme confidence and devil-may-care attitude irresistible to her. When he asked her to marry him – they were at a bar, of course – she'd said yes, assuming it was a joke. Six months later she was propping him up as they hurried through their vows, Ellie thinking the entire time, *For Christ's sake, Jason, I like to have a good time, too, but aren't you taking it a little far?* Worried about what her parents would think, sickly mortified of what Katherine would say, Ellie did what she could to mask her groom's inebriation, his cussing and lewd jokes during the picture-taking with the families, the grandmas smiling stiffly as Ellie blushed and prayed her new husband would stop dropping the F-bomb.

At the country club reception:

Beautiful night, beautiful crowd. Everything perfect except Jason, still nipping from a flask he'd smuggled in his tuxedo pocket. Removing her garter with his teeth in front of the hooting crowd, Ellie certain for one terrible moment he would attempt cunnilingus right there in front of everyone she knew. Jason smashing the cake in her face so hard he damn near broke her nose, Ellie pretending it was all a great time.

Standing with Katherine at the edge of the dance floor as Jason danced and flirted with the bridesmaids, Katherine saying, "Quite a man you've chosen for yourself, El."

Ellie giving Katherine what she hoped was a withering look: "At least I'm married. Bet you never thought your kid sister would beat you to it, did you?"

Without missing a beat: "I only plan on doing it once."

One wedding becoming another, Ellie's ceremony with Chris:

Ellie sick with worry about whether her parents would show, knowing Katherine would come but wishing she wouldn't. Katherine and her plain but steady husband and her too-adorable children...

Added strain from Chris's stodgy parents and his horrid Aunt Lillith. She could feel the weight of Lillith's stare, scrutinising her, following her no matter where Ellie went in the outdated banquet hall they'd chosen for their reception. Cheap food, no dancing, the whole affair a pathetic shadow of the reception she'd had with Jason, which was painful and ironic, since she actually loved Chris. What was more, Chris was not only sober, he actually treated her like a human being.

Which made it a shame that she spent the entire day dreading what Katherine would say, what her parents would say, wondering if at any moment Aunt Lillith would sprout devil horns and lunge at her from her seat in the banquet hall. The reception half over before Katherine made her way over, Ellie's mind an instant frenzy of defensiveness and anger.

But Katherine said, "I'm so proud of you, El."

Steeling herself for the punch line, waiting for the dagger to jab and twist.

Kat went on, "We all make mistakes, and I don't need to tell you that Jason was one of them..."

Ellie preparing to slash her sister's face with her newly manicured nails.

"...but this time you got it right."

Staring at Kat in astonishment.

"I mean it, El. Chris is a keeper. He's sweet and sincere and intelligent." Kat's voice dropping to a whisper: "And he's better-looking than Jason too."

It was the only time that day Ellie cried, and not because her sister's kindness had touched her, but because she'd lost most of what she considered her real wedding day worrying about nothing.

Now in her bedroom Ellie squirmed under the sodden sheet, moaning and sweating and enervated. She lacked the strength to cry out to Chris; she lacked the ability to stem the flow of memories.

And inside her head the haunting newsreel of the past continued to play.

⋆　　⋆　　⋆

The flashlight still pressing his belly and the cans of beer finished, Chris entered the main clearing at just before eleven. The hands of his watch glowed, but he suspected he'd be able to see their positions even had they not, so bright were the moon and stars tonight. Grinning like an idiot but unable to suppress his joy, Chris charged up the hill and did not pause until he reached its crest. The beer had given him a buzz – since his college days he seldom drank more than one or two – and the combination of alcohol and physical exertion was creating a sweaty kind of euphoria. The sweet fragrance of wildflowers drifted over him. Pivoting slowly on his heels, he took in a panorama of the meadow, even more glorious tonight than it had been the first time he'd visited. He chided himself for not yet bringing Ellie here. Before today's incident with that stupid Rottweiler, she'd seemed to be coming around to the charms of the place. Not convinced they'd made the right move yet, but definitely regarding it with more of an open mind. Standing atop the hill, he had no doubt this view would erase whatever misgivings she still harboured. How could it not? The clearing, he now estimated, was closer to twenty acres than fifteen. Perhaps even more. The entire meadow was bathed in a ghostly silver; the tall grasses undulated in the warm spring breeze.

Chris surveyed the western horizon, where the ancient oaks and poplars rose higher even than the hill upon which he stood. He continued his turn until the pond came into view, the moonlight glimmering on its unbroken surface.

He caught sight of the other clearing, and all at once his good spirits disappeared.

Impossible, he told himself. *I'm not really seeing this.*

But he was.

Firelight. Flickering luridly on the trunks of the trees on the far edge of the smaller clearing.

But how…

Chris's lips became a thin line.

Trespassers. That was how. The sons of bitches had parked along one of the country roads and hiked across his land to spend the night here. Who knew how many times they'd done this?

His chest began to heave, his fists to clench.

Goddamn them, they had to know he'd taken possession of the estate. The way Campbell acted at the library, the whole town knew everything about Chris and Ellie and their move.

He pictured the trespassers down there, burning his wood and defiling his land. Probably saying, *Who gives a fuck about the new owner, he'll never be the wiser anyway.*

Wanna bet? Chris thought.

Skin ablaze, he started down the hill.

★   ★   ★

Ellie sucked in a hissing breath and sat up in bed. She realised she'd been crying. Her upper lip was coated with mucus and her eyes were bleary. Worse, her throat felt like she'd gargled acid. The awful cough medicine taste still lingered on her tongue.

She gazed at the open door and frowned. If she'd been yelling all that time, why hadn't Chris come?

Perhaps he did, she told herself. *Maybe he came and held you. Who knows what he did or didn't do? When you take Vicodin, all bets are off, remember? You might have stripped naked and done the chicken dance, so calm down before you condemn the poor guy.*

She blew out foul-tasting breath and made a face, the noxious taste so bad she felt as though she'd been dragged across a river bottom with her mouth open. She peeled the clammy sheet off. At least her leg no longer ached. She supposed the Vicodin would ease the pain of her accident another few hours. Then, maybe, she could get some sleep that didn't feel like a drug-induced haze.

Her arms weak and rubbery, Ellie reached over and twisted on the bedside lamp, which splashed its dim, buttery light across the room. She tugged a tissue from the box and wiped her upper lip clean. Then she blew her nose and lay on her side, panting from the effort. Maybe, she speculated, God was getting even with her for running over the dog.

She slid her legs toward the edge of the bed and slowly got to her feet. The wood floor bit like frost, and the soaked nightgown clung to her parasitically. She shuffled into the bathroom, reached down and, shimmying a little, she peeled off the nightgown and slapped it over the edge of the tub. The exertion made her light-headed, and she leaned against the tub, her naked rear end mooning the open doorway.

If Chris comes now, he'll get an eyeful.

Yeah, she thought, *that's all he'll get. Right now sex is the last thing I need.*

The skin on the backs of her legs tightened, and she suddenly felt very vulnerable.

Someone was staring at her.

She whirled and saw Petey watching her from the hallway shadows.

The animal's eyes on her crotch.

Ellie forced a laugh. "Nice view, huh, boy?"

Petey stared at her sex, his body strangely still.

But that wasn't quite right, she realised with growing alarm. His body wasn't unmoving. To the contrary, his glossy black coat shook with barely perceptible tremors. His glassy eyes gleamed with a voracious need that made her reach back, pull a towel off the shower rod and cover herself. Wrapping the fuzzy yellow towel around her breasts, her mid-section, she said, "Where's Daddy?"

The animal moved quietly away.

She exhaled pent-up breath. *The sedative*, she thought. *Your imagination's running away with you, Ellie.*

The way Petey looked at me wasn't imagination.

Oh right. Your sweet family dog wants to rape you. For goodness' sakes, would you get it under control?

Head clearing, she went back to the bedroom and put on underwear, sweatpants, and a T-shirt. She checked the clock, realised she'd been out for less than an hour. She'd certainly packed some unpleasant memories into a short period of time.

She'd find Chris and join him in whatever he was doing. If he was writing, she'd find a book to read and sit near him. He surely wouldn't mind this once. The combination of Petey's leering and her bad experience with the Rottweiler had fried her nerves; she needed the salve of her husband's presence. She started down the stairs. Halfway to the first floor a knocking sound arrested her movements.

Dull, persistent, like a broken machine struggling to find a gear.

Damn. She blew a bit of hair out of her eyes. If it was the plumbing, they'd have to call someone first thing in the morning. Combine that bill with the deductible for the wrecked Camry, and this week would take a hefty bite out of their checking account.

So much for building their dream home.

She chuckled at her own impatience, as if they were going to break ground any time soon. She hadn't even seen the site yet; perhaps she wouldn't like it. Ellie flipped on the kitchen light and froze.

The basement door stood wide open.

Okay, she told herself. *What's the big deal? Chris went down there earlier and left the door open. Or he's down there now investigating that thudding sound.*

Ellie bit her lip, a new brand of fear causing her heart to speed. The problem sounded as if it were growing rapidly more severe. What if it was the furnace or the water heater?

Ellie reached the open doorway and gazed down into the dimness. The odour wafting up the grungy cement walls reminded her of her ill-advised backpacking trip. In rural England she and her boyfriend had been caught by a sudden downpour and had sheltered under an ancient stone bridge. From the road the idea had seemed both logical and romantic. She had followed the boy down the shallow embankment assuming they'd make love in the sand, build a fire, and eventually spend the night listening to the creek bubble beside them. What they found instead was a dank, foetid wasteland littered with jagged rocks and a dismaying array of refuse. The bridge had been built over a bend in the creek and the result was that every cigarette butt, every wrapper, and every dead tree limb that had fallen in the water had washed up here. They cast about searching for a suitable place to sit – their potential lovemaking a distant, curdled memory – and chose a low-ceilinged spot only to find moments later that there were several used condoms and rusty hypodermic needles half-buried in the mud. As for what happened next... Ellie shivered and thrust the memory away.

But the smell under the bridge, God that *smell* was very much like the odour plaguing her now, and the connection was enough to give her pause before plunging blithely down the steps in an attempt to diagnose the thud.

"Chris?" she said in a hushed voice.

She wondered why she was being so quiet.

"Chris?" she said, louder this time.

Still no answer.

Shit.

She backed away from the top step and leaned against the counter. If Chris wasn't down there, where was he?

More importantly, Kat's voice spoke up, *if Chris didn't open the door, who did?*

That's easy, she returned. *It's an old house. The damn thing groans and creaks all the time. Is it really such a stretch to assume that the door got blown open by a draft?*

This is the first time it's happened, El. Peculiar timing, don't you think?

Shut up, Kat.

Ellie flipped on the basement switch.

A disheartening lack of light issued forth. She knew waiting any longer would only psych her out, so she took a couple steps down and winced at the way the stairs groaned. She paused and gazed down at the shadowed concrete floor. From her vantage point she couldn't see much of the basement, but she could tell it was even darker down there than it was in the stairwell.

She'd need a flashlight.

Remembering the one under the sink, Ellie trotted back up the steps and across the kitchen.

She opened the cabinet, squatted, and frowned at the bottles of bleach and window cleaner.

Then it clicked. *Two mysteries solved*, she thought. The flashlight was with Chris, who'd gone exploring. It was the only logical explanation.

Relieved to know where her husband had gone, but slightly wounded he'd abandoned her, she stood and considered. Clearly, something was amiss in the basement. The thudding was becoming a booming. She could simply wait the sound out, see if it stopped on its own. Or she could head to town, find someone who could help.

It's going on midnight. It's pointless to go all the way to Ravana.

The sound heightened, thumping, pounding, the floor beneath her seeming to pulse. The idea rose in her that the entire house had awakened like some long-buried beast and she was now listening to its cruel heart circulating its lifeblood until it could suck her down its ancient gullet.

Ellie moaned. Maybe she'd go sit in the car.

Wimp.

She peered into the basement. She damn well wasn't going down there without some kind of light.

She strode over and opened one of the kitchen drawers. Inside she found the bulky silver lighter Chris had once purchased as a prop for a story he taught. Something about a man who bet people they couldn't make their lighters light ten times in a row. If the lighter failed once, Chris explained, the man got to chop off the little finger of the person's left hand. Shivering a little, Ellie tested the lighter, watched as it flared to life.

Then, she made her slow way back to the basement door.

She couldn't believe Chris had left her again. The insensitive jerk.

Take it easy on him. You were out cold. He thought you'd be conked until tomorrow morning.

She sighed. He still shouldn't have left. She was worried enough about her gynaecologist appointment tomorrow as it was. What if she found out there really was a reproductive issue?

Making her way down the steps, she focused in on the noise. God, it was loud, a maniacal horde of blacksmiths down there hammering a seething row of forges.

What the hell could make that kind of noise?

She reached the base of the stairs and peered into the murk. To her surprise and dismay, there was only one yellow bulb down here, and it was spattered with what looked like decking stain.

Or dried blood.

Don't even go there, she told herself. *It's not blood, and this is not the Amityville freaking Horror. You're safe, Ellie.*

There was a dog in that movie too.

That's right, there was a dog. There was also James Brolin, Margot Kidder and Rod Steiger as a priest besieged by flies, and that movie bears absolutely no resemblance to this, so quit being a child and figure out what the hell is making that noise!

She made a fist, tapped the side of her leg for courage.

Though she'd never been down here, she thought she could guess the layout of the basement easily enough. This rectangular room followed the outline of the kitchen and dining room exactly. She ventured a few paces farther and realised that, yes, there was another door that led under the foyer and, presumably, the living room. The mechanicals or whatever the hell you called them had to be in one of the other rooms because this one was empty.

Almost empty, she amended. There were several old boxes and what appeared to be a cobwebbed set of andirons. A dusty, full-length mirror.

A thunking sound made her jump. She covered her chest with a trembling hand and stared at the wall. The thud grew faster, louder, something else mixed in now, a jittery clicking that made her, for the first time, fear for her safety. Not from anything otherworldly, but from the possibility of something exploding and ripping her face off.

She crept toward the door and grasped the cool knob.

And drew her hand away.

Wait for Chris. He'll know what to do.

Or better yet, get out of the house, go sit in the car and listen to some tunes. Then, if the place blows sky high it won't take you with it.

Abruptly, the noise stopped.

She became aware of another sound beyond the door: an anguished whimper. Her eyes widened.

Petey.

Couldn't be. If the basement door had blown open somehow,

he could have gotten down here, sure. But this door was closed tight, perhaps even locked.

She reached out, twisted the knob.

Not locked.

She opened it a crack and was assaulted by a new odor: a gamy, nauseating smell that reminded her of rancid meat.

Petey whined, his voice very faint.

Ellie opened the door and stared into the darkness. Skin prickling, she pawed the cinderblock for the switch but couldn't locate it.

Petey whined again.

Why did Chris have to take the flashlight?

She stepped into the gloom and bent forward to see. She strode deeper and a little more light spilled in.

But not enough. She could just make out more boxes, several unidentifiable shapes.

And another door.

Great. Just what she needed.

There could be another switch over there, she told herself.

Yeah? And what if the door behind you swings shut? This old house is drafty as hell. What happens if you get stuck down here in this stinking dungeon? What if Chris doesn't come home for several hours? Are you really willing to subject yourself to that for a dog?

Yes, she realised. She was.

Petey might act strangely at times – she'd be a long time forgetting the way he'd gawked at her naked body a few minutes ago – but he'd become a member of their family. A loyal, good-hearted member. And if he'd gotten himself stuck down here, it was her responsibility to get him out. Chris would be proud of her. Hell, she'd be proud of her*self*. It would prove she didn't always quit, could actually stare down a hairy situation and see the damned thing through.

Jaw firm, she continued into the room.

*　　*　　*

The men would have long hair, Chris thought, the women the type who rode on the backs of motorcycles with their lower back tattoos showing.

Jesus, man, would you calm down?

He barely heard the faint, rational voice. As he reached the base of the hill and began to skirt the edge of the pond, he wondered if this was how Petey felt when sensing the presence of other dogs.

Like the one he'd killed.

Interlopers. Threats. Creatures to whom he needed to send a message, to destroy if necessary.

Relax! They're probably teenagers, for chrissakes, harmless teenagers sneaking out for a few kicks. They'll be scared shitless when they see they've been discovered, so there's no need to march in there like a backwoods Dirty Harry.

But what if they weren't scared of him? What if they were hellraisers looking for trouble, the kind who'd welcome a confrontation?

What if they're armed?

That stopped him.

Yeah, he told himself, *what if they have guns? Just what the hell will you do then?*

With a sinking heart he cast about for a weapon. Nothing presented itself but a few smooth stones and a larger rock that was too cumbersome for practical use.

You could find some poison ivy and threaten to give them a rash.

He chuckled softly and glanced back the way he'd come. He'd made better time tonight – the trip had taken just over an hour. He supposed he could go back home and arm himself with something a little more imposing than a flashlight. But that would take another couple hours round trip, and then what? By one in the morning they might be dozing peacefully in their sleeping bags, perhaps even making love under the moonlight. He'd feel like a schmuck barging in on their campout brandishing a kitchen knife and demanding they pack up their things.

He regarded the mouth of the trail indecisively.

They're teenagers and they're on your land. Tell them to get the hell off. You're completely within your rights, and the only reason not to do so is your own fear of confrontation. Stop being a pussy and do it.

And then what? he demanded. *Granted, there's a chance they'll be scared to death, but if they're the kind of teenagers you sometimes encountered in the classroom – the type of kid who'd tell you to fuck off and couldn't care less about your authority – what will you do then? What if they laugh at your Clint Eastwood act and tell you to get lost? Or worse, what if they threaten you? What if they do more than threaten?*

The voice went on, its logic growing more persuasive by the moment: *The point is, you have no idea what's waiting for you in that clearing, and the only sensible move is to head back to the house and return in the morning. If you want to bluster at them then, when they're hung over and eager to go home anyway, you go ahead. You want to call Bruder, have him accompany you, have at it. But tonight? Home is the only choice.*

He'd all but decided when he heard the baby crying.

Can't be, he told himself. No one would carry a newborn over acres of tangled trails to spend the night on someone else's land. No parent, no matter how irresponsible—

The baby's cry shrilled higher, unmistakably a cry of pain, of suffering. The hairs on the back of his neck stood up, his stomach roiling and sour.

He remembered having the flu once. Unable to keep anything down, dehydrated and weak, he'd finally allowed Ellie to drive him to the ER, where he spent the small hours of the morning attached to an IV and feeling even worse than before. But just as awful as the nausea and the discomfort of the stiff hospital bed was the sound of an infant wailing in agony. The nurses had at first been concerned for the baby, then apologetic toward Chris for having to listen to its cries, and finally visibly agitated by the unceasing noise. The baby had been colicky, according to the brusque doctor who treated Chris, but to him and Ellie it had sounded as though the child were undergoing the worst pain imaginable, in agony yet unable to express it in any manner save that ear-shattering wail.

This cry was like that but worse, much worse. The power of the child's voice grew and grew, setting Chris's teeth on edge, causing his scrotum to shrivel until his balls ached.

My God, he thought. Was someone hurting the child?

A flood of images tumbled through his mind:

A circle of faces, their expressions devoid of emotion save the hunger in their eyes.

A writhing, squalling newborn carried naked to the centre of the circle.

A fire awaiting the child, its acrid scent like brimstone.

Sacrifice.

"*Oh my God*," Chris whispered and began to run.

In an instant he reached the trail. He thundered down the dim corridor, a memory of the first visit informing his steps. As he dashed through the darkness the child's caterwauling grew louder and now he did hear chanting, did hear other voices tolling in unison.

Dear God, the voices. And not just a couple, a legion of them. He heard chanting, the baby's cry and something else, as well, something that broke through the anaesthesia of terror and slowed his movements to a jog.

Moaning. Voices moaning in sexual pleasure.

That couldn't be right, he told himself as he rounded a corner. But it was. The sounds were unmistakable. It all swirled in a witches' brew of discordance and made his head hurt.

"*Chris*," a female voice said.

The other voices were still present, but they were fading. The firelight, so distinct earlier, had diminished, had lowered to an occasional flicker between the sparse trees separating him and the clearing.

"Closer," the voice urged.

And now, far from feeling scared, Chris was overcome with desire. The voice was purring, supplicating. Full of want and the promise of pleasure.

But...Ellie, he tried to remind himself.

"*Closer...closer...closer...*"

Chris moved deeper. A curve left, then right. The trees opened up. There were no hooded figures, no chanting cult.

No child, writhing in agony.

And though the fire was extinguished — if it had been there at all — he could indeed see a woman. She stood at the far edge of the clearing, naked, her slender arms dangling at her sides, the starlight whitening her pale flesh and blackening her large eyes, her red hair, the knowing curve of her mouth, the twin blush of her nipples, the chestnut-coloured V between her legs.

Closer.

The voice grew louder.

Closer, Chris.

He approached, the supple grass cushioning his shoes. He made out more of her now. Tall body, her hair so curled it looked like ringlets cascading over her shoulders, ending just above the curves of her perfect breasts, which were not large but drove him crazy all the same. Slightly upturned, creamy.

Like Ellie's.

Yes, he told himself, *think of Ellie. At home in bed. Needing you. Your wife, Chris, your wife.*

"*Closer,*" the woman urged.

And Chris obeyed.

*   *   *

Ellie ventured closer to the black basement door. Amorphous shadows and sooty smudges on the walls floated past. A faint whiff of sulphur tinged her nostrils and tickled her throat.

She succeeded in keeping her fear at bay until a deep rumble vibrated the floor beneath her, made her teeth champ together painfully. It was a low, growling bass note accompanied by the creak of something about to burst. She imagined a gigantic bellows breathing superheated air into the hull of an iron ship, the walls of the hull bending, groaning. A great oak tree being torn apart by a sadistic giant, its ancient bark twisting, a million tiny ruptures popping within.

And beneath the sound, she heard Petey whimpering.

My God, had he gotten himself stuck down here? Had he come to investigate the noise out of protectiveness or simple curiosity and somehow gotten caught in the gears of whatever antiquated machine powered this place?

Forgetting for a moment how scared she was, Ellie took the last few steps at a jog, reached out and opened the door.

And felt her heart lurch.

Though it was nearly black within the small, closet-like room, she could see Petey's shiny body lying sideways on a workbench. She could see his trusting eyes flickering in the scant light that filtered from the doorway, which now seemed a thousand miles behind her. She discerned his sinuous shoulders, a dark space where his mid-section should have been, then his hind legs. He appeared comfortable, unalarmed. How he could have gotten up to the workbench, why he was lying on it, she had no idea, and further, she no longer felt the need to protect Petey, was only concerned with getting back upstairs and getting into the light. There was a fundamental wrongness here, and though she had no idea why this feeling should fall upon her with such certainty, she felt it all the same.

But when the shadows shifted and the scene before her clarified, Ellie lost the ability to think.

The reason she couldn't see the middle of Petey's body was the man obscuring it, the enormous man who had tensed, who was now aware of her presence, who was turning slowly to face her. Ellie had never experienced such mind-shattering fear in her life. She tried to back away from the man who was turning, turning, his wild black shock of hair spreading out like a lunatic halo, his huge staring eyes and broad thunderous brow crashing over her with the full force of insane malice, and he was reaching out for her now, striding toward her, and without thinking she wheeled and fled, the man's heavy footfalls echoing behind her. Ellie dashed for the door, knowing she would have to turn, scamper across the last section of basement and up the steps, and she could barely see to do any of it.

She cast a glance over her shoulder but it was too dark to see the man. Somehow, this was worse than spotting him. She cried out as she lunged through the door into a brighter dimness, and in moments she was clattering up the stairs, hands slapping the wooden slats as though she were a child again, and above her the doorway beckoned. *Oh please be back, Chris, please be there at the top.*

Sure at any moment a powerful hand would seize her ankle and drag her screaming into the darkness, Ellie leaped forward, reached the kitchen on hands and knees. She slid forward on the linoleum and with a palsied hand reached out. Her fingers had just brushed the door when she chanced a look at the basement below and screamed in horror.

The man was clambering up the stairs.

His wide eyes pierced her with depthless hunger, his grinning mouth a scar of vicious lust.

Ellie slammed the door on him, hurled herself against it and twisted the lock. The door jumped as he crashed against it, and Ellie stumbled away, appalled by the man's strength.

She sprinted through the kitchen, sure at any moment the door would splinter and the man would burst through. She careened around the corner, through the screened-in porch, and into the backyard. She no longer trusted her senses to help her; the man could tackle her from behind and she'd never hear him coming. Oh God, that *face*. Those sadistic devil's eyes.

It doesn't matter now, she thought as she reached the Camry. The car was in bad shape, but the damn thing had worked earlier. It would sure as hell work now.

She shut the door and reached for the keys.

And slammed her forehead against the steering wheel when she realised the keys were in the house. What an idiot! Of all things, how the hell had she forgotten the keys? She reached for the handle intending to get out and make a break down the lane, to run all the way back to town if necessary, when she realised a shadow had fallen over her.

Oh my God.

The man.

Ellie swivelled her head slowly and looked up at the face peering through the window beside her.

Chris.

He opened the door as she exploded into tears. She threw herself into his chest, buried her face in his shirt, shook her head as he asked questions. She couldn't make out his words, could think of nothing but the man in the basement. The man—

"We've got to leave," she said, pulling away.

The concern on his face only heightened her frantic need. "Ellie, what—"

"*Now*, Chris. We have to leave *now*."

★   ★   ★

His mouth worked a moment, then he gestured weakly toward the house. "The keys are upstairs on the nightstand."

She pushed out of the car to get a clear view of the house.

The back door was closed, and no figure stood watching them from the other side.

"Ellie, what's going on?"

"There's someone inside."

"In the house?"

Tears threatened again. "God, it was awful. He was *after* me, Chris. He...he had Petey."

His voice went tight. "What do you mean 'He had Petey'?"

A fleeting pang of indignation hit her. *You're more worried about the dog than you are about me?*

Then she remembered the man's mad eyes and her anger passed.

"We have to get out of here," she said. "Something's wrong here."

Chris glanced at the house, his face uncertain. "Was he... *hurting* Petey?"

She shook her head. "I don't know...I couldn't tell. It was dark down there."

He turned to her, a questioning look in his eyes.

"The basement," she explained. "He was in the basement."

"Why were you—"

"Who gives a shit, Chris? *He wanted to kill me.*"

He ran a hand through his hair, and for the first time Ellie took in his dishevelled state, the rumpled shirt, sweat-soaked and ripped near the neckline. And his complexion, ordinarily so fair, was flushed a deep crimson. A new species of disquiet wormed its way through her belly, and for one horrible moment her husband resembled the man from whom she'd fled.

"Okay," Chris said, more to himself. "Okay. We'll find a place to stay in town tonight, but we can't get there without the keys."

"Then let's walk," she nearly shouted. "Anything's better than standing here."

"It's twelve miles to town. You talk about dark—"

She grabbed hold of his shirt. "He's *in there*, Chris. I locked him in the basement, but the door won't hold him. He's...huge...strong, crazy. Now dammit, let's go already!"

His hands went to her shoulders, his condescending expression infuriating her. She wasn't some hysterical woman gibbering nonsense; she was totally lucid, perfectly able to differentiate what was real and what was—

Her thoughts broke off when she saw the woman watching them from the forest.

"Listen, Ellie," she heard him say from far away, "if the man is as dangerous as you say he is…"

The woman was naked, her bare breasts pallid and small in the moonlight. She stood beside an oak tree, one hand poised on the rough bark, the other hanging loose at her bare hip, which was also stark white, luminous against the sylvan backdrop.

"…we're not going to be any safer hiking to town through the countryside…"

The woman took a step toward them, one slender leg crossing the other, and Ellie noticed a disturbing thing. A moment earlier she was sure the woman was watching her, but now she realised the glittery sable eyes were fixed on Chris. Unwavering, as if she were obsessed with him.

"Ellie?" he asked and shook her a little. "*Ellie?*"

Ellie's eyes shifted to Chris, then flitted back to the naked woman, and in that time the figure somehow vanished.

If it had been there at all.

Of course it was there! her mind screamed. She could describe the woman in perfect detail: long, curly hair; pearlescent skin; the strange, haunting eyes that weren't quite human. The figure filled her with the same atavistic dread as…as…

As the man you supposedly found in your basement.

Supposedly?

She searched her husband's face and discerned the same thought scrawled on his features. She fought to repel it. It was *real*, she told herself. It wasn't some stress-induced hallucination, some product of the drugs she'd taken.

Was it?

"We're going to be fine," Chris was saying. "You wait here while—"

"You think I'm waiting out here by myself?"

"In the car," he said, as if it were obvious.

"No way."

"You can lock the door if—"

"*I'm not waiting in the goddamn car.*"

He let go of her shoulders. "All right, fine. Then stay right behind me. It won't take long."

He started toward the house.

"Wait a minute," she said.

"Ellie, it's the only way. If there is somebody inside, he could follow us wherever we went. All we need is the keys—"

"He'll kill you."

He stopped, put his hands on his hips and Ellie thought, *Not now. For God's sake, please don't let your wounded male ego complicate the situation.*

"Give me a little credit, El. I think I can take care of one man."

Not this man, she thought. But she knew where that would get her. She struggled for the right words, a way to take his pride out of it...

She took his arm. "He might have a gun."

His face clouded. He glanced irresolutely at the house. "I guess it's possible..."

"It's more than possible. What if he snuck in to rob the place and I surprised him? He's probably mad as hell and ready to shoot anyone that comes inside."

And that tidy explanation, she reflected grimly, ignores several salient questions, such as why would he have gone to the basement if he were a thief, and even more importantly, what the hell was he doing to Petey on the workbench?

Chris raised an index finger. "The garage," he said and set off in that direction. She followed, and as she did, she cast a glance over her shoulder to see if the naked woman had reappeared.

But the forest was darker than ever.

*   *   *

He felt a good deal more confident with the axe in his hands.

He'd offered it to Ellie, but she claimed it was too unwieldy for her and opted for a hard-toothed rake.

As they exited the garage, he said, "What're you gonna do with that, comb his hair?"

She brandished the rake playfully. "Would *you* like to be smacked with one of these?"

"Not particularly," he said, and smiled for the first time since the clearing.

Since you cheated on Ellie.

You don't know that, a small voice in his head pleaded.

Then the other voice, insistent, implacable: *Yes, you do. You know exactly what happened in that clearing. You're an adulterer, buddy. How's it feel?*

He turned away so his wife couldn't see his face. As he moved cautiously toward the house, a gauzy filmstrip of images flickered through his memory:

The naked woman urging him closer.

The soft grass under his bare feet.

Her fingertips on his chest.

A dream, he protested. *All a dream.*

He could feel Ellie behind him, her alarm growing with every step they took toward the house.

That's right, he told himself. *Focus on that, focus on Ellie. She's the one you're supposed to protect. She's the one you*

(*betrayed*)

need to keep your eye on. After that incident with the Rottweiler, when you failed her

(*because you were with another woman*)

you better not fail her again

(*and you went back, didn't you? Went back because you knew who you'd find, the woman's body easing down on yours, the feel of her warmth*)

"Wait a second," Ellie whispered.

Chris looked back at her, his head clearing.

She was staring at the ground, listening.

"What is it?" he asked and peered up at the back door, only ten feet away.

"I thought I heard Petey scratching at the screen door."

"So?"

"He was locked in the basement."

Chris gaped at her. "You locked him in the basement?"

"Would you rather I let the man murder me?"

He dropped his head, disgusted with himself. *Husband of the year*, he thought. "I'm sorry, honey. It's just…"

Just what? It's just been a tough night, what with the extra-marital sex and all?

Ellie watched him.

He shook his head. "Just nothing, there's no excuse. I'm just happy you're safe."

"If we were safe, we wouldn't be standing outside the house with gardening tools."

He saw the fear in her eyes, and some of his composure returned. He inhaled a deep lungful of air, gripped the axe in his right hand and took hold of the back door with his left.

He glanced back at Ellie. "You ready?"

She gave him a sardonic glare. "No."

Despite his own fear, he grinned. He raised the axe and slowly drew open the back door.

Petey lay on the floor in the doorway between the screened-in porch and the kitchen. At first Chris was sure the dog was dead. Then Petey twitched, opened his eyes, and gazed sleepily up at him.

Chris inched his way forward, ready to swing the axe at anything that moved. He could hear Ellie behind him, her breathing strained and shallow.

He reached down and scratched the dog between the ears, whispered, "Where is he, boy? The kitchen?"

Chris glanced that way and saw the room looking like it always did, the ugly overhead light casting its sallow glow over the outdated appliances.

His gaze moved to the unlit living room. Nothing out of the ordinary he could see. He leaned into the kitchen and frowned.

The basement door stood open.

"You said you locked it?"

"That's right."

Ellie peered around his arm.

"Oh hell," she said.

"Doesn't mean anything," he said, more to convince himself than Ellie. "Petey might've pushed it open to get out of the basement."

Ellie didn't respond. He didn't blame her.

He didn't believe himself either.

*   *   *

The house seemed empty.

When they'd searched upstairs and retrieved the car keys, they returned to the kitchen, where the basement door stood open like the hungry maw of some subterranean monster.

"Let's leave," Ellie said from behind him.

He paused. "You positive you saw someone down there?"

"*Chris.*"

"I'm just asking."

"You think I made it up to get attention?"

He half-turned, not wanting to completely lose sight of the blackened doorway. "I'm not saying that. But you had an awful day with the dog and the hospital. The pills you took on the way home..."

"None of that made me hallucinate a man who looked like a muscle-bound Satan-worshipper."

"Then let's make sure he's out of our house."

"Are you crazy? Chris, let's *go.*"

"Go where? I didn't see a hotel in town, did you?"

"We'll go to the police station then, tell Bruder what happened."

"Bruder's probably in bed sleeping," he said. "We'll get some buck-toothed deputy who'll think we're nuts."

"Great! I'd rather be laughed at than chopped into little pieces."

"I'm the one with the axe."

"Goddammit, Chris, would you please stop being such a macho idiot?"

"I'm checking the basement," he said. He stepped over to the doorway, reached in, flicked on the light.

"Damn it," Ellie said, but she followed him just the same.

They made their way down in the meagre basement light.

They reached a door in the far corner of the room. Chris opened the door and waited for Ellie to illuminate the room beyond. When she did, he couldn't make out much of anything save a few hulking piles against the wall.

"Where was he?" Chris asked.

Ellie's voice was strained. "Over there." The beam rested on the far wall. Squeezing the axe handle for courage, Chris stepped closer.

Halfway across the room, he stopped and indicated a door on their left. "Where's that lead?"

"The utility closet," she said.

He heard something odd in her voice. Before he could respond, she moved past him and stopped a few feet from the wall.

As she passed the light over the grimy grey cinderblocks, Chris asked, "Where's the room with the workbench?"

"Son of a bitch," Ellie muttered.

"Honey?"

"Right here," she said, the flashlight beam dancing wildly on the wall.

"You must've gotten turned around," he said. He nodded toward the wall on their right. "Maybe it's over there."

"It was *here*, Chris. This exact spot."

"Ellie—"

"I know what I saw, dammit. There was a doorway and a workbench, and a man had Petey. Had him...hooked up to something." She reached out, trailed a hand over the rough surface.

"You think maybe it was the medication?" he asked and immediately regretted it.

"Thanks a lot."

"Where's the door then?"

"I don't know," she said. "But I know what I saw."

They left the room in silence. When they got to the stairs leading up to the kitchen he stepped aside to let Ellie pass. He followed her up. He was about to close the basement door when he decided, on a whim, to shine the flashlight into the darkness one more time.

He braced himself for the monstrous figure, the eyes full of rage glowering up at him through the gloom.

But nothing stirred in the flashlight's dull glow.

Chris exhaled and shut the door.

CHAPTER SIX

She barreled down the country road, Dr. Stone's terrible words repeating in her head like some ghastly taunt: *I'm so sorry to tell you this, Mrs. Crane, but we've found something troubling.*

She was tempted to go faster than her current eighty, but each time she flirted with ninety, the loose gravel threatened to hurl her into a ditch. The sky portended rain the whole miserable way, and when she swung the Camry onto the lane, the rain cut loose and began to pelt the windshield with merciless force. For a wild moment she was tempted to let the back end continue its nauseating roll toward the trees and ruin the car for good. Then she jerked the wheel into the spin. Ahead she spotted the bridge leading home.

What if I overcorrected? she wondered. *What if I aimed the car not at the bridge but to the right of it and plunged down the embankment to the creek? What if I found myself upside down in the water?*

Ellie got control, manoeuvered the car between the wooden guardrails.

At the far end of the bridge the Camry jounced, Ellie's butt actually leaving the seat and the top of her head rapping the ceiling. Then she picked up speed again, the tyres lurching as she marauded over the gravelly potholes.

She checked the speedometer. Forty-five. If Petey were to dart out of the forest now he wouldn't stand a chance. Which was tragic, she told herself, since he was probably the closest she would ever come to having a child. Nature or God or whatever cruel presence presided over her life had decided to deprive her of the one thing she truly wanted. Her eyes flicked to the speedometer.

Fifty.

An overhanging branch whacked the Camry's antenna, but Ellie only pushed the accelerator harder.

Fifty-five.

The house would appear soon, and she knew she should slow down, but the picture of her crashing into the garage didn't disturb her. Chris would hear it and come out, and she supposed he'd be worried about her.

That was, until she told him she could never bear a child, was as fallow as a scorched field in a nuclear winter. *But it's a good thing we found out when we did*, she'd tell him. *Now you'll have time to find a suitable replacement for me, someone who'll give you the little boy you always talk about, the one with whom you dream of playing catch.*

A voice spoke up, clear and clinical but not unkind: *You're hurting, Ellie, but you're feeling sorry for yourself. Not to mention endangering your life by driving like an idiot.*

She checked her speed.

Sixty miles per hour.

And the house and garage were now in view. Eighty yards away. Sixty.

You know Chris will love you no matter what, the voice insisted, and Ellie was taken aback to find it belonged to Katherine. *You're in pain, and you have every right to be angry...*

The garage was very close now, the Camry racing at it with appalling rapidity.

Thirty yards and closing.

...but there are still options, Ellie. Babies get adopted every day. You and Chris could make great parents to one of those babies.

With a choked sob, Ellie stomped on the brake with both feet, yanked the wheel sideways, the Camry skidding toward the garage, the cracks in its paint clearly visible now, getting clearer, and for the second time in a minute the back end slued toward the front, but this time it kept on going, its looping swipe missing the garage by inches, the car bouncing to a stop in the narrow swath of grass between garage and forest.

She leaned against the steering wheel and wept. She pounded the dash with a shaking fist, the adrenaline of the near crash endowing her blows with added force.

After a long time she slumped back against the seat and listened to the rain. There was no thunder, just the solid thunk of the raindrops on the roof.

Find your husband, El. You need him now.

She concentrated on breathing, on calming the uneven hitches in her chest.

Okay, she thought. *Okay.*

Find Chris.

Ellie opened the door and climbed out. As if sensing her presence, the rain grew more intense, icy freshets plastering her hair to her scalp and soaking her clothes to the skin. She thought of a warm bath, a glass of wine. She could sure as hell have one now, no baby to worry about.

A fresh wave of grief blurred her eyes. She fought it, made it to the back door, stepped inside.

And stared.

The waves of sorrow diminished, a pulsing shock taking their place.

Where before there had been a single chair on the back porch, there were now two wicker couches and a loveseat. The tabletop was frosted glass, but its legs also were made of wicker. The couch fabric was gaudy pink roses on a lighter pink background. The furniture seemed to laugh at her, delighting in her dismay.

Hideous, she thought. *And somehow familiar.*

She continued inside and gazed confusedly into the living room.

Where before the room had been spartan, now the space was packed with two more couches, a leather recliner, a chaise longue with a high back that blocked a sliver of the northern window. She'd seen it all somewhere, and for reasons she couldn't pinpoint, the sight of it all plagued her with a bewildering sense of doom. There were paintings on the walls, awful, outdated paintings of country roads and windmills and seacoasts. On one yellowing print she beheld a pair of little boys climbing a tree.

She made her way through the living room on legs that threatened to buckle. She felt like an intruder, and had theirs not been the only one for miles, she would have turned and escaped, embarrassed for having entered the wrong house.

She rounded the corner into the foyer, where more surprises awaited. Another painting, this one of a country field bisected by a rock wall. Another table, one that jutted out too far into the room.

And a grandfather clock. Gazing at the brass finials, the plain beige clock face, Ellie finally remembered.

Aunt Lillith.

Dear God, Chris had retrieved her belongings from storage and littered the house with them.

"So?" a voice asked from the dining room.

She turned and stared at Chris.

"What do you think?" he asked, gesturing toward the clock.

When she didn't answer, he raised his eyebrows, mopped sweat from his forehead. "I was upstairs arranging. Must not have heard you pull up."

"I can't have children."

He frowned. "What?"

"I can't have children," she repeated. "I had an appointment today, remember?"

"How can they…"

"Endometriosis. The chances of my getting pregnant are virtually nil."

"Ellie," he said, reaching for her.

"Don't."

He dropped his arms. "Ellie, I'm—"

"You can leave me if you want."

"You think I'd leave you?"

"I wouldn't blame you."

He led her into the living room, where they sat on their old couch. She cried for a while, and he held her. She put her head on his shoulder and snuggled into him.

After they'd sat in silence for several minutes, Chris said, "What do you think of my surprise?"

"You mean your aunt's old furniture?"

She felt him tense. "You said we needed more furniture."

"I have to tell you something," she said. "But you have to promise not to get mad."

"What?" he said, his voice guarded.

"Promise."

He sighed. "Fine, I promise."

"I hated Aunt Lillith."

He didn't respond right away, but Ellie could tell he was struggling to quell his anger. Or was it hurt?

He said, "I knew you didn't care for her much."

"She didn't like me either."

"How could you know a thing like that?"

"She said I wasn't worthy of you."

He pulled away, an expression of disbelief twisting one corner of his mouth. "She didn't say that."

"She called me names and said I'd hurt you."

"Ellie…"

"Lillith was insane."

"She was not in – Ellie, she helped raise me for chrissakes."

"She was jealous of me."

His eyes narrowed. "What's that supposed to mean?"

"She wanted you all to herself."

He seemed to recoil. "Where the hell do you get off…you talk like she was attracted to me."

"Call it what you want."

His eyes drew wide with disbelief. "I can't believe you." He glanced about the room. "She gives us everything she owns. Gives us a *house*. And you talk about her like she was some kind of pervert."

"What would you call her?"

"A nice old woman," he said, voice rising. "Jesus, I guess I'll leave the rest of her stuff in the garage."

"There's more?" Ellie said. "I didn't know a spinster could accumulate that much junk."

Chris got up. As he left the room, a storm of guilt assailed her. He'd made a mistake, yes, but he'd been trying to please her. And she was so distraught over the news at Dr. Stone's that she'd taken it out on—

"*Wait*," she called, rising.

The screen door slammed.

He was halfway to the Camry, still parked crookedly in the yard, when she burst out the back door. "*Chris*," she called.

He didn't stop.

Ellie sprinted after him, and suddenly it all felt like a self-fulfilling prophecy, her thinking he'd no longer want her after the news about her infertility. She'd picked a fight with him, driven him away, and as he opened the car door and got in she started crying again, but this time the tears were different. They were hot, scalding. If he left her now she'd have nothing, she'd—

She dashed around the front of the car and slapped at the driver's window.

The engine started.

"*Please*, Chris," she said, her voice breaking. He didn't make a move to roll down the window, but he didn't put the car in gear either. The raindrops fell harder but she barely felt them, and now there was a muffled booming in the west.

"*Please don't leave me*," she yelled, but her voice was failing. This was what she deserved for her meanness and self-absorption. He *did* deserve better than her. He *would* be better off with someone else. The tears taking hold, she crumpled against the window and sobbed.

Distantly, she heard the engine die. Beneath her palms the door was moving, opening. She stepped out of the way and stared down at Chris, who was peering up at her with red-rimmed eyes.

"I'm so sorry," she said.

His mouth worked.

"I'm so sorry," she repeated.

He climbed out of the car and embraced her.

CHAPTER SEVEN

They made love that afternoon and lazed in the bedroom all evening.

Outside, the storm worsened. Winds buffeted the house, the old planks groaning under the strain. At around ten they were startled by a bloodcurdling screech from below. They hurried downstairs and discovered the rain gutter had torn loose from its moorings and was now dangling from the covered porch.

Staring out the front door, Ellie watched the wind rocketing over the front lawn, the grass driven flat by the rain. Chris slipped his hands around her waist.

"How about we give each other backrubs?" she suggested.

"Backrubs, huh?" he said, and they were soon making love again.

The next day they slept in till nearly noon.

When they awoke, Chris checked the basement and announced that no water had leaked in during the storm. Their happiness vanished when he turned on the kitchen tap only to have his glass fill with a dark, sludgy substance that smelled like slow decomposition.

Ellie eyed the glass. "We're supposed to bathe in that?"

Chris made a face and dumped it into the sink.

They were surveying the damage outside when a sound from the pocket of her sweatpants startled her. The phone.

She brought it out and stared at it. Though she didn't have any bars, she'd somehow gotten enough reception to see she had a new message.

"Your sister?" Chris asked.

"I don't recognise the number."

"Let's go for a ride and see who it is," Chris said. "We need to call a plumber anyway."

★   ★   ★

To his surprise, the cell got reception less than a mile from the lane. When the single bar flickered, Ellie told him to pull over.

He watched Ellie dial her voicemail, and soon a change came over her.

Concerned, he opened his mouth to ask her what was wrong, but she brought up an index finger and continued listening. Judging from her face, which was pinched in a mask of perplexity, the news wasn't good. *Big surprise there*, he thought.

A moment later she took the phone slowly from her ear and stared at it thoughtfully.

"Everything okay?" he asked. But Ellie seemed not to hear him.

"El?" he said and put a hand on her shoulder. "What's wrong, honey?"

She faced him, uttered a breathless little laugh. "I'm pregnant."

Chris stared at her.

"It was Dr. Stone's office," she explained. "One of his nurses, she wants me to come in for another examination...you know, to determine the risk of the pregnancy, all that stuff. But she said I'm definitely carrying a child. The blood tests came back a little while ago."

"Didn't they say yesterday you can't..."

She nodded.

"Is the baby healthy?" he asked.

"They don't know. It's too early."

She started to laugh, tears already streaming down her face. He leaned across the console and kissed her.

"You believe it?" he asked.

"I don't know what to believe." Her chest shuddered, and soon she was sobbing. Chris wrapped her up, rocked her, kissed her hair.

"You're going to be a mommy," he said, crying now himself.

"I want to be."

He pulled away, gazed at her terror-stricken face. "It's the best thing that ever happened to us."

"I don't know," she said, glancing out the windshield and wiping her nose. "There are so many things that could wrong. Miscarriages, birth defects...what if I can't carry it to term?"

"You will."

"We don't even know if it's healthy yet. What if it's...what did Kat use to call it...ectopic. What if the foetus is ectopic?"

"When we get home, I'm taking the books away. We've got enough to worry about without scaring ourselves half to death with that crap."

"Chris..." she said. She shook her head slowly.

He started, remembering something. "Didn't they say they wanted to see you?"

Ellie dialled the number.

CHAPTER EIGHT

Dr. Stone's appraisal was frank but encouraging. He told them they had better than average odds of a miscarriage during the first trimester. However, he reasoned, they were already a good way through it. According to the ultrasound, Ellie was eleven weeks' pregnant, give or take. With each successive week, the chance of losing the baby diminished.

On the way home Ellie began to cry again. When Chris asked her what was wrong, she said nothing, she was just happy.

Which was almost true. Most of her tears *were* for joy. Yet a small part of her, the part that sometimes kept her awake in the small hours of the night, had already begun to remind her of her past failures. She wiped her nose and stared out the passenger's window just in case Chris should see how scared she was.

You quit the dance team in high school, the voice wheedled. *You quit the musical your senior year even though you had an important solo. It took you forever to finish college, and when you did you didn't do a darn thing with your degree. Then you mooched off Jason while you were married.*

No.

When your marriage failed too – which was bound to happen given your track record – you answered phones for an insurance agent who only kept you around because he wanted in your pants, and when that didn't work out he fired you. And you didn't put up a fight. You were relieved you didn't have to get up early each morning. And lately you've longed to give up on the move to Indiana, haven't you? The quitting urge is overwhelming you the way it always has.

No, she thought dismally. *No it isn't.*

But there'll be no quitting this time, will there? You can't quit with a baby. It's either carry the child through to the end or—

She shook her head to scatter the thought, the awful, awful

thought. *No quitting*, she told the voice. *I'll never fail this child. I'll be a great mom and see this through, I'll—*

"Ellie?" Chris asked.

She glanced at him, her cheeks colouring.

"What?"

He held up a conciliatory hand. "Nothing," he said. "I just wanted to make sure you were okay."

"Why wouldn't I be?"

He shrugged, studying her face. "You were grinding your teeth."

"Oh," she said, turning to the window again. "I didn't notice."

*   *   *

Aaron Wolf arrived an hour after they called him. Ellie was taking a nap when he pulled up, a fact for which Chris was later grateful.

The man was shorter than Chris, but he was thicker, his shoulders broad and beefy. His russet beard was long and well groomed. The ruddy cheeks and red nose appeared to be a sunburn and not a product of hard living; to the contrary, Aaron Wolf exuded good health and virility. The clothes he wore were exactly like Daniel's: navy blue work pants, a light blue work shirt and a black hat. The only difference was the pair of navy blue suspenders Aaron wore. He had a bit of a gut, yet even this served to enhance his powerful aura.

The kitchen faucet worked flawlessly when Aaron tested it, so they descended into the basement with a work light. Chris followed and did his best to suppress the lingering chill brought on by Ellie's story about the man down here.

After making their way to the utility closet, Aaron asked, "You know where there's an outlet?"

Chris glanced about feebly, and though it was silly, a familiar feeling of uselessness began to sour his stomach. It was the same way he used to feel when his stepfather would ask for his help doing a job. When Chris was asked to perform some task, he never quite knew how to complete it. *Hand me the needle-nosed pliers*, his stepdad would say, and Chris would stare dumbly down at the multitudinous tools having no idea at all what needle-nosed pliers were. Eventually his stepdad would sigh in exasperation and grab the pliers himself while Chris looked on miserably.

"Ah," Aaron said and strode over to an empty light socket. On the conical white bulb housing there were two outlets. "Not grounded," Aaron muttered. He produced an adaptor from his shirt pocket and slid it over the three-pronged plug. He plugged in the work light and a brilliant glow filled the room.

"Hold this a moment," Aaron said as he opened the utility door. Chris raised the work light and Aaron moved past the hulking furnace to a dingy white cylinder. Chris detected a clammy trace of moist steel in the air.

"That the water heater?" Chris asked.

"Older than Moses, isn't it?" Aaron said, smiling. He got down on his knees, rubbed grime off a small brass faceplate. "1954," he read.

Chris asked, "Did your brother tell you I ran into him the other night?"

A queer stillness seemed to settle over the Amish man. In a voice very unlike his usual one, he said, "He did."

"Did he say what happened?"

Aaron slid the metal cover back in place, stood up, and relieved Chris of the work light. "Something about an argument."

Chris grunted. "Wasn't much of an argument. He beat the crap out of a grocery clerk."

He waited for Aaron to respond, but the bearded man was frowning and holding the work light aloft.

"Funny," Aaron said.

"What?" Chris asked, following his gaze.

"There used to be a workshop there."

Beneath him, Chris felt the muscles of his legs liquefy. "Workshop?"

Aaron nodded toward the wall, strode over to it. "See?" he said, holding the light against it. "You can still see the outline right here."

And Chris did see it. A faint rectangle exactly where Ellie claimed she'd beheld a man hulking between her and Petey.

"Here's the mortar line." Aaron traced it with a finger. "And right here's where the top of the doorway was."

Chris's throat had as gone dry as chaff. "Why would someone seal it off?"

Aaron shook his head wonderingly. "I wouldn't know." He rapped on the sealed doorway. A dull echo resounded from within.

"So why'd your brother beat up Campbell?"

Aaron seemed not to hear him, instead made his way past Chris and unplugged the light. In the darkness, the big man looped the cord on his thick forearm. "How much do you know about the history of this place, Mr. Crane?"

"Only what Doris Keller told us."

"What was that?"

"I don't know...it's all crazy. Doris said there used to be a cult here."

Aaron didn't look up from the coiling cord.

"Something about weird rituals, sacrifice. Of..." Chris swallowed. "...of infanticide."

"What else?" Aaron asked in a quiet voice.

Chris thought of Doris's raving about demons and vampires; he thought of Campbell's knowledge of the woman in the woods. How to say all that to Aaron Wolf? How to explain it when he didn't understand it himself?

"That all?" Aaron asked.

Chris opened his mouth, paused.

"I suspect not," Aaron said, but he didn't probe any further. Instead, he moved toward the stairs. When they'd reached the kitchen, Aaron said, "I'm not sure what's wrong with your plumbing, Mr. Crane. Well water's a funny thing. If it doesn't happen again, I'm tempted to write it off to rust. These pipes haven't been used in ages, so even if your inspector ran them, he probably didn't get all the rust out of the lines."

Chris nodded, but the water was the last thing on his mind.

"As for your question," Aaron said and moved toward the back door, "I know why my brother used his fists on that man."

Chris followed Aaron to his black pickup truck. Aaron opened the passenger door, set the work light on the seat, then swung the door shut. Leaning against it, he said, "If you go digging, you'll find a lot of folks who'll claim there's something wrong with the land itself. That Destragis was only a symptom."

"Like the land attracted him?"

Aaron nodded. "Some say so."

"You believe that?"

"I don't know," Aaron said. "I can only tell you what happened with Daniel's wife."

Aaron drew in a deep breath, as if steeling himself. "The cult was going strong in the early nineties. Right around the time my brother married Sarah."

"Was the marriage..." Chris sought for the most inoffensive way to put it, "...you know, arranged?"

Aaron grinned. "We don't usually do it that way, but no, it wasn't. Daniel met her at the county fair.

"We all thought she was a great little gal. Sharp, too. She'd gotten her degree in nursing. Things started off real well for her and Daniel."

Aaron's face clouded. "Then she started wandering around the forest."

Chris had an idea what was coming, the memory of the other night rippling his skin into gooseflesh. He knew a little about wandering in the forest.

"You're probably aware how close Daniel's land is to yours?"

"Just across the road, right?"

Aaron nodded. "I'm on the north side of you, Daniel's on the east. Sarah crossed the road to these woods one night, and from what we could gather, she stumbled onto Destragis's cult."

"Campbell was one of them," Chris guessed.

Aaron's eyes did a slow pass over the trees. "Campbell wasn't one of the ringleaders, but yes, he was part of it."

He sighed. "I don't like to gossip, so I'll spare you all the personal stuff. Let's just say Sarah didn't resist joining in for very long. Soon she was sneaking out every night after Daniel had gone to sleep.

"She got pregnant, though we'll never who..." He trailed off, a sour, introspective expression darkening his ruddy face. "About the time she told Daniel she was expecting, he decided to follow her into the woods. He'd awakened one night to find her gone, and he'd already grown suspicious of the way her..."

Aaron stared at the upper reaches of the trees. "You sure you wanna hear this?"

"Yes."

"I suppose you have a right to, this all belonging to you now."

Chris felt another chill. He assumed the plumber meant that the land and the house belonged to him, but the way he said it, he couldn't escape the impression that it was the story he now owned, the events that took place two decades ago.

"Sarah was on some sort of altar," Aaron said. "She was surrounded by several people, and though she was stark naked, she acted as though that didn't bother her at all.

"By this time my brother'd realised that every last person in that clearing was naked, too. Then, they started in...

"Evidently, they'd known Daniel was there. Must've had people hidden nearby keeping watch because my little brother was always a good hider. But they found him, and though he bloodied a couple noses, they forced him into the clearing. Told him to join in, but he refused."

Chris scuffed the dirt with a sneaker. "Did Sarah...resist at all?"

"Not a bit," Aaron replied. "Not even when they started cutting on her."

Aaron took in his sickened expression and explained, "A lot of what they did involved blood."

Aaron went on, "The long and short of it was that Sarah went to live with them."

"They *lived* here?"

"Not in the house. That was only for the man and woman they followed. The rest lived underground." Taking in Chris's confused silence, he added, "There are caves around here, Mr. Crane. You'd be best served to stay out of them."

He felt like he'd been gut-punched. How had he missed them? He'd spent dozens of hours in these woods. Had the entrances been covered in the intervening years?

"Those caves," Aaron said, "were where she had her baby."

"Was Daniel the father?"

"We'll never know. The child disappeared. Sarah did too, just days after she gave birth."

"What happened to them?"

"Your guess is as good as mine. Cult members were questioned, but no one knew anything."

Aaron heaved a sigh. "Sarah and her baby were just two in a long line of missing persons linked to this place."

Chris said, "That's why your brother got so enraged with Norman Campbell."

Aaron nodded. "Said Campbell was bringing up the past again, trying to relive all the old horror."

"Was Campbell one of the men who slept with Sarah?"

Aaron's lips curled in a disgusted frown. "I suspect he was."

Chris sought for Campbell's words that night outside the library, then remembered them. "When Campbell was arguing with your brother, he said 'She came because she wanted to.'"

Aaron folded his arms. "As much as I hate to admit it, he was probably right about that."

"Daniel thinks they drugged her?"

Aaron was quiet a good while, thinking something over. When he finally spoke, his voice was scarcely louder than a whisper. "I don't think he suspected drugs, Mr. Crane. The group that worshipped here believed in all sorts of bad things. Daniel thought there were supernatural forces at work in his wife. He couldn't imagine her changing that abruptly. She was everything you'd want in a woman. Caring, bright, hard-working..." Aaron shook his head. "It didn't make sense she'd change without some influence."

"You agree?"

The blue eyes locked on his. "I don't know what to believe. There's certainly evidence to support Daniel's theory, I don't dispute that at all. It's just..." He paused, thinking. "...it's just that people have a tendency to do the wrong thing even when – *especially* when – they know it's the wrong thing to do. It's like we have this need to hurt ourselves, to hurt the people we love...to kill the good things for no other reason than that we know we shouldn't."

Chris thought of a Poe story he once taught, "The Black Cat." How had Poe worded it? "...this unfathomable longing of the soul to *vex itself.*"

Yes, a voice whispered. *Like cheating on the person who means everything to you.*

Aaron was watching him. "That make any sense?"

Chris nodded, a tightness in his throat. "It does."

"Anyway, Daniel wouldn't think so. He can't imagine a woman so good-hearted doing such wicked things. So he blames Campbell. Even more, I guess he blames those things we can't see for what happened."

"He never remarried?"

"Uh-uh...the last eight years or so, it's been Daniel living out here with only his dog Levi to keep him company."

Chris bit the inside of his mouth. He knew what was coming even before Aaron frowned and added, "And even Levi's gone now. Last week he either ran away or got himself run over." He turned to Chris. "You haven't seen him out here, have you?"

He thought of Ellie's incident with the monstrous black dog, thought of Petey's muzzle glistening with blood.

"I haven't seen him," he said, "but I'll let you know if I do."

"Let Daniel know," Aaron said. "He's been beside himself with worry over that Rottweiler."

PART THREE
SACRIFICE
CHAPTER ONE

The storm began after Chris went into town for groceries. Ellie was sitting on the front porch poring over baby names when brilliant light strobed over the woods to the north. She got up and walked barefooted across the lawn to gain a better view. As she moved, she marvelled at how warm it had gotten, how swiftly the weather in Indiana changed. Ellie stretched her arms, glad she'd chosen the black tank top and beige shorts.

Lightning again, three quick flashes this time, followed by a louder rumble. The air was redolent with fresh green life, with the pleasing fragrance of the coming rain. Ellie savoured the feel of the bluegrass on her arches. Soothing, like the touch of a baby's fingertips.

She stopped and a warm smile spread over her face. She put a hand to her belly, slowly caressed.

A droplet of rain splashed over her cheek. Another in her hair. She sighed. It would be nice to stay out here, but foolish. It would be just her luck to get struck by lightning the day she found out they'd finally conceived.

Yet she didn't feel like being shut indoors either. She'd get a book and read on the porch.

The open garage door drew her attention. She walked to the garage, careful to keep to the yard so the driveway gravel wouldn't bite her flesh. When she could go no farther in the grass, she tiptoed across the gravel, wincing as the jagged limestone shards stabbed her tender soles.

Lightning bloomed, closer this time, and the succeeding thunder sounded much more insistent. Ellie tasted the electricity in the air, the tingly flavour of ozone.

She moved deeper into the garage and found she could see pretty well despite the lack of an overhead light. A stack of boxes bulged against the back wall.

Ellie frowned, approached them. She was sure they'd unpacked everything...

Then she remembered.

Aunt Lillith's things.

The woman's hateful face rose like a stench in her mind. Ellie pictured her in one of her expensive St. John outfits, residing in one of her antique brocade chairs and sipping hot tea. In her vision, Lillith was watching Chris with that somehow obscene expression, a speculative grin etched in her wrinkled face. Then she'd turn to Ellie, and what life had been in Lillith's face drained away and was replaced by a dead mask of loathing.

Christopher has always been my boy, and no vulgar little slut is going to change that.

Ellie shut her eyes against the woman's zombie stare.

Christopher will always belong to me.

Thunder crashed behind her and made her jump.

"Damn," Ellie said and covered her palpitating heart. *Calm down, girl*, she thought. *It's not just you now, remember? You've got a little person in there, and it won't be good for him to get so worked up.*

Ellie chuckled at herself. She realised that ever since the news she'd been thinking of the foetus as a *him* instead of a *her*. Why, she had no idea. She certainly wasn't against having a girl. In fact, the thought of it was exciting. There would be shopping excursions, watching pageants together, girl talk...

Absently, Ellie fingered the cardboard edge of a box. Though it was dim in the recesses of the garage, she could make out the words PICTURES and PERSONAL EFFECTS.

Personal effects, huh? She couldn't imagine what sort of personal effects a wretched old crone like Lillith might have owned, and the thought of riffling through them filled her with both anticipation and disgust.

She began to lift the box when she thought of Chris and paused.

How would he feel about her going through Lillith's things?

She considered this a moment and realised she had no idea.

Well, she thought as she hoisted the box and prepared for the dash to the house, at least she'd have something interesting to do while he was gone. And though it made her feel guilty, she realised she wanted him to be gone a good long while.

Long enough for her to find out if Lillith had any juicy secrets.

Smiling, Ellie squeezed the box against her chest and sprinted for the back door.

*   *   *

The smudges bothered her.

Many of Lillith's photographs of Chris were framed, but the ones that were not were in albums or the original store envelopes. The latter featured Chris at various ages, but all of them shared one common trait: smudged edges. Lillith had examined these pictures so many times that their borders were ruined with overhandling.

Not for the first time Ellie found herself chilled by the depth of the woman's obsession with Chris. It was impossible to study those smudges, the purplish marks sometimes forming a perfect fingerprint, and not also imagine the spinster's fierce gaze, the cracked lips open slightly, her breath rasping like two yellowed sheets of parchment scraping together.

Ellie shoved the pictures back inside the box and debated whether to remain here in the kitchen where Chris would see her upon returning or to take everything upstairs, where she could reseal the box and pretend she hadn't gone snooping. If he asked why she'd brought the box inside, she'd make something up. *I was afraid the moisture would be bad for Lillith's things.* It almost sounded believable.

Ellie cast another glance at the box, saw picture frames, albums, a stack of videotapes and a bundle of newspaper clippings. The tapes she could save for later. The clippings she could go through upstairs.

The matter decided, Ellie gathered up the stuff and carried the box upstairs to Chris's office. As the contents jostled, she tried to ignore the stench of mildew wafting out of the box.

She twisted on the desk lamp, which did very little to mitigate the growing gloom, and settled herself in the leather chair. She fished out a photo album and felt her insides go cold.

Every picture showed Chris as an adult, and every single one had been cropped to exclude other people. She flipped through the crackling pages, which were arranged chronologically, and beheld Chris at his college graduation, as a young teacher with a roomful of students, as a junior high track coach. And in every photograph the faces of his fellow graduates, his pupils, his runners and throwers had been excised.

She flipped to the back of the album and gasped.

The pictures were from their wedding, and of course Ellie's face had been removed. But rather than neat ivory circles taking their places, she discovered black and white images of a young woman with long, curly hair.

With dawning horror she realised why the woman she had seen staring at her from the forest had looked familiar, the naked woman with dark red ringlets.

She'd been the woman in these pictures.

She'd been the young Lillith Martin.

Ellie rose from the office chair, the album still clutched in her fingers. Distantly, she heard the rain drumming on the roof, the continual growl of thunder, yet these hardly registered. The only things she noticed were the woman's dark eyes, the expression that radiated malice. Pasted in Ellie's place, it appeared as though Lillith was the one standing beside Chris at the altar, Lillith gazing up into Chris's happy face as they said their vows, Lillith on their honeymoon in Cancun.

Ellie closed the album and tossed it inside the box.

Christopher will always belong to me.

"Sick," she whispered.

Breath quavering in her nostrils, she backed away from the box. She no longer cared if Chris discovered she'd opened it. He needed to know. He needed to *see*. See what a psychopath Lillith was, see the evidence of her unholy obsession. Christ, Ellie had always suspected something was amiss behind that coolly pensive face, but until now she never understood how deep that wrongness ran.

She stopped. Beneath the din of the storm, she was certain she'd heard footsteps on the stairs.

Chris is home, she told herself. *You were so immersed in the photos, you didn't notice him driving up.*

But that was wrong and she knew it. It was nearly dark, and the sky was moonless. She'd have seen his headlights.

She listened, unable to move her body. She couldn't be sure, but she thought she heard creaking, the kind that wasn't made by high winds or driving rain.

The kind made by footfalls.

Lightning shredded the horizon, a titanic cracking sound on its heels. A moment later she heard a sickening thump, a large tree felled by the strike. It broke her paralysis, enabled her to stride to the doorway, and so far she couldn't make out a pale, nude figure with dark red hair in the hallway or on the stairs that led down. And *down* was her only thought now. *Get downstairs, get out of this accursed house and make your way down the lane so when Chris finally gets home you can tell him you've had enough, that the experiment failed and it's time to cut your losses.*

They could spend the night in town, and in the morning they could put this place up for sale again. They could live in an apartment, they could live in any town he chose. Just not here, this horrible place where Lillith had led them, Lillith who'd somehow beaten death. Lillith who'd become young again. Lillith who roamed naked through these woods…

She took the stairs two at a time. She lost her balance and, remembering the baby, clutched the banister for a long, breathless moment. When she'd gotten control again, she continued her descent, moving methodically now, using all her will to suppress the fear that threatened to plunge her into panic.

It was warm outside, she reminded herself. She wouldn't take ill as long as she covered up a little. She was antsy as hell to get out of the house, but she flipped on the foyer light and forced herself to check the hall closet for an umbrella. There wasn't one, of course, because that would have been too organised for the Cranes. She substituted one of Chris's jackets for the umbrella, draped it over her head and pushed through the front door.

She longed to remain under the sheltering porch roof, but she could not rid her mind of the photo album, of the dead, staring eyes of the young Lillith. She'd nearly convinced herself it had been the Vicodin that made her see the naked woman that night. Yet deep down she'd known the woman was real, known the expression in that pale face had been familiar for a reason, because she'd seen that look before, on their first visit to Indiana, during their wedding weekend, and finally the last time, just before Lillith's death, when the woman told Ellie she could never have Chris, that he would always belong to...

The image of Lillith in her cold, sterile parlour was enough to get Ellie going. She hopped off the porch, her feet squelching in the sodden grass. Crossing the yard toward the lane, she chanced a look back at the third-floor office window and half expected to see the young Lillith watching her. But the window was vacant.

Feeling better, Ellie leaped a puddle and started down the narrow jade island that unfurled between the saturated wheel ruts of the lane.

When she reached the edge of the yard, she was heartened to note a slight let-up in the storm. Ellie lowered Chris's jacket and slid her arms inside. It hung to her knees and made her feel like a child trying on her parents' clothes. But wearing Chris's jacket made her feel closer to him. She still wanted to move to another house, but she no longer felt like she was in immediate peril. She no longer worried she'd see the naked young woman again...

She swallowed dryly, fighting off the dreadful realisation that had just arisen within her.

If the woman really had been standing at the edge of the woods that night, that meant it hadn't been the medication that had caused her to hallucinate. And if she hadn't been hallucinating, that meant...

That meant the man in the basement had been real too.

Calm down, a distant voice pleaded.

Calm down? How can I be calm when there's a maniac on the loose? How can I think of those crazed eyes and that monstrous grinning mouth and be calm?

She took off at a jog, throwing frequent glances over her shoulder. She wished the woods weren't so dense. A little rain she could stand. The darkness, though...the darkness was a terrible thing. Why hadn't she brought a flashlight, or better yet, a weapon? If she had the axe, she wouldn't feel so helpless, so much like a woman in one of the horror movies she'd been stupid enough to watch. Sure, they were fun at the time. Sitting safely beside Chris, she could watch with clinical detachment as a machete-wielding psycho carved up some bimbo. But now, oh God, now those scenarios seemed all too plausible.

She picked up the pace, her sneakers splashing through puddles. She no longer cared how wet she got.

Lightning exploded to her right and Ellie shrieked. Self-preservation drove her to the other side of the lane. She peered into the forest and witnessed an enormous branch tilt and crash to the forest floor. She ran faster, scared not only of Lillith and the man now, but of being struck by lightning or being crushed by a falling tree. It had been dumb to leave the house, perhaps, but how could she have known the forest would grow so dangerous?

She was thinking this when the lane angled left and she saw the Camry's hood gleam in a flash of lightning.

Relief flooding over her, she waved her arms and called out, knowing Chris could neither see nor hear her because of the storm. She drew nearer, wondering why the car was still so far away, even more curious about the headlights being off. Visibility was already bad enough – why on earth had he killed the lights?

She moved forward but made negligible progress. Chris had to be driving at a crawl. She continued on, and the outline of the car grew clearer. Odd, but it almost looked as though the car were parked on the opposite side of the bridge. For what reason Chris had stopped she couldn't even guess. At least she didn't have to worry about him running her over by accident.

When she got within twenty yards of the bridge, she realised why Chris had stopped.

The bridge was gone.

Numbly, Ellie approached the expanse where the bridge used to be. On the far side of the creek she discerned the concrete pylons, the rebar torn loose and pointing crooked fingers across the gap. Closer, she made out the other side of the creek, the turbulent water having swollen to triple its normal height, ripping away their one means of passage from this horrible place to the outer world.

What now? she asked herself. *Just what the hell—*

Her thoughts broke off as a black shape poked up from the near side of the valley.

She took a step backward.

The head was black, large. It was the Rottweiler, returned from the dead and ready for revenge.

Then she saw the rest of the body rising, lifting, almost as if someone were pushing it up the...

"Oh thank God," she said and started forward. It was Petey, and the hands pushing the dog forward could only belong to Chris.

The dog slunk toward her, then glanced back at the figure scrabbling up the bank. Chris's hair was plastered to his head, his face pinched with the strain. He'd gotten his chest over the rim of the drop-off when he noticed her, his face stretching in a look of almost comical surprise.

As she grasped his besotted shirt and hauled him toward her, he said, "What're you doing out here?"

He climbed the rest of the way and stood.

"You're drenched," he said.

"What about you?"

He nodded toward the churning creek. "Petey and I had to swim across."

They regarded the place where the bridge used to be.

Ellie asked, "What now?"

He spread his arms. "Beats me. I guess we go home and wait for the storm to end."

"I don't want to go home."

"Huh?"

She had to raise her voice to be heard above the pounding rain and the peals of thunder. "I went through some of Lillith's things."

He scowled at her. "Why'd you do that?"

"I found pictures of you and your aunt."

"So?"

"So the pictures were supposed to be of you and me."

He stared at her uncomprehendingly.

"She cut me out and inserted herself."

He shook his head, still not getting it.

She blew out frustrated breath. "Fine, then. We'll go home. But only long enough for you to see what a nutjob Lillith was."

CHAPTER TWO

When they'd dried off and changed, Ellie led him to the office. She gave him the chair and knelt next to him before the desk.

The first picture she showed him was on the beach in Cancun. Chris paled.

Pleased by his reaction, she flipped the page. His mouth tightened to a grim line as he stared at the pictures of their wedding day, the black and white face of his aunt. She waited for it to sink in, waited for him to speak, but the shock had apparently robbed him of the ability.

"Well?" she asked.

"What do you want me to say?"

"Lillith was psycho."

He was quiet a long moment before reaching out, flipping to another page, one that showed Lillith in place of Ellie as she stood with Chris before a fountain.

Ellie shook her head. "Batshit crazy, right?"

"That's a bit harsh."

"Doesn't this make you want to throw up? That's your *aunt* for God's sake."

"I know who she is."

"Maybe Doris was right."

A pause. "There's got to be an explanation."

She arched an eyebrow. "Yeah? Like what?"

He fluttered a hand, pushed away from the desk. "I don't know... She was a lonely old lady. Maybe she was thinking about someone she used to know."

"The pictures are of you."

"An old boyfriend maybe..."

She tapped the album with an index finger. "She wanted to *be* with you."

He shook his head.

Ellie stared at him, aghast. "Honey, you two are *kissing* in some of these pictures."

"This is about your vanity," he said, rising from the chair. "You're offended she replaced you."

She followed him out of the room. "She called me a vulgar slut, Chris—"

"You told me that story."

"What do you mean 'story'? You're saying I made it up?"

He started down the stairs. "You never gave Lillith a chance."

"I can't believe you're siding with her."

"She's dead, El."

"How do you know?"

That stopped him. On the second floor landing, he said, "What are you talking about?"

"The night I saw the man in the basement, I also saw a woman. At the edge of the woods. She looked just like the pictures in the album."

"How do you know? Lillith was clothed in all the pictures."

A powerful hand clutched Ellie's heart.

"I didn't say the woman was naked."

He looked away. "Yes you did."

She took a step toward him. "You've seen her too."

"I don't know what you're... Ellie, this is ridiculous." He walked away.

She gripped the handrail with a quivering hand. "Honey? What's going on?"

He rounded the corner of the foyer and disappeared.

"Chris?" She jogged through the living room. "*Chris*?"

He slammed the screen door and moved into the backyard. When she came down the steps after him he was already nearing the woods.

"Where're you going?"

No answer. Almost to the trail.

"You're gonna leave me here?"

A black shape scampered by her. Petey, following Chris into the trees. She hastened after them and felt the ominous beginnings of a migraine. She stopped, dumbstruck, at the edge of the forest. Around her, the rain fell harder.

CHAPTER THREE

Teeth mashed together, Chris shoved aside a branch barring his way. He slipped, the trail gone to mud in the storm. He sensed Petey padding along behind him, the dog's toenails providing better stability in the puddled soil. Chris jogged down a slope, hurdled a brackish stream of runoff and climbed another hill. Whining a little, Petey scrambled up the path beside him. Chris made it, stood with hands on knees.

"You believe her?" he asked. "Saying all those awful things?"

Petey watched him, mouth open, pink tongue lolling to the side.

"I don't believe it either," Chris said and stood erect.

He started off again, moving unhurriedly this time. Ellie had nearly convinced him about Lillith, and he had to admit seeing the photos was a shock. But one needn't be a psychologist to realise there were many possible interpretations of the doctored albums. Ellie was so strident sometimes, so controlling…

He stopped.

Ellie and her control problem. Ellie discovering the pictures. Ellie at home alone with Aunt Lillith's personal items for how long, two hours? He and Petey had stopped at the hardware store to buy a mosquito fogger, then to Ike's, and finally a swing by the liquor store because the grocery had been out of his favourite beer. He'd probably been gone closer to three hours, and three hours was a hell of a lot of time for Ellie to work on Lillith's things…say, to crop pictures and paste new ones in. Later, he'd go through the office, see if he could find the remnants of Ellie's duplicity, but already he was quite certain what she'd been up to.

Ellie despised Aunt Lillith. Had told him so just yesterday. Conveniently ignoring all the woman had done for them, the kindness she had shown Chris throughout his life.

Maybe, he reasoned, Ellie was jealous of the love he felt for his aunt. Maybe she begrudged Lillith that loyalty and had orchestrated this nasty little revelation in a desperate play for sole control of Chris's emotions.

It made sense. Ellie *did* love to be in control. Perhaps this was her way of alienating him from the estate. Poison his memories of his aunt, and the land would no longer possess the same meaning for him, would forever carry the taint of betrayal and depravity.

You really believe that? an incredulous voice demanded. *What the hell's wrong with you?*

Not a damn thing, he thought and shouldered past a tall shrub. *The problem's with my wife and her refusal to give this place a chance.*

But she's already warmed to it. Don't you see that? The other night in bed, while you were talking about your future home, your children, Ellie was dreaming right along with you. Christ, man, give the woman a chance.

He frowned, the argument taking hold.

That's right, the voice urged, *give her the benefit of the doubt. Didn't she just ask you this morning when you were gonna show her the clearing?*

He brushed the thought away. Up ahead he saw Petey trotting toward a bend in the path, the one that led into the lowest part of the forest, the swale that would almost certainly be flooded by now. As if in confirmation, the unwholesome odour of brackish water surrounded him. Above, the rain continued to gust in stinging torrents. It made him thankful for the sheltering trees. He was soaked to the bones, but at least he could see.

He followed Petey around the bend and began the long, shadowy descent into the thicket.

*   *   *

Maybe, Ellie reflected as she poured herself hot cocoa, the maternal instinct had already been aroused in her. Perhaps it was why she'd done such a good job of calming herself down and reassuring herself that she and her baby were in no real danger here in the house. Yes, she still hoped Chris would consider a move elsewhere – there would always be too much of Lillith here for Ellie to be completely at ease – but for now it would do. She hated not being able to leave, and she couldn't begin to guess at how much it would cost to fix the bridge, but those were matters for tomorrow.

For now she would drink her cocoa, take her book up to the bedroom and wait for her husband to return. If he was contrite, she'd forgive him and let him sleep beside her. If he still insisted she was being unfair, she'd tell him to sleep in the garage with Petey.

A small smile on her face, she stared out at the rain, which showed no signs of letting up. The lightning continued to flash with almost metronomic regularity. The thunder soothed her. Still, she was disquieted about something.

She took another sip, but the mug paused at her lips.

The videotapes.

Now was actually the perfect time to see what was on those old videocassettes. Chris was gone – might be gone all night for all she knew – and she sure as hell wasn't getting back to town tonight.

Maybe she could learn something about Aunt Lillith that would show a different side of the woman. Maybe Ellie could learn to feel something for her other than fear and contempt.

Not likely, but possible.

Ellie refilled her mug and, grabbing her novel, began the long climb to the third floor.

*   *   *

He crested a hill and spotted the little clearing.

Even with the unrelenting storm raging above, even with nightfall rapidly approaching, he found the smaller of the two clearings somehow cheerful, a place of harmony.

A sanctuary.

He gave an inward chuckle at Campbell's ominous references to this place. What a creep. There was nothing to suggest this was anything save a natural open spot in the forest, a site of tranquility and peace. In fact, he might just make this his writing spot. He could lean against a tree on the clearing's edge, gaze out at the butterflies chasing one another over the soft bluegrass, the white clover.

"You came back," a voice whispered.

Chris whirled, breath sticking in his throat, and spotted the woman twenty feet away, her body obscured by an elm tree. The pale oval of her face peeked coyly around its edge.

(*the woman you made love to*)

No! his mind shouted. That had been a dream, a fantasy.

But this was no dream.

He could make out her features in the dying evening light, yet he still couldn't see her as well as he'd like. When he started in her direction, her face clouded, and she seemed to withdraw. Certain she'd dart away, he put up his hands to show he meant her no harm and began walking toward her.

"Please," he said and winced at the severity of his tone. Then, more softly, "Please wait."

The face hovered beside the tree, but the uncertainty remained.

He stepped closer, taking care to keep his movements slow and fluid. For once, he wished he were a smaller man. How could he prove with words he was non-threatening? The very act of saying it seemed to prove the converse.

She hadn't bolted yet, and he'd halved the distance between them. He remembered their hazy, dreamlike lovemaking and wondered why that didn't imbue him with confidence. If it had been real, shouldn't there be a familiarity, a sense of trust established between them? Why should he feel like a stranger, why should this

(*Lillith*)

sweet, lovely woman be afraid of him?

He drew nearer and bit the inside of his mouth. *Let me touch you,* he thought. *At least let me know I'm not imagining all this.*

The sliver of pale skin grew smaller, smaller, and though he knew he shouldn't run the final few yards, he was sure if he didn't she'd disappear forever. He ached at the recollection of the way her way her skin tasted, sweet and rich like some rare tropical fruit.

"Where are you?" he called, but all around him there was only a funereal stillness, as though the woman had taken all life with her.

"*Please,*" he said. He gasped as cool fingers skimmed his neck.

She reached for him, her face clearer this time. Not totally discernible – the shadows were too long for that – but the shape of her nose, the maddening curve of her mouth, those he could see.

"*Darling*," she breathed as their lips came together.

CHAPTER FOUR

Ellie's plans were almost ruined when she realised they didn't own a VCR. Determined to view the tapes, she returned to the garage and rummaged through six boxes before finding one with a VCR that reminded her of her early childhood: dark grey, the kind you loaded from the top. But when she lugged it into the living room and hooked it up, it appeared to work fine.

The first cassette she inserted began with one of those polychromatic bars and an irritating, sustained beep. Finally, both the bar and the beep went away and were replaced by a shot of an empty dining room. The camera had been fixed in an upper corner of the room. Ellie squinted and moved to the front edge of the couch cushion, but the room remained unfamiliar to her.

Then she spotted something on the far wall that was just large enough for her to make out. A painting of two boys climbing trees.

Of course, she thought. *This was the dining room of Lillith's main home, the one in Chris's hometown.*

A moment later she was startled to see herself enter, followed by Chris. They were both three years younger, and her hair was a foot shorter. Chris hadn't liked it so short, so she'd grown it out. She was also dispirited to note that her legs appeared thinner in the blue skirt, which was surprisingly tight.

Probably to piss off Aunt Lillith, she thought.

Speaking of the old bag, there she was, entering from beneath the camera and hugging Chris.

All three of them sat, Ellie and Chris with their backs to the camera, Lillith at the head of the table. Lillith reached out and took Chris's hand. He nodded and bowed his head. *That's right*, Ellie thought. *Lillith always liked for Chris to say grace.*

As the prayer began, all three of them bowed their heads. But a moment later, Lillith's large eyes opened and fastened on Chris. The woman's gaze flitted up toward the camera, a secret, ghoulish smile curling her thin lips, then she turned back to Chris and watched him avidly, dark eyes glittering with jealous need.

Ellie cinched her robe tighter.

The dinner was uneventful, and try though she might, Ellie could not remember what it was they had spoken about that day. The audio quality was poor, but she could make out snatches of garbled conversation.

What came through with clarion lucidity, however, was the predatory gleam that settled into Lillith's face whenever her eyes fixed on Chris. Often, when Ellie spoke, Lillith's gaze would wander to Chris, and as it did the large doll's eyes would lose their uninterested glaze and begin to sparkle with an intensity that was difficult to behold.

She remembered there hadn't been just one tape in the box, but several. Ellie leaned over and examined the rest of the tapes.

L.R., one label read.

Living room.

Kit., read another.

Ellie spotted another that read *Bath* and brought it out of the box with a sinking feeling. Surely the depraved old woman had not stooped so low, surely she hadn't filmed them using the restroom, taking showers.

She took out the dining room tape, put in the one labelled *Bath* and pushed Play.

A bright red fury took hold of her.

It was funny how earlier, watching herself eat, she hadn't considered the violation taking place, hadn't felt outrage at being videotaped without her consent.

But now, watching herself on the toilet – fully dressed – brushing her teeth while Chris, wearing only a light-coloured towel around his waist, shaved before the vanity mirror, Ellie found her hands balling into fists and her heels drumming on the wood floor.

The camera was situated above the shower. On the bottom left of the screen Ellie distinguished the rounded surface of the showerhead; the rest of the tub could be seen plainly.

"Damn you," she whispered.

Chris leaned toward the camera, his muscular chest flexing as he reached out and twisted on the water. The water shot out at a diagonal, and through the spray Ellie could see the towel fall, Chris's naked body.

Her mouth quivered. "Damn you to hell, Lillith."

It was only a shower, but Ellie watched it with tears in her eyes. How could a woman who helped raise a child come to regard him as a sexual object when he grew into an adult?

Mercifully, the shower ended. The camera captured Chris as he stepped out of the shower and dried off. When he went out, Ellie expected the scene to end.

Seeing herself enter the bathroom alone, however, came as a big surprise.

"Oh no," she said, and on the couch in her living room, Ellie brought her knees together, clutched the edges of her robe tightly against her throat.

She watched herself unzip her shorts, sit down, and urinate.

With tears in her eyes, Ellie shuffled forward and stopped the tape. She was about to go back to the kitchen to wait for Chris when a terrible thought dawned on her. With a queasy feeling in her belly, Ellie bent over the box of Lillith's things and touched the second stack of tapes. She lifted one out and glanced at the label, already knowing what it would say.

Bed.

She shivered and set the tape on the couch. She reached down and came out with two more tapes.

Labelled the same way.

She inserted one bedroom tape.

An eerie green light lit up the middle of the screen. The bed sheets and their faces were stark white, everything else a mixture of green and black. *You gotta be kidding me*, she thought. *Lillith's cameras had night vision?*

Of course they did, a voice in her head answered. *Because it wasn't Lillith who was responsible for setting it all up. She paid some unscrupulous jerk—*

Her thoughts broke off as, on screen, Chris's hand slid under the blanket and came to rest between her legs. The bulge of his hand began to rise and fall; Ellie's face melted with pleasure.

Watching herself, she could scarcely breathe.

As in the earlier shots, the camera had been fixed in a corner near the ceiling, yet in this instance, the framing was a little tighter; the bed and about three feet on either side were visible in the shot.

Chris fingered her under the blanket, and Ellie, three years younger, writhed with pleasure.

"God damn you, Lillith," she whispered on the couch. "God damn you, you vile bitch."

She watched her arm snake out of the covers and slip over Chris's bare shoulders. She said something at his ear – Ellie couldn't hear what – and he slid on top of her.

Ellie had never seen herself on tape, and now she was amazed at how relaxed she appeared. How…experienced. Her fingertips played over Chris's shoulders, the sinews of his triceps. She heard herself moaning, no words, but very audible nonetheless.

She frowned.

In the bottom right corner of the screen she'd sworn she glimpsed something dart in and out of the picture, something as pale as their bodies. Ellie pointed the remote control, rewound it, and peered harder, but the object still passed in and out of the frame before she could identify it. She glanced at the counter on the VCR and made a mental note to return to the spot when she'd finished the tape, to study the moment in slow motion, or even freeze-frame it until she figured it out. Probably nothing, just an odd fluttering of the covers.

The session ended and was replaced by white noise.

Ellie hit fast-forward. She'd begun to think there was nothing else on the tape when the bedroom swam into focus again, the shot farther away this time.

In the greenish darkness, Ellie watched her younger self pass the camera on the way to bed. Chris, evidently, was already sleeping. She could just make out the pale curve of his shoulder as he lay facing away from the camera.

She tried but could not suppress a grin as she watched herself turn to stare at Chris. Ellie knew exactly what she'd been thinking at the time: she badly wanted sex, but her husband had gone to sleep. As if to confirm this, the videotape Ellie heaved a sigh and threw an arm over her forehead. Then, after a few moments of gazing at the ceiling, she curled up behind Chris, spooning him, her right arm slithering over his and her lips nuzzling the base of his neck. He stirred, and she caressed his arm, obviously trying to coax him out of sleep. He glanced back at her, a pleased grin on his face.

Ellie sat forward on the couch.

The supple lines of her back curved as she rode Chris, her buttocks reacting to the pressure of his body without showing any cellulite. She heard her pouty moaning, and though she often faked it with Chris – his insecurity sometimes demanded it – she knew from the sounds that no acting had been required that night.

On the couch, Ellie pushed her legs together, reminded herself that now was not the time to get so worked up. She and Chris were in a fight, and he deserved her wrath. When he came home she'd make damn sure he witnessed all this and understood what a sick, demented ghoul Aunt Lillith was—

Aunt Lillith stepped into the frame.

Ellie sucked in breath, her arousal instantly curdling into revulsion and dread. Dressed in a light-coloured sleeping gown that draped the woman's bony arms all the way to her walkingstick fingers, Lillith stopped next to the bed and watched them making love.

"Holy shit," Ellie muttered, her thumb pressed to her front teeth. "What are you…"

Ellie rode Chris with growing enthusiasm, her shoulders rolling with their movements. Less than three feet away, the gaunt, wraithlike figure stood unmoving, the expression on her puckered face impossible to make out from this angle. Ellie could see the woman's profile, but Lillith was turned partly away from the camera, so that the eyes remained veiled.

Sickening, she thought. How could they not have known? Yes, the bedroom was dark – unusually dark, she remembered thinking – the room situated at the back of the house and bordering a wooded ravine. But shouldn't they have heard the woman enter, seen the outline of the door as it swung inward?

The old woman bent closer, shook her fists at them in rage.

No, that wasn't right. Lillith wasn't shaking her fists at *them*, she was shaking her fists at *Ellie*. All the woman's ire, all her snarling jealousy, was laid bare before Ellie's eyes, and though she knew this would prove to Chris beyond all doubt that his aunt had been a fiend, she didn't know if she could watch this bizarre scene played out again.

The younger Ellie leaned back, her short, glossy locks swaying. Lillith collapsed, sobbing, the tears streaming freely down her wrinkled cheeks.

Oblivious of Lillith only two feet away, Ellie climaxed, her hands grabbing hold of Chris's splayed legs, her body tremoring once, twice, three times, before she collapsed forward and lay gasping on her husband.

Their lovemaking ended with the old crone still at their bedside.

Numbly, Ellie reached out, her fingers closing over the remote, but rather than shutting off the VCR, rather than putting an end to the unholy scene playing out before her eyes, she simply sat there watching herself climb off Chris and lie next to him. Lillith was mere inches away, her face inching toward Ellie's.

"Oh hell," Ellie whispered. Her eyes were closed, but even if she'd opened them, she'd probably not have sensed Lillith watching her because she wasn't *looking* for Lillith, had no reason to suspect the woman had slipped into the bedroom to engage in some up-close voyeurism. Ellie touched her throat, told herself to shut off the goddamn tape, but some perverse impulse demanded she wait, compelled her to see the thing through to its end. Surely Lillith wouldn't go on watching her as she descended into sleep; surely the woman's vigil would end soon. What possible reason would she have to continue this—

Something in the corner of the bedroom shifted. The shadows there, just beyond Chris's side of the bed, stirred and came to rest again. Ellie sat forward, strained to make out what it was. She brought the remote up to rewind the tape, and as she did she saw what she'd been too distracted to notice earlier.

There'd been another figure in the bedroom all along.

It sat in a wooden chair, the completely black figure, and though she knew that couldn't be – the night vision should have illuminated this person the way it had illuminated her, Chris, and Lillith – she was nevertheless certain of what she was seeing: a large, inky figure, its legs crossed, hands folded in its lap, observing Chris and Ellie's lovemaking.

Lillith whispered something. Heart stuttering, Ellie leaned forward to better hear the woman's voice. Lillith whispered again, and this time Ellie could make it out – "*Can't take this*" – and in the corner of the screen, one shadowy hand came up, silencing her.

Ellie's skin tingled as the broad figure rose and pointed an index finger toward the camera. Lillith stared up at the figure and, after a moment, nodded. Ellie watched Lillith stand, move out of the room. Whoever it was, he was able to control the old bitch in a way Ellie would never have thought possible.

The figure turned slowly, its stygian gaze never leaving the sleeping couple, and strode deliberately around the bed. For a moment Ellie was sure the figure would follow Lillith out, but it kept moving, kept to the edge of the bed, and now the hulking shadow loomed toward her sleeping body, reached the head of the bed, and gazed down at her. She strained to see the figure better, but she could not.

The shadow lowered, and she realised with sick fascination that he – it was undoubtedly a he, a monstrously *large* he – was leaning closer and closer to her slumbering face just as Lillith had done.

The rain tumbled harder outside, the thunder boomed closer, but Ellie was hardly aware of it. She drew her feet onto the couch, hugged her knees to her chest and wondered why she was still watching.

The face drew nearer, nearer. My God, he was less than a foot away now, the outline of his nose drifting ever closer to her face.

The man froze.

Then, to Ellie's infinite dismay, he began to turn toward the camera.

For the first time she could make out the face, and she screamed as the man from the basement leered at her, the huge eyes rabid in their intensity.

From somewhere in the house – it could only be the basement – Ellie heard the low thudding sound she'd heard the other night, the unearthly chorus that had presaged her confrontation with the man in the workshop, the workshop that was no longer there.

She stood as the man on the tape stood, his eyes locked on the camera, locked on Ellie's eyes, traversing three years of time and many miles of physical distance, and now she could see more of him, his gleaming, malicious grin, his satyr's jaw, and he was stepping closer, closer to the camera, his ghastly face swimming into focus, and she realised he was nodding, his dark, naked body rippling with muscles, his huge phallus tumid with lust, and she brought a hand to her mouth, crept sideways toward the doorway, her eyes never leaving the figure that loomed larger, larger, and below her in the basement the demonic thumping swelled. The great hands reached toward the camera, and Ellie was certain the glass television screen bulged outward.

She broke into a run. She burst through the front door and leaped onto the lawn. She was leaving forever this time; she didn't care what it meant for her marriage. If she didn't escape for good, she would die, her baby would die.

She bolted across the lawn and threw a glance behind her, sure the man would be there, bearing down on her, completing his pursuit and forcing himself on her. Was there any doubt that's what he'd intended to do? Rape her and murder her and exalt in the pain he inflicted? Yes, she thought, and ran faster. The man was a sadist and a monster, and he would slaughter her if she stayed.

The night was black as pitch now, and the rain soaked her to the skin, the wet robe falling open. She didn't bother closing it; she didn't care if it came off if that would help her flee faster. Soon she would reach the bridge, and this time she wouldn't stop. Chris would've left the keys in the ignition, and if he hadn't, she'd run all the way to the road. From there she'd continue hoofing it, and if she was lucky, she'd hail a motorist. She'd ride into town with anyone, as long as he didn't have those mad eyes, that appallingly muscled body.

She grunted as a sharp pain dug into her belly.

Better slow down, she told herself. *Don't wanna overdo it.*

She let up a little, but another pang seized her insides, this one powerful enough to make her cry out. The pain swelled and she was forced to slow. As the claws in her belly drove deeper, Ellie had to stop.

No, she thought frantically, but the word rising up from the foul depths of her mind would not be denied.

Miscarriage.

"*No, no, no,*" she whispered. She bent, hands clutching her belly. She shook her head against it, but it drove her to her knees, the water sloshing over her calves. She cast a feverish glance down between her legs expecting to see a gush of blood spraying the ground, but it was too dark, the gusting rain too harsh for her to see anything.

Another starburst of pain clenched her body. Ellie howled in agony as her vision greyed. Desperately, she rolled onto her side, where the gravel shoulder of the lane began. With the last of her energy, she crawled up onto the limestone, the white, jagged rocks piercing her flesh like wet needles. She flopped onto her back, the pain unbelievable now, and she shoved a palsied hand between her legs, brought it up to her eyes to see if she was bleeding. The world was darkening, dying. Soon there was nothing save the pain.

CHAPTER FIVE

The sensation was not unlike being at an amusement park, riding one of those attractions she used to enjoy as a very small child. The airplanes that rose and fell. The colourful boats that lurched drunkenly to simulate ocean waves.

Only this rising and falling was quicker and less pronounced, and she recalled another memory, an even older one: her father carrying her to bed after she'd dozed off in front of the TV. She'd pretended to be asleep because she liked the feel of her father's arms beneath her; he wasn't ordinarily an affectionate man. She remembered the warm musk of his aftershave, the button on one of his sleeves pressing against the side of her calf.

Ellie opened her eyes, saw trees overhead, brilliant sunlight knifing through in dazzling bursts. She was being carried, the arms cupping her strong and steady.

She stared at the underside of Chris's jaw. He hadn't yet noticed she was awake, and she supposed that was fine. At least he wasn't the man in the basement. At least he wasn't going to hurt her.

In her periphery the woods opened up and were replaced by lawn. Disturbed by their passage, a large robin fluttered out of the grass, which glistened in the post-shower dawn. Chris's feet made wet, sucking sounds each time they rose, and Ellie had time to wonder where he'd been, why he was just now bringing her inside. God, her throat was dry, like she'd inhaled a handful of dust.

How much time had passed? Judging from the chill in the air, it was still morning. But not early morning. Nine o'clock? Ten?

Without pause, Chris trudged up the porch steps, manoeuvered Ellie's body so he could grasp the doorknob without dropping her, and somehow got them both inside. She knew she should be terrified of the house, yet the solidity of Chris's arms under her body, the warmth of the foyer after the shivery bite of the outside air, had lulled her into a contented malaise.

He carried her up the stairs. To their bedroom, she assumed. It would be nice to be tucked in.

They rounded the landing and approached the bedroom. Ellie glanced up at her husband again and noticed something that troubled her – red lines striping the side of his neck. She considered asking him about it but couldn't muster the energy. The angry red slits reminded her of her pain last night, the talons shredding her guts. She brought a hand up and placed it on her belly. If he noticed the movement he didn't let on.

They reached the bed, and she was lowered onto it. Not roughly, but not delicately by any means.

As Chris straightened, she watched him with wide eyes, waited for him to meet her gaze.

But he departed without a word. She assumed he'd gone to the bathroom for a glass of water, maybe to bring her some Tylenol, but his heavy footfalls were tromping down the hall. She leaned over to see if he'd continue down the steps – to make her some soup perhaps, or to go fetch Dr. Stone – but instead he curled around the banister and moved up the next flight, ascending to the third floor. Why he'd go there, she had no clue.

A chilling thought scuttled through her mind: What if he had no interest in helping her?

Lending credence to this notion was the waterlogged robe still shrouding her. What the hell? Had he thought he'd infringe on her privacy if he got her out of this horrid, musty-smelling thing? Dull rage began to pulse in her head. The fact was, he considered his work done, his wife out of the elements but the fight they'd begun last night raging on.

That he had the gall to extend their battle, that he refused to set aside his grudge to help his pregnant wife was unbelievable to her. Had he really changed that much in the weeks since they'd come to this place?

Staccato clicks from above.

Typewriter keys.

The son of a bitch.

She nearly dies – their *child* nearly dies – and he reacts by plopping her and her wet bathrobe in bed, sauntering upstairs, sitting down casually at the desk and cranking out some prose?

The question rose again: Where had he been last night?

And...where had those scratches come from?

Or the better question, from whom?

Ellie's lips drew a grim line as she threw her legs over the edge of the bed and shed the freezing robe in jerky, livid movements. Naked, she shuffled over to the dresser – God, her back was sore – and not bothering with underwear, she picked out the first pair of shorts and T-shirt she found.

Still shivering, she moved down the hall, the sounds of the clacking keys becoming clearer. Dull threads of pain squeezed tight around her leg muscles as she began the climb to the third floor.

The typing grew louder. She winced as a nasty twinge of pain flared in her right calf. She was a mess, should really be in bed right now. *Would* be in bed right now if her husband were treating her better. She approached the study. He was typing faster than she'd ever heard him type, and for a moment she wondered if he were simply playing at it, depressing the keys as briskly as he could in order to give the impression he was being productive.

She passed through the open doorway, crept silently toward his broad back. She wondered what she'd find if she lifted his shirt. More scratch marks, or the same smooth skin she'd always known?

"You should be in bed," he muttered without a pause in his typing.

She stopped, abashed. She'd expected him to be sheepish, to beg her forgiveness for dumping her in bed and forgetting her.

She arched an eyebrow. She didn't know what to say, but if she got a little closer, she'd be able to read what he was typing.

He swivelled around, his face blocking her view of the typewriter.

"Need something?" he asked.

"Is it going better?" she said, nodding toward the typewriter.

He shrugged noncommittally and continued staring her in that same annoyed way.

She hugged herself, rubbed her arms to warm them. "I was surprised you left me," she said. "Did you plan on coming back?"

A sarcastic grunt. "Don't thank me or anything."

He returned to his typing.

"*Chris?*"

The keys went on clacking. "Yes?"

"I need your help."

"Sure," he said. "Make a list of stuff you need."

"I don't need to make a list," she said. "I need to see Dr. Stone."

"For what?" Still typing.

"To see if the baby's all right. Going through what I did last night, being outside in the rain…"

"All the more reason for you to be in bed right now."

"Will you take me to town?"

No answer. His fingers flew over the keys.

"Fine," she said. "I'll drive myself."

"Ellie," he said, swivelling to face her. "You need to rest, not hike all the way back to the car." He smiled without humor. "Not to mention the creek being up. With all that rain last night, it's probably ten feet deep."

She desperately wanted to be furious, but an irrational fear was growing in her that the Chris she knew had somehow been replaced by a new creature, one who gazed at her with dead, unfeeling eyes.

She said, "You act like you had nothing to do with what happened."

"I see," he said. He tented his fingers with professorial smugness. "So I'm the one who dragged you outside during a raging thunderstorm. I'm the one who made you go to sleep in the lane."

"Chris, I—"

"No?" he interrupted. "But I *was* the one who carried your ass back to the house."

"You *left* me last night."

"*You deserved to be left.*"

Ellie recoiled. "What's happened to you?" she asked and hated herself for the break in her voice. "It's like you don't care about me anymore."

"Jesus *Christ*," he said, rolling his eyes. As his chin rose, she noticed something she hadn't previously. There was another set of claw marks, this one beginning just at the collar line, a few inches below his Adam's apple.

"Who did that to you?" she asked in a tight voice.

He made a contemptuous sound, regarded the ceiling as though he couldn't believe he was being asked the question.

"Well?" she prompted.

"Well, what?"

"Your neck. It looks like someone scratched the hell out of you."

He grew very still, something happening in his eyes she didn't like or understand. *Leave it*, the eyes told her. *Don't you dare go there, Ellie.*

The hell she wouldn't. "Take off your shirt."

A lascivious grin darkened his face. "You in the mood?"

"I want to see your skin."

"Why don't you just say it, El?"

Ellie swallowed. "I think you were with someone last night."

His grin grew. "Someone?"

"A woman," she said. "Take off your shirt, Chris."

His grin became sharklike. "Sure, honey. It's good to know you trust me."

He got up, shadowing the room around her, and for one horrible moment she was reminded of the man in the basement.

"Feast your eyes," Chris said as he reached back, grabbed fistfuls of his shirt, and with one smooth motion pulled it over his head. Though the light in the study was dim, Ellie could see there were no more marks on her husband's chest, that the ones she'd seen around his collar were very faint.

So why didn't she feel relieved?

"Petey had trouble crossing the creek last night," Chris said. "I helped him, and he clawed me a couple times."

Ellie stared at the scratch marks on his throat, realised that they very well could have been caused by the dog's frantic struggles.

He took a step closer. "Anything else you'd like to accuse me of?"

She couldn't think with Chris towering over her like this. Part of her felt guilty for thinking him untrue, but an equally large part of her couldn't ignore the way he was menacing her, that he was scaring her as if to divert her attention from some essential truth.

"After you told me Aunt Lillith had a thing for me," he said, "I went for a walk in the forest. I was mad at you, El, and if you'll stop playing the martyr for a second, I think you'll understand why."

Ellie took a steadying breath. "You need to see something. There's a tape—"

"What happened was this," Chris interrupted. "Petey and I went to the forest. When we got back, I slept on the couch. Figured you'd locked the bedroom door. When I woke up, it was daytime. I searched everywhere and couldn't find you, so I went out looking."

"I still need to show you something."

His hands went to his temples, his biceps flexing. "Can't you give it a rest? You just talk and—"

"You have to—"

"—talk and the only things you say are my aunt was some monster and I'm an adulterer—"

"—see this tape, the man on it—"

"—when *you're* the one who's been around."

Ellie froze. "*What?*"

"You heard me."

"Chris, I—"

"'It was largely physical,'" he said, quoting something she'd let slip while they dated.

She stared at him, incredulous. "Chris, that was years ago."

"'Jason was *fun*,'" he went on in a bitter singsong, "'but the sex wasn't enough to keep our marriage going.'"

"I can't believe you're bringing this up."

"*You* can't believe it?" he said, bringing his face close to hers. He punched his chest. "*I'm* the one who just got accused of fucking someone else."

Ellie retreated a step. "What does one have to do with the other?"

"*Everything*, Ellie," he said, teeth bared.

She took another step back, but he followed. "I was twenty-three when I married Jason."

"And you're still married to him."

Ellie shook her head in puzzlement. "Chris—"

"In your *mind*, goddamn you, your *mind*." He tapped his temple, his eyes suddenly brimming with tears. "You never stopped thinking about him, and I've had to live with that."

Her breath came in harsh, wet heaves. She realised he'd backed her through the doorway. "Honey, I need you to calm down."

"I can't believe you have the *guts*," he said, a tear tumbling down his cheek, "to accuse *me* of cheating." He gripped the open door. "When every time we have sex, I see you going somewhere else... thinking about *him*."

She shook her head. "Chris, no—"

"*Him, goddammit!*"

She reached for his face, but he slammed the door, the concussion loud enough to shake the house.

Ellie stood in the dark hall staring at the door. She heard Chris sobbing within, and all her love for him rose in a flood of self-recrimination.

Nice going, El. The man does everything he can for you, and you accuse him of infidelity.

Her fingertips went out, brushed the cold wooden door.

Why don't you do him a favour and stay away from him awhile?

She leaned against the door, its surface frigid against her forehead. She closed her eyes, heard him weeping.

Listen to him in there, the voice accused. *Haven't you done enough for one day?*

She thought, *But the tape...*

Forget the damn tape! What about your marriage? *Accusing a man of adultery is serious business, Ellie.*

That's right, she thought. *And so is what's happening in this house, on this land.*

She made a fist and was preparing to knock when the clacking of typewriter keys started again.

Leave him, she told herself. *For now, Ellie. Just leave him.*

Reluctantly, she let the hand drop to her side.

Okay. She'd get something to eat. She'd wait a few hours. When he got done, she'd apologise for accusing him.

And then they'd talk. They *had* to talk. She had to get back to town.

And more importantly, they had to get away from this house.

CHAPTER SIX

An hour after Ellie finally ceased her character assassination, Chris unrolled the last sheaf of paper and studied it.

With a satisfied sigh, he placed the sheet facedown on the others and stretched in his chair. Outside, the clouds portended another thunderstorm.

He reached up, massaged his scalp, and wondered what to do about Ellie.

He went to the bathroom, splashed cold water on his face, towelled the oil off his nose. He rubbed his cheeks, the hard stubble scraping his fingertips, but decided against shaving. Back when he taught, he came to loathe shaving every morning, and now that he was done with that career he could forego a shave any time he damn well pleased.

Yes, he thought as he went downstairs to find Ellie, he really did feel finished as a teacher. Circumstances might dictate a reentry into education later on, but only if the writing gig didn't pan out.

He suspected it would. He wouldn't share this suspicion with Ellie, not yet, because her reaction would be what it was to every decision he made.

The decision to move to Indiana: hysteria.

The decision to not interview for a job right away: hysteria.

The decision to move Lillith's stuff in here so they weren't living in an empty house.

Hysteria didn't even begin to describe her reaction to that one. You'd have thought she'd be happy to have furniture, appreciative of him busting his ass all day to get the stuff moved.

But not Ellie.

He came into the kitchen and saw her sitting at the little round table. She looked up at him, but he stared at the table a moment longer. It would need to go. It reminded him too much of California. Too much of her past.

"You okay?" he heard her asking.

"Fine," he said absently. He went over to the coffeemaker, lifted out the plastic filter and tapped the grounds into the wastebasket.

"You don't seem fine."

He could feel her eyes crawling over him, probing for a weakness she could exploit. Marriage was always a battlefield with Ellie.

He chuckled to himself. Who'd said that? Pat Benatar? Sheena Easton?

"Wanna share?" she asked in her wheedling voice.

Washing out the filter, he said, "Not particularly."

He removed the pot from the coffeemaker and held it under the tap. He waited, knowing she was working up to it.

"Honey," she began. "We need to talk."

When he didn't answer, she added, "We need to talk about yesterday."

He positioned the coffee pot and thumbed on the machine. "Great," he said and leaned against the cabinet. "Let's talk some more."

Ellie frowned at him, but he folded his arms and kept his expression neutral.

"Can't you sit next to me?" she asked. "You look like a bouncer."

"I'd rather stand."

She seemed to deflate. She scooted her chair around to face him and said, "Why do you suddenly hate me?"

"Why do you feel the need to vent your spleen against the woman who gave us all this?"

"All this? You mean this place that's isolated from the rest of the planet?"

"You're such a drama queen."

"*The bridge is out*," she said, hooking a thumb toward the lane. "We might as well live on an island."

"Would that bother you?" he asked and could not suppress a grin. "Would that cut down on your prospects?"

She drew back. "What's that supposed to mean?"

"It's just a question."

"You can't be that insecure."

He felt his grin waver. "I'm not the one freaking out."

"You'd freak out too if you witnessed what I did last night."

"For heaven's sake, they're just pictures." He turned to get a mug from the cabinet.

"I'm not talking about the pictures," she said, her voice rising. "There're *videos* of us, Chris. Videos of us in the bedroom."

"That's absurd," he said, but he suddenly needed to be out of the kitchen, away from Ellie and her mosquito-like persistence. The woman didn't know when to quit.

Pouring his coffee, he heard her say, "She watched us make love, Chris."

When he didn't answer, she said, "Come watch the tape."

He crossed to the fridge, plucked out a couple ice cubes. "I'm not going anywhere."

"Just come to the living room, dammit, it's in the VCR now."

"We don't own a VCR." He plopped the cubes into his mug and hissed as steaming coffee spattered his fingers.

"It's your aunt's," Ellie said. "I figured you'd be excited to have more of her things in the house."

"Why don't you shut your mouth?"

Her lips parted in shock. She uttered a breathy little laugh that made him long to hurl the hot coffee in her face.

"What's happening to you?" she asked in a small voice.

The look in her eyes did it, broke through the black veil of his anger. He knelt before her and put his hands over hers. Her body remained stiff, but she didn't pull away.

"I'm sorry, El. I shouldn't have said that."

"Which part?"

"I don't know…all of it, I guess. It's just that…" He trailed off, unable to maintain eye contact. "I'm tired of fighting, Ellie. I don't know why we're going on and on about this."

She said, "Look at me."

Though a ripple of foreboding coursed through him, he did.

She said, "This is important."

"She's dead, Ellie. *Dead.* She can't hurt you."

"Will you watch the tape?"

"I don't need to," he said and picked up his mug. He took it out of the kitchen, meaning to go upstairs again, but Ellie followed him, grabbed him by the elbow. Coffee sloshed over the rim of the mug, scalded his wrist.

"Dammit, Ellie."

"Why can't you do this for me?"

"Because it's unnecessary."

"So that's it?" She threw up her arms. "You don't acknowledge it, so it all goes away?"

He shook his head disgustedly, continued toward the foyer. "That's right, El. It all goes away.

"You really are Lillith's boy, aren't you?"

His body tightened. He placed the mug on the dining room table.

"Oh, what," she said. "You're gonna hit me?"

That's what she deserves, a voice whispered.

"That'd be the perfect ending to the day," she said. "Punching out your pregnant wife."

He bit his lip a moment, fought to control his hands, which were balling into fists.

That's right, the voice whispered. *She's going to keep this up until you do something about it. It's time to stand up for yourself, take back some of the power in the relationship.*

"Your problem," he said, "is a lack of self-discipline."

"I'm not the one—"

"*Shut the fuck up, Ellie!*"

Her mouth dropped open.

"Now," he went on in a quieter voice. "If you'd have brought all this up last night in a reasonable way, I might have indulged you. I would have seen through your theatrics, but to make you happy I would have indulged you."

"May I talk now?" she asked.

"Absolutely."

"I'm going to the hospital," she said, "to make sure the baby's all right. And unless you apologise for the way you just spoke to me, I'm moving back to California."

He smirked at her. "Where will you live?"

"I don't know," she said. "But I'm not staying with a man who threatens me."

"More hyperbole."

"You bastard," she said, pushing past him.

"Where're you going?"

"I'm leav—" she began, then froze, her shoulders bunching together as she bent at the waist.

"Ellie?"

"I...I...*oooh*—"

He jogged to where she stood swaying in the foyer, one arm held out for balance, the other clutched to her belly.

"Ellie? What's wrong?"

But her moaning grew louder, higher, and her body continued to fold in on itself. His arms around her, he helped her lay on her side. She held her belly with both hands, her face a rictus of pain.

"Ellie," he said.

"*Can't...*" she whispered through tight lips. "*I can't breathe...*"

He moved behind her, slid his arms under her quivering body.

"*Hospital,*" he heard her say.

He scooped her up, moved through the foyer. "Not carrying you a mile just to get caught in another storm," he said and started up the stairs.

He hurried to their room, deposited her as gently as he could on the bed. He'd fucked up once; he realised that now. There was no excuse for treating her the way he had. But one bad night didn't erase three great years of marriage. Besides, he thought as he hustled to the bathroom, he could make it up to her by taking care of her now.

After filling a glass of water and getting some things from the medicine cabinet, he returned to find her lying on her side holding her abdomen. She wore grey shorts, and he took a moment to see if she'd soaked through them.

No blood yet.

"Honey," he said, coming around the bed to face her. "Here's something for the pain."

"Is it safe for the baby?"

"Of course it is," he lied. He had no idea if it was safe, but if she didn't calm down soon, something terrible really would happen.

She raised her head slightly and opened her mouth. He placed the pill on her tongue and brought the glass to her lips. She swallowed, winced and laid her head on the bed again.

He sat beside her until she fell asleep.

Then he took the box of Lillith's things outside and burned them.

CHAPTER SEVEN

Ellie opened her eyes in the gloom. She peered at the window and saw spider-thin rivulets wending their way down the panes. She endeavoured to roll onto her side, perhaps even get up to relieve her aching bladder, but the lassitude enveloping her sapped every ounce of energy she possessed. Defeated, she lay on her back and gazed at the ceiling. She could feel the drug working in her, an enervating inertia, and soon even keeping her eyes open was too great an effort...

Ellie let sleep wash over her.

When she opened her eyes, it was storming harder. The dream weather was even worse than it had been in waking, and Ellie realised with an uneasy tremor that she was back in England on her backpacking trip. Just as it had been during that long-ago time, the rain was punishing her and...

Jake Henderson. Her boyfriend had been Jake Henderson, and she remembered how it had taken her a while to get past the fact that Jason Halliday, her first husband, had possessed the same initials.

She didn't want to follow Jake under the bridge now, didn't want to hear the deafening rush of the river. She'd blotted out what happened under that bridge, but somehow she knew her mental shield was about to crumble.

Ellie watched her younger self huddle next to Jake, the odour of overripe blueberries tainting the air. He offered her the bottle of cheap wine he'd stolen from a general store run by a nice old man, and she drank too much from it. Then came the whiskey. They were both drunk within half an hour, and soon the slimy rocks strewn with condoms, hypodermic needles, and other detritus became almost cosy. The stench of rotting blueberries faded.

She watched herself laughing as Jake nuzzled her neck, but remembered too how badly her tummy had hurt, how scared she'd been of having a diarrhoea attack with this handsome boy.

From her distance of years, she watched him clear off a place under the bridge and beckon her to sit next to him. She watched him kiss her younger self and immediately start to unzip his jeans.

She saw herself shaking her head, attempting to dissuade him without coming out and stating the real reason. How could she tell him such a thing?

Jake laughed off her protests, and why shouldn't he? They'd already had sex, had been screwing since before the trip, so why should this night be any different?

"Let's just wait," she tells him. "Let's wait till the storm ends." The last word comes out a pained whisper because she's been gripped by a violent stomach cramp. In her dream Ellie feels that serrated blade twisting in her gut, feels the baking heat sheening her skin with perspiration. If she doesn't get out from under the bridge soon, she really will shit herself, and that might just kill the mood permanently. Grown women weren't supposed to be incontinent and certainly not before sex, but Jake's hand is squeezing her wrist, something more than simple arousal tightening his grip. Another stomach cramp wallops her as he yanks her down beside him, the damp sand stinking of rotten grapes, and before Ellie realises it, her rain slicker is unsnapped.

"Jake," she says, but his expression brooks no argument. He isn't just horny, he's possessed. *I'm gonna punish you, honey*, his eyes seem to say. *I'm gonna pound you till you beg for mercy.*

As if to confirm this thought, Jake bulldozes over her and in one bewildering motion, shoves her arms above her head and with one hand pins them. *As if he's done this before*, she thinks, and perhaps because her fear has risen above all other emotions, she no longer has to relieve her bowels. With his free hand Jake unbuttons her jeans, unzips them, and though she struggles, he has them down within seconds.

Practised movements is the phrase that comes to her, and the rapturous glaze in his eyes...yes, she realises he's done this before. He's enjoying it. There's an eagerness in him far surpassing any he has so far exhibited. The fulsome odour of rotten fruit begins to gag her.

"Now, now," he says as her thrashing becomes frantic, and

when she spits in his face he actually laughs. She is screaming, but the river drowns her out.

Jake's face begins to change.

She struggles madly to free her hands, but his grip is unbreakable. She gapes at him in terror, and yes, he has become the man from the videotape. She knows the man is Gerald Destragis, knows he has followed her into the past to do what he wanted to in the basement. His brow is wide, furious, his black eyes like polished obsidian. He revels in her terror, her shame, and his monstrous grin spreads wider, his teeth pointed and shark-white. Destragis is grunting like an animal, and she screams herself raw. And when he's done he sprawls on her a moment longer, face full of contempt. The voice, at least, is Jake's again, the boy who invited her to backpack through England so he could rape her under a crumbling bridge. Conversationally, he informs her he will kill her if she tells, and though she can no longer look him in the eyes, she believes him.

An eternity later he climbs off, spits into the sand, and tells her they're moving on. As if it never happened. She does as he commands, and somehow this is worse than the rape, because she's obeying willingly; out of fear, yes, but this is something her older self cannot accept. *You coward!* she screams at the half-naked, quivering body under the bridge. *How dare you let him control you after what he did.*

Ellie awoke, gasping, in her bed.

The self-loathing, the stench of the exhumed memory, took her breath away, caused her to rock onto her side, but still the sobbing persisted, her chest so tight it felt like a medieval breastplate, the palms that hugged her knees too slick to keep hold.

Shoulders quaking, she sucked in enough air to keep from passing out. She buried her face in the sweat-soaked sheet and ground it there, relishing the pain, wanting more than anything for her consciousness to be taken from her.

Then, distantly, the thought came to her: *Chris.*

He couldn't absolve her of her self-condemnation, and he couldn't cram that dreadful jinn of a memory back inside its bottle. But he could hold her, could moor her to this time, which was terrible but still better than it had been under that bridge. Under Jake Henderson.

Under Gerald Destragis.

His horrible, leering face was enough to compel her legs off the bed, the icy wood planks beneath her bare feet a welcome discomfort because they were *present*, they were of this time and not part of some long-ago nightmare.

She concentrated on the floor, on drawing in deeper breaths. Gradually, it worked. She was still sick with shame and anger, but at least she felt safe. Her husband was in the house somewhere, Jake Henderson was long absent from her life and Destragis, despite what she'd imagined in the basement, had been dead for years.

Ellie sat forward on the bed and was just preparing to stand when something from her periphery caught her eye. She glanced that way and gazed out the window. The front yard was steeped in shadow, the moon and the stars were swallowed up by the storm clouds, so she couldn't be sure...

But one shape near the edge of the yard, just a few feet from the treeline, looked uncannily like a human being.

Ellie got up, moved closer to the window, and braced herself on the sill.

Yes. The shape was long, but it was unmistakably human. The legs were sapling thin, the torso similarly slender, broadening only slightly at the shoulders. The head was elongated, and like the rest of the body, unmoving. She could make out no features, but she sensed the figure was gazing up fixedly at her window.

Gazing at her.

The wind gusted, and the shape seemed to dissolve. The branches overhead trembled like the fingers of magicians. She'd almost dismissed the figure as another drug-induced apparition when it pivoted and stalked into the forest. This time there was no mistaking its substance; she could even see the leaves of a low-hanging bough pendulum as its impossibly long head brushed against it. In the moment before it disappeared, she realised why the head was so long. The figure wore a hat, one of those tall things favoured by the horse-and-buggy crowd.

So an Amish man is spying on you, she thought. *It could be worse.*

Or maybe he's waiting for you to go to sleep again so he can break in here and have his way with you.

Ellie's arms went numb. *Get Chris*, she told herself. *Now.*

She hurried down the hall, made the foyer, and was heartened to see light emanating from the left, the direction of the living room. Chris would be here, reading a book.

Or watching the tape.

No, she thought as she approached the corner, she found that she no longer wanted him to view that spookshow, at least not tonight. A week from now, maybe, when the daylight showed bright and reassuring outside and they were getting along the way they were accustomed to, then maybe they would watch the tape together so he could see why she'd reacted so strongly. But right now all she wanted was his presence, his kind smile and his steadying solidity.

The television came into view, and no, it wasn't on. She stepped farther into the room and spotted his feet on the couch, the athletic socks with holes in both heels. Her gaze travelled up his body and rested on his peaceful face, his eyes closed in sleep. She took in the rumpled blue T-shirt with a dark stain just under the neckline: barbecue sauce, probably, or ketchup. His grizzled cheeks aged him a little, but this too comforted her, reminded her of winter breaks when he'd let his beard grow out in celebration of his momentary freedom from students. She'd always take vacation time then, too, and they spent those breaks curled up on the couch watching movies or reading books or sometimes just talking.

Standing over him now, the lamplight yellowing his skin, Ellie felt the memories of Jake Henderson and Gerald Destragis slip from her like filth under a hot shower. The vision of the figure by the forest, too, washed away in the glow of this man she loved, this man who had fathered the child now growing in her belly. She knelt and kissed one whiskered cheek. She rested her head on his shoulder, closed her eyes and for the first time that day, felt there would be a future, felt that a world without horror was within reach.

*   *   *

She awoke on the couch, the morning light spilling over her a glum grey. She sat up and wondered how she'd ended up on the couch. She listened for Chris and heard the sound of running water from the kitchen.

Her stomach a hollowed-out pit, Ellie got up and ambled through the house. As she neared the kitchen the smells of bacon and fried potatoes wafted over her. She rounded the corner and beheld the steaming plates of food.

"Wow," she said.

Chris turned from the stove, smiled at her. "Figured you'd be hungry after skipping supper last night."

She realised with surprise that she *had* skipped supper. Ordinarily that would've been unthinkable – she became a bear if food was half an hour late – but the last couple days had been anything but ordinary.

She moved next to Chris, stood on tiptoes and kissed him on the cheek.

"Sit down," he said, nodding at the table. "There's orange juice, hash browns, bacon. These are almost done."

He was frying eggs on the skillet. Sunnyside up, the way she liked them.

She sat down and breathed in the aromas. Chris put the skillet in the sink and sat across from her. "You didn't have to wait for me," he said as he forked a mouthful of hash browns into his mouth. Watching him chew his food, she decided she liked the shadow of beard he'd let grow.

They ate in silence, and though her plate was soon half empty, she found she couldn't shovel it in fast enough. Chris was refilling her orange juice when he said, "Sorry again for last night."

She swallowed a bite of eggs. "Me too."

"Don't, Ellie." He put the empty orange juice carton on the counter. "Don't apologise for anything. The things I said to you…" He trailed off, shaking his head. "I deserve a good punch in the nose."

"I thought I was the one who was gonna get punched."

Chris slouched, an expression of utter misery on his face. She realised he was holding back tears. "I'm so sorry, Ellie. God, I don't know what got into me. It's like…" He pressed the heel of a trembling hand into his eye socket. "…it's like I was someone else."

"You seemed like someone else."

"That's not the only time, though," he said and glanced at her sharply. "It's been happening for a while now. I don't know why, but… it's as if I can't let myself just relax and enjoy what we have here."

She felt a stirring of dread but kept quiet about it. She could leave the question of moving for another day. There'd been enough fighting.

She reached across the table and took his hand. "We're the same people we were." She squeezed his hand. "Except, of course, that we're going to have a baby in seven months."

Chris gave a start, uttered an amazed little laugh. "Jeez, I keep forgetting. When did Stone say your due date was?"

"Early January."

He smiled. "A New Year's baby."

She watched his face grow troubled. "What is it?"

He shook his head, averted his eyes. "You still want to talk about Lillith?"

"Let's let that go for now, huh?"

"You sure? You seemed—"

"We both need to calm down and put that stuff aside."

He nodded, the relief plain on his face.

"That'll give us time to get back to normal," she continued, "and get the bridge fixed."

His expression was rueful. "I can't imagine what it's gonna cost."

"It has to be done," she said simply.

He didn't argue.

*   *   *

Ellie crossed the yard and stepped onto the lane. She wanted to check out the bridge herself. Maybe the job wouldn't seem so imposing in better weather; maybe getting the darn thing fixed really wouldn't require them to drain the rest of their savings. Before she got fifty yards down the lane though, something about the woods made her stop and stare.

No, she thought, that was wrong. It wasn't only the woods, it was the lane, too. Just yesterday the gravel path had been more distinct than this, both wheel ruts several feet across with only a slender filament of grass between. Now the island bisecting the gravel strips was wider, the weeds sprouting there high enough to whisper over her shins.

So? her mind rejoined. *What's the big deal? Plants grow during*

May, or did you miss that part of elementary school science? It's warmer now, and it's rained damn near every day. What'd you expect the weeds to do, wilt?

Yet it wasn't just the weeds that had grown; the forest, too, now seemed to encroach more closely on both sides of the path.

Kat's voice, mocking her: *Yeah, El. The trees are coming alive, Wizard of Oz-style. And Lillith is the Wicked Witch of the West.*

But the trees *were* closer, she was sure of it. She assumed their branches had been growing due to the rain and warmer weather, but was it possible they had really grown this much?

Not possible, she thought. *Except they have.*

Where before there had been six or seven feet of grassy shoulder on either side of the lane, now there was only half that much, and in some places the undergrowth actually bulged to within inches of the wheel ruts. Further, the woods were ominously quiet, the birds and other animals either having fled or grown too frightened to make noise. It was seventy-five degrees at least, but Ellie shivered just the same.

Time to head home, she thought.

No, the obstinate part of her bit back. *You aren't going to hide inside the house like some superstitious fool, throwing salt over your shoulder and jumping at every chirping bird. You're going to keep going and do what you came here to do — you're going to survey the damage to the bridge so when Chris comes back with the estimates, you can discuss it intelligently.*

She slapped her forearm, teeth bared. *The famous Indiana mosquitoes*, she thought. Another twinge of pain in her calf, the damn things hunting her now. She should have worn repellant, but she didn't know if it was safe for the baby.

Safe for the baby? Kat's voice demanded. *You think this haunted plot of* land *is safe for the baby?*

Ellie gave an inward chuckle at the word *haunted*. Yes, she'd seen some peculiar things since arriving here, but they had nothing to do with ghosts.

Savaging your hands on the razors?

Bad luck, she thought.

The creature licking your fingers?

Petey, she thought angrily. *That was Petey, and you know it.*
The man in the basement.

Uh-uh, she thought. *Now's not the time to go there.* She wasn't sure there'd ever *be* a time to revisit that macabre memory, but if there was, it sure as hell wasn't now.

"*Shit*," she said through clenched teeth as another mosquito drilled her flesh, this time just below her right ear. She'd begun to sweat, and the mosquitoes were swarming her now like she was a walking blood distillery. Definitely time to go back.

She was about to turn when something ahead arrested her thoughts.

"Oh man," she muttered. "You gotta be kidding me."

Not just one, but two gigantic trees had been felled by the storm. And despite having heard falling trees during the storm, the reality of these dead giants was somehow unbelievable to her. They seemed unrelated to the storm, colossal roadblocks meant to trap her here.

Her entire body went numb, a scent enveloping her like a shroud.

Diorissimo.

It wasn't possible, had to just be her overactive imagination, but it was there just the same. Cloying, smothering. She took a step toward the fallen trees when a voice from the forest whispered, "*Eleanor.*"

And the only person who'd called her that since earliest childhood was the owner of the smell. Oh God, it was now so powerful it threatened to knock her unconscious, a corrosive ether that seemed to breathe from the very trees, which were reaching for her now, clawing branches and black eyes fringed by leafy faces.

Ellie turned to run, but it was happening again, the undertow sucking her energy, the smell filling her head, blasting away thought, painting everything a dreary grey…now the colour of old gravestones…

Fight! Kat's voice bellowed.

As if doused with freezing water, Ellie jolted. Without waiting for the murky whispering to drag her under again, she bulleted for home as fast as her legs would go.

But even when she stepped inside the house and stood panting in the foyer, she knew what she'd experienced. And the smell of Lillith's perfume still clung to her nostrils like a pestilence.

CHAPTER EIGHT

The little white house with green shutters was easy to pick out even before Chris could read the address number on the mailbox. The yard was meticulously landscaped, the overflowing window boxes a riot of purple and yellow. The brick walkway curved a little as it wound toward the wooden front door.

Norman Campbell's place reminded Chris of an enchanted cottage.

Chris knocked and waited. After a short pause, the door swung inward and the little man, his black hair parted neatly on the left side, regarded him with a look of open hostility.

"Lost?" Campbell asked. Beyond him, Chris glimpsed a living room as stylish and neat as the façade. Campbell crossed his arms, waited.

Chris said, "I need to talk to you."

"About?"

"The caves."

Something changed in Campbell's face, but the look was gone before Chris could identify it. Surprise? Fear?

Campbell shrugged. "I don't know of any caves."

"That's not what Aaron Wolf said."

At mention of the name, Campbell donned a bitter smile. "You buddies now?"

"You're not very grateful," Chris said. "I could've let his brother keep beating on you."

"I'll send you a fruit basket."

"Listen," Chris said, stepping closer, "I need to know some things, and you can help me. If you don't get in my car, I'll make what Daniel Wolf did to you seem gentle."

Norman Campbell held Chris's eyes a long moment. Then the little man grunted, the flabby neck below the chinless face jiggling, and said, "Wait here."

Chris put a foot on the stoop. "How do I know you won't sneak out the back door?"

"I'm going to pee," Campbell said. "You wanna watch?"

CHAPTER NINE

"How much did you spend?" Ellie asked.

Chris lugged two gallons of milk from the counter to the fridge. "Quite a bit," he said, "but at least we're set for a while."

Ellie studied the piles of vegetables, the row of bread loaves lined up on the counter. "We'll never be able to fit all this."

"Some'll go to the basement. We can freeze most of the bread."

"You act like we're in a bomb shelter."

Chris laughed. "We might as well be." He started stacking cans in the unused bottom drawers. "The estimates on the bridge aren't good."

Her chest tightened. "What were they?"

"Thirty grand," Chris said, without looking at her. "And that's the low end. One guy said it'd be closer to fifty."

"You're kidding."

"Wish I was." He knelt, shoved several cans to the back of the cabinet. "So I figured since we couldn't afford to fix the bridge, we might as well stock up."

Ellie spread her arms, dropped them. "How can you be so nonchalant about it? I can't be stuck here."

"I'm stuck too," he said, "or don't I count?"

Her lips thinned. "Did you call Dr. Stone?"

"I did," he said and shelved a can.

"And?"

"And he said he wouldn't need to see you until November."

She hesitated, the words sinking in. "Honey, that can't be right. He said I was a high-risk pregnancy. When Katherine had her first child she went to the doctor every couple weeks."

"Stone said the tests came out better than he anticipated. Said you were totally healthy."

Ellie stared at him. "What tests?"

"I don't know," he said. "I'm not a doctor, how am I supposed to know what he meant?"

"We need to find out."

"We *did* find out," he said and finally turned to look at her.

"Well," she said and gestured feebly toward the lane. "Did you at least check to see if I had any messages?"

"No messages for you," he said. "Just one from my mom." He gave her a sardonic glance. "Satisfied?"

"No I'm not satisfied," she said. "I can't just wait around. I need to talk to my OB, ask him questions."

"So I'm a liar again," he said, and as he did, she noticed a tiny muscle under his right eye twitch.

"Chris, I didn't—"

She broke off when a small, pudgy man appeared in the doorway. He smiled at her apologetically.

She glanced at Chris. "What's going on?"

He nodded at the small man. "This is Norman Campbell."

Campbell looked embarrassed. "I needed to use your bathroom. I'm sorry if I startled you."

She turned to Chris. "Honey?"

He held her gaze a moment, then glanced at Campbell. Chris gave him an exasperated look – *Women. What're you gonna do?* – that made her want to pick up one of the cans and brain him with it. He got up and went toward the door saying, "We'll be back in a minute, Norman. My wife wants to discuss something."

When they were in the back yard, Ellie said, "I thought you were going to be nicer to me."

"I'm perfectly calm."

"You're talking to me like I'm an idiot."

He sighed. "I spent the last three hours running errands to come home and have you snap at me."

"I wasn't snapping."

"You're acting like my kindergarten teacher. Campbell probably thinks I'm an abused husband."

"What, I embarrassed you in front of your new friend?"

And for the briefest of moments, she saw the black rage flicker in his eyes. Then he seemed to deflate. "We're not fighting, Ellie. Even if you want to."

174 • JONATHAN JANZ

She bit her bottom lip. "I'm scared."

"If we had the money, we'd get the bridge fixed today..."

His voice was stilted, unnatural, like he was reading from a script.

"But we *are* going to get it fixed, right? It's either that or move."

He seemed about to argue, but before he could, he glanced up at the house and a change came over him. "Norman will give us some ideas."

"He knows how to fix a bridge?"

"He got his degree in engineering. We're going to troubleshoot, figure out what our options are."

Chris's eyes flitted to the house, where Campbell was holding the back door open.

"Am I okay to come out?" Campbell asked.

"Of course," Chris answered. "I was just saying we're gonna take a look at the bridge."

"Yeah, I heard that," Campbell said as he came down the steps.

Ellie watched the little man, thinking, *He knows how ludicrous it sounds too. He's not even wasting the energy to participate in the lie.*

Chris clapped his hands together, said, "Well, better get going. It's after four already."

And as Ellie watched the two set off down the lane, she passed a hand over her belly. It was too early, she knew. But whenever Norman Campbell spoke, she was sure her baby had stirred.

★   ★   ★

As soon as they were out of sight of the house, they took a narrow path into the forest, Campbell in the lead.

"Your wife doesn't like me," Campbell said.

"Neither do I."

"What'd I do wrong?"

Chris watched the little man's short strides, the khaki pants and leather shoes so incongruous with the forest. "You didn't do anything, but you have this quality about you...it's off-putting."

"I tend to be that way when I'm taken from my house by threat of violence."

"Relax."

Campbell stopped, hands on hips.

"Let's keep moving," Chris said. When Campbell refused to budge, Chris heaved a weary sigh. "I'm sorry for the way I talked to you. But you weren't exactly chummy with me at the library."

Campbell didn't respond to that, but he started down the trail again.

To his back, Chris said, "What'd you think of the house?"

"It's a work-in-progress."

"That another way of saying it's ugly?"

Campbell shrugged and stepped daintily over a puddle. Chris couldn't imagine the man behaving the way Aaron Wolf had said he had. Guys like Campbell didn't participate in gangbangs; they attended poetry readings.

"That your dog?" Campbell asked.

Ahead, Petey waited in the middle of the trail. The dog sat on his haunches, his eyes not on Chris, but on Norman Campbell. For the briefest moment Chris was worried Petey would attack the little man the way he had Doris Keller, but instead of lunging at him, the black lab sauntered over and began licking Campbell's proffered hand. Watching them, Chris almost felt jealous.

"So tell me about Destragis's cabal," Chris said when they'd set off again. Petey trotted along just behind Campbell.

Campbell said, "Destragis believed that souls, like energy, couldn't be destroyed."

"They go from solids to liquids, that kind of thing?"

Campbell eyed him coldly. "You want to hear this or not?"

Chris studied the path between them and did his best to hold back a grin.

"Most souls," Campbell went on, "leave their bodies and become like ether, just floating around in space. Aware of their condition but ignorant of how to proceed."

"That Destragis's idea of damnation?"

Campbell shrugged. "He never used that word, but yeah, being powerless, being directionless would be akin to being in hell."

"So what's heaven?"

"Purpose," Campbell said. "And the only way to learn one's purpose was to follow Destragis."

"So he set himself up as a messiah," Chris said. "Sounds like every cult in the world."

A small smile began to form on Campbell's goateed mouth. The effect was singularly unpleasant. "Maybe you won't feel that way for long."

Chris made what he intended to be a scoffing sound, but it came out high and reedy.

Campbell's grin widened. "You're right to be scared."

"Oh, for Christ's sake," Chris said, and shouldered past him, "let's move before it gets too dark to see."

But Campbell didn't follow, only leaned against the oak and spoke in a meditative voice: "The more I think about it, Chris, the more I realise we're a lot alike."

"We're nothing alike."

"Sure we are," Campbell said. "We both suspect there's something to all this, but neither one of us has the courage to embrace it."

Chris blew out disgusted breath. "Ridiculous."

"I'm the only one left, you know."

"In Ravana?"

"The others all took their lives shortly after Destragis died. It was what he told us to do."

"They drink Kool-Aid?"

"Uh-uh," Campbell said. "They dug themselves graves, climbed in and slit their own throats."

"Jesus."

"I couldn't do it," Campbell said, his voice suddenly miserable. "I meant to come out here with the rest...but when the time came I was too afraid of dying..." Campbell swallowed. "...too afraid of pain."

Chris did his best to hold back his growing dread. "I suppose they did all this here."

"In the little clearing."

A memory rose in Chris, and the words escaped him before he had time to reconsider. "I heard voices the last time I was there."

Campbell glanced at him sharply. "What sort of voices?"

"It sounded like children," Chris said. "Babies."

"New blood."

"It's true then?"

Campbell's voice was barely audible. "I never killed."

Chris clenched his jaw, took a step toward the man, who stared at the ground as if in a trance. "You let them murder children?"

"I wanted to believe him," Campbell said, his voice breaking. "I wanted to believe we'd come back, the way he and Lillith did. He said they'd done it twice, that they'd lived nearly two centuries."

Chris shook his head in disgust. More wild theories, more madness.

A question occurred to him. "Why were you watching me in the library?"

Campbell glanced around as if afraid of being overheard. He stepped closer, peered up at him through the forest gloom. "You really want to know?"

This close Chris could smell the man's body odor, like old urine fermenting in a bedpan. Campbell uttered a nervous little laugh, licked his lips and looked around again.

"I want some guarantee," Campbell said, "that all the stuff we did will come to something."

"And you think I can help you? I don't know anything."

"Not you, necessarily," Campbell said and cast a furtive glance behind him. "But you're involved in it somehow."

He opened his mouth to protest, but Campbell overrode him. "Destragis said we'd die and come back, but he didn't say how long the interim would be. Some of the first ones who bought in have been dead going on thirty years."

"Let me get this straight," Chris said, "see if I understand this demonic evolution thing."

Campbell watched him with wide eyes.

Chris said, "After you die you're supposed to come back as what, a vampire?"

The man nodded eagerly. "The bestial form."

"And you *want* that?"

Campbell's face twisted. "Look at me, dammit. Overweight, bald, high cholesterol. Anything's better than this."

"Then you die again?"

"The first realm is the human," Campbell said. He counted on his fingers. "The second is the vampiric."

"You're a fucking lunatic."

"The third life combines the two forms," Campbell went on unperturbed. "That's how you knew your aunt, though she never showed you the vampire side."

"Lucky me."

Campbell held up four fingers, eyes wild, rapturous. "You go through some kind of double-bodied stage – it's what Destragis called the demonic. Then the final realm – the fifth – is the immortal. The perfect fusion of human, vampire, and demon."

"We should head back."

Chris started past him, but Campbell clutched his arm. "Do you hear it?"

Chris jerked his arm away, but as he did he became aware of a rustling to their left, where the trees were thickest. The forest seemed to stretch and crackle as if the trees were straining to tear free of the ground that held them.

"He's been following me," Campbell whispered.

"Who?" Chris said, but he knew the answer already.

"Daniel Wolf. He wants to kill me." Campbell uttered a strained little laugh. "He considers himself some sort of guardian. Thinks he can contain the evil that resides here."

Chris peered into the thicket but could make out very little in the failing light. "Did you really steal Daniel's wife?"

Campbell's face spread into a prurient leer. "Sarah didn't require any stealing."

A branch cracked like a gunshot. Both Chris and Campbell whirled and peered into the forest.

Chris said, "Maybe it's because of the storm."

He glanced at Campbell, who looked like he might be sick. "I don't think so," the man answered. "Someone's here."

Chris gazed into the darkening woods. He took Campbell by the arm, compelled him down the path. "Come on. I wanna get this over with."

CHAPTER TEN

At the bottom of a ravine, Campbell stopped and pointed. About twenty feet to their right and ten feet above them, Chris saw an opening just tall enough for a man to walk through without ducking.

"You wanted to know where the caves were," Campbell said. "There you go."

Chris maintained a level tone. "This the only one?"

"There are others," Campbell said, "but you said you wanted to be home by nightfall. Besides, it's been a long time since I've been out here."

Chris started forward.

But Campbell hung back. "You're going in?"

"I didn't come all this way to chicken out."

"This isn't some dare, Chris. We don't know if it's safe."

"Then wait out here."

Behind him, Chris heard the little man grumble, but when he glanced back, Campbell was following. As he neared the cave he became aware of a faint odor. The smell grew stronger, eye-watering and putrid. Campbell covered his nose with his shirt, and his fish-white belly drooped over his belt.

Chris wrinkled his nose. "Something must've died in there."

His voice muffled by his shirt, Campbell said, "Let it stay dead."

Chris took a couple steps into the murk.

From behind them, a powerful voice shouted, "*Hands up.*"

Chris froze, and Campbell uttered a shocked gasp. Daniel Wolf stood behind them, blocking the entrance of the cave.

Chris exhaled. "You scared the hell out of us," he said and started forward.

"*Don't move,*" Wolf commanded.

Chris's stomach dropped. He realised with growing terror that the man was holding a shotgun.

"What's this about?" Chris forced himself to say.

A beam of light splashed over him, and he brought up a hand to shield his eyes.

"Look behind you," Wolf said.

Chris heard Campbell suck in a startled breath. He faced the inner part of the cave and saw why Campbell was so aghast. He also understood where the smell had been coming from.

A thick strip of leather had been affixed to the ceiling of the cave. From it hung the corpse of a Rottweiler, its fur crawling with maggots. The belly had been torn open.

Chris had a sudden memory of Petey's bloody muzzle and suppressed an urge to vomit.

"You're a real tough guy," Wolf said to Chris. "Bringing your buddy out here to admire your butchery."

Chris could scarcely breathe. "What?"

But instead of answering him, Wolf marched forward, seized him by the shirt and shoved him backward into the darkness. Chris lost his balance, fell, and when he looked up, he saw the animal dangling directly overhead. Gagging, he averted his eyes. When he gazed up at Wolf, the man's teeth were clenched in a feral snarl. "*Lenny*," he said viciously. "That's yours, right?"

He followed Wolf's pointing finger and saw that the dog had been strangled with a belt. The buckle had bitten into the animal's fur, and though part of it was obscured by a ragged flap of skin and the rest of it was painted a squalid red with the Rottweiler's blood, he could plainly make out the word LENNY on the buckle.

"Should've known," Wolf was muttering. "Should've guessed you were just like that old witch."

Chris realised with silent alarm that the shotgun was lowering toward him. Campbell cowered against the wall, edged slowly toward the exit.

"I told my brother," Daniel said. "I told him it was all true, that stuff they used to practice out here." He gestured with the shotgun at Campbell. "You send that harpy to my house the other night? The one stood outside my window and told me to follow her into the woods?"

Campbell's eyes shot toward Chris, but Chris barely noticed. He kept staring at Daniel Wolf's trigger finger, which was white from the pressure of the man's grip. At any moment...

Campbell's voice shook. "I don't know what you're talking about, Daniel."

"The *hell* you don't!" Wolf shouted.

Something plopped in Chris's hair, and when he shook it free and beheld the maggot wriggling on the cave floor, he gasped and scrambled away.

"Don't move, Mister—" Wolf began, but Chris had to get out of there, had to get into the daylight again. He turned and saw the shotgun's stock swinging toward him and just had time to flinch before pain exploded in the base of his skull. He stumbled and saw, though his vision swam, Campbell clambering down the verge, away from the cave. Wolf stepped forward, aimed and before Chris could cry out, the shotgun erupted.

Campbell jolted, then tumbled down the hill, the top of his head a glistening soup of blood and brains. His body somersaulted several times, and when it came to rest Campbell lay glassy-eyed on his back. Chris watched nervelessly as the pinkish-grey contents of the man's skull oozed over the decaying leaves.

Wolf spun, his eyes huge, and raised the shotgun. Chris instinctively threw his hands up, but just before the shot exploded, he heard a beastly roar. The ceiling of the cave burst as the shell rebounded, a puff of dust sprinkling Chris's arms. Then he watched in shock as Petey drove the man down, his fearsome jaws clamped in a death grip on the man's throat. Blood began to drizzle from the puncture wounds. Wolf thrashed beneath Petey, the shotgun slipping from his flailing hands. Wolf grasped a jagged rock and thrust it at Petey's head, but Chris dove forward, caught Wolf's arm. Petey let go of the man's throat and started in on Wolf's heaving chest, the teeth grinding the man's flesh, the sharp claws digging the blue work shirt to ribbons.

But still Wolf's free hand scrabbled toward the shotgun, his eyes blazing at Chris. Without thinking, Chris leaped forward, seized the gun. Straddling Wolf, he raised the shotgun and swung it down at the man's face. The handle bashed Wolf's jaw, dislocating it and sending the man into a flurry of convulsions. Chris lifted the shotgun and brought it down again, even harder this time, and the man's nasal cavity imploded. A gout of syrupy blood splashed over Chris's legs. He smashed the face again and again while Petey stood witness, teeth bared in a crimson snarl.

PART FOUR
DUALITY
CHAPTER ONE

It took Chris until midnight to bury the bodies.

Now he stood naked at the pond's edge and gazed down at his silhouette, clearly limned by the half-moon overhead. Seeing himself that way, faceless, a figure only, it was easier to believe he had slain someone earlier that evening. Self-defence or not, he had to think this thing through to make sure he wasn't caught.

He didn't think anyone had seen him at Campbell's earlier that day, but there was no way of knowing for sure. It was possible some nosy octogenarian had looked away from her crocheting long enough to identify him, and if that was the case, he was pretty well fucked. He could explain how everything had gone down – sans the part about the Lenny belt and the Rottweiler; he hadn't the first clue how to explain that – but he doubted Troy Bruder would buy it. The sheriff would blame both murders on Chris – all three if you counted the dog – and he'd lose everything: Ellie, the baby, Petey, even the estate.

The estate most of all.

He breathed deeply of the air, the dank, fecund pond-smell mingling with the sweeter scents of lilac and jasmine. His hands were cracked and bleeding from digging the holes. He'd seen plenty of crime shows in which buried bodies had been found by well-trained police dogs, but deep down he suspected any search of these woods would prove fruitless.

The land would make sure of it.

That the forest was a sentient thing he'd long suspected. This place was alive, had perhaps always been so, had only needed the right person to coax it fully awake. And now he could drink it all in: the water, the moonlight, the fragrant air.

Chris crouched, leapt outward, arms extended in a tight V, and felt the water surround him. The pond was frigid, but after the exertion of the burials, the chill was welcome. He rolled over and began a leisurely backstroke.

He thought of his wife and how skittish she was. Nothing like that other woman, the one who'd come to him in the woods, that gorgeous, knowing, incredible woman, her touch like the kiss of the water, the sensation of her sex enveloping him unlike anything he'd ever felt before.

As if summoned by his thoughts, he saw, coming slowly toward him through the water, the top of the woman's head. He could see the hair flattened against her scalp, the subtle underwater stirrings like secret promises, portents of the transcendent experience to come. He treaded water, waiting for her, and his body was already responding, his erection blazing, and in moments she would wrap those supple, creamy legs around him, the eyes lingering on his as she impaled herself on him. She'd read his thoughts, understood his need for her. Soon the memories of the blood and the burials would be lost in a sea of rapture. Only five feet away now. He readied for her.

A face rose out of the water, a horrible demon face, the eyes glowing white, the fanged maw stretched wide in a ghastly leer.

He screamed, thrashed away from the monster, but its talons closed over his bare heel, yanked, and he felt himself jerked backward with appalling force. He ventured to push away, but when his fingers brushed the icy, moist skin a galvanic shock made him recoil, a silent shriek twisting his face.

Then he was paddling for dear life, slapping the water and kicking, sure at any moment she'd haul him back again, and this time there'd be no escape, the demon ripping him apart while it chortled with pleasure. The pond seemed to have no end. Chris wearied, the creature somehow sapping his strength. God, he could hear it back there, its breathing heightened not from exertion but from hunger.

His hands scraped mud. He realised he was near the edge, the shallows leading him to safety. If he could only reach dry land he'd –

He glanced back and bellowed with horror. The monstrous creature, its skin agleam with beading water, had risen above the surface, was floating nearer, nearer, Jesus Christ, defying gravity, its fangs glistening with slaver. He stumbled through the pond scum. Whimpering, he reached the shore and bolted across the meadow toward the rise. He'd never run so fast, yet he'd never felt so helpless. Any moment the creature would lift him from the ground, his legs still pumping, and bear him toward its forest lair.

He risked a look back, sure he was already caught, but there was nothing behind him but waving grasses. Somehow this was worse than before, the creature vanishing into thin air. Hell, she could be anywhere, in the water, underground, anywhere.

Get moving!

He did. He set off, finding a pace he could sustain. He ascended the hill and felt very little strain in his legs. He was in better shape than he'd been since college. The thing he'd seen in the pond might not have been real, might just have been his guilt and emotional turmoil geysering up in one unsettling psychic blast.

He reached the hilltop and chanced another look behind.

Nothing.

He started down the slope to the forest, and from there it would be twenty minutes before he reached home. He'd be able to come up with a good reason why he'd gone back to the forest tonight. Why he was naked and sweaty...

Damn. Just what the hell *would* he say? *I felt like skinny-dipping, El. I always like to go for a nice nude swim after I kill an Amish man.*

Chris ran faster.

*   *   *

Safe for pregnant or nursing mothers, the label read. Ellie wasn't sure about that, but she knew if she didn't sleep soon, she'd be worthless again tomorrow, and feeling that way couldn't be good for the baby. With a shaky sigh, she shook out two of the sleeping pills and plucked the glass from the edge of the sink. She popped the little blue pills in her mouth and tossed back half the water at a gulp. She stared at herself in the mirror and thought, *You've aged ten years since coming here.*

She switched off the light, shaking her head ruefully at Doris's insane story. Gerald Destragis, demonic evolution. It was all so ridiculous. She'd scoured Chris's books for the phrase – everything from *The Dictionary of Theology* to *Man, Myth & Magic* – and come up empty every time. She shook her head and climbed on top of the covers, the lace of the peach-coloured nightgown rasping unpleasantly against her skin.

The ironic thing about the Realtor's claims were how poorly researched they'd been. Even if such things as demons and vampires really did exist, all the occult literature Ellie had pored through disproved the link between them. Vampires, according to legend, were spawned by bites from other vampires. Doris gave the impression that Lillith and Destragis had made a conscious decision to be *reborn* as vampires; there was never any mention of a transformative bite. Conversely, demons were wholly evil and had never been human beings. Yet Doris claimed that people, by enduring a protracted and bloody series of rituals, deaths and rebirths, could enter the demonic realm.

She yawned. The pills were working already.

Demonic realm, she thought and smiled. *What a silly, childish phrase.*

*   *   *

By the time Chris caught his first glimpse of the garage's peeling façade, he felt almost normal. Winded and sweat-soaked, perhaps. But safe.

He passed the garage and gazed up at the house. The kitchen light glowed, but upstairs all was dark.

Time to go in, he thought. *Either Ellie's sitting at the kitchen table laying for a fight, or she's in bed asleep. Either way, you can't stay here all night, not buck-naked.*

He shivered, took one last look at the forest, and headed up to the house. Taking care not to let the door slam, he padded quietly into the kitchen.

The room was empty.

He blew out pent-up breath, realising for the first time how nervous he'd been. Not as terrified as he'd been in the pond – not even close – but nervous enough to understand he still valued Ellie's favour a lot more than he'd been showing. Yes, she'd been irrational earlier, but according to her, pregnant women were often controlled by the many hormones gushing through their bodies.

He wasn't the least bit drowsy, but the right thing was to join his wife upstairs. Before he did, though, he'd have a cold glass of water. Goodness knew he needed it after the ordeal in the forest.

He filled his glass and drank. As he did, he peered out the windowpane, thinking maybe he'd spot Petey out there.

Chris froze. On the other side of the lane, against the backdrop of the forest, wasn't there a paleness? A shape framed by the shadows?

Heart pounding, he crossed to the light, switched it off and returned to the window.

He swallowed. There, amidst the gently stirring leaves and branches...

He peered deeper, his hands cupped against the pane. He focused on one particular spot. An oval, the curve of a chin. The delicate slant of a nose.

Two white eyes shuttered open.

He shoved away from the window and stood in the lightless kitchen, his heart a painful slamming, and watched in horror as the pale figure emerged from its place of concealment. The eyes never left his, the white ovals vast and triumphant. He backed away until his shoulder blades bumped the wall. Then he was swinging around the corner and scrambling up the stairs. His mind shouted a dim reminder that he'd forgotten to lock the back door, but there was no time now, no way to go back, she would be there waiting for him, leering, fangs dripping, demon eyes glinting with obscene need. He burst into the bedroom and saw right away that Ellie was asleep, and maybe that was best, maybe he could spare her this horror. Maybe if he locked the door, they'd both be spared. He bumped the foot of the bed with his rear end and nearly cried out. A hand over his mouth, he stared at the door, listening for footsteps on the stairs, listening for the demon as she approached.

A minute went by. Two.

He felt an uneasy smile begin to curl the edges of his mouth.

Then he heard it. The sound began as a low, subtle creaking but soon clarified, growing, and he realised the door was *bulging*, some force from the other side crowding into it with irresistible force.

He felt a chill on his bare ankles. He looked down and saw the mist swirling around his feet. He followed the mist and saw, under the door, how it was rolling in, a writhing white cloud.

And now the cloud was curving, coalescing into human form.

No. Not quite human.

Moaning, he backed along the edge of the bed, climbed into it, unable to peel his eyes away from the fair skin reflecting the moonlight, and the long arms were reaching for him.

The shape swam over him. He lay flat on his back to escape it, but it swirled closer, a pressure forming on his chest, stealing his breath, and the worst part about it wasn't the suffocating weight of the creature or the jagged tendrils of pain as its claws razed the flesh of his arms, it was the way his body responded to its insatiable lust, his erection, molten and dirty and ringed with slippery heat. She was using him, the revoltingly cold tissue of her sex tickling his genitals like a million tiny tongues. He whipped his head sideways to escape her foul, sweet breath, but also to see if Ellie had awakened, was witnessing this befoulment, and this much at least he'd been spared, his wife asleep during his betrayal.

As the creature's gripping hot vagina slid up and down his member, he experienced an arousal he'd not thought possible, and the debasement of being raped was somehow, oh God, making it all better. He thrashed, moaned, willed Ellie to stay asleep, and not just to prevent her from seeing, but to prolong this sweet, excruciating pleasure as well.

He glanced up at the white eyes, the sensual line of nose, and as he did a black tongue, slimy and cold, slid over his lips, back and forth, plunged into his moaning mouth. An atavistic revulsion rippled through him at its sluglike touch, the taste of it like decomposing fruit. Below, the glistening hips continued their pumping, massaging him, roasting his erection with microscopic embers.

The creature began to chortle, its pumping accelerating. He was nearing the most powerful climax of his life, the tongue circling his, one slender black finger slipping inside his anus and penetrating him, deeper, the hips slamming down on his pelvis.

Ellie, he thought as the demon riding him clenched in a long, satisfied orgasm, *I'm so sorry, Ellie.*

Chris let loose, too, his seed spurting into the foulness. The demon's face loomed closer, the white eyes slitted in blissful release. It clotted his vision, its stench unbearable. Then the darkness swallowed him.

CHAPTER TWO

He awoke and knew immediately he was going to vomit. Mouth slightly open, he drew the sheets aside and made his way across the bedroom, moving with a panicky haste.

He reached the toilet, but the nasty tide of puke splurted out before he could kneel and aim properly. A good third of it splattered on the rim of the bowl and slapped the linoleum between the toilet and the bathtub. His body clenched again and another tide of vomit sprayed from his mouth. The room filled with the odour of spoiled meat, and that too made Chris puke.

After what seemed an eternity, he rested his forehead on the cool bowl and waited for the shaking to stop. As he did, he became aware of the many aches in his body. The skin of his torso burned, and a downward glance explained why. Nasty red wounds striped his chest and upper abdominal muscles where the flesh had been harrowed. He noted with revulsion that his pubic hair and inner thighs were coated with a dark, viscous substance that reminded him of cranberry sauce. Worse, there were chafe marks on his shrivelled penis. Yet that was nothing compared to the humiliating ache issuing from his rectum.

Real. It was all real.

The room listing wildly, Chris staggered to the bedroom door and stared at his sleeping wife.

I'm so sorry, he thought. *I've let you down and done things I'd never dreamed I'd do, but that's over now. From this moment on, I'm different.*

He stood and watched her uncertainly. What *could* he do to make it up to her? What could he do

(that didn't involve taking her into town)

No goddammit, that didn't matter! He felt like he'd been drugged lately, was still lost in the haze

(she reaches town she'll never return)

but it was hard, *so* hard to think clearly, so hard to hear himself think through that ugly, buzzing static

(*can't let that happen, have to keep her here*)

Dammit, why couldn't he focus? The buzzing was growing louder, and it started in his mind but now was maybe in the house, the walls

(*here goddammit, here, it's the only way*)

Leave me alone! he nearly shouted.

He wanted to put his head on his wife's belly, connect with the baby. And though he desperately wanted to feel Ellie's skin, longed to draw back the blanket, he didn't feel worthy of the gesture, sensed that if he touched his wife he would sully her, the wickedness overtaking him communicable, infecting her and her baby—

"Our baby," he muttered desperately, "it's *our* baby."

You really believe that? a voice asked, and Chris stood rigid not only at the buzzing, malevolent rasp of the voice, but from the implication of the words as well.

What the hell's that supposed to mean? he demanded, but he knew already, knew it before the buzzing answer came, the voice like a chorus of flies trapped inside a glass jar.

You never conceived before coming here, did you? You never could. You *never could.* You, *Chris.* You *were the problem.*

She never conceived with her first husband, he argued.

Jason, the voice buzzed. *His name was Jason. Say it with me, Chris. JASON. She never tried with Jason, and had they tried, they would have succeeded, HE would have succeeded, JASON would have succeeded in sowing his seed, but you, Chris, you only shoot blanks because you aren't the man he was, the man he is, which is why you stashed Ellie out here...*

"No, no, no, no, no," he muttered. He was moving down the stairs now, hands tossing idiot gestures into the air.

But it didn't work, did it? It didn't work because there are still others, Sheriff Bruder, to whom you know Ellie was attracted. You sensed it, didn't you? The way she watched him, her eyes large and brown...

"Stop," he pleaded. "*Please stop.*"

Or Aaron Wolf, you were threatened by him, he reminded you of a story you once read in college, "The Amish Farmer," the wife in the story cheating on her husband because the farmer had possessed a raw virility that

he lacked, and you identified with the husband, didn't you, Chris? Even
then, you identified with the cuckolded husband and not the farmer, because
you've always worried about things being taken from you, being inadequate,
because you ARE inadequate.

His hands clutched his hair, yanking

You can't stop it from happening, you can't keep Ellie from other men

Tearing out his hair, the pain a distant coldness

Even if you do stop Bruder and Aaron Wolf from sniffing round Ellie,
which they'll surely do, there'll be others. Dr. Stone who had his hands
inside your wife

Pummellling his bleeding scalp

The doctor has more money, Bruder has better looks, Aaron has more
strength and you have none of it, you fucking wimp

Staggering to the kitchen

The baby isn't yours, Destragis fucked your wife, like he did again last
night, fucked her in your bed and left her like the flea-bitten slut she is

No

How else to explain it, do the math, you pussy, the first night you were
here, she conceived. You didn't fuck her, Destragis did

Reeling toward the stove

Now rectify it. Cut it out of her, cut that mewling filthy foetus out of her
stinking whore's womb

Twisting on the burner

Bring it to the clearing, feed it to Petey

The coils reddening

Let the dog's jaws crunch through those hairline foetal bones

Grasping the glowing orange coils, steam hissing

Kill her Chris KILL THE BABY KILL YOUR WIFE

Flames shooting up his fingers, the pain a shrieking holocaust—

Chris bellowed in agony and lurched for the sink, plunged his
hand under cold water, his teeth grinding and the tears streaming,
the pain worse than any he'd ever felt, a hundred times worse. He
pounded his forehead on the sink edge, wailing prayers to anyone
who would listen, Please take away the pain, please forgive me.

A long time later, he lifted his sweat-drenched face and stared at
the glowing coils of the stovetop. He removed his quivering hand
from the flowing water and ventured a glance at the livid maroon

burn marks, the blood that flowed into the cracked, scorched skin. Then he thrust his face away, unable to bear the sight any longer.

Returning his hand to its place under the faucet, his gaze wandered to the knife rack. He wondered which one was the sharpest, which would make the cleanest cut if he held out his arm, sliced the veins and tendons of his wrists. Or better yet, he could slit his throat, a smiling red curve from ear to ear, the underjaw a happy scarlet gush. Would he have time to make it to Ellie, to die beside her? It was a better fate than he deserved.

The agony from his burned hand spread through his entire body. He couldn't do this any longer, not today. He went slowly upstairs, gritting his teeth against the crawling rage of his roasted skin, and made it to the bathroom. There, he swaddled his hand in a towel, shook out a handful of sleeping pills. Before he swallowed them, he started to count but lost track at nine.

No, a distant voice pleaded. *Have to take care of Ellie. You owe her that at least.*

Chris flushed the pills and went up to the office.

He'd been in there twenty minutes weeping over his hand and cursing himself when he beheld someone walking across the yard toward the house.

CHAPTER THREE

Ellie heard voices, soft laughter.

One voice belonged to Chris, of course. The other she couldn't identify right away. It was familiar yet somehow alien. She closed her eyes and was back in her childhood home again, pretending to be asleep so her parents wouldn't make her go to church. Now she heard her sister, her sister talking to Chris, laughing again.

Ellie came fully awake. She opened her eyes but squinted at the harsh white light. She got out of bed, wrapped a blanket over her shoulders, and staggered to the stairwell. Out here the voices were clearer. Yes, it was Katherine speaking to Chris. That couldn't be, but she'd recognise that voice anywhere. Hell, she was tortured by it every freaking day. She went downstairs.

Chris and Katherine, seated at the little round table, looked up at her.

"Decided to join the world of the living?" Kat asked her.

"Come sit with us," Chris said.

Ellie noted the tightness in his voice, the artificiality of his expression, and wondered, *What are you hiding?*

She sat down between them, Katherine on her left.

"What time is it?" Ellie asked.

Kat checked her watch. "Three-thirty."

Her sister's hair was drawn back with its normal tortoise-shell barrette. As always, Kat looked pretty, but there was something else in her sister's face, something strained around the eyes.

Ellie let it go for the moment. "When did you get here?"

"At your property or your house?" Kat asked, cocking an eyebrow. "You two might as well live on Mars. As if this place weren't in the boonies already, there's not even a bridge over your creek. I had to take off my shoes and wade across like Laura Ingalls Wilder."

Ellie felt her pulse quicken. "The creek is down?"

Chris said, "It's about waist deep now, but the current's still fast."

"Then I can go see Dr. Stone," Ellie said.

Chris looked away.

"Your husband needs to see a doctor, too," Kat said. For the first time Ellie noticed the white dressing around Chris's right hand.

"What—" she began.

"I was stupid," he said. "I was trying to heat you up a bowl of soup, but I tripped and grabbed the burner."

"Third degree burn," Kat said. "I'm sure of it. He wasn't even going to let me see it until I threatened to rip that silly towel off his hand."

"It's fine," Chris said, but Ellie could see the pain in his eyes.

Ellie said to her sister, "How did you – when did you decide to come?"

Kat gave her a sarcastic shake of the head. "I've been leaving messages for over a week, El, but you never call back. I thought about hiring a skywriter, but I doubt you'd have seen it through all these trees."

Ellie turned to hear Chris's explanation, but he was studying the woods beyond the lane.

No messages for you, she remembered him saying. *Just one from my mom.*

You deceitful jerk, she thought.

"Earth to Ellie," she heard her sister saying.

She looked at Katherine.

"I said, why don't we go to town tonight?"

Ellie opened her mouth to respond, but Chris said, "Tonight's not good. There's a storm on the way."

Kat peered outside. "The sky is crystal clear."

"At the moment," Chris said, an edge to his voice. "The bad stuff's supposed to hit later."

Kat affected a country twang. "I don't mind. Put on some clothes, girl. We're headin' to Ravana."

Ellie smiled, but it faded when she took in the grim set of Chris's jaw, his eyes blazing at Kat.

"That would be—" *Fine*, Ellie had meant to say, but a smouldering livewire of pain sizzled through her abdomen, cutting off speech.

"El?" Kat asked, a hand on her shoulder.

"It's okay," Ellie said. "Really, it's—"

"You need a doctor," Kat said.

Ellie gasped as another blaze seared her guts.

Doesn't want me to leave, she thought dimly.

"Better not tonight," she said with difficulty. "It's probably... something I ate."

"You haven't eaten *anything*," Kat said. "You've been in hibernation the past fifteen hours."

"That long?" Ellie said, struggling to her feet.

Kat got up with her. "Where are you—"

"Bedroom," Ellie explained. "I need to lie down till this passes."

"You need anything?" Chris asked, and she thought, *You lying bastard, you know exactly what's happening. Maybe you're even helping it.*

"No," she told him. "Kat'll take care of me."

"You bet," her sister said and put a steadying arm around her back.

All of a sudden Ellie was very thankful Kat had come.

*   *   *

An hour after that, Kat was sitting beside the bed stirring an ice cube in a hot bowl of chicken noodle soup. Ellie watched her sister move the diminishing cube around and wondered when they'd last been together.

That's easy, she thought. *The wedding.* She'd scheduled three or four visits to Ann Arbor since then, and many times Kat had asked when she and her family could come to Malibu, but it had never materialised.

Because Ellie hadn't allowed it to materialise.

Kat finished blowing on the soup, handed it over. "Try it now."

Ellie spooned some into her mouth. "Mm," she said, relishing the hot feel of it in her throat. "You make this?"

"Straight from the can," Kat said. "I'll gladly take the credit though."

"I'm glad you came," Ellie said quietly.

"I got the impression you wanted me to leave you alone."

Ellie averted her eyes, took another spoonful of soup.

"What?" Kat said.

Ellie shook her head, all at once worried she'd break down bawling.

Kat leaned forward, a hand on the blanket covering Ellie's knee. "Hey," she said. "What's going on, kiddo?"

"I'm such an asshole."

"Why—"

"You're the only one who put forth any effort," Ellie said. "I've treated you so badly."

"C'mon," Kat said and sat next to her on the bed. "You act like you took out a contract on my head or something." She leaned closer. "You didn't, did you?"

Ellie laid her head on Kat's shoulder and closed her eyes. "I'm so sorry."

"Hey," Kat said and put her arm around her. "You could never treat me badly enough to get rid of me forever." Kat squeezed her. "You'll always be my girl."

Ellie straightened and shoved a couple pillows between her and the headboard so she'd be more comfortable. She felt as though someone had lodged an axe between her ribcage and her left hipbone. The only advantage of pregnancy she'd so far experienced was her swollen breasts, though she suspected the novelty would wear off soon enough.

Leaning against the pillows, Ellie said, "It's been three years. We need to catch up before I spill my guts about my problems."

Kat scooted around to sit cross-legged on the bed facing her. "We'll do small talk later," she said. "What's the matter with you?"

"You mean the stomach cramps?"

"I mean everything. Purple bags under your eyes, you've lost weight—"

"I needed to."

"Believe me, pregnancy wreaks plenty of havoc on your body. You don't need any extra stress."

"I look stressed?"

Kat tilted her head, eyes widening sardonically: *Isn't it obvious?*

Ellie sighed. "Okay, I'm stressed. It's just..."

"Go on."

"I don't know... I'm afraid you'll make fun of me."

"I won't make fun of you. Much."

Ellie blew out a tremulous breath. She knew how crazy it would sound, knew the chances were excellent Kat would roll her eyes and chalk it up to her overactive imagination. The one thing, however, Ellie was sure would strike a chord with her sister was the pain in her belly, the titanic, soul-ripping pain she experienced every time she tried to escape this place. And if Ellie wasn't well enough to make it out, Kat was sure as hell persuasive enough to get Dr. Stone here to examine Ellie. Then she'd have the peace of knowing her baby was still healthy, still alive in her womb.

She opened her mouth to tell Kat about that first night in the house, the grisly discovery of the razor blades; and then later that first week, the sensation of being licked on the fingers even though the dog had been outside; she opened her mouth to share everything that had happened, to unburden herself of the whole macabre tale, but a sudden tightness in her stomach stopped her.

She gripped the swell of her belly.

"What is it?" Kat asked.

When Ellie didn't answer, only bent forward as the tightness spread lower, her innards squeezed by an invisible vice, Kat rose to her knees and put her hands on Ellie's shoulders.

"Seriously, El, you're scaring me."

You don't know what scary is, she thought.

"We've gotta get you into town," Kat said.

A rocket of heat shot through Ellie's abdomen.

"*No*," she said in a tight voice, "I don't need to go anywhere. I just need to—" Another wave of pain. "—*stay here and*—"

"*Ellie*," Kat said in disbelief, "you could be in real danger. If something—"

Searing pain, stealing her breath.

"—is wrong you need to see—"

"*Stop*," Ellie hissed through clenched teeth. "*Just stop. Please. It's...*" A slight alleviating. "*...not helping me.*"

Kat fell quiet. Ellie stayed leaned over that way for several moments, and gradually, by infinitesimal degrees, the pain dulled to merely an uncomfortable throb.

"Better?" Kat asked.

Ellie nodded.

"I really think we need to—"

Ellie grabbed Kat's arm, stilled her with a warning look.

"Okay," Kat said. "I'm just trying to help."

Her breathing grew slower, almost normal. "I know you are. But for now, let's just hold off talking about it, okay?"

Kat searched her eyes a long moment. Then she nodded. "Okay."

★   ★   ★

"So what kind of stuff do I have to look forward to?" Ellie asked later that evening as they sat on the front porch. "Health-wise, I mean."

She leaned against a post, her sister a few feet away sitting barefoot on the concrete.

Kat leaned back on her palms, warming to the subject. "Oh, it's a carnival of delights. I assume your back is hurting?"

"Some."

"Just wait. Pretty soon your boobs'll feel like bowling balls."

"They're getting there." Ellie frowned. "And my hair's been falling out."

"It'll get worse. Chris'll think there's something living in the shower drain."

"Ugh."

"It gets better. When you shed the hair on your head, the stuff down below starts growing like crazy."

"My pubic hair?"

Kat nodded. "Everywhere south of the border. The first time I was pregnant my husband said I looked like I sat on a squirrel."

"That was sweet of him."

"Vintage Roland."

Watching her sister's face, something Ellie hadn't considered struck her like a stone. "Where are your kids?"

Kat straightened her legs and regarded her toes. "Mom and Dad's."

She felt a stirring of foreboding. "They're not...with Roland?"

After all this time, she still hated saying the man's name. He didn't pronounce it the way she'd always heard it, like *Poland*. He insisted on rhyming it with *Holland*, and somehow, that always seemed to summarise the man for Ellie.

Kat opened her mouth, and Ellie could see she was debating how much she should share.

Finally, Kat said, "Roland and I are separated."

Ellie could only gape.

"Don't look so stunned."

"I can't help it."

"I'm relieved," Kat said, some of her old brusqueness returning. "The last couple years we've been running on fumes. If it weren't for the kids, things would've fallen apart long ago."

"I don't..." Ellie began. "I mean, what happened?"

"You mean did Roland cheat on me?'"

"No," Ellie said. "Did he?"

"Who the hell knows."

She sat thunderstruck. She couldn't imagine her sister letting anything she was a part of fail. It was one of the fundamental laws of Ellie's reality: Kat succeeded; Ellie was the one who screwed up.

"I'll tell you about it on one condition," Kat said. "You have to tell me exactly what's going on with Chris."

Ellie wanted to look away, but Kat's stare transfixed her. There was something almost fierce about her sister's expression, but beneath that she sensed a hurt she'd never imagined possible.

"Okay," Ellie agreed.

Kat began to talk then, and soon the twilight deepened. Ellie lay on her back staring up at the porch ceiling planks, her hands folded behind her head for a pillow.

Roland, Kat told her, had begun to behave distantly around the time Ellie had gotten married to Chris, and one of the many shocking facts Kat revealed was that Roland had accused her of being attracted to Chris at the reception.

"You're kidding," Ellie said. "Roland thought you wanted my groom?"

"Sexually."

"Why would he think that?"

"I made the mistake of mentioning that I thought Chris looked handsome in his tux."

"And because of that he thought you were after him?"

"That's Roland," Kat said. "Painfully insecure. He thinks I want every man my gaze happens to linger on, like I'm constantly on the prowl for new lovers."

"My first husband cheated on me," Ellie said.

"No kidding?"

Ellie was surprised at herself for mentioning it. In fact, the whole ordeal had been so painful, she rarely allowed herself to think of it.

Not unlike being raped under the bridge.

Ellie shut her eyes to blot out the memory.

"Well," Kat went on, "Roland didn't cheat on me, but in a way that might have been better."

"Believe me, it wouldn't have been better."

"Yeah?" Kat said. "I'm not so sure."

Ellie shifted on the unforgiving concrete, striving for a more comfortable position.

"Hold on a sec," Kat said and got up. Ellie heard her open the screen door. A moment later, she returned. "Sit on this," she said, placing a couch cushion beside them.

Ellie did as she was told, and felt an almost immediate lessening of the pain in her left side.

Kat went on. "He didn't cheat on me because that would have required him to perform sexually."

Ellie raised her eyebrows.

"After we had our second child, he was barely able to get an erection."

"How'd you get pregnant the third time?

"Luck, I suppose."

Ellie let it digest. She couldn't picture Roland becoming impotent; then again, she couldn't picture him having sex either. There'd always been something strangely robotic about him. She thought of him as a Stepford husband, but instead of being glamorous, he was like a million other American husbands: clean-cut, pale, not unattractive, but not remarkable either. He was just…there.

They sat in silence awhile, the sky darkening to navy blue. There were stars out tonight. Not many, but enough to make it nice on the porch.

All at once, a weird whirring sound erupted from the woods, making Ellie start and grab her sister's arm. "What the hell is that?" she asked.

"Cicadas," Kat said. "We didn't have them in California, but around here they're all over the place."

"What an awful noise."

"You get used to it. I'm just surprised they're out this early. In Ann Arbor they usually don't start until July."

Ellie sat back on her cushion. "So…when's the last time you two had sex?"

"Probably the night we conceived Jacob."

"You've gotta be kidding."

"I wish I was."

"And Jake's how old now? Three?"

"Four in October."

"Jesus, Katherine."

Kat smiled, but there was pain in it.

"Why do you think Roland…"

"Couldn't get it up?"

Ellie waited.

"Who knows?" Kat said wearily. "I guess he stopped finding me attractive."

"But you're gorgeous."

"I wouldn't go that far. Having babies does a lot to your body, El. My stomach looks like a dried prune."

"That's not so bad."

"Sometimes I pee when I laugh."

Ellie laughed, her enlarged breasts jiggling painfully. Still, it felt good. She hadn't laughed in weeks.

"It's true," Kat said, laughing now too.

Ellie lay back on the cushion, struggling to catch her breath. Kat lay back beside her, laughing as well, and as she did she gasped and squeezed her legs together.

"No way," Ellie said.

"I can't help it," Kat said, wiping her eyes. "I can't control it anymore."

Just then, Chris opened the screen door and stared down at them. "What's so funny?"

But try as Ellie might, she couldn't catch her breath to explain.

*   *   *

The burned hand made typing a bitch.

Chris pushed away from the desk with a frustrated sigh. He examined the medical tape with which Katherine had wrapped his hand, the bulging gauze beneath. He'd need to change the wrapping tonight before bed. Once, when his mom had used gauze to cover a nasty scrape he'd gotten while sliding into second base – a strawberry was what his coach had called it – he'd nearly screamed himself hoarse when his mom peeled the white bandage off several days later, the scab having attached itself to the gauze. It resulted in a wound that was worse than the original.

His bladder throbbed, but below, he could hear the shower going. He checked the small clock on the corner of the desk: 10:17 p.m.

He stood and stretched, his lower back a tangle of knots. He went down to the second floor and passed the guest room, which was closed, and the room in which he kept his weights, which was open. He made a face at the realisation that his burn would likely prohibit working out for at least a week.

Stupid thing to do, he thought as he reached the bathroom door. He frowned. Ellie seldom closed the door. In fact, she never did unless she was taking a dump. But he could hear the shower spraying within. Maybe it was because her sister was here.

He opened the door and blinked at the amount of moisture in the air. The mirror was completely steamed up, the room like a sauna.

He glanced at the shower curtain.

It *was* Ellie in there, wasn't it?

Kat's door had been shut, and he was pretty sure she'd turned in for the night. He didn't know his sister-in-law all that well, but she seemed like an early sleeper. Most people with kids were.

Chris stepped over to the toilet and raised the lid.

He grinned. It would be funny though, wouldn't it? Him walking in on Katherine taking a shower? How would she react? Even better, how would Ellie react? Would she take it all in good fun, recognise how innocently it had happened, or would she be pissed off, assuming Chris had done it intentionally? Like he was some kind of adolescent, desperate enough for a look at some tits to walk in on his sister-in-law. Well, it would be embarrassing for him too, right? Him standing here with his dick in his hand taking a leak?

He was thinking this when the water shut off and the curtain slid open.

Katherine had her eyes on the bathmat, one leg extended out of the tub, when she looked up and uttered a gasp of surprise.

"Hey, I didn't mean—" he began, but she was already jerking the curtain over her. Before she did, though, he got a good look at her naked body. Nice-sized tits, small pink nipples. Below that...

And what was more, her eyes had flickered, just for a moment, to his penis.

Through his surprise at having encountered her this way, he felt a powerful surge of arousal. It was difficult to zip up.

"Could you..." she began. He met her gaze and followed it to the towel bar.

"Oh, sure."

When he handed her the towel he noticed she was blushing. Embarrassed, yeah, but not angry. That told him a lot. When she had the towel in hand, she receded into the shower. A moment later, she drew the curtain aside again and stepped out, the towel low enough to show a little cleavage, but not quite long enough to cover much of her legs. In fact, if he had a better angle...

She glanced at him, and he realised he'd been staring too long.

"I'm sorry," he said and forced a smile. "I'm just—"

They heard footsteps below. Ellie.

Without a word, Chris slipped out the door and into the bedroom. He crossed to the closet, occupied himself by studying neckties.

He listened as Ellie climbed the stairs. Then she was in the room beside him.

"Hey," she said.

"Hey, honey," he said as casually as he could.

"I feel bad for Kat."

"Yeah, why's that?"

"We only have one shower. I hate that she has to share it with us."

"We'll make it work," he said.

And turned away so Ellie wouldn't see his smile.

★   ★   ★

Katherine had a hard time making eye contact when Chris came down for breakfast. It wasn't only that he'd seen her naked, which was bad enough — hell, she hated to see *herself* naked — it was the way they'd both reacted to the incident. No nervous laughter, no talking over each other to ease the tension of the moment.

Chris said good morning and went to the fridge to pour himself some orange juice. Katherine noted that Ellie hadn't even looked up when her husband came in, had only continued pushing her scrambled eggs around her plate.

The tension...that was the real problem. It had been the wrong kind of tension percolating in that small, humid bathroom last night. It hadn't been the tension of two embarrassed people who wished the moment had never happened. It had been the tension she sometimes felt when her husband's — soon-to-be *ex*-husband's, she reminded herself — best friend came over for dinner and drinks. Ross wasn't remotely her type, but there was a knowingness about him that she reacted to, couldn't *help* reacting to. Her only defence with Ross was to avoid making eye contact, which worked during dinner. It was always later on, after they'd started on their second round of drinks, that she allowed herself an occasional glance at Ross as they all talked. She told herself she was simply being polite — after all, in a party of six, how could she *not* look at him at some point in their conversation? But whenever he'd look back at her she'd have to squeeze her legs together to stifle the heat he kindled there.

After Roland ceased initiating sex between them, and later, after they stopped having sex completely, there'd been a yearlong period in which Kat had not experienced an orgasm or even indulged in a sexual fantasy. Then again she'd been pregnant for nine of those months, and after her last child was born she was too busy or too tired to think of anything other than survival.

But slowly, as her nursing decreased and her libido returned, she

206 • JONATHAN JANZ

indulged in fantasies of Ross, of her college boyfriend Francesco, of George Clooney.

And eventually, of her sister's husband.

The ironic thing about her blow-up with Roland upon leaving Chris and Ellie's wedding reception had been that a cruel part of her had wanted to confess to her husband that yes, she did in fact want to sleep with Chris Crane, did want him to ravage her the way Roland would not.

Katherine forked in a bite of hash browns and stifled a laugh. Who was she kidding? Roland had never ravished her in his life, and definitely not in the manner Chris did in her fantasies.

The first time she met him, he and Ellie were just dating, and Katherine assumed he was only another in a long line of her kid sister's flings. Some of them had been handsome in a vapid, puerile way, but none of them had been memorable.

But Chris…

The first time he entered the Italian restaurant at which they were to meet for dinner, Katherine knew she had a problem. As he smiled and shook her hand, his sincerity incongruous with his gorgeous looks – the sandy hair, the broad shoulders, the knockout smile, even the dimples in his cheeks and chin – she secretly hoped it wouldn't work out between him and Ellie. There was a part of Katherine that wanted the relationship to fail out of a primitive, nasty jealousy. Chris was everything Roland was not. He was bigger, sunnier, more charismatic, and Katherine was sure he could get erections just fine. Ellie'd certainly never stay with a man who couldn't.

Katherine realised Ellie had been speaking to her.

Ellie chuckled. "Jeez, Kat. Talk about zoning out."

Katherine steadied her breathing. *If you only knew.*

She said, "I was just thinking about Gigi." She glanced at Chris. "She's my oldest. I was just thinking Mom and Dad better make sure she gets plenty of sunscreen or she's liable to fry."

"Always a mother, huh?" Ellie said and went back to playing with her eggs.

Katherine swallowed, her throat thick with guilt.

Chris set his glass on the table, a few inches from Katherine's fingers. He tented his hands, looked at his wife and said, "I don't suppose Kat told you what happened last night?"

Katherine felt her heart lurch. She shot a warning look at Chris: *What are you doing?*

Chris caught it, a hurt expression rippling through his features. He went on in a less jocular tone, "I feel sort of bad about it, it was really an—"

"It was nothing," Katherine interrupted. She risked a glance at Ellie in the hope that she was still staring down at her uneaten food, but her sister had picked up the nervous energy hovering over the table.

"What happened?" Ellie asked.

Chris shifted in his seat, but Katherine cut him off. "He almost walked in on me in the shower," Katherine said. "Apparently he thought I was you."

"Did he..." Ellie began.

"No, thank God." She grimaced. "Probably would've given him nightmares."

"Oh," Ellie said, but she didn't seem to relax any. If anything, her expression grew more troubled.

Katherine forged on, "He asked if I'd leave the water running for him. I told him sure, but could he give me time to put on a robe first?"

Ellie was watching Chris now, her face difficult to read. She said, "Guess you'll knock from now on, huh?"

Chris nodded, gave Katherine a sheepish grin. "You bet."

Soon after, Ellie excused herself and went upstairs.

When she was gone, Chris seemed to deflate. "Shit, I'm sorry, Katherine. I didn't mean to—"

She stilled him with a hand on his forearm. "It's okay," she said. "Really."

He suddenly seemed very vulnerable, almost like a little boy. Though they were roughly the same age, she felt like a rapacious older woman.

She took her hand off his arm.

He said, "Sorry about last night."

"You really got an eyeful, didn't you?"

His cheeks reddened. "I'm not the only one who got an eyeful."

It was Katherine's turn to blush.

"You have a great body," he said quietly.

She shrugged. "After three kids…"

"You look fabulous," he said. "Seriously."

She stared up at him. "Yeah?"

He nodded. "I know I shouldn't have, but…"

"What?"

He favoured her with a sidelong glance. "Tell you the truth, I sort of enjoyed it."

Katherine fell silent. She had no idea what to say to that.

*   *   *

"There's something I was wondering about," Ellie asked as they made dinner that evening.

Kat said, "Shoot," and went on chopping celery.

Ellie opened the oven a crack to make sure the garlic bread wasn't burning. "I wondered why Chris walked in on you."

In her periphery she saw the knife pause, then slowly begin chopping again. "I told you why," Kat said. "He thought I was you."

"You said that earlier."

"Well," Kat said and uttered an impatient grunt, "that's because it's the truth."

"What I don't get," Ellie went on, "is why Chris didn't take a shower last night."

Kat stopped chopping and set the knife on the cutting board. Palms on the counter, she said, "Why don't you come out and say it?"

Ellie returned her glare. *No*, she thought. *I'm not buying it, not this time. You've been caught, and you're doing a poor job concealing it. But what exactly are you concealing? What happened between you two?*

Ellie kept her tone level: "You said he came in and asked you to keep the shower running after you were done. You said, 'Sure,' but would he give you time to put on a robe first."

"Good memory," Kat said. "You should've been a court recorder."

"He asked you to leave the shower on so he could take a shower." She leaned forward to drive home her point. "But he didn't take a shower last night."

"So?"

"So what happened between the bathroom and the bedroom? Did Chris suddenly decide he wanted to go to bed dirty?"

Kat faced her. "I don't know, El, why don't you ask him?"

"I'm asking you."

"What, you think I drove all the way out here so I could screw your husband?"

"I didn't say that."

Kat's eyebrows went up. "Then what *did* you say? It sure sounded like an accusation to me."

"Asking you to clarify is not the same—"

"The hell it isn't."

And dammit, they were right back to arguing the way they had in their teens and twenties and would have in their thirties, had they stayed in touch. Ellie shook her head and took the cover off the soup. She put the bowl of washed lettuce and cucumbers next to the cutting board, nodded at the celery. "You can put that in with the rest."

Katherine's tongue made her cheek bulge. "I'm not hungry anymore."

Ellie sighed. "I'm sorry, okay?"

Katherine watched her with pitiless eyes.

Ellie went on, "It's just that...you've always been the one with her life together."

Katherine scowled. "What does that—"

"Nothing," Ellie interrupted. "It's got nothing to do with it. At least it shouldn't. I don't want..."

But Katherine was already turning away, her expression stony.

Ellie watched her go and tried to convince herself she hadn't just lost the only ally she had.

* * *

The forest flew by. Chris veered left, galloping down the trail into shadow.

He'd been wrong about Katherine; he knew that now. At first he'd pegged her as a country club snob, too stuffed with affectations and rich friends to connect with.

Yet the woman who'd shown up yesterday bore little resemblance to the one Ellie had railed about for the past few years. This Katherine was more vulnerable and more alive than the one he remembered. Granted, she seemed worn out – marital problems? – but the raw vitality within her still flickered whenever she smiled or her eyes locked on his.

He stumbled over a root, staggered, but narrowly regained his balance. He shook his head, picking up speed again. That's what he got for daydreaming about his wife's sister.

Not telling Ellie about Katherine's messages on their cell phone had been a miscalculation. If Ellie confronted him about it, he'd muddle his way through, claim he figured it would only stress her out, and that he'd hoped that not returning Katherine's calls would keep her away.

Actually, this last part was true.

How surprised he'd been when she appeared at the front door yesterday. He'd been even more surprised at the powerful attraction he felt toward her.

It was too bad, really, that Katherine couldn't stay here a good long while. He knew that wasn't possible though. Her kids surely knew where their mother was, and even if she hadn't told them, she could still be found here. For one, her car was parked at the edge of the bridge. Also, couldn't they trace a cell phone signal?

His stomach did a somersault. He stopped, implacable fingers of dread closing over his throat.

Campbell had been carrying a phone.

He'd buried the phone with Campbell's body.

Jesus Christ, could they trace a signal underground? He had no idea. Maybe, he thought hopefully, the phone's battery had gone dead by now. It had already been, what, two days since Campbell could have conceivably charged it?

How long did their own battery last? Chris scanned his memory feverishly. Up to five days, he remembered with a sinking feeling. That meant Campbell's phone, if it was as good at holding a charge as theirs, would continue to put out a signal for two or three more days.

Campbell had probably already missed work, so he'd likely been declared missing. Weren't cell phones one of the first things the authorities checked? He thought they were.

Relax, he told himself. *It probably can't even be traced. The damn thing's underground, for God's sakes. And remember, you can't even get a signal here.*

Chris chewed his bottom lip, the acrid taste of bile boiling in the back of his throat. He strongly doubted they could trace Campbell's phone way out here, especially through several feet of dirt.

But what if they could?

He began running back toward the house.

*　　*　　*

Ninety minutes later, he leaned on the shovel and mopped his brow with a red bandanna. He estimated he was halfway to Campbell's body, give or take a few inches. A robust wind had begun to sweep through the forest, which made digging a hell of a lot more bearable.

Of course, the job would soon become considerably less pleasant.

Chris had read several stories involving the exhumation of a body. His favourite was Ray Russell's "Sardonicus," though in Chris's own case the revenge angle of the Russell tale was blessedly absent. Chris hadn't shot Campbell – Daniel Wolf had – and though Chris had been responsible for bringing Campbell out here in the first place, he'd never intended to hurt the man.

Why, then, was he so frightened?

That was easy, he thought. The bare fact of what he was doing to begin with. He was literally becoming a ghoul. Human bodies, once buried, were supposed to remain that way, and those who didn't observe this axiom were committing some sort of sin, weren't they?

Yeah, and coveting your sister-in-law isn't sinful?

Good point, he thought.

He tossed the bandana aside and began digging again. What would have happened last night, he wondered, had he locked the door and climbed inside the shower with Katherine? Twisted the hot water back on and made feverish love to her in a cloud of steam? Would she have surrendered to him? Would Ellie have heard and come rapping at the door? Would it have mattered?

The questions scattered as the shovel blade hit an obstruction. Chris didn't remember any rocks in the dirt with which he'd filled in the grave. It could only be Campbell's body.

He leaned on the shovel, tested to see how much give there was. If it was Campbell he'd struck, there'd soon be a puff of foul air. He lifted the spade, jabbed it into the soil, steeling himself for the noxious odour of congealed flesh.

But he smelled only the forest, a hint of manure borne by the wind.

Frowning, he tested the soil again with the shovel tip, and again he felt the same hardening of the earth. He was tempted to drop down on all fours and begin pawing the dirt aside until he reached whatever he'd found, but the possibility of inadvertently coming into contact with Campbell's putrefying skin precluded that. Even worse, what if he happened on the dead man's ruined head? What if he scooped out a gelatinous glob of brains? He shivered, held tight to the shovel handle until he got control of his imagination.

Okay, he thought. *You know you've found something, and if it is Campbell's body, that's a good thing, right? Isn't that what you came out here for? It's no vacation, that's true enough, but neither was burying two men and a dog – which, by the way, had already become a maggot-infested horror. If you can endure all that, you can certainly do this. Just dig a little more, find Campbell's pants, check his pockets for the phone, then shut the damn thing off. That is if it's even working. But the main thing is to by God do it.*

With steadier hands, Chris set about exposing the body. Five minutes' work revealed the first glimpse of Campbell's red shirt. As he set to work probing with the shovel, he told himself he wasn't stalling, wasn't putting off the inevitable – going through a dead man's pockets and coming into contact with his rigour mortised body. But as his shovel sought the contours of the man's hips, he found an odd thing; there was no stench emanating from the corpse. Momentarily forgetting his dread of contact, Chris knelt and brushed dirt off the shirt. At first there was just red fabric, but after a little more work he uncovered a small ivory button. Then another. With trembling hands, Chris undid the two exposed buttons and spread the fabric apart. Campbell's white belly gleamed up at him like a milky cataract.

Without thinking, Chris reached over and swept a patina of soil from Campbell's face.

And gasped.

The bugs've been at him, he told himself. *They've chewed away at his flesh and that's why he looks different.*

"Bullshit," he whispered. Bugs didn't change the shape of a man's eyebrows, transform them into thick, black arches. And bugs didn't make a man's lips curl into a savage snarl, as though the canines within had grown longer.

And bugs sure as hell didn't change a man's eye colour – not just the irises, but the whole goddamn things – to a soulless obsidian.

No! he wanted to scream. *It's impossible!*

Then what the hell was wrong with Campbell's face?

"*Fuck me,*" Chris murmured. He didn't want to do it – hell, he no longer wanted to be anywhere *near* this hole in the ground – but he had to do what he came here to do, had to find Campbell's phone.

Studiously avoiding the unsettling, vulpine face, he scuttled back a couple feet, clawed more dirt aside. His hands trembled as he worked, certain at any moment the too-pale fingers would batten onto him, haul him toward Campbell's growing maw with inexorable slowness. He struggled to thrust away the thought, to ignore the sensation of the loose dirt beneath his knees shifting. Soon, he distinguished the muddy creases of Campbell's khaki pants. In moments he'd exposed the right hip pocket, which disgorged only a leather key ring and a couple coins. He dug down until he found Campbell's other pocket, and inside, *finally,* he found the phone.

Chris activated it. His heart dropped as an orange AT&T logo appeared, accompanied by a brief but shockingly loud jingle. He waited for the screen to say "New Voicemail," but the only thing that appeared was a picture of a tropical beach that probably came with the phone.

Momentarily, he forgot his fear of the corpse beneath him. The poor bastard didn't even have any family to use as wallpaper. For some reason, this filled Chris with a desolation that made him want to cry.

Then a far more terrible thought took its place.

Daniel Wolf had been a German Baptist, an upstanding man who wore the traditional beard and clothing of his faith, and for this reason Chris hadn't even considered one important possibility.

Daniel, like his brother, had driven a newer pick-up truck. Also like his brother, Daniel was a businessman. So if Daniel wasn't against using technology, wasn't it possible – likely even – that he'd also carried a cell phone?

Yes, Chris thought. It was very likely.

Campbell's battery was still working, which meant the phone could still be traced.

Which meant Daniel Wolf's could be too.

Daniel Wolf, the man Chris had murdered.

What if the authorities were tracing Wolf's phone right now? What if—

With a start, Chris depressed the *Off* button on Campbell's phone. Jesus, he thought. He was one slick criminal. By digging up the man's cell and turning the damn thing on, he might just have led the police to the body.

Why not just turn yourself in and save them the trouble?

Trembling badly, he climbed out of the grave. It would take a while to fill the hole back in, and it would take even longer to repeat the process with Daniel Wolf's body. With any luck he'd be home by suppertime, and though he desired nothing more than a shower, some food and a good long nap, he'd no doubt have to account for every goddamn minute.

Chris scowled, imagining how Ellie would react.

Where've I been, Ellie? Oh, I forgot to mention that in addition to all the other bullshit gripes you've voiced about this place, you can now add the following:

Campbell got his head blown off the other night by an Amish man who was pissed because his Rottweiler – yep, the one that tried to eat you – was strangled to death with my belt.

What's that? Oh, I forgot to mention...it's sort of funny, really, but well, it's like this: I staved the Amish man's head in with the butt of his shotgun. Yeah, it was self-defence, and I did have some help from Petey, but yes, I'm the one who actually murdered him.

To escape these thoughts, Chris filled in Campbell's grave, and though his hands beneath the work gloves were yowling again, he went immediately to work exhuming Daniel Wolf.

But there was no phone within Wolf's navy blue work pants.

★   ★   ★

Ellie peered out the office window. Despite the lengthening shadows, Kat was still laying out in the front yard. Why she'd chosen the front yard was obvious; it was sunnier. Why she insisted on displaying so much skin was another matter. The bikini was normal enough. Just a two-piece, red bathing suit that tied at the neck. But Kat had folded the waistband down two or three times to reveal the top of her buttcrack and in doing so had given herself the world's worst wedgie. If pressed for a reason, Kat would no doubt tell her she was trying to avoid tan lines, and if Ellie kept asking, they'd be right back to where they'd been before lunch: at each other's throats like two snarky teenagers.

God, she thought, *if we could only leave here everything would be okay.*

The land won't let you leave, a malefic voice whispered. *The land won't even let you speak.*

But that wasn't quite true, she thought. It wasn't the land. At least not *entirely* the land. It was the man in the basement, the woman in the woods, Ellie's own husband who was turning into Jack Nicholson in *The Shining* for chrissakes. It wouldn't surprise her if she picked up a page of his manuscript and read "All work and no play makes Chris a dull boy."

Impulsively, she reached down and opened the drawer. Her right hand lowered toward the stack of pages.

No, a voice spoke up. *Don't do it. You remember what happened the last time you snooped? You found that damned videotape.*

Shivering, Ellie rose and went downstairs. The last thing she needed was another reason to fear her husband. In the kitchen she poured a glass of water and went out to the lawn if for no other reason than she could no longer bear being alone in the house. Ellie went outside and saw as she drew closer that Kat had not only untied the back of her bikini top, but that she'd tossed the top aside as well, apparently not worried that Chris would appear and see her half naked.

Because he's already seen all of you, hasn't he, Sister Dearest?

Knock it off, she told herself. *It was an accident, nothing more.*

Kat asked, "You ever hear of something called astral projection?"

Ellie handed her the water, and as her sister grasped it, Ellie caught a glimpse of nipple. *Not as shy as you used to be, are you?*

She brushed the thought away, said, "Astral projection… Is that like using the stars to predict the future?" She sat in the grass next to the blue beach towel on which her sister lay. The scent of coconut tanning oil hung in the air.

"That's astrology. This is like an out-of-body experience, only you're still in control of your spiritual self. The body remains where it is – in bed usually – and the ethereal self is able to move around and explore."

Ellie could not suppress a grin. "Ethereal self?"

"Believe it or not, Roland was the one who told me about it." Kat pushed up onto her elbows. If Chris did appear now, Ellie thought, he'd get quite a show.

Kat said, "I hardly listened when he explained it…Roland has a way of making even the most fascinating concepts sound dull. But that night I had a dream. "

Oh crap, Ellie thought. *Here we go.*

"You wanna hear about it?"

Ellie shrugged.

"It was like astral projection, only reversed. My body got up, but my spirit stayed in bed next to Roland."

"You watched yourself?"

"My body left the room. It was gone for several minutes. When it finally returned it didn't even look like me. It looked like—" Kat broke off, a sick look on her face.

"You probably dreamed it," Ellie said.

"That's not the worst part."

"Kat—"

"I watched the woman stand over Roland with a carving knife."

"It was a dream."

"Was it?"

Ellie stared at her sister, unable to speak.

Kat's eyes were pleading. "What if it wasn't?"

Ellie ignored the tingle at the nape of her neck. "It had to be."

Tears shimmered in her sister's eyes. Kat pressed white knuckles against her mouth, said something Ellie couldn't make out. Ellie put a hand on her back, leaned closer.

Kat said, her voice hardly audible, "I think I'm losing my mind."

*   *   *

After finishing his novel, Chris downed several beers by way of supper and plopped down in bed beside Ellie. Within minutes he fell asleep.

Later, he dreamed.

It began pleasantly enough. The beautiful woman − not the demonic predator, but the one to whom he'd first made love in the forest − beckoned him into the woods. Naked, Chris hastened after her. And though it was dark, he discovered she was naked too, the tantalising glimpses of her buttocks and the feminine curves of her legs driving him crazy as he strove to draw even with her. In moments they'd somehow reached the large clearing, but here was where pleasure faded and horror took its place. The hill was crawling with white, humanoid shapes that wriggled and growled with desire. He approached them, not at all curious but unable to prevent his legs from carrying him forward. Toward the great hill, which blazed with several bonfires. Though he couldn't make out what awaited at the crest, he was overcome with an inescapable dread, a certainty that whatever evil lurked up there was waiting for *him*.

Something brushed his ankle. He told himself to leap away, but his leg wouldn't cooperate, the cold, clammy fingers inching their way up his shin, his knee. He refused to look down at whatever groped him, but the fingers continued upward, caressing the skin above his knee, his bare thigh. Then confusion set in because the firelight was fading, the familiar touch of the pillow under his head supplanting it.

But the touch on his thigh persisted.

Was Ellie waking him up for sex?

Eyes still shut, Chris wondered what had gotten into her. How long had it been? A week? Two? They'd scarcely even spoken lately.

Yet the summery touch of her fingertips was working its magic on him. He was already rock hard.

Chris debated. He could teach her a lesson, abstain tonight in protest of her bad attitude, but really, what would be the point? Sure, she deserved it, but the fact remained that he needed to get laid, especially after the last couple days. He could make love to Ellie and pretend she was Katherine, and given his wife's bitchiness of late, he really wouldn't feel too bad about it either. Smirking, Chris opened his eyes.

And saw the figure standing over him.

His first impulse was to scream. The room was dark and the figure was darker, and even in this dimness he could see it was a woman, and he'd rather leap out the window and risk serious injury than gaze into those soulless white eyes again. He actually did scoot toward the headboard to get away from the probing fingers until his night vision kicked in and he distinguished the crooked grin on the woman's face. This wasn't a vampire or a demon.

This was Katherine.

Katherine with her fingertips skimming the waistband of his boxer briefs, her nails tickling the flesh of his belly in the most wonderfully maddening way. Propped on his elbows, Chris watched the fingers teasing over him, then gazed at her forearm, her shoulder. Above that, the sheer nightgown draping her delicate frame.

The moonlight slanting through the panes illuminated the diaphanous white gown she wore, made more distinct her lovely body beneath. He eased himself down, lying as he'd been when she'd first awakened him, and from this angle the limpid glow allowed an exhilarating glimpse of the sheer gown. He could actually make out the shadowy thatch of pubic hair, the supple lines of her inner thighs limned by the flimsy fabric.

Katherine drew down his waistband, Chris raising his hips to help her, and as the briefs slithered down his legs he remembered Ellie, slumbering beside him. He shot a glance that way and saw her lying peacefully on her side, the way she always did, facing away from him, and thank goodness for that. His attention returned to Katherine, who was bent over him now, massaging the flesh of his upper legs.

Reason demanded he delay their liaison until they could go to another room, but obviously Katherine had other ideas. If she wanted to make love in her room, why was she still teasing? Why not simply walk away and trust him to follow?

Because she wants you to make the decision, he told himself. *She'll do it either place, but she wants you to take charge. You do know how to do that, right?*

Hell, yes, he thought. Not that Ellie would ever give him credit for his assertiveness. Her every word was designed to emasculate him. And she'd succeeded, at least for a time.

But not any longer, he thought. *Oh no, not any longer.*

Chris reached up with his free hand, hooked his fingers in the neck of her nightgown, and drew her down so he could kiss her. Her tongue met his, and she moaned so loudly he feared Ellie would awaken. But that was part of it, wasn't it? The excitement of doing it right beside her?

Chris climbed on top of her.

She'd cinched her nightgown up so there'd be no encumbrances to their lovemaking. *Perfect*, he thought. He lowered himself on top of her, but as he did, he detected something new and entirely unwanted seeping into Katherine's pretty face, a combination of fear and utter bewilderment. As their bodies came together, her eyes shot down to her bare breasts.

"What are you—" she began, then she swung her head toward Ellie and gasped.

Ellie was sitting up, her eyes wide with horror.

"Katherine?" she asked in a breathless voice. Then to Chris: "*What are you two doing?*"

Isn't it obvious? Chris almost said, but there was no time for wisecracks now because Ellie had climbed out of bed and was switching on the lamp. Katherine was doing her best to scramble out from under him, but Chris was in no hurry. They were busted, and nothing could change that now. The light spilled over them as Katherine scuttled away from the bed, her arms thrown over her breasts as if she'd just realised the nightgown was damn near transparent.

"I can't believe you," Ellie whispered in that same aghast way.

Chris stood but made no attempt to hide his erection. Several feet to his left, Katherine hugged herself, made little keening noises that reminded Chris of someone who'd just stubbed her toe. Ellie shouted something at him.

He faced her. "Huh?"

Her lips drew back. "I said, I want you out of this house."

He grinned. "It's my house, too, dear."

"Don't call me that."

"What would you rather be called?"

She cracked then, palsied hands twining in her hair. "*Goddamn you both!*" she spat, but her voice dissolved on the last word. She stormed out of the bedroom. The bathroom door boomed, the lock clicked and Chris glanced at Katherine, who was staring at the floor, a shell-shocked expression transforming her face into that of a frightened dullard.

He gave her a grin. "You sure know how to surprise a guy."

She shook her head. "I don't know how it happened."

"Nothing did, but if you want, I'm still game."

Her bottom lip quivered, and she gave him a brief, doleful look. "Please don't."

He shrugged and went to his dresser. When he got his clothes on and went out, Katherine was still standing there.

And Ellie was still in the bathroom.

*   *   *

"El?" she heard Kat say through the door again. "Ellie, please? I don't know how to make you believe me, but..." Her voice trailed off in what sounded like a sob.

Fuck you, Ellie thought and gripped the edge of the vanity tighter. *Fuck you, you vicious, heartless slut. I'll just bet there's more to your divorce than you said. Did you jettison your whole family so you could steal my husband?*

Kat's voice, plaintive: "Please open the door."

Through the stinging tears, she stared absently at her makeup case, the toothbrush holder. Next to that, a half-used tube of Crest.

Beside that, a razor.

Ellie picked it up, considered using it on her wrists. Or better yet, on her sister's throat.

No, it was a safety razor. Bright orange plastic with a white handle. More useful for shaving legs than slitting throats, but maybe if she got lucky she could catch Kat off guard, swipe at her nose, her eyes, disfigure the husband-stealing bitch or at the very least seriously impair her vision. Whatever forces resided here weren't allowing Ellie to leave, that much was obvious. She might as well exact some revenge, spread the suffering around a little.

"For God's sakes, Ellie, I'm scared," Kat said. Though the voice was muffled by the thick door, Kat's fear resonated nonetheless. And though her sister had always been a good enough actress, Ellie didn't think the terror was feigned.

Exhaling, she dropped the razor in the sink and opened the door.

"What?" she asked in a dead voice.

Kat moved forward, and for one insane moment, she was sure her sister would try to embrace her. But Kat turned sideways in the door, hurried into the bathroom. She wrested the door from Ellie's grip, closed it, and pushed the lock button on the old brass knob.

"What do you think—" Ellie began, but Kat's strident whisper arrested her in mid-sentence.

"*We don't have much time.*"

"Time for what?"

Kat looked bewildered a moment, then her eyes brimmed and, bending over, she sat on the closed toilet lid.

You think I'm going to comfort you? Ellie thought. *You try to screw my husband, and you think I should comfort you?*

Yet she found herself crossing her arms, biting her bottom lip. She hated it when her sister cried, probably because it happened so infrequently. What if she really had been driven by some other force to come on to Chris? What if she'd been sleepwalking?

Bullshit, Ellie's anger insisted. *She's wanted Chris since she met him, and you know it. She didn't even have the courtesy to make her move behind your back, had to attempt it in your marriage bed. If you hadn't awakened when you did, they would have been humping like rabbits, and can you imagine waking up to that?*

Kat said, "You must think I'm the worst person in the world."

Ellie stared down at her and said nothing.

"I'm so sorry, Ellie. I—oh, *God.*"

The depth of pain in her sister's voice nearly softened Ellie, but she fought it, forced herself to think about what had happened only ten minutes ago. Kat practically sprawled across her husband, their two faces mashed together.

"I want you out of here," Ellie said. "Now."

Kat stared up at her with naked fear, but rather than evoking pity this time, it only hardened her resolve.

"I mean it," she said. "You couldn't have hurt me any worse."

Her bottom lip quivered. Ellie'd never seen her look so small, so lost.

Kat sniffed, reached forward and tore off a strip of toilet paper. She blew her nose on it, and Ellie watched with satisfaction as it disintegrated in her hands.

"There's something I need to tell you," Kat said.

"You slept with my first husband too?"

Kat flinched, hung her head abjectly, and again Ellie felt a tug of sympathy. She struggled against it, but it was there and for the time being ineffaceable.

Kat ripped off a longer strip of toilet paper, but the result was no better this time. As she swabbed her eyes with it, the white tissue balled into messy fragments and clung to her eyelashes, her nose.

Ellie sighed. "Oh, for chrissakes, here." She grabbed a towel and shoved it into Kat's trembling hands. Her sister gave her a grateful look and began cleaning her face.

"I suppose you hate me," Kat said, "and I don't blame you at all. In fact, I'd hate me too."

Ellie remained silent, a hollow weariness taking hold.

"I told you about the fight I had with Roland the night of your wedding," Kat said. "I told you it was about Chris looking good in his tux, but that was only part of the truth."

"Do I wanna hear this?"

"Something happened at the reception."

"You threw yourself at Chris."

"It wasn't Chris," she answered. "It was his aunt."

Ellie felt a stirring of dread.

Kat exhaled a shuddering breath, stared down at the towel in her lap. "I was standing at the bar waiting for a drink. I felt someone staring at me – you ever have that happen? Where you can feel someone watching you?"

Ellie waited.

"It was a beautiful woman. Gorgeous face, these old-fashioned red ringlets."

Ellie's heart thundered. *Oh my God. Please stop.*

"She had pale skin, the kind the Victorian romance novels would've called 'porcelain.'"

Ellie didn't think she could support her own weight much longer, so she slouched on the edge of the sink.

Kat didn't seem to notice. "The woman was staring at me, I could tell that even before I turned to look at her, and what was more – what scared the hell out of me – is that my body reacted to her in a way I'd never experienced before. I was...aching."

Ellie had a fleeting thought of the scratches on Chris's back, but her sister was going on.

"I faced her, and the woman staring back at me took my breath away." Kat glanced up at her. "I mean it, Ellie, no matter how cliché it sounds. I couldn't breathe. I realised I was also perilously close to having my first orgasm in years, and the woman hadn't done anything but look at me."

Kat blew out shaky breath. "Then she got off her barstool and walked away.

"I thought that was the end of it, but later, when I went to the bathroom, I had the same feeling as before. It was one of those single-toilet bathrooms, and I'd locked the door. I was reapplying my lipstick when the door opened.

"That couldn't be right, I thought, because I'd been sure to lock it, but it was swinging open, and what was more, I smelled a woman's perfume."

Ellie closed her eyes. "Then what happened?"

Kat was quiet a moment longer. Then, her voice scarcely above a whisper, she said, "I thought it was strange that a woman so young would wear an old-lady perfume, and when she appeared behind me in the mirror, I saw something even stranger. I hadn't noticed it before, but she was wearing the same red gown Chris's aunt had worn at the wedding. I just had time to make the connection before the woman reached around and began massaging my breasts."

Ellie fluttered a hand. "Kat, please, I don't—"

"*I have to*," she said, eyes fierce and pleading.

Ellie closed her mouth, but her heart throbbed harder.

Kat said, "I've never been attracted to women before. I swear to God. Even in college, when my roommate wanted to experiment a little...you know, kiss and all that...I never had any interest."

Kat stared down at the towel she was clutching. "But when I felt those fingers touch my nipples...then move lower, lifting my dress...I turned and let her...put her mouth on me."

Despite herself, Ellie saw the scene playing out in her mind. She felt a little sick, and beneath that was an undercurrent of fatalistic doom.

"I held the dress up around my belly while she...did what she was doing to me, but it had only gone on a couple minutes or so when I felt her tongue stop, her mouth pulling away. I was disappointed – I'll admit it – and a little confused, but what happened next was the biggest shock of my life."

Kat's voice lowered to a whisper. "The woman bit me."

Ellie's mouth fell open.

"Slightly to the right of my...you know, where the leg begins. I felt this incredible pain. I looked down and saw her face writhing, the tongue lapping up the blood pouring into her mouth...her teeth, lips, stained red..." Kat closed her eyes, shuddered. "She was feasting on me, El. I understood even then that this was why she'd come onto me, why she'd picked me out at the bar. I've had dreams of her ever since. Especially in the last year or so."

Ellie started. "Do you remember when the nightmares... accelerated?"

"Like I said, about a year—"

"*Do you remember the date?*" Ellie nearly shouted.

Kat drew back. "El, why would I—"

Ellie took her by the shoulder. "Was it when Lillith died?"

Kat's expression remained confused a moment. Then a slow fog of horror seeped into her features. "Yes," she said.

Ellie went to the sink, turned on the water and splashed some on her face. When she'd done this, she stared at her dripping skin in the vanity. "You said the woman appeared behind you in the mirror."

"So?"

"She cast a reflection."

For a moment, the sarcastic Kat she'd always known flickered. "Oh for God's sake, this isn't some silly vampire movie."

"But that's what we're talking about, isn't it? Vampirism?"

"Ellie—"

"She drank from your femoral artery. You said so yourself."

"I know what I said." Kat made a face. "But vampires, Ellie? Really?"

"Call it what you want. Regardless, we have to find a way out of here."

The faintest of smiles played on Kat's lips. "What, you think we're being held against our will?"

"I do."

Kat's grin turned rueful. "Nothing is stopping us, El. It hasn't rained in days, I'm sure the creek is down. Let's go now."

Ellie shook her head. "I can't." She opened her mouth to say more, but the memory of the stomach agony stopped her.

"What do you mean, you can't?"

Ellie thought it over, chose her words carefully, "Maybe it'll let you."

Kat's eyebrows rose. "It?"

"Whatever you want to call it. The forest, Chris. Aunt Lillith."

Kat drew back. "You think he'd try to stop us?"

"You're leaving tonight to get help."

"For what? There hasn't been a crime, El. Am I supposed to tell the sheriff we're worried about a dead woman coming back to life and drinking our blood?"

Ellie felt herself careening toward panic. "I don't care what you tell him, I just want you to get him here. He'll be able to notify the doctor, get someone out here to take care of me."

"Shouldn't I just go to the doctor directly?"

Ellie thought it over. Then she said in a quiet voice, "I'm afraid Chris would...hurt him."

"Ellie," Kat said, a look of disbelief furrowing her brow, "he's your husband, not a killer. I know he's been doing unusual things lately, but he's still the same person."

"Were you the same person a few minutes ago?"

Kat recoiled as though she'd been slapped. "You know that wasn't like me."

"It wasn't like Chris either."

Kat's mouth worked. "God, I'm sorry, Ellie. I never—"

"We don't have time for that," Ellie said. "You've gotta get help."

And when Kat's eyes finally locked on hers, her sister's face gained back some of the steel to which Ellie had grown accustomed.

"Okay," she said. "Tell me what to do."

Ellie returned her gaze a moment, then shook her head and looked away. "I don't know what to do. But I have an idea where we might start."

* * *

When Kat beheld the picture of Lillith, she didn't speak for a long time. What Ellie first mistook for uncertainty, she soon realised was dread.

"She's been in my dreams," Kat said, "haunting me since that night at the reception."

They sat on five-gallon buckets in the garage, rummaging through boxes of Lillith's things. They'd found an old Coleman lantern buried under a half-disintegrated tarp. Amazingly, the lantern worked, but they kept the light dim. Ellie had an idea if Chris knew they were out here, these boxes would disappear the way the box of videotapes had.

Kat couldn't stop staring at a leather-bound album from Lillith's childhood. The edges of the paper were gilded with dark gold, the spine burnished to a dull shine despite the album's age. Ellie was eager for her sister to move on to help her find something of use, but she suspected this was a kind of therapy for Kat, a struggle to understand the most uncanny experience of her life. Staring at her sister's knitted brow, something occurred to her.

"How did it end?"

"How did what end?" Kat asked absently.

"The...incident in the bathroom."

"It's hazy, El. I have a hard time remembering..."

"Did she say anything?"

Kat cocked an eyebrow. "She was too busy doing other things."

"So...she just left?"

"There was one more thing." Kat cleared her throat, and this time it wasn't pain in her voice, but deep embarrassment. "She wanted me to do to her what she'd done to me."

Ellie held her breath. "Did you?"

Kat was silent a moment, her head down. "You mean the... pleasuring? Or the drinking of blood?"

"I don't know," Ellie said. "Both, I guess."

Without looking up, Kat nodded. "She opened her leg with a fingernail."

Unable to say anything to that, Ellie pretended to be absorbed in the notebook. But try as she might, she couldn't get the image of her sister kneeling before the woman from the forest, the younger Lillith. The vision made her both queasy and sad, the big sister she'd always idolised debased by a creature that defied human logic.

She imagined Kat sucking at the creature's femoral artery, and a question arose. "Did drinking her blood...change you?"

Kat gave her a wan smile. "You mean other than the insomnia?"

"A thirst for blood."

"Christ, Ellie."

"Well?"

"Did she cast a reflection, did I transform into some blood-sucking ghoul?" Kat closed the album with a thump. "For God's sakes, El, why don't you drive a stake through my heart to make sure I'm human?"

Ellie sighed, stared dejectedly at a box of books she'd opened but hadn't yet been through. Her sister ambled out of the faint circle of light cast by the lantern, but Ellie hardly noticed. One of the titles had caught her eye, both the words and the cheap appearance of the book setting it apart from the rest. She slid it out and read *LIBIDINEM*.

Beneath that: *THE LUST.*

"I think we've got something," she said.

Kat's voice from the darkness, not a question: "What."

Ellie didn't bother answering, opened the book to the table of contents and made a silent wish that the thing would be in English rather than Latin or whatever the hell language the title was in.

Ellie scanned the chapter names, evidently made with a typewriter and then photocopied:

Preparation and Purification

First Death and Thirst

Second Death and Sacrifice

Third Death and Duality (Remnant and Ether)

Unification and the Demonic

Ellie read and reread the chapter names, but her eyes were repeatedly drawn to the word "Remnant."

She opened to that chapter and began reading.

Another minute went by before Kat said, "What's wrong?"

Ellie looked at her. In a voice that shook, she said, "You have to leave this place."

*   *   *

On the way through the yard, Katherine stopped and stared at her sister. "This is crazy."

Ellie's jaw went firm, the way it always used to when she was digging in for an argument. "It's the only way."

Dammit, Ellie, Katherine thought. *Is this our salvation or my penance?* Katherine gestured toward the trees lining the forest, the inky canvas of sky above them. "Why does it have to be now, in the dark? Why can't I just wait till morning?"

"Chris will stop us in the morning. It has to be now."

Katherine glanced at the carving knife. It felt ridiculous in her hand. "What if he catches me?"

One corner of Ellie's mouth curved. "You said yourself, he's not dangerous."

"But you don't believe that."

The humor drained from Ellie's eyes. "Explain the keys."

Katherine didn't have an answer for that. The keys to her Jeep had inexplicably vanished, and she didn't carry a spare. She turned toward the lane and shivered. "What're you gonna do?"

"Read more of Destragis's book, I guess."

"You really think that'll help?"

"I don't know if anything will help."

Katherine drew in a deep breath, took a step toward the lane.

Turned back to Ellie. "You sure you can't come?"

Ellie's Adam's apple bobbed and her eyes lowered. "I can't."

Katherine opened her mouth, but Ellie said, "Something will happen to my baby."

She felt a thickness in her throat at the desperation in Ellie's voice.

"The forest won't let us leave," Ellie went on. She ran a trembling hand over her tummy. "I've almost lost her so many times already."

Katherine smiled despite herself. "Is that what you think you're having? A little girl?"

The hope in Ellie's smile did it, got her moving. Walking backward toward the lane, Katherine said, "If Chris comes back, tell him I'm ashamed of myself for what I did. Tell him I went to the woods to cry about it."

The last thing Katherine saw before turning and stepping onto the lane was a flicker of pain on her sister's face.

I'm sorry, she thought as the woods closed in around her. *I'm so sorry for hurting you, Ellie.*

CHAPTER FOUR

Katherine climbed over seven fallen trees before she stopped counting. Most of them appeared perfectly healthy – towering, robust trees that had no business lying across the lane like slain giants. And though they were a hindrance, she hadn't yet experienced any of the physical pain to which her sister had alluded.

Maybe it only works on pregnant women, she thought.

More than once Katherine had considered veering off the trail and trying her luck in the forest, but one thing stopped her from attempting it.

The woods had closed in.

At first she'd attributed the notion to the blackness of the night, then to faulty memory. The idea that these trees, all this green life could *move*, could shift bodily like tectonic plates was absurd. She told herself she'd been too absorbed with seeing her sister again – seeing Chris again – during her arrival here to truly mark the distance between lane and forest.

But there sure as hell hadn't been branches reaching across the wheel ruts.

In fact, the groping boughs so crowded the lane that Katherine had to keep to the grassy median to avoid being scratched. A few times her shoulders and thighs had brushed against the silent leaves, and as this contact occurred she could not escape the sensation of microscopic movement within the pale green veins. Whenever she climbed over a fallen tree, she did so in a breathless scramble because the bark under her palms felt as though it were squirming, rubbing itself against her skin with feverish longing.

Keep moving, she told herself. *Don't give the woods any more time to work against you. Pretty soon the whole lane might be swallowed up.*

She attempted a smile, but it faded quickly. The idea didn't seem at all farfetched. Just what would she do if the lane suddenly disappeared? If she found herself surrounded by unbroken wilderness?

No way in hell, she thought, her steps quickening. *No way I'm gonna let that happen.*

She carried the flashlight like a baton, and though her fingers itched to click it on, the idea of Chris spotting it and running her down prevented her from using it.

You're speedwalking down the middle of the freaking lane, a voice reminded her. *You obviously aren't too worried about being inconspicuous.*

Still, she felt safer in the dark.

The swath of lane curved, and ahead Katherine spotted a gap. She'd reached the bridge.

Beyond it, where her Jeep and the Camry had been, there was only that same narrow swath of lane. Had Chris moved the vehicles? Had the forest? She stifled an insane urge to laugh.

She forced herself to maintain a steady pace. If she broke into a run, she might be heard. Though she knew this also made little sense, she believed it just the same.

Katherine focused all her will on the black place where the bridge had once been. If she stayed focused, remained intent on her goal, she'd be there soon.

Yes. She grinned as the distance shrank. It was heartening to feel some of her old composure return. *Stay strong*, she thought, *and you can make this work.*

Unlike your marriage.

Katherine walked faster, kept her body aimed at the washed-out bridge.

You also failed as an older sister, don't forget that either.

Katherine's breathing became ragged.

You wanted him, Katherine, you wanted him so much that you mounted him in your sister's bed.

Shut up! she thought angrily. *Just shut the hell—*

You still want him, don't you? You want him to carry you off to that place in the woods, the high place, the altar.

I don't know of any altar!

But you do, Katherine. You do. And you'll go there soon enough, willingly. You'll spread yourself for him and feel his hot strength pushing inside you.

"*No!*" she shouted, then flung out her hands for balance. She'd reached the verge of the drop-off, had nearly tumbled over it and landed in the shallow creek. She whipped her head from side to side, eyes darting about for

Him

some movement, some sign of

Chris

who was following her, who was about to clutch her shoulders with bony fingers.

"Oh, this is crazy," she muttered and started down the steep decline. The water had been up to her thighs upon arriving, and according to Chris, that had been just after the storms. The creek shouldn't be above her knees now, and she'd cross it without problem. Katherine staggered, flailed her arms until she regained balance, then took the last few steps to the muddy bank.

She stared at the black water. The oppressive odour wafting up from it made her think of dead things. Here and there tiny glimmers played over its gently flowing surface, but despite its probable shallowness, she couldn't see the bottom. She stretched out a foot to test the water, but drew it back, not wanting to get her tennis shoes wet. But she didn't want to take the time to shed them and her socks either, so that meant she'd have to slop through the creek and spend the rest of the evening with wet feet. She sighed. There were worse things in life.

Katherine's breath caught as she remembered her phone. The idea had been to make it to the road and then walk toward town until she got a signal, but what if she could get one now? There were clouds, but no storm was imminent. Perhaps, she thought as she extricated the phone from her jeans pocket, she wouldn't even have to get wet.

Kat powered on the phone and felt her heart sink.

No signal.

In fact, there was hardly any battery left, which couldn't be right. She'd charged the damn thing this afternoon. How could it already be...

The forest won't let us leave, she remembered Ellie whispering.

Ridiculous.

As ridiculous as you performing cunnilingus on a ghost?

Touché, she thought. She cleared her throat, crammed the phone into her pocket. Then, without allowing herself time to reconsider, she stepped into the creek. The mud squished beneath her sneaker, conjured images of cattle pens and rank manure. Katherine blocked it out, took another step. Keeping her shoes on had definitely been a smart move. Even though the icy feeling of the creek soaking her socks was a bit startling, it was a small price to pay for preventing that runny, sucking mud from squirting around her bare toes.

Katherine took another step and felt the ground drop away.

Her strangled cry was cut short by the engulfing water, the *freezing* water that dragged her lower and lower in its virulent undertow, pressing against her lips, stealing her breath. She thrashed her arms, her mind a frenzy of confusion and terror, but a bump against her toes superceded all. Katherine flailed her hands at whatever had touched her foot, but instead of raking her fingers over a leering goblin face, her nails scraped painfully on stone. It was a ledge, she realised with frantic hope. She hoisted herself onto it, felt the top of her head breach the surface, and then she was thrusting her face up, spluttering and gasping. She lurched forward into the shallow water, only a couple feet deep here, and continued coughing out the nasty creek water until her breathing regained something approaching normalcy.

Her chest heaved, but the panic was dissipating. In moments she'd made it. She leaned against the nearly vertical bank, stared down at the sable water, and wondered if Chris had known the deep place was there. Maybe he'd purposely not mentioned it, had counted on it as a snare for her or Ellie should they attempt escape.

Yes, she realised, with new uneasiness. It *was* escape. Before, moving furtively down the diminished lane, she'd felt like an ornery teenager tiptoeing past her parents' room to sneak out for some boy and a session of harmless kissing. She'd been scared, yes, but not for her mortality – simply of being found out.

Now though...now, as she took in the trees milling impatiently on the opposite bank, the coarse leaves scraping like the flesh of carnivorous reptiles, she felt as if her momentary plunge into the freezing abyss had been her one warning. *We're not fucking around,* the trees seemed to rasp. *You try to leave again, you won't like what we'll do to your sister or her baby.*

Despite the steepness of the bank, she clambered to the top and resumed her trek down the lane. She noted without surprise how suffocatingly near the branches were the farther she went, as though the very forest had drawn in on itself while she was in the water.

It won't stop me, she thought. *In a minute or two I'll be out on the road, and soon after that I'll finally get reception on my—*

She froze.

Her phone had gone under water.

A caul of doom swooping over her, she patted her pockets until she found the one with the cell. She shoved a hand inside, wiggling a little to fight the damp denim.

With a grunt she tore it free and pushed the power button.

Its face was black.

No!

With a palsied hand, she thumbed the *Send* button, squeezed the phone until it was near breaking.

"*No, no, no, no, no...*"

She uttered a small cry of relief when the picture of Jacob, her youngest, appeared, his innocent smile a much-needed elixir for the darkness around her. Just to be sure, she pushed a couple buttons, and when they worked the way they were supposed to, she blew out pent-up air.

Still working, then. But for how long?

The battery, she saw, was nearly dead, would go dead any minute. She bit her lip, debating. Shutting it off might save the battery, but it might prevent her from turning the damn thing on again. One thing was certain, though. She couldn't put it back in her pocket; her jeans were so wet it'd be like submerging it a second time.

She clutched the phone and gazed up at a gnarled old sycamore. The tenebrous knots peppering its white face gave it a wicked, leering appearance. *Are you going to do to me what you did to my sister?* she wondered. *Tear my insides apart?*

A rush of hatred swept through her. *Damn you,* she thought as she glowered at the tree. *Damn you for hurting my Ellie. And damn you for trying to hurt her baby. It's the only thing she has, and I won't let you take it from her.*

A breeze worried the sycamore, and in the stygian gloom the tree appeared to nod.

It got her moving again. She remembered the creek being very close to the road, and within a minute she was stunned to spot the end of the lane, the gravel road beyond.

Of course, the thin swath leading there was scarcely wide enough for her to navigate without turning sideways. But that didn't matter. Had she waited another day − hell, another hour even − she might not have made it. Thus far none of the branches had lashed her skin, but she no longer considered the possibility so farfetched. There was unquestionably a presence here in the forest, a malevolent will. She wasn't meant to leave.

Katherine started to jog.

The end of the lane was only fifty or sixty yards away, and though she remembered there being woods on both sides of County Road 1200, she was sure passage there wouldn't be as claustrophobic as it was here.

Getting closer.

Her pumping elbows brushed leaves, a wiry branch or two, but nothing more impeded her.

Almost there.

A black certainty exploded within her, that Chris had bided his time here at the edge of the lane, that he would step into her path at the last moment and drag her screaming into the woods.

Katherine burst onto the gravel road, veered right and did not stop, so sure was she that Chris would appear.

But he didn't. Other than the dusty stones under her sneakers and the rusted barbwire fence flanking the road, there was no indication that *anyone* else resided out here, as though this place were still part of a primordial world from millennia past. She shot a glance upward and saw an only slightly wider strip of sky attending her steps. Still, it was better than the suffocating canopy covering the lane.

A stitch started in her side. She experienced a moment's misgiving. *Was it the forest?*

Take it easy, she told herself. *It's the sprinting that's making your insides ache, not some supernatural curse. Just take it easy and walk awhile. You're safe now.*

God, how she wanted to believe that. But how could she with the haunted forest still lurking to her right? She wasn't remotely safe yet, and she knew it.

Abruptly, she remembered the phone in her hand.

She activated it. Her hands shook in desperation when the screen remained black. Had she turned it off?

No. She hadn't.

Dead, it's dead.

No. She thumbed the circular button but nothing happened.

Impossible!

Not impossible – completely logical. You got it wet and it's dead.

"*Please*," she muttered, mashing her thumb on the button.

Or something else *sucked the battery dead, sucked it like blood from an artery.*

She uttered a harsh sob.

Dead, Katherine. Just like you're gonna be.

"No," she growled and, whirling, held up the dead phone to the trees. "This won't stop me, you hear? *This won't stop me!*"

And though the forest remained silent, Katherine's skin rippled with gooseflesh. It was a mistake to provoke the presence. She suddenly felt very naked, very small.

Hugging herself, she cast a glance down the gravel road. Town was how many miles away? Twelve? Fifteen? She'd have to walk for hours to reach it.

Then she saw it. About a mile down, maybe farther, on the left-hand side.

A security light.

A kindly farmer maybe, or a reclusive old woman. It didn't matter. There'd be a phone there, and a phone would mean salvation.

Ellie's salvation.

Keeping as far away from the estate as she could, Katherine started down the road toward the light.

* * *

Sitting at Chris's office desk, Ellie pored over the "Remnant" chapter again. In a way, she almost wanted him to discover her here, wanted him to know she understood, at least in part, what was happening to them.

The spirit who seeks transference from demonic infancy to demonic maturity, after preparing his table, must exist in two forms during his purgatorial state. One form is non-corporeal, the other corporeal. However, each shall take on characteristics of the other.

Ellie read the paragraph again and tried to keep her eyes from crossing. When she thought she had the sense of it, she slogged on:

The non-corporeal shall at times, given the proper mindset and power of will, discover the ability to manifest itself in physical form. Though this body will be a primarily disincorporated entity, it will, when necessary, become tangible. Such times may coincide with certain dates of the calendar, moments of agricultural importance, the moon and sundry other factors. The end result is an ability to effect a change in the human world, sexual or otherwise.

Ellie's heartbeat quickened as she remembered Katherine and the red-haired woman.

Acid boiling in her throat, she continued:

The corporeal self shall satisfy two requirements only: that the chosen vessel's life should cover the interim between third death and final birth.

Final birth, Ellie thought. What a disturbing phrase that was. It was the next sentence, however, that chilled her to the marrow:

The second requirement involves the symbiotic transfusion of the life-blood. Should either aspect of this transfusion be neglected, the remnant shall be trapped in his purgatorial state eternally.

She thought of her sister's words: *The woman bit me.*

Did that mean that Kat was Lillith's *vessel*? My God, it was all so outlandish. Demons and vampires and dual existence and a dozen other things that flouted what she knew of the world, what she'd scoffed at in movies and books.

If it's so outlandish, Ellie, why are you frightened?

Shutting her mind against it, she forced herself to continue.

Once infected with The Lust, the vessel must either complete the cycle and midwife the demon into final birth or be destroyed for breaking the covenant. The latter course of action, of course, must be avoided at all costs due to its impact on the waiting spirit.

Ellie put the book down. The skin of her hands felt greasy and befouled, acrawl with some terrible, unseen rash. The walls seemed to close in on her, animated by the same diabolical impulse controlling the forest. She suddenly wanted to be anywhere but in this office, but a new urge stopped her from fleeing.

Her eyes slid down the cherry surface of the desk and came to rest on the bottom right drawer.

Chris's manuscript.

When she lifted out the bundle of pages and placed them before her in a neat white pile, she steeled herself against whatever she might find.

But when she saw what was on the first page, Ellie knew her defences were useless.

*   *   *

The house was much larger than Katherine originally thought. A dark colour she couldn't make out, New England saltbox-style architecture. Behind it hulked a huge barn with a name spelled out in the roof shingles. Though the clouds had scattered somewhat, it was still difficult to see, the security light leaning over the road providing most of the illumination. As Katherine crossed the yard toward the house, she screwed up her eyes to make out the name on the barn.

WOLF, she finally saw.

Not particularly reassuring.

She jogged up the steps, reached out, pushed the illuminated doorbell.

She cringed, hunched her shoulders at the exaggerated ding-dong that reverberated from within. She didn't know how late it was, but it had to be well past midnight. Whoever answered the door — assuming someone eventually did — wouldn't be happy.

That was fine. Anger she could live with. It wasn't like she was seeking a long-term relationship here. She just needed to borrow their phone for a minute. Hell, she could even wait out here for the cops to pick her up, though she greatly preferred the safety of a house.

Katherine peered at the woods across the road and shivered.

She was reaching out to try the doorbell again when heavy footfalls sounded from within. A moment later, the porch light spilled a harsh halogen glow over her, and the inner door creaked open.

A broad man with a long red beard regarded her with unconcealed suspicion.

"You break down?" he asked.

"No," she said. "I don't...have a car."

"Don't have a car?" the man repeated. "How'd you get all the way out here?"

She cast a glance back at the road, turned to regard the man, whose doubtful eyes never wavered. She shook her head to clear it, sought for the words she needed, but the chill of the night air, the stillness of the country conspired to keep her mute.

"You a friend of the Cranes?" the man ventured.

Katherine opened her mouth in surprise and nodded. "Yes. Yes, I am. I'm Ellie's sister."

She thought that might thaw the man's glacial stare, but the hardness in his eyes only intensified. "I'm not sure I want to help you," he said.

Katherine stood speechless.

The man's eyes flitted higher, his steely gaze taking in the forest across the road, as if he too expected it to attack.

"It's my sister. She's pregnant."

"I know," he said distractedly.

"She needs help," Katherine pushed on. "There's something... wrong with her husband."

The man seemed to notice her again. "Like what?"

"He's..." She shook her head, bemused. "He's changing. For the worse, I mean. He's holding Ellie prisoner out here, he won't let her leave, won't let her see a doctor even. He..." Katherine swallowed, a dry clicking sound in her throat.

The man nodded over his shoulder. "You better come in." He stepped back to allow her passage, but his body went rigid. He put out his arm, barring her way. In a tight voice, he asked, "Have you been bitten?"

Katherine thought of Ellie's wedding, the woman in the bathroom.

"No," she lied. "I haven't been bitten."

The man turned. "We better call Bruder." He spoke in hushed tones as he moved past a staircase and into the kitchen. "He doesn't work nights, but his deputies are too green to do us much good."

She stopped just inside the kitchen, noticing how modern it was. From the man's appearance she'd assumed the place would be filled with butter churns and wooden washboards.

He dialled a number, waited, and soon began explaining the situation. He listened, said thanks, and hung up.

Katherine watched him approach with wide eyes.

"Bruder'll be here in a few minutes," the man said. "I woke up his dogs, so he'll be in a sour mood."

"Thanks, Mister..."

"Wolf," the man said. He took her gently by the shoulder and led her over to a chunky wooden table. From somewhere came the soothing smell of cinnamon potpourri.

"Name's Aaron," he said and pulled out a chair for her. "It's a good thing my wife's a heavy sleeper," he said as he sat next to her.

"I'm sorry for bothering you, Aaron. I didn't know where else..."

"It's fine," he said, and for the first time he smiled. If not for the long red beard, he would have been very handsome. Even with the chin whiskers, she found him ruggedly attractive. "My Anna wouldn't wake up for the rapture, but she still insists on running the box fan and a sound machine to make sure nothing disturbs her beauty rest."

She returned his smile, told him her name. "I can't tell you how much I appreciate your helping me."

"Least I could do."

She hooked a thumb at the ceiling. "You probably have kids sleeping up there."

He sat forward. "How old do you think I am, Katherine?"

It was difficult to tell in this light, but she made an honest guess: "Early forties?"

His smile was pleased. "I'm sixty-two this August."

"You've taken good care of yourself."

Aaron gave a little shrug and dropped his eyes humbly, but a moment later his expression grew troubled. "Has your sister or her husband said anything about a man named Daniel Wolf lately?"

She shook her head. "You're related to him?"

"My kid brother," he said. "He went missing several days ago. Bruder said he's spoken to most of the neighbours, but I thought..." He trailed off, frowning. "What about someone named Campbell?"

Katherine shook her head.

He opened his mouth as if to ask her something else, but he was interrupted by the doorbell. They stared at each other a moment.

Katherine asked, "The sheriff?"

Staring in the direction of the door, Aaron shook his head vaguely. "He wouldn't have gotten here so fast."

He glanced at her, and she saw her fears confirmed in his narrowed eyes.

"Wait here," he said.

Before she could protest, he'd risen and moved through the kitchen. She sat at the table and listened.

A door opening. A muffled question.

Chris's voice.

Don't let him in! she thought.

Aaron's deep voice, firm.

Chris's voice, equally loud. The two of them arguing now.

She gnawed on a thumbnail, glanced out the window over the sink. If Chris did something to Aaron, could she escape through that?

She cast about for a better escape route and found it, just a few feet beyond the table and to the left: sliding glass doors. Probably leading to a deck. She peered through the glass and felt her stomach lurch.

A naked woman stood on the deck watching her.

The woman from the bathroom. Oh Jesus.

Katherine stood on legs she couldn't feel. She tried to look away, but those big, avid eyes transfixed her. The woman's red ringlets spilled over her pale shoulders, her beauty so profound it made Katherine ache, and now the woman was grinning, and Katherine saw the elongated canines, the ancient hunger in the woman's expression.

Katherine barely heard the livid voices echoing down the hall, didn't care that Chris was dangerous, perhaps had already threatened

Aaron Wolf. She had to escape that knowing gaze, that radiant lust. She was appalled to find she was aroused by the sight of the woman, could not prevent her eyes from crawling down the pallid skin, from lingering on the fiery thatch of pubic hair. She gasped as her back struck the doorjamb and felt a sudden flare of anger when the woman's hungry grin widened.

Katherine fled down the hall, toward the voices. She saw that Aaron had stepped onto the porch, was arguing with Chris there. She hated going outside, where the woman could move around the house and enfold her in those chalky white arms, but she feared being alone even more. She moved through the doorway in time to see Chris poking Aaron's chest with an index finger, angrily driving home a point. Aaron's face was down as though he was trying to control his temper.

Chris noticed her and seemed to forget Aaron. "*There* you are," he said, taking a step forward. "We were scared to death something happened to you."

"I'm fine," she said to Chris, but when he put his arm out to lead her toward his car, she stiffened. "Something frightened me at the house, so I had Mr. Wolf call the sheriff."

A look of naked ferocity flitted across Chris's face, but he replaced it quickly with unconvincing concern. "Why didn't you tell me about it? I'd have—"

"You weren't there," she interrupted. "You took off after what happened with Ellie."

Chris smiled nervously, his eyes darting between her and Wolf. "That was a misunderstanding," he said, and endeavoured again to lead her toward the Camry.

When she wrenched her shoulder from his grip, Wolf stepped between them. "Let's just wait for the sheriff."

Chris's easy manner vanished. He moved chest to chest with Wolf. She cast a desperate glance down the road, but so far there was no sign of Bruder.

Chris stared down at the man's averted face. "This has nothing to do with you, Aaron. Now get the fuck out of my way."

Wolf looked embarrassed, but he didn't back away. "Surely you don't mind your sister-in-law talking to the sheriff, do you?"

Chris pushed past Wolf and seized her arm. "I've had enough of this shit," he said and started dragging her toward the car.

"Let her go," she heard Wolf say, and when she turned, she saw the Amish man's hand on Chris's shoulder. Before she knew what was happening, Chris wheeled with a balled fist and smashed Wolf in the face. As he followed through, he let go of Katherine. She lost her balance and landed awkwardly on the lawn, one wrist pinned beneath her hip. Gasping, she flopped onto her back and saw Chris swing again. This time Wolf took the blow in the shoulder and swung hard at Chris's mid-section. She watched in satisfaction as Chris doubled over, a look of comic surprise on his face.

As she made to rise, she heard Wolf saying, "That's enough, Mr. Crane. This doesn't need—"

But Chris pounced before the man could finish. Then they were brawling, Chris aiming wild blows at Wolf's face, the older man patiently absorbing them and jabbing at Chris when he could. One of these jabs snapped Chris's head backward, his jaws clicking together. Then Wolf came out of his defensive posture, swung a looping fist and connected with the side of Chris's face.

Chris grunted and went down.

"Now, that's enough," Wolf said, panting. "I don't like to fight, and you don't need whipped any worse."

Chris rolled onto all fours and launched himself at Wolf, who met his face with a knee. The impact was wet and meaty and made Katherine's gorge rise. *Broken nose*, she thought vaguely, but something to her right scattered the thought.

Headlights.

She staggered toward the road, for a moment certain it was not the sheriff, but rather some factory worker heading home after third shift. Then she spied the sleek line of lights mounted atop the car and moaned in relief. Behind her she heard the men scuffling, but that wouldn't matter anymore. The sheriff would have a gun, even if he was off-duty, and Chris wouldn't be able to argue with that.

In moments the cruiser was crunching to a halt on the shoulder. The man who emerged was handsome and well built, but Katherine didn't allow herself time to linger on his looks. "It's Chris," she said. "He's lost his mind."

The sheriff was nodding, his eyes kind and composed. He put a steadying hand on her shoulder. "We'll get Mr. Crane the help he needs, but for now I need you to have a seat inside the car."

She nodded, allowed him to lead her to the passenger's door, which he opened. She got in and smiled gratefully up at him before he shut the door and strode across the lawn. Chris lay on his back, Wolf standing over him as though the older man had just delivered a knockout blow. The windows were closed, so she couldn't make out what the sheriff said, but whatever it was brought a weary grin to Wolf's face. Then Bruder was helping Chris to his feet and leading him toward the cruiser. Thus far, she noted with some misgiving, the sheriff hadn't used handcuffs to restrain him.

Mistake, she had time to think before the back door opened.

* * *

The only sound of which Ellie was aware was the distant drone of cicadas. Her saliva tasted like blood; her breathing had slowed to an occasional, quavering sip of air. She stared at the front page of the 'novel' her husband had been writing, which she now realised wasn't just a work of fiction.

It was a suicide letter.

Yet it didn't just chronicle Chris's death – it encompassed their entire time here. More, it told their story through a perverse revisionist lens that transformed Ellie into a monster. Verbally and emotionally abusing her husband. Murdering a dog. Even threatening an abortion if Chris didn't do her bidding.

Ellie cast a glance outside the office window. Her legs itched to make a run for it, but she'd learned her lesson. There was no escaping this place. And though she now feared her husband more than ever, she felt for the first time she was truly grasping the enormity of the power these woods possessed.

Again, Ellie read those terrible opening paragraphs:

I am sorry for what's happened. I wish I could have been strong enough to save us, but I wasn't.

When we came here I didn't know what the isolation would do to Ellie. I didn't understand how important it was for her to remain in contact with the world. Had she maintained healthy social relationships she never would have begun drinking and taking long rambles in the forest. Many nights I've wondered why she went out. After talking with Aaron Wolf, however, I understand that my wife, like Gordon Wolf's deceased wife Sarah, has fallen prey to the allure of the forest.

I believe Ellie intends to kill me and then herself, and in doing so, murder our child as well.

She leaned forward, elbows on the desk, and mashed her palms into her eyes, as if by the very act she could destroy the words imprinted in her memory. My God, did Chris even know what he'd written? She suspected not. She thought it far more likely that he really did see a story before him as he typed, perhaps one that was unrelated to the dreadful things contained in this neat stack of pages.

Her mouth a grim line, Ellie silently cursed this place.

With a sick, acrid burning in the back of her throat, Ellie turned to the final page of the manuscript.

Ellie's sister Katherine has proven to be a boon in all this turmoil. Ellie would have wanted Katherine to have everything, so please consider this our dying wish: that Katherine Chambers should inherit our house, the property, and all our worldly possessions.

Signed,

Chris and Ellie Crane

She read over the signatures again. Chris's, of course, was authentic since he himself had penned it. But Ellie's, too, was unmistakably her own despite the fact it couldn't be. She sat there numbly, both fascinated and appalled by the scope of this place's power.

Katherine had gone out to get help for her, but that had been how long ago? An hour and a half? Two hours? It was a long way to town, but surely in that time she'd have placed a call to the police, found a sympathetic driver to give her a ride.

No, more likely Chris had captured her, talked her into finishing what they'd begun in the bed.

Her lips twisted in contempt for her husband. He thought he was becoming the new Gerald Destragis, as though he and Katherine could recapture the old magic Gerald and Lillith had created.

But you're not part of the picture, she thought. *Somehow, Lillith means to get rid of you. And you're helping it happen.*

While Ellie was stuck here protecting a baby who'd never see the light of day.

She shut her eyes against the tide of sorrow flooding over her, a darkness so complete she felt like curling up in a ball and waiting for the end to come.

Ellie grew still.

Sucking in a breath, she realised there was indeed a way to prevent all of it — at least there *might* be. Without bothering to tidy the stack of pages her husband had typed, she grabbed the whole bundle, dropped it inside the drawer, and slammed the drawer shut.

I'm not dead yet, she thought. *And I'm sure as hell not going without a fight.*

Her eyes fierce, she slid the Destragis book in front of her and found where she'd left off.

★　　★　　★

As the cruiser gained speed, Chris said, "Take me home," in a voice Katherine thought strangely calm.

Bruder glanced at him in the overhead mirror. "You just attacked a man on his front lawn."

"You weren't there," Chris said. "It's my word against his."

Bruder nodded. "Aaron Wolf's as honest as they come."

"Because an Amish person would never lie, right?"

Bruder's lips formed a hard line. "That's got nothing to do with it, Mr. Crane. Now, it'd be best if you'd just calm down."

The forest crawled by, Bruder taking his time about getting them to town. Perhaps he wanted to conduct part of the interview here, see what he could learn about Chris's behaviour before they found themselves in one of those sterile, official-looking rooms, the kind of place that practically coaxed the words "I want a lawyer" out of a suspect's mouth.

"I need to see my wife," Chris said, his voice subdued.

"You'll see her soon," Bruder said, but he drew out the last word, his eyes narrowing at something in the rearview mirror.

Katherine fought off a new surge of fear.

"What is it?" she asked.

Bruder shook his head faintly. "Funny."

The cruiser crunched to a gradual halt.

"What?" she said, searching his face.

"That security light," he said, still staring into the rearview mirror. "The one in front of Aaron's house."

"What about it?"

"It just winked out."

Who cares? she wanted to scream. "That happens sometimes, right?"

Bruder's frown deepened. "Sure, it happens. But the timing's kinda odd, don't you think?"

"Better check on it," Chris said from the back.

Bruder gave him a hard look in the mirror. "I don't need help from you."

Chris grinned. "First Daniel, now Aaron."

This time Bruder turned in his seat. "What do you know about Daniel Wolf?"

"Only what Aaron told me, that he'd gone missing."

"Aaron didn't say anything about that," Katherine said, watching Chris's silhouette.

Chris shrugged. "Maybe I heard it somewhere else then."

Bruder eyed Chris a moment longer, then leaned forward and picked up the CB. He frowned, then tapped the handset on the steering wheel.

Katherine thought of her phone and felt her insides go queasy.

"Damndest thing," he said. "Just got new ones last fall."

The fear spread icy tendrils through her body. "Can't we just go? Please, Mr. Bruder?"

Bruder glanced at her, seemed about to speak, but Chris said, "I'd check on him if I were you."

Bruder gave Chris a sour look, but then he was sliding the cruiser into gear and cutting the wheel.

Katherine tensed. "You're not going back?"

As they completed the U-turn, Bruder said, "You've got nothing to fear from him," and nodded back at Chris. "Those doors only open from the outside."

It's not Chris I'm worried about, she wanted to say but knew she'd sound like a lunatic. *There's a woman back there, Sheriff Bruder. She's a vampire. You see, she drank my blood and I drank hers, so we know each other pretty well.*

They drew even with the farmhouse and stopped. Bruder killed the engine and opened his door.

She grabbed Bruder's arm with both hands. *"Please don't leave me here."*

He put a hand over hers. "You're totally safe, ma'am. I'll only be gone—"

"Let me come," she pleaded.

"I can't bring you with me," he said. "Besides, Aaron and Anna are probably fine. I just need to make sure."

Before she could protest further, he was gone. The slam of his door made her entire body vibrate. She stared out at the road, which was partially illuminated by the headlights. Ahead, less than a mile away, was the lane leading back to Ellie's.

She wished Bruder had faced the car in the opposite direction.

"We should've gone to your room," Chris said behind her.

For a moment, she had no idea what he was referring to, and when it came to her, she closed her eyes in guilt. *Just wait for Bruder,* she told herself. *He'll be back in a minute.* She watched the sheriff, who stood on the porch waiting for someone to let him in.

Chris said, "I thought for sure I'd have to make the first move, but damn, Katherine, I gotta hand it to you. Wanting it in your sister's bed...with your sister *in* it..."

She pushed hair out of her eyes, wondered how impregnable the Plexiglas barrier between them was, how reliable the locks on the back doors. She couldn't bring herself to glance at the man sitting behind her, a man she hardly recognised anymore. When Ellie had married him, he was lean, tall and baby-faced. And while he was obviously still tall, his size was an intimidating thing now, a threat. His neck and shoulders were broader, his arms thicker. His facial hair made him look more like a construction worker than a schoolteacher.

As if reading her thoughts, he said, "Afraid of me now, sweetie? What if I called you Kat the way Ellie does? Would that make us friends?"

Katherine turned and stared at the dark figure. She was grateful for the shadows obscuring his face. They blotted out the bloodshot eyes and the glaze of madness that had lately seeped into them.

"I think you need help," she said as evenly as she could. "I think this place has done bad things to you. Or..." She trailed off as his white teeth showed through his grin.

"Or brought the bad things out of me?"

She frowned at him. "I don't know, I—" But the words died on her lips as his door swung slowly open.

As though he hadn't noticed, he said, "You need to make a choice, Katherine. I've decided Ellie isn't in my future. You, on the other hand..."

He swung a foot over the edge of the opening and climbed out. She watched him round the back of the car. Then the shadows seemed to swallow him up. Nervously, she lunged toward the driver's door and hit the automatic locks. She knew he could still get in if he really wanted to, but it was better than nothing.

She saw that Bruder had taken the keys.

She cast a feverish glance at Aaron's door, but Bruder had apparently gone inside; the outer glass door was shut, but the wooden door within hung open. Should she warn Bruder of Chris's escape? And just how would she accomplish that?

Honk the horn, idiot!

With a cry of relief, she leaned over to do just that.

Then Bruder stepped out the front door.

She saw, even from this distance, how rigid his steps were, how unnatural his movements. When he drew closer to the cruiser, she realised why. His face had gone stark white, an expression of unutterable shock imprinted on his slack jaw, his gaping eyes. Numbly, she reached across the seat and unlocked his door.

Bruder opened it and slumped in the seat beside her.

"What is it?" she asked.

He looked at her, his eyes dead and glassy. "There's blood everywhere."

Katherine's breathing grew reed-thin.

"I've never seen..." He trailed off, stared at the dark dashboard. "Something got ahold of Aaron and his wife..." His voice weak and throaty. "...pieces of them all over the place." She glanced at Bruder's door, hanging wide open.

She opened her mouth to say something but it was too late, a huge shadow leaping at the sheriff, slamming him against her. She was driven against the passenger's door, the car suddenly filled with growling voices, the sounds of blows. The weight left her body, and she watched Chris drag Bruder by the collar out the open door into the road.

"*Mr. Crane*," Bruder was saying, but the gun Chris had wrested from him swooped up, pointed at his face.

"Shut your pretty mouth," Chris said.

His back to Katherine, Bruder put his hands up. "I don't want to die, Mr. Crane. Just tell me what you want."

Chris gave him a sly grin. "I only want to go home."

CHAPTER FIVE

They rolled away from Aaron's house in silence, Bruder locked in the back seat, Katherine riding next to Chris.

The gun in his left hand.

Bruder asked, "You have anything to do with what happened?"

Chris didn't respond.

"That bloodbath?" Bruder prompted.

Chris shook his head once. "I didn't do anything to those people."

Bruder's voice was edgy. "I know you didn't do it. You couldn't've because you were sitting back here. What I wanna know is, did you have anything do with it?"

The headlights illumined the narrow turnoff ahead. Without signalling, Chris swerved onto the lane. The cruiser was immediately besieged by branches as thick as baseball bats, palmate leaves that slapped the cruiser like abusive parents. The impacts were deafening, like they'd ventured into the world's roughest automatic carwash.

"*Jesus*," Bruder shouted, "*slow the hell down.*"

But Chris compelled the cruiser deeper into the jungle of boughs. Katherine had no idea how he knew where the path was. The antenna snapped off with a discordant twang. She threw up her hands as the windshield starred on her side. Bruder shouted and pounded on the Plexiglas barrier, but Chris drove on undeterred. She knew the washed-out bridge was coming up, and for a delirious moment she wondered if Chris would try to jump the gap like some suicidal daredevil.

The thought dissipated as, thankfully, the cruiser began to slow.

A sharp rap on the Plexiglas made her glance at Bruder, who was staring wide-eyed at the forest savaging his police car. "Would one of you tell me what the fuck is going on?"

Chris brought the cruiser to a halt, jerked it into park. Ahead, through the tangle of foliage, Katherine could just make out the opening that marked the creek. Somehow, Chris had stopped within ten feet of it.

"You hear?" Bruder demanded. "I want some answers, Crane. What the fuck is happening? This path didn't look like this before."

Under his breath, Chris said, "Plants grow."

"*Bullshit!*" Bruder shouted. "You took a different road or something, one I didn't know about."

"You don't believe that," Chris said in that same quiet voice.

"The hell I don't," Bruder said, but his voice broke on the last word. He'd huddled against the seatback, his face that of a young boy afraid of monsters. Katherine noted with a pang of real sympathy that he'd chosen the centremost point of the back seat, as though the forest couldn't reach him there.

For her part, she was more frightened of the man sitting next to her.

"Come on, dear," he said to her, a hand on her knee. He shut off the cruiser and pocketed the keys.

As Chris opened the door, Bruder's voice teetered on the verge of panic. "What are you gonna do? I've got a family at home, goddammit."

Chris climbed out, slammed the door.

Katherine and Bruder exchanged a frightened glance. His eyes white and wild, the sheriff looked like a caged animal back there.

Her door swung open.

"Out," was all Chris said.

She glanced again at the sheriff and saw tears streaming down his cheeks. It was pathetic and gut-wrenching, and she hated Chris for terrorising him. Bruder didn't deserve this. Whatever Chris had planned, Bruder didn't deserve it.

"My daughter's only three," Bruder was saying. "My son started little league this summer. I'm coaching his team..."

Chris gripped her wrist, hauled her up and out of the car.

"*...wife won't be able to do it by herself...*"

Sharp branches raked her face. Katherine covered her eyes with her free arm so she wouldn't lose an eye. Chris squeezed her wrist, the bones grinding together. She grimaced and asked, "Where're you taking me?"

No answer.

From inside the car: "*They'll know something happened to me,*" Bruder yelled, his voice rising. "*They'll lock you up for good if you don't let me go.*"

"What about the sheriff?" she cried out, but the slapping, ripping forest muffled her words.

Chris led her through a nasty thicket, and behind them Bruder screamed, "*You can't leave me here!*"

The crack of breaking glass rang out like a gunshot. Bruder let loose with an inarticulate wail. Then came the unearthly shriek of ripping metal, the ravenous branches puncturing the doors and roof. Katherine glanced back at the cruiser and just had time to see, through the webbed windshield, Bruder's kicking legs, his flailing arms. A fountain of blood spurted against the side window, and the sheriff's madly scrabbling fingers streaked a frenzied Z in the bright red splash. Katherine looked away, no longer able to breathe. From the swirling snarl of branches, the sound of rending metal deepened, and beneath it, Bruder's high-pitched death howl.

Then they emerged on the creek bank, and mercifully, the cacophony behind them diminished. But the odors of spilled gasoline and sheared metal still hung in the air.

Katherine wasn't aware she'd been crying until she heard herself ask, "Why didn't you stop it?"

He'd taken a step down the steep bank, but now he stopped, an amazed grin on his face. "*Stop* it? This is everything I've ever wanted."

She struggled to jerk her wrist free, but his fingers held fast.

She stared down at him incredulously. "Do you hear yourself? Those people back there – Aaron Wolf and his wife – they're *dead*, Chris."

He dragged her downward. "They're better off."

"Who is she?"

"Who?" he asked absently.

"The woman who killed them."

"You know who she is."

She stumbled, her knees squishing into the muddy bank. "I don't know…" she began, but a wave of dizziness swam over her, the moonlight glinting off the creek growing hazy, diffuse.

"Yes, you do," he said. He was ankle deep in the water, she on her knees before him.

She shook her head, a languid heat engulfing her. The smell of the creek, dank and darkly pleasing, filled her head.

"You *do* know, Katherine. You've known for three years."

His voice was muffled, the sight of his reaching fingers gauzy. They slipped under her chin, lifted her face. She stared up at him, at the broad, burly shoulders, the T-shirt clinging to his rippled chest.

"It's okay now, Katherine," he whispered through the fog. The warm fingers resting against her cheek. "The death is behind us now."

A snapshot of the sheriff's thrashing body strobed through her mind, but it was gone as quickly as it came, replaced by the smell of warm flesh, the sound of gently lapping water. Chris pressed the side of her face against the belly of his shirt. The scent of musky sweat made her flesh tingle, her breathing deepen. His fingers twined through her hair, caressed her scalp. The ache in her wrist was gone, her hands embracing his thighs. Against her cheek the damp T-shirt slithered up, and then her skin pressed against his abdominal muscles, her fingers sliding over his erection, the hardness pushing taut the denim of his jeans.

He suddenly jerked away, gasping. Katherine stared at him uncomprehendingly.

"Not now," he said. "Not yet."

"Please," she said.

"The clearing," he said, his voice louder. "We need it to happen in the clearing."

A gust of frustrated rage swept through her. "Why do we—"

"It *has* to be there," he said, pushing to his feet. "It's the only way."

Katherine watched him extend a hand. All thoughts of Ellie had vanished, and in their wake was only a pulsing, aching desire for Chris's body. Ellie had gotten to make love with Chris for years, and dammit, Katherine deserved him now.

She sighed, her whole body quivering.

Then, lips thin, she accepted his hand. Once on her feet she felt better. Together they waded through the creek, scaled the bank. On the other side she saw a path leading eastward. Dimly, Katherine wondered why she hadn't seen the path before, it was so wide and clear.

But the beauty of the trees, the thrumming sound of the cicadas and the chirping of crickets drove the question from her mind.

Side by side, she and Chris moved through the forest.

PART FIVE
DEMONIC
CHAPTER ONE

Two bodies, Ellie's mind repeated. *Two bodies.*

She tried to focus on chapter five, "Unification and the Demonic," because she knew it was somehow crucial, yet that idiot mantra – *two bodies, two bodies* – wouldn't release its dogged hold on her.

This section was even more cryptically worded than the chapters preceding it, but there were a few points that stuck with her:

During unification the temporary carrier of the host's essence shall succumb. However, the appearance of the carrier shall remain accessible.

Two bodies, Ellie thought. One was clearly the demonic figure – Gerald Destragis, for instance. But the other...? If the man in the basement was Destragis's "disincorporated" self – and Ellie had a hell of a hard time thinking of the man who had chased her up the stairs as a disincorporated being – who was his corporeal self?

Not Chris, else there wouldn't be a suicide note.

Unless, a voice suggested, *the old Chris will be absorbed into the new Destragis, in which case a suicide note would make perfect sense.*

No, it wouldn't, she argued. If the text were to be believed – "However, the appearance of the carrier shall remain accessible" – Destragis would don Chris's appearance whenever suitable, but when exactly would it be suitable to resemble a man who'd taken his own life? Ellie doubted impersonating the dead would help an immortal maintain a low profile.

Further, if Destragis didn't look like Chris when he came back, he'd presumably look like himself, and that wouldn't do either. People around here would recognise him.

Wouldn't they?

Maybe not, she realised with dawning fear. He'd been in his eighties when he died, so the vast majority of Ravana wouldn't recognise him as a younger man. If, of course, that was how he came back to life.

What guise would he choose?

She drummed her fingers on the open book, considering.

He could come back as a man in his twenties or thirties. Or he could go even younger. A teenager or...

Her eyes opened wide and her hands went to her belly.

No, she thought. *Not that.* The idea that she was carrying the creature that had orchestrated this macabre drama was too much to bear.

No. The child growing inside her was normal and healthy, and she refused to believe otherwise. If that wasn't true, nothing else mattered.

Still, the fear would not abate.

Troubled, Ellie glanced down at the book. As she continued to read, her sense of disquiet was replaced by a faint flicker of hope.

The reversal of the unification process can only be achieved when the distilled life is consumed in the furnace of desire.

She read it over again, her hope fading. Just what the hell was the "distilled life"? And how could it be "consumed in the furnace of desire"? She bared her teeth in frustration. Even if she did solve the riddles in the book, what toll would that take on her and the baby? The evil presence that monitored her whereabouts – that had nearly *killed* her baby on several occasions – might be delayed, but did she really believe she could stop it? What if she defeated it but lost her child in the process?

That's fear talking.

She closed her eyes against the voice, but she knew it was correct. She realised with wry surprise that the voice had belonged to Kat.

She remembered what her sister had asked before leaving: *Is that what you think you're having? A little girl?*

She remembered Kat's smile as well. A genuine, loving smile, not the expression of someone who meant her harm. Kat had been forced into doing what she'd done with Chris, or at the very least *influenced* into doing it. Hell, maybe Chris had too.

Now Ellie was the only one who could save them all. She'd either succeed or die in the attempt.

But where to go, dammit? What to do?

She bit her lip, scanned the wall distractedly.

It came to her.

There was only one place in this house she hadn't explored, and she hadn't explored it because she'd convinced herself it didn't exist.

But what if it did?

It had been nearly pitch black in the basement the night she and Chris had ventured down there, and since that time she'd avoided the place with a superstitious dread, all the while telling herself there was nothing to discover.

But what if there was? What if they'd missed the doorway or not found it because it had been concealed?

Ellie rose from the chair and raced down the stairs. In moments she'd made it out to the garage. She found the lantern. The other object was lying atop the workbench.

Then, the lantern in one hand and the sledgehammer in the other, Ellie headed down to the basement.

CHAPTER TWO

Take it easy, she told herself. *Just take it easy. Don't overdo it and hurt the baby.*

Ellie leaned on the handle of the sledgehammer, doubled over and panting.

Her hands were a nightmare of blisters and aches, but she gritted her teeth and forced her fingers to close around the handle anyway. She broadened her stance, reared back, and swung. The flat edge of the hammer smacked the cinderblock a solid blow and smashed through the outer shell to expose the hollow area within. She was eager to begin destroying the inner layer of cement, but she wanted to create an aperture wide enough to climb through first.

Patience, she told herself. *Patience.*

But Kat's voice protested: *Fuck patience, Ellie! Patience won't save me from Chris!*

And though Ellie didn't believe in telepathy, she was sure Chris had gotten Kat by now, perhaps even had sex with her, whether she wanted to or not. The "Unification" chapter in Destragis's book had mentioned coupling several times, and she seriously doubted Chris intended to couple with anyone but Kat now.

Quit stalling.

"All right," she said and swung again. Despite the awful reverberation brought on by the impact, she felt a surge of satisfaction as a football-sized segment of cinderblock imploded.

Another strike, and she thought she'd made a hole wide enough. She caught a whiff of some chemical, sulphur maybe. She clenched her jaw against the braying nerves of her palms and swung again.

The rusty sledgehammer crashed through the wall.

Hurriedly, Ellie wrestled the rectangular head out of the hole and dropped the sledge. The sulphur smell invaded her mouth, the flavour vile and eggy. She hooked her fingers through the wire handle of the lantern and raised it to the hole. At first all she could see was swirling dust.

Then, bringing the lantern right up to her cheek, she made out the workbench, the many shapes resting on its wooden surface.

I knew I wasn't crazy! she thought triumphantly. She gazed into the room and made out some of the objects: a saw, a number of glass beakers and vials, what looked like a long plastic tube suspended between two steel braces.

Yes, this was the place. If there was any hope for them, she'd find the answers here. Her heart thundering in her chest, she set the lantern out of the way and hefted the sledgehammer again. She reared back, ready to punch out a big enough hole to stick her head through.

The sledgehammer wouldn't move.

Slowly, Ellie turned and saw the large knuckles grasping the head of the sledge. Above that, the viciously grinning face.

"Naughty girl," her husband said.

CHAPTER THREE

When Ellie opened her eyes, she knew where he'd taken her even before she saw the gently stirring grass.

The clearing.

Overhead, the night was absolutely clear, the deep blue sky alive with glittering stars. The moon was merely a pallid sliver.

She sat up, glanced to her left and saw the starlight reflected on a pond about twenty yards away. A pulsing luminescence to her right caused her to turn and gaze up the rise. Though it was difficult to see from this distance, the tall grass blocking a good deal of her vision, she could make out multiple fires ringing the crest of the hill.

A single figure stood within the ring.

Her husband.

Solitary, rising atop the majestic hill, he looked like some kind of god fallen to earth. His shoulders were broader than she remembered, the V shape of his back more pronounced. Face upturned, he paced the ring, the lurid red firelight flickering on his face. He was naked, his bare buttocks sculpted and powerful. His leg muscles flexed as he walked, his long fingers limp at his sides.

She remembered those fingers closing around her throat in the basement, squeezing, her hands first swiping at his eyes and then scrabbling to pry loose his fingers. Then his grinning face followed her into darkness, his teeth alabaster within the shadowy nest of beard.

But you didn't kill me, did you? she thought. *Why not? Because you wanted me to witness what you were about to do? Because you wanted to visit upon me this one final degradation – watching my husband make love to my sister – before the blasphemous transformation takes place and my baby and I get killed?*

Unless, a voice whispered, *your baby is Lillith or Destragis.*

No!

She got to her feet, listing drunkenly, and started toward the rise. She kept waiting for the stomach pain, for the cruel dagger to split her belly and prevent her from intervening, but she was being allowed to move freely.

Its attention is diverted, she thought, and continued toward the hill. As she climbed, she watched her husband wheel slowly in her direction. He didn't see her though, was too immersed in his thoughts, too eager to complete the process to notice her approach.

She became aware of a dull ache in her right hand, and when she discovered the ragged flaps of skin crossing her palm she remembered the last thing he'd done to her before hoisting her up and bearing her out of the basement: the knife embedding in her open hand, the flesh parting as the blade ripped through it.

Halfway up the hill.

She kept expecting to see Kat join him and begin their erotic rite, but so far he remained alone, his magnificent body one moment black, the next a blazing orange. His face, too, was alternately glorious and ghastly.

Ellie closed in, most of her haziness burned away by the sepulchral scene awaiting her.

As her head rose even with the hilltop, she finally spotted her sister. Kat lay in the middle of the circle, writhing in sexual desire. Ellie watched sickly as her sister's fingers slid over her jutting nipples, massaged her thighs, her hips upthrust as if in offering to the stars. Woodsmoke stung Ellie's eyes, but she couldn't look away.

Kat turned and saw her.

At first there was no recognition in her expression. Then a look of utter loathing twisted her pretty features.

When Kat spoke, it was in Lillith's voice. "So you've come, Eleanor."

And the pain exploded in Ellie's midsection, worse than it had ever been. She fell forward and narrowly avoided landing on her stomach. Groaning, her breathing thin and tortured, she saw Chris approach her sister. Kat got to her knees, the hatred in her face nearly as awful as the waves of pain ripping through Ellie's body. Kat faced Ellie on all fours, and for the briefest of moments Ellie thought the woman might lunge at her like an animal. In a way, Ellie thought dimly, it would be a welcome respite from this soul-destroying agony. Chris reached down and touched Kat's shoulder, obviously meaning for her to roll over so he could make love to her.

But rather than facing him, Kat lowered her head and arched her lower back so her buttocks raised higher, offering herself to him.

Grinning wickedly, Chris got on his knees, reached down and inserted himself inside Kat, and then they were pulsing together like animals, Kat's breasts quivering each time his hips met her buttocks. Ellie bit her lip. The heat within the ring was unbearable, the taste of smoke mean and withering. The naked, undulating bodies shimmered in the firelight. Ellie moaned, held the small lump in her belly, and waited for it all to be over. She'd failed her baby, failed herself. Neither of them would escape this unholy place, this ceremony in which demons would be born.

Through the awful, blazing pain Ellie saw her sister gazing at her, and though the lovemaking continued, harder and faster now, Kat's expression had again become her own, and she was staring at Ellie with heartbreaking guilt. Kat's eyes twitched to the right, over Ellie's shoulder.

Though the pain was raging worse than ever, Ellie was just able to swivel her head and follow Kat's gaze. At first she saw nothing, just the silent forest framing the clearing.

Then a pale figure started to materialise.

A second one appeared beside it. Another. The humanoid shapes were crawling like maggots, their wasted legs squirming behind them, the obsidian hollows of their eyes sparking with the fires' reflections.

Ellie realised there were several more dragging themselves out of the forest, and to her left she spied a single pale arm poking out of the earth. Another arm joined it, and then the figure was wriggling out of the ground, its glistening white face already fixed in a rictus of deepest hunger.

The first figures she'd spotted were crawling better now, their legs working more efficiently, and Ellie realised she was watching newborn vampires, remembered the chapter titled "Second Birth."

She now understood why Chris had taken the time to slice open her palm. Though she could see the black, idiot eyes of some of the creatures, many of them appeared sightless, a milky translucent membrane keeping them, at least momentarily, blind. It was these creatures whose snouts twitched and bobbed, sniffing for food, and one by one she watched these creatures freeze in recognition as they picked up the scent.

Ellie counted at least twenty pale, gleaming bodies squirming their way up the hill.

They were crawling toward her.

Instinctively, Ellie scrambled to her knees and started to clamber away from the pale figures, but a gust of pain so powerful it turned her limbs to rubber dropped her facedown in the grass. She howled in agony. She flopped onto her back and thrashed her head from side to side and thought, *The baby can't survive this – even if I somehow make it through this torture, there's no way a foetus can withstand this punishment.*

With what energy she had, she clawed herself forward, toward the centre of the ring. She didn't want to be nearer the couple making frenzied love only ten yards away, but anything was preferable to the obscenities that were rising on unsteady legs and staggering toward her. Not only had their movements grown more refined, but she saw with deepening horror that their awareness of their surroundings had as well. At least a dozen of the creatures were leering at her with ravenous need now, their dripping incisors bared in anticipation.

The first vampire had nearly reached the crest of the hill.

Ellie crawled forward, and as she did, she noted that Kat's head hung low and was swaying eerily from side to side, like some tribal shaman in the throes of a magical trance. Chris was squeezing Kat's hips with animalistic greed, his expression primal and sadistic as he slammed into her harder and harder. Kat's limp body juddered with each impact. Ellie felt a cold mist of dread drowse over her.

Kat was changing.

Transforming, she saw, into another woman. It shouldn't have surprised her – the sight of the dusky skin paling, the arms and legs elongating, the black hair threading into shimmering red curls – yet it did. All at once, the body Chris was making love to seemed to tense, the fingers splayed wide in the grass, the sinuous shoulder muscles bunching.

Lillith's face swung up and grinned at Ellie.

Ellie tumbled back, brought a hand to her throat, but the blazing eyes refused to release her. The fury and raw lust in those eyes were unspeakable, endowed with the power of countless centuries. Lillith, a demon in human form, watched Ellie with a look of such utter contempt that for a moment Ellie forgot all about the vampires who were now surely right behind her. Then she turned to see that they'd indeed closed the distance, were nearly within arm's reach, and there were too many of them, half of the ring clotted with their mud-smeared bodies, and they were slavering for Ellie's blood, for the tender flesh of her innocent baby. The white creatures stank of decayed soil and old blood.

She closed her eyes and waited for the end.

A second went by, then two more. When nothing happened, she opened her eyes and saw the vulpine faces upturned and staring fixedly at something beyond her. She too turned and watched Lillith rising, her back curving like a serpent's, her arms reaching up, contorting to close around the back of Chris's neck.

No, Ellie thought desperately. *Don't hurt him.*

Chris continued his feverish pumping. Ellie saw the signs of impending climax in his body – the straining jaw, the tendons in his neck jumping and tightening, the eyes closed in desire.

Had they been open they would have seen Lillith's beautiful face becoming hideous, the cheekbones stretching, the eyes slitting vertically like some ancient reptile's, the teeth tapering to voracious points as the open maw leaned toward his exposed throat.

Wait! she wanted to scream but the hideous face plunged into Chris's neck. His eyes shuttered wide, and then Lillith was feasting, her long red tongue flicking out gluttonously as the fearsome jaws chewed, rent, tore the muscles to jetting ribbons. Chris let loose with a gutwrenching bellow and beat at the creature affixed to his mutilated throat, but the blood-drenched face continued its convulsive burrowing. Chris's limbs flailed. Ellie's stomach lurched as one of Lillith's scimitar fingernails hooked inside his left nostril and peeled it back until the flesh parted with a horrid, wet, ripping sound.

Something bumped against Ellie's shoulder, and before she had time to react, they were pushing by her, the newborn vampires flowing hungrily toward the writhing, blood-soaked man whose gurgling death cries Ellie could bear no longer.

Pushing to her feet, she realised the pain in her gut had dissolved, knew her time was short, Lillith's attention momentarily on her prey.

Soon she would slaughter Ellie too.

She shouldered past the pale, naked monsters who were moaning lustful dirges to their queen, their deliverer. Seemingly unaware of Ellie, they shambled up the hill, teeming in a noxious flood toward Lillith and the feast she had prepared.

Ellie ran between a mewling pair of the creatures and made for the forest. Running with the full force of terror, Ellie spotted the mouth of the trail that she hoped would lead her home. She cast one final glance at the hilltop and witnessed it all in a ghastly tableau worse than any Bosch painting. The pale bodies swarmed over the corpse of her husband, and above all she beheld the tallest figure raise her glistening red hands and smear her fingers over her breasts, Lillith bathing in her nephew's blood.

*   *   *

Ellie was certain the pain would cripple her before she reached home.

It didn't though, and soon she found herself bursting from the imprisoning forest and veering through the yard. The night was cloudless, so Ellie would have a clear view of the lane, the twin paths of gravel that would deliver her from this horrible place.

But her heart sank as she lurched to a stop. Within her, the last thin strand of hope snapped with terrible finality.

The lane was gone.

She'd known it was diminishing by the day, and earlier tonight she'd watched with foreboding as Kat disappeared down the narrow corridor bisecting the trees.

But now even that was gone. Ellie knew Lillith would not allow her to leave. No wonder there'd been no reaction when Ellie hoofed it out of the clearing, no resistance from the vampires as she dashed through the forest. They had nothing to fear from her because she was entombed here as surely as they'd been entombed in the earth only minutes earlier.

Except, she suspected, unlike those stinking, bloodthirsty creatures, she would not someday rise from the dead.

When Lillith killed her, it would be forever.

Without thinking, she drifted toward the house, and as she did an unexpected tide of sadness washed over her at the thought of her husband. The fool. He'd actually thought he was meant to be a part of this, the new era of evil that had already cast its shadow over these woods. And who knew where it would stop? How many followers had Lillith and Destragis readied for this night? Who could possibly prevent them from—

On the bottom step, Ellie paused.

She thought of Destragis, then of the workshop in the basement. She'd been about to enter the small room when Chris had stopped her.

Why had he stopped her?

Because, Kat told her, *you were about to disrupt Destragis's plans in a major way.*

Destragis. Obviously Chris wasn't intended to be Destragis's vessel the way Kat had been Lillith's. Maybe one of the obscene creatures that had swarmed up the hill had been Destragis's resurrected body.

But that didn't seem right.

If Lillith was the queen of this sect, Destragis was the unquestioned king, and a king did not reclaim his throne on his belly, or in a jostling mass of vampires. No, in life Destragis had been a charismatic leader, and when he returned it would be with a flair for the dramatic.

Unless she could prevent it.

Casting fearful glances behind her, Ellie mounted the steps and headed for the basement. Moving as swiftly and quietly as she could, she made it to the black room, saw the lantern burning feebly against the half-demolished wall.

She rushed forward and picked up the lantern. As she climbed through the jagged hole, the light flickered, the kerosene nearly gone. It wouldn't burn much longer.

That's fine, she thought grimly. *It won't be much longer before Lillith and her minions descend on me and tear to shreds either.*

She stepped through the aperture and stood erect. She breathed through her mouth to fight off the sulphurous odour permeating the air. She noticed designs on the wall beyond the tubes and beakers.

Though many of them were crude sketches of naked women and vampires, one drawing, larger than the others and centred above the workbench, commanded her attention.

She took a step closer, frowned. She brought a hand up, was about to trace the contour of the demonic face with an index finger, when a skittering sound filled the basement and made her cry out in shock. Heart thudding, Ellie whirled and stared through the hole she'd made. In the room she'd just vacated, a shape was moving. She brought the lantern up, certain it was Lillith.

But the shape wasn't human, was darker and closer to the floor.

Petey.

"Oh, thank God," she said, exhaling a pent-up breath. She slumped against the jagged cinderblock hole and chuckled at the dog, which was lying on its side, the kind brown eyes gazing up at her. "You scared the shit out of me, boy."

Petey sat up, suddenly alert, and Ellie felt her bowels freeze.

Oh no, she thought. *Not that. Please don't tell me they're here already. I haven't even had time to find something that might help us. I can't—*

Her thoughts broke off as something in Petey's face began to worry her in a different way. Like that night she'd stepped out of the shower, Petey was watching her with an uncannily human expression, the intelligence in his eyes unsettling her in the pit of her stomach.

She tried to laugh. "C'mon, boy, my heart can't take much more of this."

Petey continued to watch her.

Blowing out air, she listened for the growling voices of the vampires, the sounds of footfalls on the wood floors above, but thus far all was quiet.

She raised the lantern, swept its yellow light over the monstrous images on the walls – unspeakable creatures with serrated fangs and glowing vermilion eyes – and the many empty beakers strewn about.

Her eyes settled on the clear tube spanning the bench.

She followed the tube to the right and saw the plastic sack hanging from the steel rod, the tube filled with some black substance that dangled down to the bench and terminated in what looked like a needle.

Oh, hell, she thought. *An IV drip.*

She spun to her left and discovered a similar set-up, the same black tube – black with someone's dried blood? – the same needle.

Her memory of that night in the basement finally clarified.

Destragis hooking himself up to the drip-sack.

The other end of the tube sticking in one of Petey's back legs.

A gurgling moan made her whirl and stare through the hole in the cinderblock. The lantern trembling in her hand, she stepped toward the sound and gazed into the room at Petey.

The dog lay with forepaws splayed, his hind legs stretched behind him as though he were trying to become one with the floor. Petey's rear end stirred faintly, the tail twitching in a perfunctory wag.

Then, he lay completely motionless.

Ellie leaned closer, held the lantern out to better illuminate the dog. "You okay, boy?" she asked. "You hear something—"

Petey tossed back his head and let loose with the most hellish wail she'd ever heard. Her insides turned to ice, her nerveless fingers threatening to drop the lantern. She'd never seen a creature in such pain, and though she knew the sound should be evoking sympathy from her, her only thought was that the vampires would hear and rush down to devour her the way they had Chris.

Then Ellie's worry turned to horror.

While Petey's bloodcurdling howl razored higher and higher, his mouth continued to stretch open to an unnatural size. She could see his tongue, vibrating with the scream, his teeth, which were sharper than she remembered, and – she told herself it was a trick of the light – the hair on his face, which seemed to be withdrawing into his skin, sucked down by some internal gravity.

Awestruck, Ellie swept the lantern down the juddering body and realised she hadn't been mistaken, the hair *was* disappearing, and even more alarming, Petey's back legs seemed to be extending, broadening, the slender bones near the paws growing pear-shaped, almost like...

"*Oh, shit*," Ellie whispered.

Almost like the calves of a human being.

An atavistic horror tightened her flesh and clogged her airways. She whipped her head and saw the forepaws extended to the sides, as though the creature were about to do push-ups. The head snapped forward, teeth clicking audibly, and the face, she now saw, had drawn inward, the snout becoming a nose, the ears rounding and diminishing.

The wail, too, was becoming human.

The transforming beast regarded her with malicious glee.

Even in this transitory state Ellie recognised the man from the basement. The man from the videotape.

Gerald Destragis.

It had been the animal all along. How stupid she'd been to think herself safe, even momentarily. The malevolence here wasn't diverted; it had everything under control. Even if Lillith and the newborn vampires were still in the clearing – a prospect she highly doubted – the other half of the demonic royal family was down here with her, perhaps keeping watch until she got too close to some dangerous revelation.

The beast sat back on its knees, its claws becoming fingernails. The skin of its arms quivered, the muscles swelling as the hair obscuring them seemed to wither. The corded neck twitched spastically, the shoulders and throat pulsing at jackhammer speed. A great cracking sound rebounded off the walls, recurred, and Ellie realised it was the sternum spreading under the widening chest. The creature still bellowed in pain, but now there was exultation in its voice as well. Ellie beheld with sick dread the canine phallus becoming smoother, longer, Destragis's genitalia taking shape.

Do something! a voice exploded within her.

She whirled and set the lantern on the workbench. Whatever chance she had lay here, but what could she do?

Oh, Christ, she could hear him even now through the gaping hole in the wall, his deep, chortling laughter, a measure of the dog's growl still present in the sound. She needed more time, more time, but there wasn't any more time, the metamorphosis nearly complete. In moments he'd come bounding toward her, make her the first meal of his new existence.

The voice sliced through her panic: *Think, goddamn you, think. Quit standing there like a useless slab of meat and fight back.*

Against that thing? she wanted to scream. *What am I gonna do, whack it with the sledgehammer? Slap it with one of those drip-sacks?*

Her eyes stretched wide as she remembered the words of the Destragis text: *The reversal of the unification process can only be achieved when the distilled life...*

Dammit, she couldn't remember the rest!

She made herself block out the gruesome creaking sounds coming from a few feet away – sounds, she thought dimly, that might just be the animal's bones expanding to human size – and scour the words for meaning.

The distilled life, she thought. *The distilled life...* What could *the distilled life* mean—

Her hands shot out, grabbing the workbench in astonishment. An overused and dimly remembered quote trailed through the theatre of her memory: *For the blood is the life.*

Ellie glanced at the drip-sack.

That had been the one attached to Destragis's arm, and yes, there *was* some dried, black-looking substance contained inside. It could only be Destragis's blood.

She reached for it, yanked it off the steel holder.

Then the hand closed around her ankle.

She gasped as she was tugged off-balance and hauled toward the hole. Her body spun as she fell, her head smacking the hard edge of the workbench, then thudding sickly on the unforgiving concrete. Her vision swam, her consciousness wavering. She felt the floor slide beneath her.

With an effort she raised her head.

And immediately wished she hadn't.

The creature, its body still convulsing with the change, had crawled through the hole and with a powerful hand was now drawing her slowly toward it, *under* its changing body, the lust on its abomination of a face far greater now than the physical agony it was experiencing. The creature opened its mouth in rapturous anticipation, and Ellie noted with revulsion how the gums were still flecked with black, the teeth still wide-spaced like Petey's had been. Propped on its elbows, it was wriggling toward her now, its hairy shoulders expanding, the muscles there jumping like game fish trapped under a net.

Her feet drew even with the crooks of its forearms, the dripping jaws hovering over her bare knees.

No! her mind screamed, recoiling at the thing crawling over her. It meant to feast on her, accelerate its metamorphosis. Her mind clearing, her terror incinerating the haze, Ellie battered at its face, hooked her nails at its gaping brown eyes. She scooped a hunk of flesh from the bridge of its nose, and it snarled at her, the hard fingers scuttling up her legs like armoured spiders.

Beneath her buttocks the floor slid again, and now its face was revoltingly near her crotch. A stinking stream of drool pooled on the exposed flesh just beneath the hem of her shorts. Groaning, she seized the hair above its pulsing temples and ripped, but rather than screaming in pain, the demonic face seemed to shudder in ecstasy, as if delighting in the injury and imploring her to inflict more. Frantically she sought to extricate her legs, but its weight, its swelling girth pinned them down, the sweaty, hairy armpits fixing her knees to the concrete.

Just when she was sure it would pull her all the way beneath her, sink its leering fangs into her neck the way Lillith had done to Chris, its manic energy seemed to coalesce, all its concentration focused now on her abdomen.

It's going to bite me between the legs, was her first thought. *Oh my God, it's going to bite me down there*. Gagging, Ellie struck its face with useless fists, but again, the thing seemed to delight in the punishment.

Then she realised something even more horrifying.

It wasn't staring at her crotch.

It was staring at her pregnant belly.

*   *   *

Ellie was under the bridge on the backpacking trip again. And even if the creature on top of her wasn't a boy named Jake, it all came to the same thing.

She was going to be violated by a monster.

Its shiny black lips curled back in a libidinous snarl, its lolling tongue darting in and out of its mouth in unholy eagerness, the monster's face moved closer and closer to the rise of her stomach. She caught a whiff of its stench, the mingled odors of sweat, semen and dog shit. Its quaking body wriggled higher, the hairy torso crushing her legs. It pushed her shirt up.

For one frozen moment, Ellie and the monster regarded each other across the dull gleam of her pregnant belly.

And at that moment, with her sanity teetering on the brink of a bottomless abyss, she remembered the second half of the passage:

...is consumed in the furnace of desire.

She bared her teeth in a tortured grimace. What the hell did that mean?

The staring brown eyes crawled over her smooth belly. Though she knew it was futile, she grabbed her shirt and tried to push it down, but even that measure of defence was denied her. She turned her face away, unable to bear the sight of the monster any longer, and spotted the drip-sack lying discarded on the floor.

Furnace of desire, she thought, furnace of desire.

The dripping fangs closed in on her stomach, a deep growl emanating from its throat. Ellie became aware of another sound and realised she was sobbing. The smell of faeces burrowed into her nostrils.

Furnace of desire, she thought weakly, furnace of—

Ellie sucked in breath. She had it.

She cast a desperate glance at the workbench. She couldn't see the lantern, but the ceiling was painted in its lurid glow.

The slimy tongue oozed out of the monster's mouth and dragged a slick trail across her stomach.

Now, the voice screamed. Now!

A moment before the fangs pierced her skin, she thrust both thumbnails into the creature's eyes. It bellowed in rage, its hot breath scalding her skin and speckling it with spit. Viscous matter leaked over her knuckles, blood and ocular fluid dripping between her fingers. The creature's huge arms swung up and grasped her wrists, tore them away from its face. She heard a dull crunch and knew her left wristbone had snapped. The creature reared back and ground its palms into its mutilated eye sockets and roared in ear-splitting fury.

The moment she was released from its weight, she rolled onto her side. Taking care not to use her useless left wrist, she pushed unsteadily to her feet and raised the lantern. She saw with dim terror that the flame had almost gone black.

The creature's hand shot out and fastened onto her broken wrist, sent white-hot pain rocketing through her arm. It dragged her down as though she were made of paper, and as she fell she slammed the guttering lantern against the side of its face. Blue fire wreathed its head, its torso, but still it pulled her closer. She interposed her good arm between her and the bellowing monster, but its power was too great. She smelled singed hair, felt her forearm blister as the flames spread to her own skin. She threw a glance at the creature and saw that one eye had partially escaped her earlier assault, and this eye was glaring at her in triumph. And though her forearm burned with the searing blue flames, the creature appeared unfazed.

She was lifted, twisted in the air, and slammed down on her back.

Starbursts bloomed in her vision, the pain unbelievable. *Concussion*, she thought weakly. The burning monster loomed closer, its blackened face again looming toward her stomach. She had been wrong about the passage, the furnace of desire, all of it.

Its teeth slowly punctured her flesh. Blood dribbled down the curve of her belly and soaked her waistband. She felt an object poking the small of her back. She reached down, touched it, and remembered the drip-sack.

The words whispered one last time: *...when the old life is consumed in the furnace of desire.*

Oh, Jesus, she thought.

With what strength she still possessed, she shoved away from the creature, its mouth detaching from her stomach, seized the plastic drip-sack and thrust it into the pool of flame on the concrete.

The reaction was immediate.

The creature descended into a wild frenzy of flailing limbs and bizarre wails. Crawling away, Ellie could see its twisted body thrashing in agony. In the guttering firelight she saw why.

Blood was seeping from its pores.

And not just seeping, but *gushing* in some places: the mouth, the eyes, the genitals. The creature flopped over, freshets of blood splattering the concrete. The misshapen body jerked spasmodically. It retched and vomited a steaming tide of what looked like mangled intestines. Ellie cried out in revulsion as a syrupy maroon liquid sprayed over her hands. The last chunk of purple guts drooled from its mouth with a plop, then the creature pitched forward into the pile like a newborn calf writhing in its own afterbirth.

Ellie could bear it no longer. She turned her head and threw up.

When she wiped a shuddering wrist over her mouth, she was appalled to see the creature's blood smearing her skin.

The gag reflex seized her again, but this time there was nothing left to void. Instinctively, Ellie held her pregnant stomach until the gagging stopped.

Taking care not to touch what was left of the creature's body – she could not avoid sloshing through its blood; the entire room was painted in it – she crawled toward the hole in the wall. She kept expecting the creature to leap up, to fasten its obscene mouth on her belly again because that's what happened in horror movies. But so far, the figure remained motionless, save the occasional death spasm.

She kept her eyes on the bloody ruin as she stretched first one leg through the hole, then the other. The flames produced by the exploding lantern still burned, but weakly now. In another minute, the basement would again be steeped in darkness.

She stood and backed away from the dimly glowing hole in the wall, still expecting the Destragis creature to appear in the hole and lunge at her, snarling and laughing.

But it didn't.

She turned and saw, less than a foot away, Lillith's pale face.

Ellie screamed.

Lillith's blood-smeared mouth curled into a grin.

Ellie tried to push away, but a taloned hand seized her by the throat. The face floated closer, only inches away.

"You thought you'd escape, Eleanor," Lillith said and traced an index finger across Ellie's forehead. The flesh unzipped and rills of blood spilled over her eyebrows. She struggled to pry the steely fingers from her throat, but Lillith squeezed harder, and Ellie's breath thinned to almost nothing.

Lillith drew her closer, and for a moment, Ellie feared the woman would kiss her.

But she rasped: "I shall enjoy feasting on your child."

Ellie smashed a knee into Lillith's naked body. The touch of the woman's pubic hair sent Ellie's stomach roiling again, but Lillith didn't even flinch. The breath whispering out of the ancient lips was rank, the stink of a flyblown slaughterhouse, and despite the blood gumming Ellie's eyelashes and blurring her vision, she beheld the depthless evil lurking in the woman's green eyes. It wouldn't be enough to slay Ellie; that wouldn't satisfy this monster. Lillith planned to inflict unspeakable horrors, to make Ellie watch as her child was torn from her still-living womb. Then Ellie would bleed to death as she watched her screaming baby devoured by this monster. As if hearing her thought, Lillith lifted her off the floor, Ellie's belly rising closer and closer to the leering, fanged mouth. Ellie rose toward the ceiling, and though she concentrated her whole will, she was unable to breathe.

Just as her consciousness began to dissolve, the fingers around her throat loosened, the woman's eyes flicking to something behind Ellie.

Lillith's voice was low, but it was stitched with the first signs of panic: "*What have you done to Gerald?*"

Ellie swallowed, her hands on Lillith's forearm. She stared down at the woman's face, which was no longer smiling, anxiety replacing hunger.

Lillith glanced up at her, teeth clenched. "*What have you done to him?*"

Before she could respond, Lillith released her and Ellie fell to the floor in an ungainly heap. She pushed to her feet, and as she did she caught a glimpse of Lillith's nude form stepping tentatively toward the hole in the wall. Soon she would see the ruin that had once been her lover and know that all their preparations had been for naught.

Ellie didn't wait around to witness it.

Moving as briskly as her injured ankle would allow, she limped around the corner and mounted the stairs.

Halfway up she heard Lillith scream.

After hearing Destragis's ghastly death cries, Ellie thought nothing could be worse. But the sound thundering through the basement walls possessed such unmitigated sorrow and fury that

Ellie was forced to clap her palms over her ears and move the rest of the way up to the kitchen in a clumsy lurch.

When she did reach the main floor another grisly surprise awaited her.

The kitchen windows were filled with pale, monstrous faces. There were dozens of them, lining the windows like wayfarers seeking shelter from a blizzard.

More, their glassy black eyes were stretched wide in concern. *They're worried about their goddess*, she thought in sick fascination.

But when they spotted Ellie stumbling toward a kitchen drawer, their expressions grew enraged.

You did this to her, their monstrous doll's eyes screamed. *You did this to our Lillith.*

The dark, bloodless lips stretched tighter, revealing sickle-shaped teeth that dripped with pink fluid.

Chris's blood, she thought weakly.

As her hand closed on the silver lighter, one of the faces drew her gaze.

Norman Campbell, she thought without surprise.

The screams from below had dissolved into wracking sobs, and Ellie knew her time was short. Any moment now the vampires would crash through the windows, the walls, and avenge the murder of Gerald Destragis. She backpedalled through the kitchen, doing her best to ignore the long, black claws scratching at the windows, the elongated tongues smearing the panes.

She backed into the dining room and glimpsed more white faces snarling at her, lapping greedily at the glass. They would move on Lillith's command. Whether that entailed a frenzied orgy of rending claws and ripping teeth or a slow, ritualistic torture, either way meant death. She made it through the foyer and had taken one step toward the stairs when the floor exploded in front of her.

Ellie landed on her back, and through the dust motes and hunks of floorboard clattering against the walls, a pale figure emerged. Lillith's face was gone, the vampire's true features replacing the lovely mask.

"*Spread your legs, Eleanor*," the vampire growled. "*I want that child.*"

＊   ＊   ＊

The vampire lunged at her.

Gasping, Ellie rolled over and shoved to her feet. A pale arm shot out, and scythe-like claws harrowed her left shoulder. Hissing from the pain, Ellie rushed up the stairs as Lillith pounced again. One taloned hand sheared through the heel of her shoe and opened her flesh, but Ellie kept climbing. As Lillith flew at her again Ellie reached the second floor and dove through the doorway into the guest bedroom. Scrambling, she lurched into the closet. She yanked the pull string and light flooded the tight space. She grabbed the sliding wooden compartment door with palsied fingers.

Please let this work, she thought. *Please let my baby live.*

She heard Lillith coming fast across the hardwood floor. Ellie jerked shut the closet door, knowing how futile the measure was, and a second later, the door smashed into her, torn free of its hinges. Ellie was driven into the wall, her shoulder splintering the small wooden compartment, dozens of razor blades spilling out. Stunned, Ellie thrust her hand into her pocket, got hold of the lighter. The door flew away, Lillith tossing it behind her into the guest bedroom as easily as a slab of cardboard.

She towered over Ellie, her face a deathmask of rage. Heedless of the pain, Ellie seized a handful of old razor blades. Lillith sank piercing claws into Ellie's ankles and dragged her out of the closet. Frantically, Ellie opened the lighter and flicked the wheel. It sparked but didn't catch. She tried again. Just as Lillith's powerful body landed on her, a pale yellow flame appeared. Ellie brought her hands together, the flame licking the blades and searing her palm. At the same moment, Lillith's razor-sharp nails raked the flesh of her belly, burrowing toward her baby. Ellie swirled the flame under the blades she clutched, but nothing happened. Exquisite pain flared in her stomach and the lighter flame winked out. Lillith's mouth was on her open wound, sucking.

Ellie flicked the lighter again. One blade, she now saw, was darker than the rest, its paper-thin surface crusted with dried blood. She guided the blade over the flame and felt Lillith's mouth leap away from her belly. Shocked, Ellie's thumb slipped off the lighter wheel. She dropped every blade save one, which she now pinched between thumb and forefinger.

For a moment Ellie's eyes met Lillith's white ones, the hateful reptilian gaze suddenly confused. Ellie flicked the wheel again, the flame licking the coated blade.

Lillith howled in pain.

Ellie pushed to her knees and stared at the woman's blood-smeared face. The eyes had flown wide in shock, and now they shifted to the object in Ellie's left hand, the razor blade with which Lillith had once probably shaved her legs. Disbelief was slowly replaced with a bold cunning that filled Ellie with dread. *But it worked*, Ellie thought desperately. Just like Destragis, Lillith would be destroyed if she set the crusted blood aflame.

So why was the woman smiling?

Ellie brought the lighter closer to the blade.

"Before you do that," Lillith said, her voice now a throaty growl, "you might take a look at them."

Ellie followed Lillith's gaze to the dark hallway and saw the white, vulpine faces, their expressions twisted with rage and terror.

Holding both the lighter and the razor blade before her, Ellie regarded Lillith. "If I burn this, they'll die too."

"They'll disembowel you."

Ellie's eyes darted toward the vampires. "Then why are they afraid?"

"They're afraid for me, dear. Not themselves."

Ellie took a breath and passed the lighter under the blade again, this time keeping her eyes on the creatures in the hall. In her peripheral vision she saw Lillith's body clench in sudden agony, but the only reaction on the part of her servants was an appalled rage.

Lillith's voice was husky with pain. "The moment you kill me, they'll destroy you and your child."

"They'll die too," Ellie insisted, but her hope was flagging.

"Do you feel anything?"

"Why would I—" Ellie began, but Lillith's spreading grin stopped her.

"Because you're one of us now," Lillith said.

The lighter wheel was sizzling her thumb, though Ellie hardly felt it. She shook her head slowly.

"You've been bitten, dear. By me and Gerald."

Ellie passed a hand over her tummy, the once-smooth skin now ragged with rips and bite marks.

"Your child," Lillith said, "is infected."

Ellie's bottom lip quivered. *No!*

She let the flame die, got slowly to her feet. Lillith rose too. Ellie glanced again at the vulpine faces, their terror now becoming anticipation.

Lillith took a step forward, but Ellie flicked the lighter, brought it within inches of the blade.

"Let us go," Ellie said. "Let us go and I'll let you live."

Lillith's grin never wavered. "You can't kill me, Eleanor."

Ellie held the flame under the razor blade. Lillith collapsed, wailing. Downstairs, Ellie heard glass shatter. A few feet to her left, another pane exploded, a ghostly white hand punching through the second-storey window.

On her knees, Lillith shot her a venomous glare. "*You fucking cunt.*"

"Let us go!" Ellie commanded.

The vampire in the window dropped inside the room. Smoke rose from the blade. Lillith's upper lip curled in a feral snarl. Blood began to seep from her pores. A window down the hall burst and more glass tinkled on the floor.

Ellie let the flame wink out. "Order them back or I'll burn you alive."

The vampire who'd punched through the window came at her in a blur. Ellie flicked the lighter, held it under the blade.

"*Wait!*" Lillith shouted.

The reaching talons stopped just shy of Ellie's throat.

"*Back,*" Lillith said.

Growling, the vampire backpedalled, but only a couple steps.

Lillith's slitted white eyes returned to Ellie.

"What do you want?"

Ellie swallowed, a painful clicking in her throat. "Only to leave."

Lillith chuckled, but there was pain in it. "I can't allow that."

"Then we'll both die," Ellie said.

"You wouldn't do that to your—"

"If we're going to die anyway, I'm taking you with me..." Ellie brought the lighter closer. "...you ugly bitch."

Lillith's eyes widened in rage.

Ellie brought the flame right up to the blade.

Lillith shouted, "*All right!*"

Then, rising to her feet, Lillith stood aside.

Ellie's hands trembled as she sidled past the woman's accursed figure. She was sure at any moment the long fingers would shoot out and pluck the lighter from her grip, but thus far Lillith was only standing beside the other vampire, watching her. Ellie backed toward the doorway, and though she didn't want to take her eyes off the monster for a second, she chanced a look behind her and saw, pale and hulking just outside the door, the scowling creature that had once been Norman Campbell.

The floor creaked as Campbell took a step forward.

"*Make him stop!*" Ellie shouted, her voice rising in terror.

Lillith raised her head and growled something in a tongue Ellie didn't understand. The meaning though, was clear enough. Not only did the vampires in the hall back away, but Ellie saw the one beside Lillith backpedal until it bumped the wall.

Ellie let the lighter flick out – she had no idea how much fuel might be left – and backed hurriedly out the doorway. Taking care to spot any creature preparing to leap at her, she backpedalled down the stairs, through the foyer and out of the house.

Hopefully for the last time, she thought.

On the lawn she beheld a multitude of pale figures. Ellie moved down the steps and into the yard. The vampires parted like curtains drawn open, and Ellie edged between them, trying to see in all directions at once. Most of all, though, she kept glancing at Lillith, who had stepped onto the porch to watch her.

When Ellie had hobbled halfway across the yard, she turned and saw with a gush of hope that the lane had reappeared, and though it wasn't as wide as it had been when she and Chris had first arrived, it looked broad enough to drive a car through. Just as encouragingly, the mass of vampires ended at the forest.

Unless more were lurking in the brush.

Ellie shook off the thought and turned to see that Lillith had, impossibly, halved the distance despite the fact that Ellie had only taken her eyes off her for a couple seconds. Ellie brought the unlit lighter closer to the razor blade.

She said, "I don't want the pain to come back."

Lillith matched her step for step. "As long as you leave that here," she said, nodding at the blade in Ellie's hand.

"When I'm safe," Ellie answered, "I'll drop it and—"

"You'll never be safe," Lillith said.

Ellie shook her head, struggling against the icy fear coursing through her.

"*Drop it now,*" Lillith said, her eyes blazing.

"No," Ellie said, her thumb touching the lighter wheel. She experienced a moment's satisfaction at the fearful way Lillith's eyes flitted there. *Not the only one who can inflict pain, are you?* Then she cleared her head. She still had a long way to go. It wouldn't be wise to get too confident now.

In a tight voice, she said, "Tell them not to follow me."

"Why should I? You're not giving me any assurances."

"You don't deserve any."

For a moment, Lillith seemed to consider.

Then, she said, "If you harm that blade, they'll find you. They'll tear out your baby and feast on its screams."

Ellie took in the vicious black eyes, the quivering, infuriated mouths. She nodded.

"Then get off my land," Lillith said, "before I decide to drink you myself."

*   *   *

The next fifteen minutes were the longest of Ellie's life. Every fibre of her being cried out to run, goddammit, to sprint as hard and long as you can and don't stop until this place is far behind you.

But that was the fear talking. Moving gingerly, casting glances all around her, she kept the lighter poised beneath the razor blade, her thumb resting on the wheel. Her broken wrist ached terribly. Her arms alternated between an enervated numbness and a howling chorus of agony, but she refused to let down her guard. Whenever the urge to rest did strike her, the forest seemed to tremble, the trees sensing an opening. Several times she turned to see a pale face withdrawing into the woods.

She thought of Kat as she made her way down the shadowy lane, the droning cicadas and the chirping crickets masking the more furtive sounds of animate vegetation and the bloodthirsty vampires tracking her movements.

She noted with faint optimism that the creek was down. Taking care not to allow the razor and the lighter to spread too far apart, she made her cautious, halting way down the bank. She knew if the vampires were going to attack her, now would be the time. Her attention was on not breaking her neck, and they might use this moment to fly at her in one gibbering mass.

But she reached the creek without issue.

Of course you did, Ellie thought. *It's not the descent or ascent you need to be careful of, it's the water. Remember, water isn't exactly conducive to setting something on fire.*

Ellie grimaced. She blew out a nervous breath and described a slow three-sixty, sure at any moment Lillith's leering face would appear.

But it didn't. At least not yet.

She took a step into the creek and was surprised at its warmth. The bed felt rocky, but at least the footing was uniform. The last thing she needed was to lose her balance, the blade – or just as bad, the lighter – dipping into the water and rendering her only defence useless. She took another step, and again found solid purchase. The water trickled past her calves, its eddying warmth lulling her, insisting everything would be fine, there was nothing to fear anymore.

The hell there isn't, she thought, and the next moment she understood how true that thought was. One moment she was stepping forward, the next she was windmilling her arms in terror. For an awful second she was sure she'd fall face first into the water. Then, some of her balance returned, but she knew she'd only bought a brief reprieve. Her momentum was still going forward, her only hope now to jump for the opposite bank, which was several feet away.

With all her strength, she sprang from the shelf of rock and thrust her arms as high as they would go. She knew her lower body wouldn't clear the water, but as long as her arms landed on the bank, there was a chance the blade and lighter would remain dry. Her knees connected first, and though the bite of the river rocks sent starbursts of pain up her legs, the landing allowed her to extend her arms all the way as she flopped forward onto the bank. She gasped as what she'd been terrified of, the splash caused by her lower body, showered her arms, but as far as she could tell very little of it had actually landed on her hands. She was about to test the lighter when she heard a skittering noise to her left, beheld the vampire lunging toward her.

Ellie flicked the lighter, and the flame shot up. The vampire hit the ground, one arm thrown up as if she held a flamethrower.

You're right to be scared, she thought. *You know what'll happen to Lillith if the dried blood ignites.* She glanced at the blade to check for moisture and glimpsed a pale blur in her periphery.

Whirling, she discovered Campbell looming toward her, the vampire having somehow traversed the creek and scuttled down the opposite side, the side on which she now stood.

"*Get back!*" she roared.

But rather than obeying, Campbell snatched at her, his monstrous face a mask of lust and madness. Instinctively, Ellie jerked the blade over the flame and saw Campbell's expression change. Blue fire licked up the edge, and behind her – terrifyingly near – she heard a shriek of agony explode in the forest. Campbell scrabbled away, his taloned hands splashing the edge of the creek, and the vampire who'd attempted to sneak up behind her growled.

She remembered Lillith's words: *The moment you kill me, they'll destroy you and your child.*

She glanced at the blade, the blue flame winking out. Around her, the forest seemed to sigh. She glimpsed them then, the faces peering over the creek banks from both sides. They'd followed her, and they'd almost succeeded in catching her unaware.

Ellie called, "If you try to stop me again, I'll kill her!"

For a moment there was no reaction in those ghostly, black-eyed faces. Then, slowly, they receded. Campbell's clawed hands were up in a gesture of supplication, and the vampire behind her was walking away, its face turned and watching her over its shoulder.

With even more care than she'd taken going down the bank, Ellie climbed up the other side and back onto the lane. Deep within the mass of trees to her right, she thought she spied the glint of a red-and-blue police light.

But surely that was her imagination.

She forced herself to keep walking, and a few minutes later she saw the lane open upon the county road. She was certain that the trees would swing toward her at the last moment, the branches become deadly spears that would impale her and her child, but the only movement she witnessed as she emerged from the lane was a blackbird taking flight, fluttering toward Ravana.

The lighter poised beneath the blade, Ellie followed.

AFTER

Toward the end of August, nearly three months since the bizarre happenings at the Crane house, Doris Keller signalled a left turn onto the lane. She remembered the attack, that horrid dog

(*Petey*)

pouncing on her as though she'd threatened its owners. Doris squeezed the wheel tighter, her knuckles white and full of tendons. At the time she'd believed Sheriff Bruder when he told her the animal had been destroyed, but now, gazing out at the leviathan oaks and the broad Colorado spruces, she had to wonder. If the nasty beast did scamper out of the forest toward her car, she'd run the bastard over. But she doubted it would fall for that. "Petey" was too canny to become roadkill. No, more likely he would lope beside the car, perhaps even wag his tongue placatingly: *Let's be friends, Ms. Keller, and let bygones be bygones.*

Doris reached out, slipped a hand inside her purse, and touched the cold steel of the Kahr E9 handgun.

She smiled thinly and thought, *I hope I see you again, Petey.*

She shifted in her seat, and as she did her bra chafed against the deepest gouge the animal had made, an ugly, ragged trench just below her sternum that still hadn't healed all the way. Stupid dog.

Stupid owners.

Doris had no doubt Chris and Ellie Crane were alive somewhere. She stared sourly at the ranks of trees drifting by. Whatever had happened out here, they'd been in on it together, of that she had no doubt.

Ahead, just like Franklin — the deputy who'd taken Bruder's place—had told her, the new bridge spanned the creek nicely and provided ample room for her car to pass. This one even, she noted with a dubious glance, sported steel guardrails, much fancier than the wooden ones that'd flanked the old bridge.

She picked up speed and waited for the black lab to come darting out of the forest. It made her nervous, and she didn't like that, not a bit. *Did they name you in honour of him, Petey? Of Gerald Peter Destragis?*

Doris found she was trembling.

To calm herself, she turned on the radio and concentrated on the unspooling lane. Thinking of the investigation and the superstitious paramedics who'd started all kinds of rumours about these woods, Doris shook her head and made soft clucking noises in her throat. One paramedic – she'd forgotten his name, but he had greying hair and was old enough to know better – claimed that an enormous branch on the Crane side of County Road 1200 had swept down toward his ambulance as he and another man pulled away from Aaron Wolf's house with what remained of Aaron and his wife. Another man who'd been part of the forensics team claimed that a ghostlike face had suddenly lunged through the brush at him, growling and snapping. Quavering fools, both of them, she thought and twisted off the radio. The reception was terrible out here anyway.

A white face, the man had said. *With eyes as black as a shroud.*

Ridiculous that in this day and age grown men still reverted back to their childhood fears when confronted with the least mystery. But there was really no mystery at all. Chris and Ellie Crane had murdered the Wolf brothers, Aaron's wife Anna, Sheriff Troy Bruder, and probably Norman Campbell. Unless Campbell was in on it, an idea she refused to totally discount. The notion that all the old business with Destragis had started up again

(*It's true, you know it's true*)

was akin to believing in the boogeyman. She aimed to get to the bottom of things today.

The sister knew something.

Katherine Chambers had said all the right things during the investigation. Rather than shying away from the press, the woman obviously relished the attention. Why, even one of the Chicago papers had sent someone down here to interview her, and while she'd answered the questions coolly enough, if one took a step back and examined the situation – the way Doris had – one could see that something was fundamentally amiss.

Ahead, the woods parted and she caught her first glimpse of the house.

Had she been able, Doris would have stopped the car and shifted into reverse. It was only a feeling, but she suddenly had serious doubts about what she was doing. The aura of the house seemed different now. She knew there'd been several workmen out here lately, and right away she spotted several changes – the siding a deep brown rather than the nasty tar colour, the cinderblock porch steps replaced by honest-to-goodness concrete, new window treatments – but the difference she sensed went far deeper than anything cosmetic.

The house was alive again.

Doris brought the car to a halt and gazed out the passenger's window. She gritted her teeth against the fear that flowed down her back. There was nothing to be afraid of, she reminded herself, absolutely nothing at all. Chris Crane had murdered those people, and Ellie had helped. That was, if he hadn't murdered her, too.

Then why is your hand on the gun?

With a start, she realised her hand had, of its own volition, slipped inside her purse again.

She did feel better with her fingers around the pistol.

Not that she'd need it.

Still, she'd take it inside with her as a talisman against her own silly nerves. After a moment's debate, she thumbed off the safety and opted not to zip the purse shut. Again, just in case something... unexpected should happen.

When she turned to get out she screamed.

Katherine Chambers stood just outside the door.

Because the woman was so close, Doris couldn't see her face from here, only the plunging neckline of her loose-fitting and rather tawdry dress. Who wore a red dress around the house anyway? On a weekday, no less. Had Katherine known she was coming?

Impossible, she thought. *Now stop scaring yourself and get out of the car.*

Doris opened the door and swung her legs over the edge. Then, smoothing her beige dress, she climbed out and regarded Katherine. And though Doris stood several inches taller – she towered over all but the very largest women, a fact in which she secretly delighted – she couldn't help feeling very small in Katherine's presence.

"Would you come in?" Katherine asked.

The skin of Doris's scalp tightened. Though she'd heard the

woman's voice on television, she couldn't get over how much she sounded like Lillith Martin.

That's just your imagination, she told herself.

"Yes," Doris said, producing a smile that no doubt looked as artificial as it felt. When the woman didn't say anything to that, Doris gestured toward the house. "You've done a lot with the place."

"Come on then," Katherine said and led her inside.

* * *

Sitting in the living room amidst the antiques and the smell of the woman's perfume — a scent that seemed oddly familiar, though she couldn't say why — Doris should have felt more at ease. After all, Katherine had so far proved a lovely host, and the tea and rye bread were welcome fare after the light lunch Doris had taken before leaving home.

But with the gorgeous — yes, she now realised that Katherine Chambers was *gorgeous* — woman seated on the couch beside her, Doris's nerves were jangling louder than ever.

"More tea?" Katherine asked, her voice honey-sweet.

Doris said yes though she had no idea why. Her cup was still half full and too hot to drink. When Katherine reached over with the kettle and put her hand on Doris's cup to steady it as she poured, the red dress sagged lower to reveal the ghost of one pink nipple. Katherine's breasts shifted as she poured the tea. Doris's breathing thinned.

"There," Katherine said, sitting back in her place and easing the kettle onto the table. "Where were we?"

Doris cleared her throat. "You were telling me your plans for the house."

"Oh yes," Katherine said, then frowned. "You aren't here to talk me into selling, are you?"

Doris laughed and shook her head, though that *had* been one of her goals. "Of course not, Ms. Chambers."

Katherine leaned toward her, the slender fingers closing on Doris's leg. "I'm sorry if I offended you, Ms. Keller." The dress tumbled open again, and this time she could see both breasts nestled in the scarlet shadows.

Doris wrestled her eyes up to meet Katherine's. "You didn't offend me. I promise."

Laughing, Katherine sat back. "That's good. I wouldn't want you angry at me again, Louise."

Doris's stomach clenched. The strength seemed to drain from her fingers. "What did you call me?"

Katherine raised her eyebrows. "Doris. Isn't that your name?"

"That's not what you said."

Katherine gave her a coy look. "I'm sure it was."

"No one's called me that since I was a little girl," Doris went on thoughtfully. "I hated my name – Louise Opal Keller – so I started called myself Doris because of Doris Day. I had it legally changed when I was eighteen."

But Katherine was staring off through the window, apparently having lost interest. A small smile dimpled her cheeks.

Doris welcomed the itching heat at the nape of her neck. Anger could be useful. Better, at least, than fear. Very slowly, she said, "Maybe you can explain something to me, Ms. Chambers."

Without looking at her, Katherine replied, "Of course, Louise."

"What I want to know," Doris said and set the scalding tea on the stand beside her, "is how a mother of three can just forsake her family the way you have."

If that bothered the woman, she didn't show it. "Roland and I are separated."

"I'm not talking about your husband," Doris said. "I'm asking about your children."

"Do you have any?" Katherine asked in that same mild voice. "Kids, I mean?"

Doris drew her shoulders back primly. "I never married."

"I'm not talking about your love life," Katherine said. "I'm asking if you ever had children."

Doris folded her hands. "I never had the desire."

"They're a lot of work," Katherine said. "I imagine Ellie will have her hands full when hers is born."

"Ahh," Doris said, turning on the couch to face the woman, "so you *do* think she's alive."

"I've said that all along."

Doris eyed her coldly. "I know what you've said. But I believe you know more."

"I only know what you know, Ms. Keller. That Chris lost his mind and murdered several innocent people. And now he seems to have taken my sister and her baby hostage."

"While you live in their house."

"I want to be here when Ellie returns."

Doris stared at the woman. "You're lying."

And now Katherine's serene expression did change, but not in the way Doris had expected. Rather than growing infuriated or defensive, Katherine turned, rested an elbow on the back of the couch and closed her eyes.

As furtively as she could, Doris slid her hand closer to her purse.

"Why are you here, Louise?" Katherine asked.

Doris's hand stopped moving. "Who told you that was my name?"

"No one told me," Katherine said, and as she spoke, Doris noticed something that alarmed her a great deal. In this light, though it was still mid-day, Katherine's hair didn't look completely black. Perhaps it was the dress she wore or some trick of the light, but she was growing sure the woman had red highlights. Or perhaps that had been the colour all along, and she simply hadn't noticed.

"I know a good deal about you, Louise," the woman said.

Doris found it was getting harder to breathe, as if the steaming tea were filling the room with wet, blistering air.

"I think I'd like to go," Doris said.

"I knew your mother very well," the woman went on as though Doris hadn't spoken. "We spent a good deal of time together..." The smile widening, growing predatory. "We ran in the same circles, you might say."

Doris felt as though she were in a trance, the woman's eyes, which a moment ago had been brown but were now a lighter colour that might have been green, transfixing her, nailing her to her spot on the couch.

"I remember your birth," Katherine said, "the agreement that was made."

In a pale, breathless voice, Doris said, "There was never any agreement—"

"But how would you know, my dear, being so young?" The woman's hand again fastened on her leg, the sultry breasts shifting. The creamy flesh so much whiter than it had been only minutes ago.

"I need to go," Doris whispered and was appalled to find herself on the brink of tears.

"Bloodthirsty harlot," the woman said.

"*What?*" Doris said in a hoarse whisper.

"That's what you called me." And somehow the face staring hatefully at her had become the one from her childhood. Passing the woman on the sidewalk on the way to the store. The pale, achingly beautiful face floating by as Gerald's car drifted past.

But that, her mind screamed frantically, *was forty years ago! When I was just a kid. How could this woman look the same now as she did then? How could she—*

Lillith Martin's eyes were now glowing moons. "I murdered your mother, Louise."

With a cry, Doris lunged for her purse. When her knees hit the floor, her fingers closed on the handgun, and she was about to whirl and shoot the woman in the face when she saw the cloven feet before her, three sets of them. She followed the white flesh upward and saw the sinewed legs, the genitalia – two of the figures male, one female – and above that...

On her knees, Doris turned and noticed that the woman on the couch had changed again, but this time she resembled nothing Doris had ever seen. The protruding cheekbones, the white, pupilless eyes, the leering, fanged mouth.

Doris swung the gun up and fired at the demon, watched the bullets punch neat holes in the dress, the flesh of a shoulder. Black streams trickled out of the wounds. But rather than writhing in agony, the demon massaged the black liquid into her skin, the sleek body undulating in slow, erotic waves. Doris gagged, covered her mouth with a wrist as the gunshot wounds began to knit, the flesh spanning the ragged holes in twitchy groping tendrils. The demon's slender fingers smeared the black blood across her throat, one shoulder strap snapping, and then over her bare, jutting breasts. Through the doorway beyond the writhing creature, several more vampires appeared.

She watched the demon's mouth open, moaning, a hand closing on its crotch, and Doris felt powerful talons seize her shoulders. The last thing she saw before a dozen sets of fangs tore her flesh was Lillith's tongue, nearly a foot in length, slip out of her fanged maw and curve in hateful ecstasy.

Doris screamed and Lillith's laughter followed her into death.

ACKNOWLEDGMENTS

There are several authors who influenced this book – authors that every lover of dark fiction should read. Ramsey Campbell, Stephen King, T.E.D. Klein, Charles L. Grant, Edgar Allan Poe, Joseph Payne Brennan, T.M. Wright, Thomas Tryon, and Algernon Blackwood all have a way of finding horror in both the natural world and in the nature of man. I am in their debt.

I'd like to thank my editor, Don D'Auria, for his unending supply of kindness and patience. I'd also like to thank my agent, Louise Fury, for her enthusiasm and expertise. Thanks also to my three children, who love me more than I deserve.

FLAME TREE PRESS
FICTION WITHOUT FRONTIERS
Award-Winning Authors & Original Voices

Flame Tree Press is the trade fiction imprint of Flame Tree
Publishing, focusing on excellent writing in horror and the
supernatural, crime and mystery, science fiction and fantasy.
Our aim is to explore beyond the boundaries of the everyday,
with tales from both award-winning authors and original voices.

•

Other titles available by Jonathan Janz:

The Siren and the Spectre
Wolf Land
The Sorrows
Savage Species
The Nightmare Girl
The Dark Game
House of Skin
Dust Devils
Castle of Sorrows

Other horror titles available include:

Thirteen Days by Sunset Beach by Ramsey Campbell
Think Yourself Lucky by Ramsey Campbell
The Hungry Moon by Ramsey Campbell
The Haunting of Henderson Close by Catherine Cavendish
The House by the Cemetery by John Everson
The Devil's Equinox by John Everson
The Toy Thief by D.W. Gillespie
Black Wings by Megan Hart
Stoker's Wilde by Steven Hopstaken & Melissa Prusi
The Playing Card Killer by Russell James
Will Haunt You by Brian Kirk
Creature by Hunter Shea
Ghost Mine by Hunter Shea
The Mouth of the Dark by Tim Waggonner
They Kill by Tim Waggonner

•

Join our mailing list for free short stories, new release details,
news about our authors and special promotions:

flametreepress.com